Letters to Mary

**a novel
by John Livsey**

Big Wave Books

Big Wave Books
P.O. Box 108, Charlestown RI 02813
bigwavebooks.com

Printed in the United States of America

First Printing: June 2005

LCCN 2005903572

Livsey, John
Letters to Mary

ISBN 0-9754979-3-6

1. Rhode Island- Fiction. 2. Grieving- Fiction.
3. Quonochontaug- Fiction. 4. Historical-
Fiction

Acknowledgements

Once again, many thanks have to go to Anne Doyle of the Quonochontaug Historical Society for letting me glimpse into the past. I am also grateful for the efforts of Cindy Walsh, Shawn Simmons, Jen Goodnow, Mickey Ranalli, and Deb Tretter. Their eyes saw what I couldn't. I am especially appreciative of The Westerly Sun and the archivists at the Westerly Public Library who have kept the elements of a bygone era alive. Much gratitude goes to everyone at Fidlar Doubleday for making this process run smoothly. I also have to show my appreciation for my ideal readers; Jon Simmons, Mallory Cole, Joshua Fishlock, Kereen Montgomery, Nancy Zabel, Robert Utter, and Art Ganz. Their spirit is with me every step of the way. This book wouldn't have been possible without the efforts of Gene Zabel. His knowledge of Quonochontaug, as well as the arts of fishing and gardening helped mold this novel. I am indebted to Mom and Dad for letting me grow up in Quonny. It has helped shape the person I have become. Most of all I have to thank my wife, Michelle, and my children; Sara, Caitlyn, Joshua, and Sean. They are my inspiration.

for Michelle

Although some old timers may recollect a few of the locations in the southern part of Rhode Island, this is a work of fiction.

1

The rhythmic clacking of the wheels on the rail, along with the gentle sway of the train, lulled Joshua Keegan into a kind of a daze. This was an escape. There couldn't be any other way to describe the journey. His mother had made it very clear to his grandmother last night. If she didn't get her boy out of the city, he would never climb out of the darkness that he had sunk into over the last two years.

Outside, the barren landscape of this dreary March morning was like something out of a bad dream. The snow tapered to a cold, wet drizzle the farther they got from the city. 1912 had been a very strange year so far, with over four inches of snow just a few days ago, and those frigid January mornings when the temperature had dipped well below zero. Joshua had never been this far south in the state before. In fact, this was only his fifth or sixth time out of Providence. Those other occasions were on beautiful, warm summer days, either north to see the Sox in Boston or down river on a trolley to Rocky Point. He had no idea where they were now. Occasionally, he saw signs, but the foggy mist made them too difficult to read. Joshua finally tried to settle back in his seat and prepare himself for what he could only imagine might lie ahead.

To Joshua, March meant death. The gloomy outside world only added to that feeling. The dismal blend of melting snow on the muddy ground, along with the bare trees scattered along the track, just made that emotion stronger. He was ten years old when the news came that his father had died. That was just two years ago, but it seemed like so much longer. It was a rainy March afternoon, and Joshua had just come home from school. Mother slumped in Dad's big, old stuffed chair in the parlor, and Mary was kneeling on the floor with her head resting in Mother's lap. In the doorway stood Father Donovan with a look of condolence on his face. At first Joshua thought it was news about Grandma. She had been sick for most of the winter, but when the priest came over to him and put his arm around Joshua's shoulder, he had a sudden vision of his father lying motionless in the mud.

"Joshua, it's your father," the priest said in that soothing Irish lilt of his. "He was down in the shipyard, and there was a problem with one of the rail cars." Father Donovan sighed and paused for a moment. "He was trying to tighten up one of the loads, when it broke loose and all fell on top of him. A few other men were injured, but they just couldn't help your father. I'm very sorry, son. James Keegan was a good man."

Joshua had been numb ever since that day two years ago. In his mind, Big Jim Keegan could never fall. His booming laugh and huge body were his strength, but the thought of him in that coffin, crushed, took the life right out of Joshua. He could remember so clearly, those evenings waiting on the front steps of their house on Foster Street. His dad would get off the trolley down around the corner, and Joshua would stretch his neck out to see the first glimpse of his father making his way through the crowd of other workingmen coming home. Joshua could see the strain and weariness on the man's shoulders as he returned from twelve or thirteen hours of back breaking work. Once his father saw him with a baseball glove in his hand, all of that fatigued gloom would disappear; replaced by a sudden smile. They'd play catch until Mother called them in for dinner. He would throw long fly balls, and Joshua would run in to catch them, just like Tris Speaker did in Boston's centerfield. Although the thought of those times warmed Joshua a bit, a deep sadness soon took over his body, and he struggled to dash the memory from his mind.

Looking back out the window again, he saw a few people gathered around an automobile that seemed to be stuck in the mud. Two men were trying to lead a horse forward. A rope connected the animal and the vehicle, and the car slowly began moving. The train rolled passed before Joshua could see if they had pulled it out. Again, woods covered the landscape outside, and Joshua wondered how close they were to their destination.

His mother sat next to him, staring straight ahead, like some Civil War general preparing for battle. Her skirmish had been the night before in the parlor with Grandma. Joshua had never heard them yell so much in his life.

"You're not leaving a good paying job to go off gallivanting at a beach resort like some eighteen year old," his grandmother shouted.

Joshua was on the stairs, just out of sight, having been awakened by all of the noise.

"Mother, I have got to get out of here, and I have to get Joshua out of this city. You've seen what he's become. There's just too many bad memories. We need a new start."

"Jesus, Mary, and Joseph; Mollie, you've lost your mind."

"Yes, I know, and I've lost a lot more than that," she answered as her voice faded away.

Mother was right, Joshua thought, he was the only one left. On the darkened stairs, he ran his fingers over the scar just above his right ear. It was early last March, and Joshua was downtown with Mary, his older sister. The horse came around the corner onto Westminster Street so quickly, that they hardly had time to react. The loaded cart behind the animal slid and slammed into both of them. Joshua couldn't remember anything else that happened that day. Sometimes he would get a glimpse of it in his mind, but mostly it was just smells that were around him, or the high-pitched voice of some Italian woman. The bump on the head blinded him for a short time, and when his vision returned, everything looked a little different. Joshua couldn't recall how long he was in the hospital, but when he came home, Mary was gone.

He didn't have any recollection of his older brother Jamie. He died when Joshua was two. Mother went to the hospital twice after that to have babies, but never came home with one. So yes, Joshua was the only one left, but he didn't really feel like he was there at all. He hadn't gone to school too much that year; in fact, he hadn't done very much at all. There was nothing to do.

"Mollie, be reasonable. You've got a roof over your head here, your brothers live upstairs, and..."

"Mother, tomorrow morning, Joshua and I will be getting on the 7:30 train for Westerly. We'll take a trolley to Watch Hill, and then get a ride to the Pond View Inn in Quonochontaug. I've got the letters upstairs. It's all set."

"But,"

"No buts, Mother. I have to get him away from here, and I don't have any qualms about leaving the Hearns. They've already got another housekeeper to take my place. Besides, there's some funny business going on there, and I'm not sorry to go."

"What kind of funny business?"

"Never mind about that. Our things are packed, and we're ready to move on."

"What about school for the boy, or church for that matter?"

"I'll teach him, and we'll see what happens down there."

"I can't believe you're actually going to go through with this, and for what?"

"You've seen him this last year. The doctors say that he's all right, but I know he's not. That knock on the head did some damage. Remember how he used to be...so full of life; chattering away...asking questions about everything...running everywhere... laughing... doing so well with his studies. You're the one who thought that he should be a priest. Now look at him; all the life has gone out of him. First his father, then Mary. The other boys don't even come over to the house anymore. Why should they? He's sick all the time now, and all he does is drift around the house. Who can blame him?"

It was quiet for a while, and Joshua could hear his mother sobbing. Tears rolled down his own cheeks too. Alone on the stairs in the near darkness, Joshua Keegan could not figure out how to get back to the way he used to be. He found that it was so hard to remember what things were like in the past. The harder he tried to act normally, the worse things became. He saw the look in his mother's eyes whenever he walked into the room. It was like she hoped that he would suddenly be all better, but Joshua had no idea how to do it.

As they pulled into the station, Mother's face seemed to change. Her strong bearing suddenly weakened, and her eyes began to shift back and forth. The conductor made his way into the car.

"Westerly, Rhode Island...Westerly Station," he barked.

Mother's hand went up to her collar, and she started to rise. The train slowly came to a halt, and there was much bustling about as passengers started to get off. Joshua and his mother each got their bags. He followed her as she made her way down the aisle and stepped off into a town where he had never been before.

People were coming and going, much like they did in Providence, but Joshua couldn't get the rhythm of their movement. He wasn't sure which way they were going, and Mother seemed to be having the same problem.

"I'm looking for the trolley to Watch Hill," she asked one of the railroad workers who was bending down by the side of the train. "Can you point me in the right direction?"

"Walk down Canal to High Street, it'll be right there," he said gesturing down the road without even looking up.

"Thank you."

They headed away from the station with their bags. The drizzle had fallen off to a fine mist, and tiny beads of water gathered around the brim of Mother's hat. As they walked, the crowd thinned. It wasn't quite lunchtime yet, so workers wouldn't be heading out for awhile. Joshua's stomach growled at the thought of food. As they came around the corner of Canal Street, Joshua could make out the different trolleys coming and going. A truck's horn made him jump as it passed by on the street. He was still a little jittery about walking along sidewalks, and simple movements or sounds could easily send him into one of his panics. The horse and carts were traveling slowly, so he knew that he could spring out of the way if he had to.

5

Westerly seemed like just a smaller version of Providence. The buildings didn't go up as high, and there weren't as many of them. The river off to the right was much smaller, but boats moved along on it nevertheless. The men wore dark brown or black suits with their bowler hats, and the women were dressed just like Mother with their long dresses and dark coats, along with hats on their heads. Many of them seemed to have fancier clothes than she did, but the women who worked were probably in at their jobs at this time of day. Joshua saw a few boys running around in tattered pants and figured most other children would be in school now.

Mother had said that the Watch Hill trolley only ran out there twice a day at this time of year, so he knew they had to catch it. Their ride would be waiting for them when they got there, and Joshua wasn't sure how long the man would stay. He scanned the cars to see which one they would need to get on, but he couldn't find it.

"Over here, Joshua," Mother said, as she grabbed the arm of his coat and pulled.

They trotted over to an older looking trolley that looked like it was ready to pull away. Mother gave the driver a couple of coins as they stepped onto the platform, and within seconds, Joshua could feel the trolley start to move. The car only had about a dozen or so people, and they each were carrying different types of bags or boxes. Joshua looked out the window as they traveled along by the side of the river. Because of the mist, it was hard to see what was on the other side. The ride wasn't as smooth as the trolleys in Providence, and they lurched back and forth as the car made its way toward Watch Hill. Once the trolley was out of the city and nearby neighborhoods, the ride became desolate. They passed through wooded areas and then open fields. Joshua thought he saw six or seven deer grazing in a brown meadow. The water was always on their right, and it came in and out of view. Small marinas were the only signs of civilized life, but it didn't seem like anyone was there.

After stopping and letting two women off, they crested a hill and came around a long swaying curve. Looming before him, Joshua could see a huge structure appear out of the mist. As they moved farther along the line, more mansions came into view and then slowly faded away. The fog made it seem like some kind of a dream. It was hard to tell where they actually began and ended. These were even bigger than the houses on the East Side of Providence. Joshua glanced over at his mother and saw that she had the same look of awe on her face that he did. Coming down a final hill, water reappeared off to their right, and Joshua could just make out the masts of a few boats in the harbor. The trolley slowed as they came into a small village area of shops and small restaurants. They passed hotels; first the Narragansett, then the Columbia. Two fancy automobiles were parked at the side of the road, and behind them was a weathered truck facing the wrong way. A boy on horseback walked along beside the trolley, peering in at the passengers.

"Bay Street, last stop," the conductor barked.

When they came to a halt, Joshua grabbed his bag and followed Mother to the front. They stepped off onto a wooden boardwalk, which was placed over the muddy road. Mother immediately looked around once she got underneath the overhang of the store in front of them. An old woman was walking along, and Mother leaned over toward her.

"Excuse me, I'm looking for a Mr. Ray Crandall."

The woman looked up at her through tired eyes, and for a moment, it didn't seem as if she was going to say anything. She turned and looked over her shoulder, and in a soft voice that Joshua almost couldn't hear, she spoke.

"That's his truck over there," she pointed. "Probably in Sisson's having himself some lunch."

Joshua looked back across the street and saw the truck, which would be their final mode of transportation. Wooden slats ran along both sides of the flatbed in the rear, and caked on mud covered almost the entire vehicle.

"Thank you," Mother answered.

Looking up and down the street, Joshua searched for the best possible place to cross. The mud was everywhere, and there was no telling how deep they would sink in it. There were some planks set on both sides of the trolley rail a little farther down the road. They backtracked and slowly made their way across. Mother almost lost her balance as she stepped from the rail onto the second board. It slid, but she caught herself before going over. The bottom of her dress dragged over the soggy ground, as she carefully made her way onto the opposite side of the street. Part way down the street, a horse and cart were struggling through the mire, splattering mud everywhere. Joshua jumped the last couple of feet, so he wouldn't be covered with the muck.

Sisson's only had a few customers when they entered, and each set of eyes turned and gawked as Joshua and his mother put their bags down in an empty corner behind the door. No one said anything for a long moment, and Mother looked as if she were waiting for someone to step forward. Three of the men at the counter were staring at her, and then the woman at the soda fountain finally broke the silence.

"Can I help you?"

"Yes, I'm looking for Mr. Crandall."

"You must be the new housekeeper at the Pond View," one of the men responded.

"Yes," Mother replied in a strange, shy voice.

"Mrs. Keirnan?"

"Keegan," Mother said quickly, "Mrs. Keegan."

"Oh sorry, I knew it was one of them Irish names."

The man next to him snorted when Mr. Crandall said this, and Joshua got a little nervous at the way they all looked at each other and chuckled. He sensed that there was some kind of trouble brewing, but he wasn't sure what it was.

"We're supposed to get a ride from you to the Pond View Inn."

"Well, I can get you to the top of the beach road, but I'm not taking my truck all the way down there today... too much mud. The Swede's supposed to meet me there, if not, it's about a mile walk."

Mother looked at the man for a moment.

"My letter says that you're to give us a ride to the inn," she said with a growing strength in her voice.

Mr. Crandall looked back at the other men with a

wide grin on his face.

"The thing is," he began, "if you showed up a few weeks ago when everything was frozen, or maybe a few weeks from now when everything's dry, I could've helped you. I gotta be back downtown for the evenin' train, and if I'm stuck in the mud down in Quonny, then I won't get there."

Mother stared at the man for a moment, then realized that she wasn't going to win this battle. Her firm jaw softened a bit, and Joshua could tell that her mind was working. All she wanted to do was get there, and a mile walk in the mud and the mist wasn't going to kill them.

"I'm just about to have some lunch, and we'll get going as soon as I'm done," Mr. Crandall replied. "Don't worry, the Swede should be there with his cart, so everything will work out."

Mother turned and sat down at one of the small tables. Joshua followed and waited for her next cue. The woman behind the counter came around and asked them if they were interested in anything.

"I've got some pork chops today with mashed potatoes and carrots."

"Yes, why don't we have a plate for each of us, a glass of milk, and a cup of tea."

"That'll be just a few minutes."

Joshua looked around the cafe. There was quite a collection of art work of beaches and other summertime activities. A large painting of a merry-go-round hung on the back wall. The men at the counter laughed and talked as the woman served them their lunch.

"We should be there soon," Mother said to Joshua. "How are you holding up?"

"Fine," he responded truthfully.

This was like some kind of adventure that they were on; an escape from the usual routine. Joshua wasn't sure what was going to happen, but he knew that he was getting tired of wandering through the rooms of their house on Foster Street. It really wasn't even their house though. It was Grandma's place, and they just lived there and helped out when they could. Uncle Steven and Uncle

Kevin lived upstairs on the third floor with their new wives. All four of them worked so much, that Joshua rarely got to see them any more. They were both married last fall and were saving up to get places of their own. Mother and Dad had been doing the same thing. Joshua's father had always talked about buying some land in Warwick and starting a farm. His vegetable garden in the backyard was the pride of the neighborhood. Joshua always helped his father with the planting, weeding, and picking; listening to him talk about plans for their future. All of that was gone now, and here he was with his mother in a strange cafe waiting for the last leg of their journey to begin.

The woman came over with their meals and leaned down low beside Mother's ear. Joshua could just barely make out what she was saying.

"Don't mind Ray, he's an old softy. He got stuck in the mud last week, and the boys've been givin' him a hard time of it. It took two horses to pull him out," she giggled. "He was covered head to foot."

Mother just nodded and picked up her fork. The pork chops were delicious; they helped to take away the chill that had been in Joshua's bones since leaving the house early that morning. The slushy walk to the Providence train station was now a distant memory. Mother nudged Joshua twice, silently telling him to slow down with just a look in her eyes. As he finished his milk, Joshua looked around for a bathroom. He watched as Mr. Crandall disappeared out through the back door. When he returned, Joshua traced the man's steps to an outhouse at the end of a narrow alley. Chickens squawked nearby, and Joshua thought that he heard the snort of a pig. Mother was at the counter handing some coins to the woman when Joshua returned. Mr. Crandall was putting on his jacket and cap.

"You be nice, Ray, and give these people a ride down to the inn."

"We'll see," he responded as he walked out the door.

Mother handed Joshua his bag, and they followed Mr. Crandall. The truck was only a few doors down. Ray held out his hands for the bags and plopped them in the back.

"Why don't you slide in from this side, it's pretty wet over there."

Mother climbed in and made her way slowly across to the other door. Joshua hopped in and sat in the middle. Mr. Crandall fired up the truck and let the engine idle for a few minutes. The whole vehicle shook violently, and Joshua was glad that he had made the journey out to the alley before getting started.

"Are we all set?"

Mother just nodded. Ray eased the clutch into gear, and slowly they slid away from the side and out into the street. They jolted into the trolley rail, and the truck seemed to finally catch on something solid. Mr. Crandall kept talking to the vehicle as if it were a horse that he was trying to coax into action. The hill that lay in front of them looked impossible, but eventually they made their way up and over. Once the truck was around the corner, the vibrations began to settle down into a rhythmic shake. A majestic hotel loomed in front of them grandly just off to the right.

"That's the Ocean House," Mr. Crandall shouted over the noise of the engine. "They say there's ghosts that roam the top floor up there... old sailors who never made it back home, or some such. Spirits just flew up from them rocks down there."

They came around another corner, and Joshua could see waves crashing in on the rocky shore. The powerful surge rolled into, and then over the seaweed covered rocks, sending huge sprays of water splashing skyward. Because of the fog, it was hard to see how big the waves actually were. The crashing swells seemed to appear from out of the gray mist. Joshua had never seen anything like this before. The few times that he went to the beach at Rocky Point, the waves were only a few inches high. That was in Narragansett Bay, but this was the open ocean.

They slid and rambled down the straight, wide open stretch of road along a marshy area. Gulls and other sea birds flew up in front of them as they passed.

11

Because of the mist, Joshua couldn't see anything that was more than fifty feet away. They passed a sign for a place called Misquamicut, and then a little farther down the road, one for Weekapaug.

"Quonny's the next beach down. We have to get up on the Post Road, and things should be a little smoother. They say the trolley's supposed to go all the way to Weekapaug this summer. They'll put me out of a job sooner or later," he snorted.

Shacks and other small cottages littered the road. Occasionally, Joshua saw some horses and cows, but there were no signs of human life anywhere to be seen. One of the bigger houses had smoke coming from its chimney, but the swirl blended into the fog so quickly, that it almost seemed as if it wasn't there at all.

"Quonny's got its own share of spirits too," Mr. Crandall suddenly said, as if he was continuing the conversation that he started a half an hour earlier in Watch Hill. "They say some slaves jumped ship a mile or so out, about a hundred years ago. They were being smuggled into Newport or Bristol, so they didn't make a big stink about it at the time."

Joshua wondered if Mr. Crandall was telling the truth, or if this was just some tale to scare him.

"They made their way up over the beach and hid out in the root cellar of a house that later burned down. They say some parts of it are still there, out in back of where the old Sheffield farm used to be, in a grove of trees all covered with blackberry brambles. They couldn't keep themselves a secret for too long though. Some people say their spirits still haunt the back path to the breachway between the pond and West Beach Road, not too far from your Pond View Inn."

Maybe it was the fog that was surrounding them, or maybe it was this unfamiliar place, but a chill ran right up Joshua's spine when he thought of those spirits wandering through the mist. He wondered what it would be like when darkness fell.

The Post Road was smoother, and Mr. Crandall seemed to loosen up a bit at the steering wheel as they passed by what a small sign said was Havisham. They

12

cruised along for a couple of miles without much change in the scenery, except for some small hills.

"I'll give it a shot, but if that mud starts to pile up, I got to turn it around," he said almost to himself.

Mr. Crandall slowed the truck and began to turn the wheel. They drove down an incline onto a rutted road.

"Not too bad."

They leveled off and passed through a wooded area. Soon the road opened up, and it looked like there was some water off to the right. Joshua strained his eyes to see, but was suddenly snapped out of his concentration when the truck came to a sliding halt, as Mr. Crandall slammed the vehicle into reverse.

"Nope, not today."

He opened the door and jumped out of the truck in one fluid movement, and then grabbed a stick from the back. Joshua and his mother watched as he walked in front of the truck and looked at a large, expansive puddle that seemed to go on and on. Mr. Crandall moved to the side of the dirt road, stepping on one of the rocks that were scattered every few feet. He dipped the stick into the water, and it sank down at least half a foot. Moving farther down the road, he stuck it in again, and the wood dropped down even lower.

"Sorry folks," he said as he returned to the truck, "this is the end of the line today. I can't get my vehicle through that water, and there's just too many rocks on the side of the road to go around. East Beach Road is probably worse."

"How far?" Mother asked, wearied by the whole day.

"It's less than a mile or there abouts on your right. The first big place that you see. Can't miss it."

Mother tried to give him some change, but Mr. Crandall waved her off.

"No, the ride's on me today. If I can't get you all the way there, then it's on the house."

"Well, thank you, Mr. Crandall."

"Good luck. You'll see me around from time to time."

He handed them their bags, and they started their

13

trek through the mud. The rain had stopped, but the mist kept the air damp. Joshua hopped from rock to rock on the side of the road. Mother chose to go around the stones on the brown, grassy areas. Her boots were covered in mud, but what real choice did they have? Joshua heard Mr. Crandall's truck crank back into gear, although he could no longer see him. The wind of the engine became more distant as they moved on. Now, Joshua and his mother were alone, trudging toward some hope of a better future.

2

The walk wasn't too bad. After a short time, the road began to rise a bit, and the surface didn't seem so muddy. Off to the right, Joshua could hear the lapping of water. The fog prevented him from seeing what it was, but he figured the pond that the inn was named for must be out there somewhere. Mother slowed for a moment to gather herself, and Josh tried to look further down the road. The mist was slowly rolling passed them from west to east across the road and into the reedy marsh on the other side. They walked in silence, passing a few small cottages that were boarded up for the off season.

Up ahead there was something in the road, but Joshua couldn't make out what it was at first. It just seemed to be some dark form. Joshua hurried his pace, but was a little more cautious in his approach. He heard the neighing of the horse before he figured out what it actually was.

"Joshua, slow down. Wait for me," his mother's voice beckoned from behind.

It was a beautiful, brown horse, and the cart behind the animal was tilted over to one side. A man crouched on one knee at the front wheel. When he noticed Joshua's presence, the man stood and wiped his pant leg with a rag. He was lanky, with white hair and a big, bushy mustache. Joshua stood and peered at the horse as Mother caught up.

"Hello, Mrs. Keegan, sorry I couldn't meet you at the top of the road, but this darn cart threw a wheel," the man said as he gripped his hat with both hands. "I was meaning to fix it last fall before we packed up, but never got around to it. I'm Luther Nilsson. The wife and I run the place for the Van Houtten family." His voice was thickly accented, but had a sing-song quality to it.

15

"Pleased to meet you, Mr. Nilsson."

"Who's this fella?" he asked with a big-toothed grin.

"This is my son, Joshua." Mother's voice was strained. "I wrote and said that I would be bringing him."

"Oh, I'm sure you did. Mrs. Nilsson handles all of the correspondence. We sure need your help. Last year she tried doing it all herself, but we're getting on in years. We hired some girls in July, but they had no sense. It made things even harder."

Mother nodded, but Joshua wasn't sure what they were supposed to do. He just stared at the horse and slowly reached his hand out to pet its nose.

"Why don't you head on up to the house, it's just around the bend. Have you had your dinner?"

"Yes, we ate in Watch Hill."

"Sisson's?" he asked, raising an eyebrow. "Did they have the roasted chicken today?"

"No, pork chops."

"Just as good, just as good," he smiled. "I'll be there in a little while. Mrs. Nilsson will get you settled."

The man stood tall, watching them as they passed by. Joshua looked back at him once, and he gave the boy a big wink. Although Joshua didn't have many things in his bag, the weight of it was starting to put a strain on his arms. He kept switching back and forth, but what he really wanted was for the inn to appear. As they came around a short bend in the road at the top of a small rise, the house appeared before them. It was a large sprawling place; nothing like the mansions in Watch Hill, but a good size nevertheless. There were three floors and a big wraparound porch. The white paint looked a little chipped and worn, but not too bad. Joshua counted sixteen windows across the second floor in the front; each with its own set of green shutters. Off to the right, he could just make out another building. Immense, leafless trees were scattered about the sweeping lawn.

A dog on the porch lifted its head up, yawned, and then slowly got up and walked down the gravel driveway to meet them. It was light brown in color, and as the dog approached, its tongue hung out in anticipation. Circling around to the back of Joshua, the animal sniffed his carrying bag. Probably sensing that there was nothing to eat inside, the dog sauntered back to its spot on the porch.

Mother walked up to the steps and tried to scrape the mud off the bottom and sides of her shoes. Joshua followed her and tried to do the same. The bottoms of his pants were caked with the sloppy wetness. Soon, the top step was covered with mud.

The front door opened, and a woman with gray hair and a stiff white collar appeared.

"I didn't hear the horse come up the drive."

"It broke down," Joshua said without really thinking.

"Excuse me?"

"Mr. Nilsson is down the road a little way," his mother answered, "the wheel of the cart is broken off."

"Oh my."

She looked off into the foggy distance for a moment.

"Please excuse my manners. I'm Anna Nilsson, and you must be Mrs. Keegan and Joshua." Her smile warmed the boy. "Please come in, and don't bother yourself about the mud, it's everywhere."

The dog got up and moved over toward the woman.

"Kip, you stay."

The three of them walked in through the large doorway, which had colored glass on both sides. The musty smell of the house struck Joshua after only a few steps inside. They passed by a wide, formal stairway that loomed in front of them and walked down a hallway lined with bookcases.

"Why don't I get you settled upstairs, and then we can do the grand tour," Mrs. Nilsson said as they passed through an enormous dining room. The chairs and table were covered with white sheets. Dishes were piled in glass cabinets on both sides of the room.

The kitchen looked like something right out of a restaurant. There were two stoves with oversized ovens. One of them was throwing off a wave of heat. Joshua couldn't quite place the smell that drifted into his nose, but after one whiff, he knew that there was going to be some good food here at this place. They went up a dark, narrow stairway between the kitchen and the pantry, and then came into a small hallway that had four doors.

"This should suit you, Mrs. Keegan."

"Please, call me Mollie."

"Mr. Nilsson and I are right in here, this is a bunk room for some of the summer help, and you'll stay in this room," she said, pushing the door open wider. "The heat from the kitchen keeps it fairly warm until May, and the big maple out front keeps it cool in the summer."

The room was small, and there was one window looking out into the fog. The branches of the maple were bare, and they swayed gently in the breeze.

"Why don't you unpack your things. There's a chest of drawers in the closet here. The washroom's just down the hall on the other side of the bunk room. Mr. Nilsson used the hand pump to get some water in the storage tank for now. I'll be down in the kitchen if you need anything."

Mrs. Nilsson gave them a small nod and backed out of the room. Mother sagged down on the bed, looking exhausted after their journey. It would be dark out soon, and Joshua wanted to get a look around the house before they lost the light. He started to unpack his bag and put the clothes on the bed next to Mother. Looking beneath, Joshua found that there was a trundle bed that could be pulled out under the box springs.

"Joshua, go and wash up, and I'll get things settled here. Don't go anywhere else."

The washroom had a small window that looked out onto the back lawn, but the fog distorted the view. It took a few seconds, but the water began to flow out of the faucet. It was ice cold, and there were flecks of rust bubbling out with the water. Looking down, Joshua saw that he was making a mess on the white, tiled floor. The mud from his shoes had soiled the whole area where he had been standing. He took them off and wondered where he could clean them off. The dirt smeared and kept spreading out in all directions. Joshua's stomach started to get that twisted feeling again; like he was doing something wrong. Wringing his hands, Joshua desperately scrambled about, trying to figure a way out of this situation. If Mrs. Nilsson saw this mess, then she would send them away. Joshua was sure of it. The more he tried to wipe up the mess, the worse it became. He banged his head on the side of the sink, but that didn't slow down his frantic movements.

"Joshua," a voice seemed to come from far away. "Joshua!"

He looked up and saw that it was his mother standing over him. Tears ran down his cheeks. He didn't know what was wrong with him.

"What are you doing down there?"

"The mud," he said in a loud, anguished voice.

She put her hand on his shoulder and then rubbed his back.

"Everything's okay, Joshua. It's just a little mud. I'll take care of it."

Slowly, his breathing returned to normal, and his heartbeat settled back into its rhythm. It was strange, the littlest things could really set him off. Whenever he looked back on one of his episodes, Joshua could never understand why he had gotten into such a frenzy.

"Go change out of those clothes and put on your nice shoes for now. I put your things in the bottom drawer."

Joshua did as he was told, and within a few minutes, Mother was back in the room; looking refreshed with new life in her. Putting the dirty things in a small basket at the bottom of the bed, she surveyed their quarters.

"Well, it'll take a little getting used to, but we'll do okay. Let's go down and look at the rest of this place."

He followed his mother as she descended the steep stairs into the kitchen. Mrs. Nilsson was at one of the counters with her back to them.

"I made some cookies to snack on if you'd like."

Joshua looked up at Mother, and she nodded, so he grabbed two from the plate.

"Let's show you two around," she said as she breezed through the kitchen into the dining room. "This is where we serve breakfast and dinner. Guests are on their own for their noontime meal, except on Sundays. We'll get a few in here for the last two weeks in May. Maybe a dozen at the beginning of June, and from then on until September, we'll have a full house. Actually on the Fourth of July, we'll be overloaded, with people everywhere."

They walked into a parlor area with couches and chairs covered in sheets. There was a dwindling flame in the fireplace. A small stack of wood sat next to it. Joshua gazed at the oddly shaped stones that made up the area around the hearth and chimney.

"Mr. Nilsson should be back in a few minutes, and he'll put some more wood on. This is one of the parlors, and the other one is through here."

This next room was a bit smaller, and it had a woodstove that didn't have any heat coming from it. Mother and son followed Mrs. Nilsson through a beautiful set of glassed doors. A large expanse opened up before them. Furniture was piled along the wall, and a dusty wooden floor spread out at least twenty feet one way and thirty feet the other. A piano sat at the far end.

"This is the main sitting room. Mrs. Van Houtten has dances in here some nights, and the guests even set up a bowling alley once in awhile. Through here is the sun porch."

Crossing the wooden floor and then going through another set of glass doors, they stepped down into a room that was lined with windows from floor to ceiling on three sides. Some of them looked like doorways with screens attached to them. Joshua surveyed the outside world. The darkening sky only added to the foggy gloom.

They retraced their steps and went up the formal stairs at the front of the house. The rooms on the second floor were cold. They were much bigger than Joshua's room, and some even had a small sitting area by the windows. The third floor was made up of two large bunk rooms with beds for about eight to ten people in each. Joshua wondered who would be staying there during the summer months.

Mrs. Nilsson kept up a steady chatter as they went through the rooms. She listed off family names of guests who stayed there during the months of July and August. She seemed to have something pleasant to say about each one.

"...and I don't know what your thoughts are for Joshua here, but we can put him to work starting tomorrow morning. Mr. Nilsson would be happy to have a boy around. Ours are back in New York with families of their own now."

Joshua brightened at the prospect of working around the property. The city didn't offer many opportunities for boys to work outside. He could have easily gone into one of the mills or factories. In fact, Mother had threatened to send him there if his school work didn't improve. Lately, Joshua had a hard time focusing on his studies. He couldn't sit still for too long, and all the days that he missed because he was sick put him behind the other children.

"There's a school up on the Post Road," Mrs. Nilsson said.

"I was planning on teaching him myself for the rest of this school year," Mother said with a bit of strain in her voice.

"That sounds fine. There are hundreds of books out in the main hall, and I'm sure we can scratch up some paper for the boy."

Joshua heard a door open and shut out near the kitchen. Mr. Nilsson must have fixed the wheel.

"You'll be responsible for getting the house in shape for the guests. All of the windows need to be washed, and the screens have to come out too. All of the floors need a good wash and wax. I'll cook the meals for now, but when the guests start arriving, you'll assist me in there. The beds need to be aired out as well as the furniture, and all of the linens need to be washed and ironed. There's some painting, but Mr. Nilsson will do most of that. He has two men who will be here in a few weeks; brothers who can't work in the quarries anymore. They'll stay out over the barn. Old Cal will be around too. He takes care of the animals at most of the places around here during the winter months while everyone's away. He lives over in East Beach."

21

Mother spent her time looking at Mrs. Nilsson, and then around at the general areas where the woman pointed as she was talking.

"We've only been here two days. We closed up the lodge in Vermont and headed to New York for a week, then up here to Rhode Island. Not much has been done yet. We'll get a fresh start bright and early in the morning."

Mr. Nilsson walked through a door on the other side of the kitchen as they were entering from the dining room.

"Oh, you're back. How's the cart?"

"I rigged it for now, but it won't last," he answered as he grabbed a cookie off of the counter. "I'll have to work on it in the morning."

They ate a light supper of ham sandwiches and tea. Joshua devoured his meal in silence. The room on the other side of the kitchen had a small eating area with four chairs around a table. Windows lined the walls, but the darkness outside made seeing anything almost impossible.

Joshua and his mother went to their room after helping to straighten up in the kitchen, while Mr. and Mrs. Nilsson did a few things around the house. Mother pulled the trundle mattress out for him. There were some sheets on the chair in the corner. The kerosene lamp made strange shadows on the opposite wall as he made his bed. The room seemed to have a peculiar, hollow feeling to it. Joshua took off his shoes and climbed under the covers. Mother settled into her bed a few moments later. She sighed and began writing something on a piece of paper. Joshua fell off into sleep before she put the light out.

A squealing noise stirred Joshua out of his dreams during the night. The pitch blackness of the room reminded him of days that he had spent in the hospital last year, blinded from the blow to his head. He lay still and tried to focus on the sound. Joshua had no idea what time it was. The wind must have come up over the last few hours because Joshua could hear the tree branches scraping and tapping against one another. The other sound, though, was a mystery. It had a metallic quality to

22

it and seemed to get louder and louder as he focused on it; as if something were approaching. Joshua's imagination made his heart thump within his chest. He envisioned the slave hunters coming to recapture the escapees; the horses' thundering hooves wildly galloping closer and closer. He didn't dare move. The wheels seemed to spin faster and faster with each gust of the wind. As the bluster slowly died down, the sound dwindled, as though they were circling back around the far side of the property.

Joshua didn't know how long he lay there listening, but slowly hints of light began to appear in the room. Thankfully dawn was coming. A little while later he saw the first glimpse of sunlight reflect off the top corner of the wall. Joshua stirred a bit, and felt as if it was safe enough to begin moving around.

He got up out of bed and tried to shake off the memories that still lingered in his mind. The morning chill hung on the boy as he made his way down to the washroom. Beneath him, the floorboards squeaked and groaned. Trying to be as quiet as possible, Joshua ducked into the bathroom. The sight outside of the window took his breath away. He suddenly realized where the name of the inn came from. Down a long rolling lawn, spotted with different shaped trees, there was a path down to a dock. Beyond that, a large body of water opened up. There were a few small islands, and on the opposite side of the water, houses dotted the wooded shoreline. Southward, off to his left, Joshua could see the open ocean. It seemed to go on forever. The darkness that had hung over him before dawn was now a fading memory.

Joshua carried his muddy shoes downstairs along with his coat. He wanted to get a closer look at his new surroundings. Something popped as he came around the corner into the kitchen. One of the Nilssons must have gotten up earlier to fill the stove with wood. Joshua quickly scanned the downstairs area and saw no signs of life though. Grabbing three of the sugar cookies from the counter, he went into the small eating area behind the kitchen and put his shoes on. The back door creaked open as Joshua pulled on the handle, and tried to keep some semblance of the silent calm which hung about the inn. As he stepped out onto the expansive back porch, the stiff wind hit him immediately. Buttoning his coat, he ventured out into the backyard.

Joshua heard that predawn sound again. It was coming from over his right shoulder. At first he didn't even want to turn; just wishing to go back upstairs and get under the covers again, but slowly he shifted around. Joshua laughed out loud for the first time since he couldn't remember when. Across the grass, out on the other side of the barn, up higher than the roof of the house; a windmill spun. He watched it turn for a few moments. The squeaking noise that had scared him so much in the early morning darkness wasn't frightening at all. It just needed to be greased.

A huge tub sat beneath the spinning slats that were rotating in the wind. Water dripped from the bottom of the oversized bucket, and a pipe ran down through the middle of the structure. A wire was stretched from just below the blades over to the barn, and then to the side of the house. Joshua planned to investigate the windmill further, but right now, he wanted to go down and examine the water's edge.

The yard was relatively flat for about a hundred and fifty feet from the house, then there was a gentle incline as the grassy area narrowed and turned into a wide path. Low bushes and vines were on both sides of him as Joshua got closer to the dock. The wind was blowing straight at him, and his eyes began to water. Pulling the collar tighter around his neck, Joshua stepped out onto the wooden dock. The tide was low, and he could see where the high water mark was on the pilings. After taking about eight or nine steps onto the dock, the water went from about two inches deep to at least three feet. The drop off was distinct, and Joshua could see how the channel ran on both sides. To his left, he followed the shoreline with his eyes down around a slow bend. Another dock jutted out less than a quarter of a mile away. Past that was a marshy flatland, and Joshua could see groups of buildings off in the distance as he turned his gaze back. Out to the right, the pond opened up. It looked to be almost a mile across to the other side. An island filled with trees sat about two hundred yards out in front of him, and two smaller bodies of grassy land extended between the island and the marshy area. Rocks, large and small, speckled the water between the island and the dock. Joshua figured that most of them would be swallowed up with the incoming tide.

He couldn't see the ocean from where he was standing, but far off to his left, Joshua could hear the waves. The brief glimpse of them yesterday in Watch Hill had stirred something inside of him. Their amazing power charged his broken spirit in a way that nothing ever had before. The salty smell in the air was more crisp than it was down in the shipyard on the bay where his father used to work. It seemed cleaner, and maybe a little more pure.

Turning his back to the water, Joshua started up to the house. It was an amazing sight. As he came back out of the path into the yard, he had to stop and take it all in. The place was truly picturesque, and the open space around it gave the structure a majestic air. Trees that would be filled with leaves in a month, served as sentinels, guarding the framework. The long back porch, now empty, would give a perfect view of the sunset. A bare flagpole stood in the center of the yard. On the opposite side of the house from the barn, there was a large fenced in area. As he approached it, Joshua couldn't figure out what it was used for. Two short poles stuck up from the ground on both sides near the middle. The fencing around the grassy area must have been eight feet high. Vines encroached the back corner.

"It's a tennis court." Mr. Nilsson's voice jolted him out of his solitude.

Joshua turned around and saw the man coming around the house with an armload of wood. Running up to the house, he opened the back door for him.

"Thank you, Joshua."

Through the small eating room, Joshua followed him. Mrs. Nilsson was at the stove, and Mother was bent down reaching for something in a lower cupboard. Mr. Nilsson left a few small logs next to the stove, and then went through the doorway to the dining room with the rest of the wood.

"Good morning," Mother said as she stood back up, "I was wondering where you had gotten to."

"I was just looking around."

"Why don't you go see if Mr. Nilsson needs any help, while we get some breakfast ready."

Joshua nodded and traced the old man's steps through the swinging door. The dining room and parlor were much colder than the kitchen. Mr. Nilsson was loading the fireplace when the boy came up behind him.

"Do you need any help?"

"Sure," he answered in a long dragged out voice. "Let me just get this going first."

Joshua watched as he stirred up the embers. Smaller twigs soon started to catch fire, and within a minute or two, the flame was creeping up through the spaces in the pile of logs. The crackling noise meant that the fire would be going strong shortly.

"Ever chop wood before?"

"No," Joshua answered.

"Well, today's your lucky day. We need to bring in some more wood first, and then after we eat, we'll get started."

He followed Mr. Nilsson back through the kitchen. Mother gave her son a cheerful smile as he passed by her. They walked over to the barn, and Josh couldn't take his eyes off of the spinning windmill that towered over them. The barn wasn't as big as he first thought. Joshua could hear the horse inside, moving about.

"Nettie's hungry. Let's bring a load in, and then you can feed her."

The wood pile stretched about a third of the way down the outside wall. An overhang kept the logs dry, and the sunlight beamed across the side of the barn. Mr. Nilsson piled four medium sized pieces of wood in Joshua's arms. When his body started to sag, the older man sent the boy on his way. The soggy ground under Joshua's feet squished as he walked. The load got heavier and heavier with each step. He could feel his shoulders starting to give, and he was only about halfway to the house. Joshua stopped for a second and tried to rebalance the weight. When he did this, one of the logs rolled out of his arms and bounced painfully off of his right knee.

"Don't worry about it, just keep walking."

Joshua felt like he was letting the man down. Mr. Nilsson passed him and continued up to the steps. Mrs. Nilsson opened the door for them, and Joshua trudged in behind the man. He put the logs next to the stove and ran back outside to retrieve the one that he had dropped. Mr. Nilsson was coming back into the kitchen as Joshua placed it on top of the others. Again, the boy followed the older man out to the barn. Around on the road side of the building, two large doors hung crookedly. Mr. Nilsson pulled one of them open, and it scraped along the muddy ground. Nettie's head bobbed up and down at the sight of them, and she moved back and forth in her stall. The smell of hay was strong, and it took a moment for his eyes to adjust to the dimly lit barn. The cart took up most of the space in the middle of the area. The wheel that was broken off yesterday hung at an awkward angle from the rest of the vehicle. Across from the horse's stall, different types of equipment lined the wall. There was a plow, a stone wheel attached to a pedal, and what looked like some kind of grass cutting apparatus. Joshua couldn't figure out what the other tools were for.

"Grab her bucket there on the wall. Her feed's over in that sack," he said, pointing to the corner. "Fill it about two thirds of the way up."

Mr. Nilsson was inspecting the cart wheel when Joshua came back past him with the breakfast for Nettie. He stood at the gate of the stall, not knowing what he should do. The horse pushed forward, trying to get to the food.

"Open the gate up, she'll be fine, and then empty it into her feed tray there. Don't let her bully you. Just go in, pour it, and then back out."

She withdrew a bit when Joshua opened the gate, but she quickly stepped forward and put her snout down to the bucket as he hesitated at the entrance. Joshua tried pushing past her, but she wouldn't let him; her strong neck muscles not giving an inch. Nettie's cold nose rubbed against his knuckles, which were wrapped around the handle of the bucket. Josh was afraid that her teeth were going to gnaw his fingers off. Frozen, he just stood there, not knowing what to do.

"Come on Nettie, Joshua's going to feed you," Mr. Nilsson's hand appeared under her neck and led her back from the boy. "If you don't let him in, then there's going to be no breakfast for you today."

Joshua used the brief opening to step forward and pour the feed. As soon as the bucket was empty, he backed out of the stall, always keeping an eye on Nettie's movements. Mr. Nilsson rubbed the bridge of her nose and made a clicking sound with his mouth. The boy stood there, outside the stall, and watched as the horse casually stepped over to her breakfast. Hanging the bucket up on the peg, he followed Mr. Nilsson back outside.

While the man closed the door, Joshua wandered over to the other side of the barn to get a better look at the windmill. It was set about ten feet from the wall. Four legs were bolted to a cement platform. The structure narrowed as it rose, and the large tub was supported by a metal platform about twenty feet up. Water trickled down into a stony hole next to the windmill. A smaller shed sat on stone blocks on the other side of the windmill. As he walked toward it, Joshua saw that there was some type of metal screening around the front. He assumed that this was a chicken coop, but right now it was empty. About forty feet away from the building a small wooded area stretched from the road down to the pond. A stone wall separated the yard from the trees. There was an opening a little way down which opened up into a large muddy area scattered with small stones. It looked to be at least an acre, if not more.

"That's our food for the summer," Mr. Nilsson said as he came up behind the boy.

Joshua looked at him strangely, not quite knowing what he was talking about.

"We're going to turn you into a farmer. That field there is going to be twenty different kinds of vegetables: potatoes, corn, tomatoes, beans, broccoli, lettuce, carrots, and on and on... row after row. We have to wait until the ground dries first though. Out on the other side of the field there's apple and pear and peach and plum trees too."

The boy could make out the trees off on the other side. They weren't that tall, and their branches seemed gnarled into strange shapes. Both of them headed back to the house. Mother was ladling oatmeal into bowls as they entered. Joshua couldn't help but think how much his father would have loved to work that soil on the other side of the barn. He looked forward to putting all those skills that his father taught him about growing vegetables to good use. The Pond View seemed like it was going to be just the place for Joshua. He began to have some optimism that things would finally get better.

3

"I thought we'd finally get a dry day, but I guess not," Mr. Nilsson said as he looked out the back window.

Joshua turned and followed his line of vision. The clear sky off on the horizon was filling with a dark line of clouds, forming a distinct contrast to the blue above the pond. He was just beginning to have high hopes for this first day at Pond View, but now the gloom was beginning to seep into him again. For some reason he couldn't restrain the feeling. Ever since the accident, this anguish followed Joshua through his days. No matter how cheerful he felt one minute, the dark despair would creep in and haunt him the next. Anything could set this reaction off. It was a shame because, as Mother said, this place was supposed to be a fresh start for them. Just like the approaching clouds, Joshua's own darkness was beginning to wrap around his every thought. Sometimes these spells would last a few minutes, and other times they could drag on for days. He knew that he had no control over this murk, and the harder he tried to beat it, the deeper he sank into its depths.

Although the oatmeal smelled delicious when he first walked into the kitchen, with the scent of cinnamon and honey, Joshua just couldn't enjoy it now. Each spoonful tasted like dripping plaster. For the whole meal, the boy attempted to hide his shaded thoughts from Mother, trying not to make eye contact with her. If she realized that he was trapped in one his spells, then her own hope would fizzle. Who knew what would happen then? By now, Joshua was well aware of the fact that she couldn't really help him. It always seemed that the harder Mother tried to make things right, the worse they became. The knots would just get tighter. Knowing that he couldn't keep his illusion up for very long, Joshua shoveled the last of his breakfast into his mouth, and with a downcast mumble, excused himself from the table.

"Joshua, finish your milk," Mother said as he put his bowl on the counter. She looked over at Mrs. Nilsson with a slight grin on her face, so Joshua knew that she didn't suspect how her son was feeling. He gave her as big a smile as he could muster, and then pulled on his coat and passed the three of them on his way outside.

Joshua's lungs exploded once he got off the back porch and onto the brown grass. Taking deep breaths and trying to keep from turning his face back to the house, he walked over toward the barn; his heart heaving in his chest. The cold air iced his throat, but Joshua had no control; the gasps kept coming. Blindly making his way around to the front of the house, he stumbled along down the driveway. Without thinking, or even actively knowing what he was doing, his body turned to the right, and he followed the road away from the inn. Visions raced in front of Joshua's eyes; glimpses of frantic memories, as well as imagined retributions.

The boy's staggering gait turned into a spastic run and then a full sprint. The road began to bend around a corner to the right, and then there was a fork. Before putting any thought into it, or even slowing down much for that matter, Joshua veered to the left, feeling as though he was being chased. Suddenly, the ocean was in front of him. He continued his mad dash, and soon the road turned sharply to the sunny east, but in front of him, a path led to the shore. Slowing, Joshua followed it through the long, stringy grass that enveloped both sides of the narrow trail. As he stumbled onto the beach, he could feel tiny grains of sand seeping over the sides of his shoes.

The wind whipped onto his right cheek and fluttered his hair. Out of breath, Joshua stopped at the top of the dune and surveyed his new surroundings. It was as if he had just magically appeared at this spot, having no true recollection of what he had passed as he approached. Everything was new to Joshua, and slowly

31

his vision began to focus.

Maybe ten miles out, sat what must be Block Island. He had heard about steamers going out there, but had never actually seen the place firsthand. Bronze cliffs stretched along the front of the island with bluffs rolling along the length of it. In front of Joshua, the waves rolled in. Spray blew off the tops of each one just as it crested, and then tumbled in toward the beach, bouncing and rolling over itself as it neared. Large rocks were scattered all along the sand, and Joshua wondered where people swam in the summertime. Following the shore eastward, he could see an open stretch without any boulders. Beyond that area, there was a small group of rocks, then the beach opened up to miles of light brown sand. Despite the winter's lingering chill on this early spring morning, Joshua could almost picture bathers scattered along the beach.

Although the view momentarily distracted him, the sense of frantic foreboding soon overtook Joshua's body again. He paced back and forth, kicking up sand and trying to will the feeling away, but knowing full well what he would have to do. Sitting on a small rock which lay buried in the sand next to a larger one, Joshua stared out at the rolling waves. The wind was blocked on his right, and the sun began to warm him from the other side. The hypnotic surf started to peel the layers of pain from the young boy's tired spirit. Tears started to roll, then flow down his cheeks; breath catching with each intake of air. This uncontrolled weeping had been washing over Joshua for a year now. He tried to shut his eyes against the vision that he knew was coming, but there was no use. It appeared in his mind just like one of those ten cent picture shows at the Union Theater, only this was much clearer and didn't have any of those jerking movements.

Joshua wasn't supposed to be downtown that day. Mother had to work up at the Hearn's on the East Side for some party they were having later that night. The boy had been out of control since his father's funeral, not caring what he did or who he hurt. Inside of him, there was this rage that he couldn't control. He remembered one winter day earlier that year when he found himself in their cluttered backyard. There was a small elm tree that sat in the back corner, over near Mrs. Sullivan's house. With his baseball bat in hand, Joshua started out pretending that he was waiting to connect with one of Smoky Joe Wood's fastballs; eyeing the great pitcher as he went through his motions, then following through. Thoughts drifted back to his birthday two years before when his dad gave him that bat. He jokingly called it Old Hickory. Joshua tapped on the tree as the pitch came in again. They played catch just before dark that day after everybody left the party. Another tap on the tree. Joshua could barely get the thick handle around when Dad lobbed pitches to his son. That was the day in the park when Uncle Kevin fell in the mud. Another tap. He wasn't even too angry the day Joshua hit the ball through the window in the upstairs hallway. Tap. Then the boy's mind drifted inward, darkly, and started to focus on the bruised bark of the tree each time he swung. That one spot became everything. Slowly, the world disappeared, and soon Joshua was smashing the wood against the tree in a frenzied madness until the bat cracked, and then finally shattered into pathetic splinters. Heaving, with the broken handle clenched in his fist, the world appeared to him again. Looking down on the ground before him, Joshua couldn't remember how he had gotten to that point or what he was even doing . After a few of those episodes, Mother took him to the doctor, but according to the serious man with the white beard, nothing was ever wrong with the boy.

　　He and Mary were supposed to be cleaning the house for Grandma. Joshua had worked for awhile, but Mary's bossiness had gotten the better of him again, so he just stormed out through the front door. Each fervent step down the sidewalk and through the gate justified his righteousness. The cold, drizzly air added to Joshua's bad mood as he strutted down Point Street and across the bridge over the river. This was all a bad dream. He hated everyone he passed, wanting to reach out with his fingers and claw at their faces. Who were they to look at him?

　　The hill up to the East Side was steep, and as his

pace slowed and his thighs burned, the rage began to dwindle. Out of breath and with unfolding fists, Joshua paused for a moment and looked back toward the city. What was he doing here? Mother would just shoo him out of the Hearn's kitchen and send Joshua home. She would take Mary's side, and he would have go back and clean the house anyway. Why was he so angry? What was bothering him so much? He had to help clean the house every single Saturday for as long as he could remember.

Deflated, he crossed back over the river at the bottom of the hill and ambled by all of the shops downtown. Slowly, Joshua settled back into himself again. People's eyes didn't look so full of pity now. The pressure that had trapped his heart and mind was releasing, like the steam from the boats that traveled along the river. The displays in the stores distracted him. The boy became lost in the decorative windows, wanting to be part of the world created there, dreaming of someday just walking inside and buying whatever he wanted. As he was moving along Westminster Street, Mary appeared from out of no where with her finger wagging.

"Joshua, I'm sick and tired of your behavior," she screeched at her brother just like Mother did. "If you don't get home right now, I'm going to drag you there by your ear."

He started to argue for a moment, sulking and pouting, but then gave in to her; knowing that she wouldn't give up, and that she truly would drag him home exactly the way she promised. They began the walk back, and soon without realizing it, both of them were laughing. Just as they were getting to Empire Street, the horse came around the corner. Joshua couldn't remember what was so funny right before it happened, but they weren't paying attention, and then there was blackness.

When Joshua's eyes snapped open, there was nothing there. He was on his back and there were strange smells; hospital smells. People were talking in the muffled distance, but Joshua couldn't see anything. There was just a gray haze in front of his eyes. Slowly reaching his hand up, Joshua could feel the cottony bandage around his head. His fingers trailed down, but oddly, his eyes weren't wrapped. Joshua kept trying to blink, but still, nothing appeared. A frantic moment passed until he realized that it must be night and all of the lights were out. Joshua's head throbbed with each heartbeat, and he tried to focus on the sounds that were around him. A female voice that he didn't recognize seemed to be walking somewhere nearby.

"Good afternoon, doctor," she said. "What a wonderful day it is with the sun finally shining."

Joshua made a gasping noise when he realized what time it was. Mother was suddenly by his side.

"Joshua, Joshua... are you awake?"

"I think so, but why is it so dark?"

"I'll get the doctor," she said, and he could hear her shuffling away.

"What happened?" he shrieked, but no one was there.

Joshua tried to wrestle the bandages from his head. When he attempted to get up, his world spun darkly, and he collapsed back down. Hushed voices entered the room, and fingers probed his head and face. They talked as if the boy wasn't even there. Joshua kept asking what happened, but all they cared about was bending his arms and legs and tapping his knees and elbows.

"I can't see!" Joshua screamed. "I can't see!" He continued, groping out at whatever was in front of him.

The doctor wrestled Joshua back down to the bed, and in a moment, there was a cold cloth with a sharp odor placed over his mouth. Joshua thrashed and tried to push it away, but soon he lost all of his strength as the ether sent him to another place.

It wasn't until later on; maybe days, when Joshua heard Mother and Grandma whispering about funeral arrangements that he began to realize what had happened.

Wracked with a numbing pain in his chest, Joshua opened his stinging eyes, exhausted. The ocean was still there in front of him, but Mary was gone. Her smile was what he remembered the most. Even after his father died, she took it upon herself to make her brother's life bearable. Mother would get frustrated with him, but it was his sister who never gave up. How did she find him downtown so quickly? It was like she knew exactly what was going on in Joshua's mind. All the anger that he had when she was ordering him around at the house had melted away after only a few short blocks of walking with her. That was her gift, and now she was gone.

Sensing that this bout with the darkness was coming to an end, Joshua picked himself up from the sand and brushed off his pants. He was getting to the point now where he almost knew how to shrug off the painful gloom, but the problem was that he hated to go through the memory of that day. Each time Joshua replayed those moments through his head, he was able to briefly ease the murky blackness from his mind. The pain of reliving it though, was almost too much, and sometimes Joshua would just rather deal with the weight on his chest, than go through it again.

The wind still blew, and the heavy, gray clouds were getting closer. Houses dotted the beach on both sides. They sat in clumps of three or four, but others were set back and isolated. Joshua saw another windmill at a house off to the east. Slowly, he started to head back up the path and retrace his steps to the inn; noticing things now with new eyes. Rabbits lazily bounded in yards and then scattered when he passed. A chipmunk scampered over a low stone wall. Somewhere off in the distance, he heard a gunshot.

It was strange how Joshua's mind worked. These sensations that he had seemed to infect his whole being, and he truly had no control over them. As he walked, Joshua tried to sort it all out as best he could. A couple of times over the last year he had seen or thought of something funny, and immediately wanted to share it with Mary because he knew that she would appreciate it. For a few wonderful seconds, Joshua imagined her laugh as he told her, then suddenly his whole body would be slammed with the realization that she was dead; gone forever. If she wasn't so bossy, then he would never have left the house that day; and if she wasn't so stubborn, then she wouldn't have tracked him down on Westminster Street. Joshua's anger, though, was soon swept away with a flood of guilt. It was his fault that she died. If he had just tidied up the kitchen and the parlor, like he was supposed to, then none of this would have happened. What had started out as a happy thought only moments before, soon spiraled into an abysmal gloom. This routine had been playing in Joshua's mind over and over again, and he couldn't make it go away. Like some violent storm, he never knew when it was going to hit or how long it was going to last. Sometimes, he just had to close his eyes and rock back and forth, knotting his forehead and taking the pain.

The inn had a different look as Joshua approached from this direction. He could see Mr. Nilsson walking out toward the barn as he came around the back corner with the dog, Kip, following at his heels. Because he didn't want to face Mother right away, Joshua followed him.

"Ready to chop some wood?"

"I guess so," Joshua answered, trying to keep his voice as even as possible.

"I'll get you started. I've got to get that wheel fixed. We need more wood, and I've got to get down on the beach and collect some seaweed."

For the life of him, Joshua couldn't even begin to understand why the man needed seaweed. He figured that the look in his eye asked the question for him.

"For the garden. Seaweed's the best fertilizer around, and the price is right. I just pile it out on the other side of the field. It smells for awhile, plus the rain has to wash some of the salt off of it. Then I just till it right into the ground."

This concept really wasn't sinking into Joshua's mind. He couldn't remember his father ever mentioning using seaweed in his garden. He just seemed to plant the stuff in the ground and weed it a couple of times a week until the vegetables were ready to pick. There was some powdery mixture that he always put in the ground with the seeds and plants, but it sure wasn't seaweed.

"I get some loads for a few of the other places around here too. They pay us or swap things. We'll get some chickens and some nails and wire for the coop if we can get enough."

"How do you collect it?"

"Nettie and me just go down to the beach with the pitchfork. It's usually lying all along the shore after the surf is up."

Joshua just nodded.

"If this rain holds off for awhile, and if I can get the wheel fixed right, then we'll go down after lunch."

Out on the other side of the wall, just before the muddy field where their vegetables were going to be growing soon, there was a pile of logs. They weren't split like the ones stacked along the side of the barn. Mr. Nilsson rolled one away from the rest and turned it up on its end. Taking the heavy ax that he carried with him from the barn, he smoothly brought it up over his head and then let it fall. His wrists snapped just as the sharp metal hit the wood. With a crisp cracking sound, the log split in two.

"It's easy. This wood has been drying since last fall, so it pops nicely. Now you just take each of these," he said as he reached for one of the split halves, "and do the same thing. Here, you try it."

Joshua grabbed the ax handle. It felt different than a baseball bat. The weight made the whole thing feel awkward, and he couldn't find a good way to hold it. With his hands held apart like Ty Cobb, Joshua heaved the ax over his head and brought it down. The ax blade slid to the left and then off the log. His body followed through, and as the wood tipped over on its side, Joshua tripped over it and fell to the ground.

"That's not quite it," Mr. Nilsson said patiently as Joshua quickly stood up. "Use your legs to balance yourself first. Tighten your muscles. Bring it up, and then let it fall back down."

This time Joshua focused more on what his body was doing instead of thinking about the ax and the log. He brought it down squarely in the middle, and the metal sunk in about an inch.

"Good, good, now you're getting it."

He had to tip the log back over and work the ax handle until the head slipped out of the log. Josh put the wood back up on its end, lined himself up, and then swung down again. The ax hit the log right on the corner, and a two inch splinter broke off.

"Keep trying, you'll get it," Mr. Nilsson said as he walked back into the barn. "It's easier without an audience. You just need to get the feel of it."

Joshua looked back at the huge pile of wood, and figured that it would take him most of the summer and some of the fall just to get through it. The way he was chopping, he would have one giant stack of kindling when it was all done. Slowly though, he started to get the hang of it. By the time lunch time rolled around, Mr. Nilsson was pulling out of the barn with the cart in tow, and Joshua had about thirty pieces of split logs around him. There was a mess of bark and smaller chips of wood, though, from where he had hacked away at most of the logs. They stacked the wood next to the barn, and went in to eat.

Joshua's shoulders vibrated, and he tried to loosen them up as he sat in the chair at the table in what was now known to him as the breakfast room. Mother and Mrs. Nilsson had taken just about everything out of all the cupboards, and pots and pans were piled everywhere. The silverware was lined up on the counter, along with other cooking utensils.

"What have you been doing all morning?" Mother asked as she ladled some thick soup into a bowl in front of him.

"I took a walk down to the shore, and then I helped Mr. Nilsson chop some wood."

"How did that go?"

"He's coming along just fine," Mr. Nilsson said as he sat down across from the boy. "We'll make a lumberjack out of him yet," he laughed.

The sun had disappeared awhile ago, and now a light drizzle started to speckle the window next to them. Taking in a deep breath, the aroma of the soup warmed

Josh's bones. After letting it cool for a moment or two, he began to spoon it into his mouth. It was a good feeling to get his appetite back. Joshua had gone through most of the winter just picking at his food. Mother or Grandma had to almost threaten him just to put a forkful in his mouth. He would just swirl the food around his plate; lost in a daydream, but thinking about nothing. Today's woodcutting had snapped Josh out of his listlessness when it came to lunch.

"Looks like it's going to let up... just a passing shower maybe," Mr. Nilsson said as he looked out to the lightening sky.

It wasn't as dark now over on the other side of the pond, and the drabness above them was slowly giving way to a whiter shade of gray. Joshua finished his bowl of soup, and Mother quickly filled it again. She must have noticed his eagerness. Mrs. Nilsson gave the boy a broken end of the loaf that she had just taken out of the oven.

"A working boy needs a full stomach," she said, chuckling to his mother.

Mr. Nilsson hitched Nettie up to the cart after they finished their noon meal. The rain had stopped, but there was a raw wind blowing through Joshua. He pulled his collar up and hopped onto the cart. Mr. Nilsson put a strange looking iron rake and two pitchforks in the back, and then climbed up next to him. Josh watched him as he lightly snapped the reins and let Nettie pull them down the driveway. Turning left, the boy wondered why they were heading away from the beach.

"It's best to get on the sand over in East Beach. There's less rocks and more open shoreline."

Remembering the wide expanse that he had seen before, Joshua nodded in agreement. They followed a dirt road that had a small pond on one side, and a marshy area on the other. Josh thought that they were going to get stuck in the mud, but Nettie pulled them through. She silently worked as Mr. Nilsson gently coaxed her along. Above, the sky brightened, but the clouds still hung. The houses over on East Beach were lined along the dunes. They were mostly one-story cottages with porches looking out to the sea. Joshua could see the cart tracks in the sand in front of them. They slowed and crept over a low rise, and then down onto the open beach. Right above the high tide line, seaweed lined the beach as far as Josh could see. It was such a strange sight. He hadn't noticed it before, but there it was. He looked to the west and could almost see the point where he had sat earlier that day. The different perspectives of the view gave him pause, as he pondered the vast openness of the Atlantic Ocean in front of him. Joshua wasn't used to wide vistas. His limited views of Narragansett Bay were nothing compared to this. Block Island seemed so distant, that the scene was not distorted by its presence.

They came to a stop after only moving down the beach a little way. Mr. Nilsson hopped down, and from the other side, the boy did the same.

"The trick is," the old man said as he handed him a pitchfork, "not to pull up much sand with each haul. Try to sweep it up and over the side of the cart without missing a beat."

He demonstrated the movement, and Joshua watched as he easily scooped up a large clump. The boy tried doing the same, but only got a few strands that ended up falling through the tines and blowing away from him. His second forkful was more successful, but still not even close to what Mr. Nilsson had done. Sand skittered about as he swung the load over the side of the cart. After a few more tries, Joshua was able to get enough on the pitchfork to be considered substantial. Small, stringy pieces still drifted away each time he lifted it up, but Joshua was happy with his progress.

They continued this way for awhile; each of them working toward one another and flipping the seaweed over the wooden side of the cart. Nettie stood patiently, and whenever they finished one section, Mr. Nilsson gently urged her farther down the shore. Josh's shoulders ached from the activity after only a short time. Thankfully, he got a rest each time the cart had to be moved. The seaweed that was still wet had some weight to it, so Joshua tried to just focus on the dried batches. The load began to grow and grow in the back of the cart. Once it was mounded over the top edges, Mr. Nilsson tossed his pitchfork in the back and called it a day. Josh followed suit, and then climbed up onto the seat in front.

"Do you want to try leading her?"

Joshua wasn't sure what Mr. Nilsson was asking him, but when the man handed over the reins, he got the message. Taking the leather straps in between his fingers, he looked at Mr. Nilsson for guidance.

"Just snap them lightly, she knows what to do."

Joshua's first attempt was laughable. The reins fluttered up, and then down for about two feet. Nettie didn't even know that he had done it. Slowly her head turned back to them as if she were wondering what was going on.

"Snap it. Bring your arms up quickly, then back down again. Give it a tug when you do it, then ease off."

This time Nettie felt the crack, and without being in any rush, she began to step forward. Joshua held on to the reins; not really sure what was going to happen. The wheels of the cart followed the horse's movements.

"Now we need to turn it around and head back to the road. It'll take a wide turn because of the sand, so gently pull the left hand rein and ease up on the right."

Joshua pulled, and Nettie came to a halt.

"Not too hard, she thinks you want to stop. Get her going again, then work the turn."

The boy snapped the straps, then once they began moving, he eased her into a turn. They came all the way around, and Josh got them back into the cart tracks where they had been before. It wasn't too hard; Nettie seemed to know what to do. She followed the path back to the opening in the dune. The houses that they passed were vacant; their front windows boarded up for the winter. Joshua wondered what this place would look like during the summer.

They came back up and over the mound of sand and got back on the road where the ride was smoother. There was a woman pumping at a well in front of a three story farmhouse as they came around the first corner. Mr. Nilsson gave her a big wave, and the woman looked up and smiled. This was the only other person that Joshua had seen since he arrived yesterday. He was paying too much attention to her, and the cart went a little wide around the corner. The wooden sides scraped against some of the viney growth that was along the road. Joshua pulled the left rein in a little harder, and Nettie got back on track.

"Take a right at this turn up here," Mr. Nilsson said as he pointed ahead.

Joshua gave the man a puzzled look.

"This load's not ours today. We'll drop it at a small farm on East Beach Road. It'll mean eggs, and then chicken dinners."

Joshua followed the road down around two more corners. East Beach Road looked to be in about the same shape as West Beach Road. The muddy rutted track slowed them some, but they never got stuck. Joshua handed the reins over to Mr. Nilsson as they approached the property. The house was smaller than the Pond View, but was built in a similar style. The porch ran around the house, and green shutters formed a contrast to the white shingled sides. Mr. Nilsson eased the cart through a narrow entrance between two sides of a stone wall. They skirted to the left and around a garage and storage area. Joshua could see a mound of seaweed at the corner of a muddied plot of land, and Mr. Nilsson pulled the cart over next to it.

With not as much enthusiasm, they emptied the contents next to the pile that was already there. In silence they scraped the last remnants of the seaweed out. As Joshua was picking the final strands out of the corners, Mr. Nilsson leaned his pitchfork against the side of the cart and walked around to the house. Smoke lazily drifted up from the chimney. Joshua watched it swirl and get lost in the white sky. A few minutes later, he returned, and they were on their way. Josh looked over at the house as they passed. Curtains in the front window parted, but he couldn't see who was peering out at them.

Mr. Nilsson let him guide the cart back to the inn. Joshua was hoping that Mother would be outside when he pulled it up in front of the barn, but she was nowhere to be seen. The boy helped unhitch Nettie from the cart, and with Mr. Nilsson's assistance, he led her into the stall.

Josh had to fill her water, and once he did, she lapped thirstily at the bucket. Mr. Nilsson wheeled the cart back inside the barn and checked to see how the wheel had done. With a knock on the side of the cart, he stood back up with a satisfied grin on his face.

"Looks like she held," he said, not taking his eyes off the wheel.

They each took an armload of wood into the house. Joshua didn't drop any this time, but his arms were sore from the hard day of work. His body wasn't used to this. Mother shared a plateful of cookies with her son after they had stacked the wood and stirred up both of the fires.

"Joshua, I'd like for you to find a book to read until dinner. You've got to at least try to keep up with your studies."

Inside Joshua groaned, but he knew that if he complained about it, she would make him go up to the schoolhouse that Mrs. Nilsson had talked about. Joshua was just so tired from working, that he knew what would happen if he sat down with a book.

"Mrs. Nilsson said that you are welcome to choose any of the books from the front hall, but make sure that you take good care of them."

Joshua nodded and made his way out to the front entryway. The light was dim, so it was hard for him to make out the titles. The bookcase ran along the wall across from the formal stairway. He looked up at the large collection of different sized books that lined the six shelves. Mother stood next to him as he looked up at the collection.

"Mrs. Nilsson says that there are some professors who spend part of the summer here. That's why there are so many books."

They both silently scanned the shelves for a few moments. Nothing of interest leapt out at Joshua. There were books about Greek mythology, wars, especially the Civil War, art, and endless novels. They all looked to be too much for Joshua.

"You pick one out and read until dinner. We'll talk about it after we eat."

With that, she walked back down the hall, through

the dining room, and into the kitchen. Joshua could hear her moving things around as he turned back to the books. There were cabinets beneath the shelves, and he opened one up to see piles of yellowed newspapers and magazines. Joshua hit the jackpot with the next cabinet. There were stacks of magazines that were written just for him. He thumbed through them; checking out the titles: *Pluck and Luck Stories of Adventure, Brave and Bold Weekly, Bowery Boy Library, Fame and Fortune Weekly,* and his all time favorite, *Tip Top Weekly.* Boys in school would always trade these magazines back and forth whenever they could get their hands on them. Joshua recognized a few of the older copies, but there were dozens that he had never laid eyes on before.

Joshua grabbed the one with the baseball pitcher on the front. These were always his favorite, because once summer came, he lived and breathed the sport; at least he used to. Joshua hadn't been able to really get interested in the sport for almost two years now. His enthusiasm started to dwindle as he thought back to the times that were gone now.

Smoky Joe Wood and Tris Speaker were the two best players in baseball, and they both played for his Boston Red Sox. Things hadn't been going too well for them lately, but Joshua knew that their time would come. He was on his father's shoulders at the Huntington Avenue Grounds when the Sox won it all in 1903. Cy Young was unbelievable in those days. Since he was only three years old at the time, Joshua couldn't remember being there, but the way his dad used to tell it, Joshua cheered them on every time the Sox got a man on base.

The magazine was about a pitcher who could throw a curve that broke both ways. Batter after batter went down in puzzled amazement after the called third strike. Joshua settled into a chair in the front parlor and read on. The heat from the fireplace warmed him, and before he knew it, Mother was rousing her boy from a nap that Joshua didn't even know that he was taking.

"Joshua Keegan," she said in a stern voice, "that's not the reading that I had in mind, and you know it. I don't want you wasting your time on these trashy dime magazines. You need to pick out something substantial or I'll do it for you. Now go get washed up, dinner is almost ready."

Joshua ate like he hadn't eaten in a year. The food tasted so good, and he was so hungry, that he didn't even look up from his plate.

"The boy did some good work today, Mrs. Keegan," Mr. Nilsson said with a smile on his face. "You should be very proud of him."

By the time dessert rolled around, Joshua couldn't even keep his eyes open. His neck kept bouncing his head back and forth as he started to nod off. Mother sent him off to bed after dinner. Joshua pulled the trundle bed out, climbed under the covers, and was asleep instantly.

4

The days that followed started to settle into somewhat of a routine. There was always wood to chop, and Joshua was starting to feel more comfortable with the whole process. He didn't seem to be expending as much energy as he split the logs. What took him seven or eight swings before, now was cut down to three or four. Occasionally, he popped the log on the first try. They collected more seaweed; sometimes bringing the load over to East Beach, but mostly forming a long mound on the far side of the garden at the Pond View. Mr. Nilsson told Joshua that in a week or two, they would begin spreading it into the garden. Then he would teach the boy how to till the ground.

The stones that were scattered throughout the garden area had to be cleared before they could plow the field. Joshua made a game of it. He would pick out a tree that was off to the side and pretend that he either had to make a quick toss to first base or a long throw to the plate, depending on how far away he was. Once he got to the middle of the field, though, he had to use a bucket to haul the rocks. This became more of a chore, and Joshua wished that he had started there first and made his way outward.

March became April, and the world started to turn green. It was slow at first, but after a stretch of five nice days, the color began to explode. Joshua and Mr. Nilsson spent a whole morning getting the chicken coop ready. The work was dirty and disgusting, but the man kept reminding Joshua how good the eggs would taste, as well as the big chicken dinners. They got the hens from the farm on East Beach. After unloading a cart full of seaweed, an old man appeared and then disappeared into the side of a storehouse. Mr. Nilsson followed, and after a few minutes, both men came out, each carrying a wooden crate. Joshua could hear the squawking coming from inside of them. As they were pulling out of the driveway, Joshua looked back to the house and saw a girl that was about his age. She was standing on the porch and staring at them. This was the first young person that Joshua had seen so far. He wondered what her name was.

"Joshua, would you please hang these sheets out on the line for me," his mother's voice said from the basement.

She was starting the process of cleaning all of the linens. Joshua didn't like going downstairs. The corners were too dark, and he could never get comfortable; especially when Mrs. Nilsson sent him down in the evening to get a jar of jam for breakfast the next day. The stone walls seemed to hold some kind of secret that Joshua was afraid to know. Mother had been held captive at the stone wash tub for the last few days. Now that the weather was getting nice, the dry air could be used to their advantage. She spent hours down there in the damp basement stirring the sheets and towels in the tub, and then rolling them through the wringer. Thankfully, there was someone who had this job during the summer months. When Joshua helped her down there, he was always afraid that his fingers would get sucked in, and then his arms would follow. An imagination was sometimes a burden.

Joshua worked diligently during the mornings and into the early afternoons. He usually spent the time before dinner exploring the area around the beach. Kip would follow along with him, going off to chase rabbits and then circling back around again. Every morning Josh looked out the upstairs window and saw the line of houses off in the distance, across the marshy flats. He knew that there was a path to the breachway, but Mr. Crandall's story of the spirits back there along the way had made Josh squeamish about taking that journey. Today was the day though. He had made up his mind when he was chopping wood that he would explore what lay to the west. Over the past couple of weeks, he had gone in every other direction, and there were no longer any excuses. He had hoped that Mr. Nilsson would have had an errand to run over there, so they could go together in the cart, but it just didn't happen.

The path was probably about ten feet across in most places, but there was growth that narrowed it in others. A horse and cart could probably go through there, but the crooked turns would make it difficult. West Beach Road wove along the outside edge of this wooded area, and as Joshua moved deeper through the shadowed trail, he wished that he had taken the longer route this first time. He wondered where that old root cellar was located; the one where Mr. Crandall had said the spirits lived. If he didn't have Kip by his side, then Joshua would definitely have turned back, especially when a large, white bird squawked and flew away right in front of him. His heart jumped, but before he could think about it too much, the path came out onto the dirt road.

He could see the buildings now. Some were three stories high, and one was taller, all lined along what Joshua figured was the breachway. Mr. Nilsson had said that was what connected the pond with the ocean. One structure sat on top of a low hill. Joshua knew that there was some life down here, because for the last few days, trucks and carts had been passing by the inn. That was probably the origin of Joshua's urge to come down here. He really hadn't seen too many people since he arrived, and the only person his age had been that girl back at the farm in East Beach.

As he approached the small village area, Joshua could hear sounds of life, but he really couldn't see anyone. There was an engine revving from inside a large garage, and somewhere nearby he could hear hammering. The first person who Joshua saw was a man pulling a fancy buggy out of a storage shed. He gave the man a small wave as he passed by.

There was a walkway between two cottages, so Joshua followed it to the breachway. Mr. Nilsson had told him about this place, but his first sight of it was amazing. The water was rushing out to sea at an incredible clip. Following the salty river, Joshua watched the current flow out toward the open ocean. There was a boardwalk that led along the shoreline. The breachway bent around a short corner, and there in front of him was the Atlantic Ocean. The water rushed out, yet waves crashed into the flow from the sea. This caused a swelling and a dangerous chop.

On the other side, Joshua could see a sign that read, United States Coast Guard Life Saving Station. The building had a ramp with some type of track running from a large door right down into the water. He wondered if it was some type of boat launch. The American flag waved proudly next to the structure. Out on the water, there was a large ship sailing by, and closer to the shore, a smaller boat sat not too far from the point. Joshua could see that two men were pulling up rope from the water. Watching for a moment, he saw what looked like a wooden cage being hauled up over the side of the boat. Joshua wasn't sure what they were doing.

Back along the boardwalk, Josh retraced his steps taking in all of his new surroundings. The shore was lined with cottages, inns, and hotels. He passed signs for the St. George, Breakers, Worcester House, The Ocean View, and the largest building, the Eldredge Hotel. All of them were closed up, but Joshua could almost picture the liveliness of these places in the months to come. Kip chased seagulls away up ahead of the boy, and Josh looked down at the swirling water next to him. The bottom was littered with shells. Mr. Nilsson said that pretty soon they would be heading out into the pond for clams and scallops, and Joshua couldn't wait.

On his way back to the inn, he passed a store and casino. Looking in through the darkened window, Josh could see a bowling alley in the back, as well as a bar with a soda fountain. The walls were covered with advertisements. The one for Moxie seemed to be the biggest. Josh dreamed of coming in here on a hot summer day for ice cream.

"Hey!"

Joshua jumped and suddenly spun around. Kip barked. There was a man standing there in greasy overalls with a wrench in his hands.

"Whatta ya doin' there?"

Joshua swallowed hard and tried to shrink away.

"I never seen you around here before," the man said through squinting eyes.

"I...I live at the Pond View," Joshua stuttered.

"Zat so," the man said as he rubbed his chin. "What's the Swede's name then?"

"Mr. Nilsson... I work with him. My mother's the housekeeper."

"Well, whatta ya doin' 'round here?"

"I don't know, just looking around, I guess."

"You fixin' ta take anything?"

"No... no. I was just looking."

"Well, you shouldn't be walkin' around on people's property when they ain't around."

"I'm sorry, I just looked inside."

Joshua couldn't tell if this man was really angry, or if he was trying to make him feel uncomfortable. He kept tapping the wrench in the palm of his hand, and Joshua wondered what the metal would feel like if the man decided to haul off and hit him with it.

"Whatta you do at the inn?"

"I don't know, chop wood... get seaweed for the garden... help get the place ready for the summer," Joshua trailed off, not knowing what else to say.

"Travis," a voice called from inside the garage. "Are you helpin' me with this or what?"

"I'm just meetin' our new neighbor," Travis called back with a strange grin on his face.

A moment later another man came out of the garage wiping his hands on a dirty rag.

"Who's this?"

"He works at the Pond View," Travis answered. "He was lookin' in the window here, so I got a little suspicious."

"Oh yeah, what's he gonna take, an old can a beans? There's nothin' in the store yet."

Joshua just watched as the two men talked.

"I'm Homer, and this is my brother Travis."

"Hi, I'm Joshua. I was just looking around."

"The Pond View, huh," Homer said. "The Swedes run a tight ship. I guess they have to, old lady Van

51

Houtten would can 'em if they didn't. She thinks this is Watch Hill or Newport or somethin'... Me, I think it's better."

Joshua just stared at Homer, not knowing what to say. He hadn't heard Mr. or Mrs. Nilsson say anything bad about the family who owned the inn. In fact, it seemed like they really looked up to them; Mrs. Nilsson especially. This was a strange side to hear about. Josh just scratched Kip's head, looking back over toward the breachway, wondering how to get out of this conversation.

"Well Travis, let's get back to that engine," Homer said. "And we'll let Joshua continue his explorations." The man smiled and nodded at Joshua, but Travis still had a scowl on his face.

Joshua decided to head back along the beach, not sure what to think about the encounter with the two men. He followed the boardwalk near the end of the breachway, and then continued on the wooden pathway as it turned around the corner. Groups of cottages lined the shore as he walked along. The sound of his footsteps on the boards served as a reply to the waves that were bouncing in over the rocks. The boarded up windows gave the houses a haunted look. He wondered how many people would actually be walking on this boardwalk during the summer. He pictured women under sun umbrellas and kids racing along in their bathing trunks. When the walkway ended, Joshua hopped down the steps and onto the beach. He began to jump from rock to rock. Suddenly, he looked forward to the future. Thinking back, he realized that this was the first time that he had this feeling since the early spring of 1910.

The problem now was that once he started to dwell on the reasons why he couldn't look forward to the future, his mind began to spiral downward. What right did he have to look ahead to anything? He stumbled on a rock and banged his knee, but got right back up. How could anything be good in his life? If he started to think that way, then who knew what would happen next? Joshua slid on another rock and scraped his hand, but he kept going. Maybe his mother would die next, and then where would he go? Back to Providence? His movements started

to get more erratic as his mind raced. He suddenly felt
dizzy, and before he knew what was happening, Joshua
fell face first onto the beach. Sand went in his nose and
mouth, as well as into his eyes. Trying to wipe it away
only made the tears flow more.

For a moment, he sat there, out of breath, but
quickly bounced up and began to run again. He swerved
around the rocks as fast as he could; occasionally
knocking his knuckles against the bigger rocks. He
couldn't control the thoughts that kept battering his mind.
Joshua remembered when his father would sit in his chair
in the parlor and listen to Mary read to him. His mother
told her son that it was their time together, and he
shouldn't go in there and bother them. The unfairness of
it all made Joshua want to scream. Here was a beautiful
summer evening, and instead of playing catch out in the
backyard, his father just sat inside with his sister. He
hated both of them that day, and secretly, he wished that
he would never see them again. Now, running along the
beach, knowing that he got his wish, Joshua Keegan
couldn't help feeling responsible for the whole thing.
Finally collapsing on the beach on all fours, he knelt and
slammed his fists into the sand as hard as he could. The
boy punched and punched. He was so sorry now that he
ever had that dark thought. He knew that he would never
be forgiven. His tears dropped down and mixed with the
blood that was coming from his mangled hands. Finally,
Joshua just lay down and sobbed.

Kip's tongue on the back of his neck brought him
out of his nightmare. Joshua sat up and looked out to the
ocean. The waves kept rolling in as if he wasn't even
there. Glancing down at his hands, Josh saw the damage
that he had done to himself. Now he would have to
explain it all to Mother. His mind started to work on a
believable tale that he could tell her. He could just say
that he fell from one of the rocks onto some smaller ones.
She would make a fuss about being more careful next
time, but hopefully she wouldn't be suspicious.

Getting up from the sand, Josh walked a little way
down the beach until he came to a small tidal pool. He
rinsed his hands, and felt the pain as the salt water

cleansed the blood. He took handfuls up to his face and washed away the sand and tears. Then, he dried himself off with his sleeve. Joshua knew that he would have to walk around for awhile to settle himself back down, so he continued his journey down the beach. Things didn't look so hopeful anymore. He barely glanced at his surroundings now; just keeping his head down and trying not to get lost in any more of those dark reflections again.

As his pace started to slow into a normal rhythm, Joshua began to snap out of his melancholy thoughts. He glanced out at the ocean, and noticed that the water wasn't really the blue that he imagined it would be. There was more of a light green quality to it. His last glimpse of the water before he went up the path to the road was of the frothy, white bubbles from the waves swallowing up the sand on the edge of the shore. Wondering if maybe the answers to some of his problems could be solved here along the beach, Joshua tried to keep the image of the water in his mind as he headed back to the inn.

Mr. Nilsson was sharpening a metal piece from the plow on the stone wheel when the boy returned. He had the pedal pumping at a good pace as water dripped onto the spinning stone. The man was just finishing up as Josh came into the barn. The weight of the plow made the whole process difficult, and Mr. Nilsson struggled to get it over his leg and back onto the ground.

"Hey, Joshua, I didn't even see you come in. You want to give this a try? I noticed the ax needs a little bit of an edge to it."

"Sure," Joshua answered, trying to sound confident, as he reached over to the wall to retrieve it.

"Alright, just hop up on the seat here, and then slowly get the stone turning with your hand. The pedals just go up and down, so you need to keep it turning."

Joshua nodded as his legs got it started.

"You need to make sure the wheel stays wet. This can here lets it drip slowly," he said, adjusting the flow. "Now, when you start to sharpen the ax, make believe that you're trying to slice off a thin piece of the stone. This'll give it a sharp edge."

Joshua followed Mr. Nilsson's instructions and

slowly touched the metal down onto the stone. It bumped and grinded for a moment, and then the boy lifted it back up.

"Hold it tight."

He tried again, and the ax seemed to fall into a groove as the stone shaved the dullness off. Joshua flipped it onto the other side and repeated the process.

"Wow, that's pretty sharp."

"Yup, more people get hurt with dull tools than sharp ones. Tomorrow we plow. We'll till that seaweed into the ground, then do it again next week. We should be ready to plant after that."

Joshua nodded, still thinking about his father. The dark thoughts from the beach had faded, but the remnants still lingered. The idea of planting vegetables for the garden only made Joshua long for the times he had done the same thing with his dad.

"I'm going to chop some wood before dinner, so I can work in the garden tomorrow," Joshua said, trying to avoid dwelling on the thoughts that were creeping back into his mind. The physical work of swinging an ax would focus him. He would have to put his full attention on the wood, so there wouldn't be room for drifting off.

When his mother called him in for dinner, his body was sweating and his mind was clear. Joshua tried to figure out how he could keep himself from breaking down so easily. There really weren't any warning signs; his brain just decided to cloud up, and then the storm came on. Joshua never knew how long it would last, or what damage it would cause. Since they had arrived at the inn, his mother hadn't seen him have one of his episodes yet, so maybe he could continue fooling her. He knew that his days were numbered though. Because he couldn't control them, he never knew when the spells would happen. The odds were that one of these times, she would be nearby. Then there would be problems.

"What did you do to your hands?" His mother asked when he sat down at the table.

"I fell when I was down on the beach," Joshua said, not making eye contact with her. "I was jumping from rock to rock, and I slid, and then fell on some other rocks.

55

I'm okay."

When Joshua finally did look up, his mother was staring at him with pity in her eyes. It was then that he knew he couldn't fool her much longer.

"I'm okay. It doesn't hurt too much."

Mrs. Nilsson came in with a roasted chicken and broke the spell.

"Well, this is the first real meal that we've had since we've been here," Mr. Nilsson said. "Thanks to all that seaweed we hauled."

Joshua cut off a large piece for himself, spooned some mashed potatoes, and then some beans. Trying to avoid eye contact with his mother, Joshua focused on the delicious meal that was in front of him. He hadn't had anything like this in weeks.

"The Drabble brothers should be here in a day or two," Mr. Nilsson said, "and then we can start painting the place."

Joshua looked up from his plate. He had heard the Nilssons talk about Walter and Henry Drabble before. They had worked in the quarries for years, but now their bodies couldn't do the heavy lifting. The brothers spent the spring and the fall painting houses all along the different beaches.

"Old Cal stopped by while you were over in East Beach," Mrs. Nilsson said. "He brought the mail."

"Oh, anything interesting?" Mr. Nilsson asked.

"No, just a few letters."

Joshua looked up from his meal. They hadn't heard from Grandma since they arrived, so he wondered if she had sent them anything.

"We got a letter from the Leightons in Springfield. It doesn't look like Mary is going to make it down to the shore this summer."

This sudden mention of his sister's name made Joshua choke on his food. He gagged on the mouthful of chicken, and then swallowed it the wrong way as an uncontrollable intake of air dragged the meat into his windpipe. The boy stood and tried to heave it back up, but nothing happened. Joshua couldn't breathe; the food was stuck.

"Joshua," his mother said somewhere off in the distance.

He stumbled into the kitchen, trying to cough it up, but was unsuccessful. Grabbing at his throat, Josh wretched, falling down on one knee. Nothing worked. Suddenly, a hard slap landed in the middle of his back, and the food came out of his mouth. Josh sat down on the kitchen floor and sucked in air. Mr. Nilsson had his hand on the boy's shoulder, looking at him with concerned eyes.

"Joshua, are you alright?" Mother asked as she knelt down in front of him.

The boy burst into tears, and then into frenzied sobs. Joshua couldn't catch his breath now. Although the food was gone, his weeping kept him from being able to settle back down. Mother came closer and put her arm around her son; gently rubbing his back.

"Why don't we go upstairs and cool off."

She helped Joshua from the floor and then up the stairs. He laid down on her bed on his stomach and looked out the window. His mother's hand made slow circles on his back. They were both quiet for awhile, as Joshua's breathing settled back to normal. In his mind, images of Mary kept flashing through his thoughts. Pictures of her walking down the street, coming out of church, and helping him with his schoolwork flooded into his consciousness.

"I miss her," he said in a quiet voice.

"I know."

The leaves on the trees were getting bigger now. They had started out as small green folds, but now they had their shape. Joshua watched as they fluttered slightly outside of the window. His wet cheek rested on the pillow.

"I don't know what to do."

"I don't either," his mother responded in a sad tone. "I wish I did."

Again, they were quiet, letting their thoughts drift.

"If I try to forget her, I get angry at myself for doing it... but if I think about her too much, then I just start crying again. I can't help it."

"Me too," his mother responded.

Joshua could hear her sobbing softly. His tears rolled down the side of his face and onto the already damp pillowcase. This was the first time that his mother had ever admitted her feelings to him. It almost seemed as if his own miserable thoughts were shared with her. In the past, she had tried to be strong, but now it was as if she was surrendering. Somehow this made Joshua feel better, but he didn't understand why.

Outside, the light was beginning to fade. Another day at the Pond View Inn was ending. Joshua wasn't sure if this place was going to be any better than the house in Providence. It seemed like his journeys into the darkness were getting less and less frequent, but the thoughts that streamed through his mind were building in intensity. He wasn't sure what would happen if they became too powerful. Joshua just wished that he could be more in control of them.

"I need to go downstairs and help Mrs. Nilsson," Mother said in a gentle voice. "I'll be back in a little while."

She slowly got up, giving her son a light squeeze on his shoulder. He continued to stare out the window, watching the long shadows disappear into twilight. He must have dozed off, because the next thing that Joshua remembered was his mother coming into the room with a small kerosene lamp on a tray. There was a plate of cookies and a glass of milk, along with a copy of *Pluck and Luck Stories of Adventure*. Joshua guessed that he wouldn't be reading The Bible tonight. Since he couldn't choose a book from downstairs and stick with it, his mother had been making him read from the good book each night. They would take turns reading parts, and then talk about it before going to sleep. There were actually some pretty good stories in the book. They had started out reading the Old Testament, especially Genesis, but for the last few nights, they had read about Jesus' life in the New Testament.

His mother felt his forehead after she put the tray down.

"Why don't you try to eat something, and then read

for awhile. I'll be back up soon."

Joshua was starving now. All of the work that he had done on this day had given him an appetite, but his first real dinner was ruined because of his reaction to Mrs. Nilsson's mention of the name Mary. He ate all of the cookies and drank the milk before making himself comfortable to start reading. Pulling the trundle bed out from under his mother's bed, Joshua drew back the covers. He pushed the pillow up against the iron rail of the bed, and began to thumb through the magazine. He hadn't seen this copy before. The first story was a tale of an African safari. Joshua skipped to the second one. It told of a ship caught in a storm. Water crashed over the bow as waves tossed the boat in all directions. Dozing, Joshua drifted off before the hero could rescue the crew.

With a loud crash, Joshua bolted up from his bed. Lightning flashed through the window, and thunder rumbled the whole house. At first, the boy thought that he was trapped on the ship, but the bursts of light every few seconds showed him the outlines of his bedroom at the Pond View. The rain battered the roof overhead, and Joshua wondered how long the storm had been going on. The brilliant flashes of lightning lit up the tree outside, giving it an odd spectral shape. The thunder rolled in off the pond and over his head. Joshua sat up and could see his mother on her elbows watching the display.

"Boy, that's quite a storm," she said as she turned to him.

Suddenly, thunder and lightning crashed at the same moment. Joshua could hear a crack somewhere nearby. He wondered if it was a tree or the windmill getting hit. The rain came on even stronger, and the lightning flared almost continuously. The thunder drummed in Joshua's heart; each clash waking him up a little bit more. Within a few minutes though, the storm started to drift away. He could hear the rumbles rolling out to sea. The lightning flashes got dimmer and fewer as the rain began to fall in a lighter and steadier way. Soon the boy drifted back to sleep, wondering what tomorrow would bring.

5

The ground was too wet to till the garden, so Mr. Nilsson said that they would be cleaning out the upstairs room in the barn for the Drabble brothers. Joshua had never ventured up to the loft.

"It's not too bad up there," Mr. Nilsson said, "we just have to air it out."

When Joshua climbed the ladder and peered over the edge, the first thing that caught his eye was the black bicycle that was leaning against the wall. He never had one to call his own, but once in awhile, his friend Michael Joyce would let Joshua ride his family's bicycle. He used to watch all the people cruising by in Roger Williams Park too, hoping someday that he would have one for himself.

"That's a nice one, isn't it," Mr. Nilsson said, pointing to the bike. "Mr. Van Houtten brought it up from New York City two summers ago. We'll grease it up, and you can try it out."

A smile came to Joshua's face. He couldn't wait to hop up onto that leather seat. The work up there was easy, but dusty. They moved a lot of boxes and other items to the sides of the loft, and Joshua swept everything off the edge and down into the barn. He could hear Nettie in her stall sneezing and trying to clear her nose. Mr. Nilsson opened the doors at both ends, and immediately a breeze started to stream through. There were four bunks and two sets of drawers. Looking around, Joshua thought that this would be a nice place for him to live. Although he didn't mind sharing a room with his mother, the loft offered something that Joshua couldn't quite put his finger on.

"Why don't you go down and toss that rope up to me. I'll lower the bicycle to you, and we can get it fixed up."

Joshua did as he was told, and in a moment, Mr. Nilsson was sending Joshua's new mode of transportation down into his waiting arms. Mr. Nilsson fiddled around with the mechanisms on the bicycle, and then lubed the tires with some of the wheel grease that he had in a can.

"It's probably too wet to ride it now, but maybe later this afternoon you can take it out for a spin."

Joshua took a rag from the bench and began to wipe the dust and grit from the seat and frame.

"Why don't we make you the official errand boy of the Pond View? You can use the bicycle to get around. It's a lot easier than the cart."

"What errands?"

"Well, let's see. You'd have to go up to the store on the Post Road to buy newspapers. We usually get them a few times a week. There's the Westerly Sun; that's the local paper. We have guests from all over, and they like to know what's going on. I used to go up and get the New York paper... Hartford, Providence, Springfield, and Boston."

"Okay."

"There's always something that has to get done or brought somewhere. We can rig a basket on the front here, and there's a bag inside the house that you can drape over your shoulders to carry things."

Joshua's mind raced. He would be the messenger of Quonochontaug; racing around from the beach to the Post Road to the breachway and back.

"I thought maybe we would try to get a few clams this morning. Mrs. Nilsson was talking about making some chowder for dinner tonight."

"How do you catch them?" Joshua asked, still marveling at the vehicle in front of him.

"Well first, let's find an old pair of pants and shoes for you. We'll take the boat across the channel over to the flats. That's where the cherrystones are. Sometimes she uses the big sea clams, they're farther out, but I like the smaller ones. Maybe we can get some steamers too. They hide deep down in mud."

Joshua watched as the man took down two rakes from the wall. They each had tines that were at least six

61

inches long. He had always wondered what those were for; thinking they were used in the garden. Mr. Nilsson grabbed a bushel basket from under the bench, and Joshua followed him outside.

In the closet at the back of the breakfast room, Mr. Nilsson dug out some shoes and an old pair of pants.

"These are probably too big for you, but they'll have to do."

"What's going on?" Mother asked as she saw Joshua walk back into the kitchen wearing his new outfit.

"We're going clamming," the boy answered with a big grin.

"Then I'll chop up some potatoes," she answered, finally smiling again.

The day was clear, and a light breeze blew from the southwest. Now that the weather was getting nicer, there wasn't that rawness to the air anymore. They didn't even need the oars. Mr. Nilsson just pushed the dinghy away from the dock and let them drift over the channel into the shallow water. They both hopped out, and Joshua pulled the boat behind them. The water was cold on his legs. Walking was a little difficult, and Joshua stumbled a few times on the rocks that littered the bottom. As they moved closer to the flats, the water became only a few inches deep.

"It's just about low tide. This is the best time to get clams."

Joshua could see the tops of rocks breaking through the surface. After they splashed through the water for about a hundred yards, Mr. Nilsson grabbed a small anchor from the front of the boat and dropped it into the water. He took the bushel basket out and picked up a rock from the pond and put it inside.

"We don't want our basket floating away from us."

Grabbing both of the rakes, Joshua handed one to the old man.

"The trick is to work the rake into the mud and gently pull it back out. Most of the muck and small stones will drop out. What you'll have left are big rocks, clumps of mud, shells, and hopefully a clam or two."

Joshua watched as Mr. Nilsson dug into the mud.

When he pulled it back up, the rake was empty. They both went at it for a few minutes without having any luck. Finally, Joshua pulled up two cherrystones. The shells were white with blue and gray lines crossing from one side to the other.

"I got some," Josh said with excitement.

"Better check them out first."

Joshua glanced over at the man with a confused look. He picked each of them from the rake. One looked a little duller in color than the other one. When he turned it over in his hand, the shell fell open and mud dripped out of it.

"That one's no good," the man said.

Joshua looked at the other one more closely, and then tried to pry it open. The clam wouldn't give.

"I think that's a keeper," Mr. Nilsson said as he put three clams that he had just hauled up into the basket.

Joshua stared at the cherrystone for a moment. The shell was very hard, and down at the bottom of the fan shaped outer covering was a black nub of some sort. Tossing it into the container, Joshua went back to his digging.

"I try to start on this side of the pond, and as the summer goes on, I work my way north," Mr. Nilsson said. "By the time September comes, I'm all the way over where the deep water starts."

Joshua looked over and could see where the light brown coloring of the shallow water turned to a deeper shade and then to blue. He figured that it must be at least a hundred and fifty yards across. That would mean a lot of clamming over the summer.

"We usually do a clambake in July and then in August. That's a lot of clams, lobsters, steamers, and fish."

"Lobsters?" Joshua asked as he looked around at the area surrounding them.

"Don't worry, they're farther out in the pond and in the ocean. I set up a few traps, but we usually end up getting most of what we need from Johnny Crandall. He's the local fisherman around here."

They dug for awhile in silence, slowly filling up the

bottom of the basket, and then Joshua watched as their catch began to pack the sides. The salt air smelled good, and the morning breeze made the memory of last night's storm fade away.

"Mrs. Nilsson and I spoke with your mother last night."

Joshua's daydreaming thoughts came to an abrupt halt.

"She said that you've been having some difficulties lately."

He was slow to answer.

"I guess so."

They were quiet again for awhile. Mr. Nilsson dropped a few more clams into the basket.

"I came to this country when I was fifteen years old. The War Between the States was just getting started. I didn't want to leave Sweden, but my uncles had made the journey a few years before and had set things up for my parents."

Joshua wasn't sure why Mr. Nilsson was telling him all this.

"My brother Lucas was eleven years old, and he'd been sick since the day he was born; always coughing and trying to catch his breath. They never thought that he'd make it to his third birthday."

The boy almost knew what was coming next, and he tried to hold back the thoughts that were trying to break through.

"It was my job to take care of him, since Mother and Father were always working. I'd take him places, but we would always have to stop, so Lucas could rest. It was during those times when he would tell his stories. We would see a man and woman walking, and he'd make up this tale about what he thought was going on in their lives. Or we'd see a shop, and he'd make up a crazy story about what they really sold inside. He was so funny. I think he tried so hard to make me laugh because he knew I hated stopping so often when we were trying to get somewhere."

Again, Mr. Nilsson paused and continued his clamming. The sun was beginning to warm the back of

Joshua's neck.

"He never recovered from the journey across the ocean. Sometimes I look out toward Montauk Point when we can see over to Long Island from the house and think about what he was like when we pulled into New York City. Lucas was only in America for about three months before he died. I kept hoping that he would get better, but it never happened."

After a moment, Joshua looked over, and he could see the somber look on Mr. Nilsson's face as the man dug for clams.

"That was fifty years ago, and I don't think that I'm totally over it... I'll never be."

Suddenly, Joshua had a vision of himself as an old man, still stumbling through a life filled with tears and a knotted up brain.

"I had a hard time when we got to New York City. We came from a small town outside of Stockholm, so I wasn't used to the fast paced life in my new home. When Lucas finally gave up, I didn't know what to do with myself. I wandered around, not knowing what was going to happen to me. Mostly, I was just sad."

Joshua was sad too; not just for himself, but for Mr. Nilsson's loss.

"Now it was my Aunt Catherine who really helped me to get back to myself again. She told me that it was okay to feel sad. That showed how much I loved my brother. His loss emptied a part of me, and my job now was to fill that space up with a part of Lucas that I could carry through my life."

Joshua now listened to the man speak with a growing interest.

"It took awhile to figure out what to do. At first I tried to remember everything I could about Luke, but that only made things worse. The more I focused on him, the sadder I got."

"I know," Joshua said in a quiet voice.

"One day while I was walking down the street, I sat down on a bench for a minute to watch all of the people go by, and it suddenly hit me. I started to think about the stories that my brother used to tell. I started to make up

65

a tale of my own. I knew that I wasn't as good as him, but every time I thought of something new, it would remind me of my brother. I started to get in the habit of doing it every day, and soon I wasn't so sad about the memory of him, I was happy that a part of him was with me. I learned English by making up stories. In my mind, I was talking to Lucas, and I felt like I was teaching him all about this new country that our family had come to."

Joshua's mind was starting to turn; not quite formulating anything, but seeing a kind of light up ahead.

"So, when I say that I'll never get over the death of my brother, I really mean it. But through all my years, I've shared my life with him. He's helped me to understand people. I was thinking about him a lot last night before I went to sleep. I think that he would have wanted me to tell you this and maybe you can figure out a way to fill up the empty places inside of yourself."

They had three quarters of the basket filled now. Mr. Nilsson picked it up from the water and hauled the whole thing over the side and into the boat. They trudged back through the edge of the flats and hopped into the dinghy to drift across the channel. Both of them grabbed a handle and walked up the path toward the inn. Something had passed between them. Joshua wasn't sure what was going to happen next.

"Mrs. Nilsson will probably get three pots of chowder out of this haul. We'll bring some over to East Beach. The Thorntons love chowder."

Since they had old clothes on and the garden was still muddy, Mr. Nilsson and Joshua had a quick bite to eat outside on the porch before heading over to the piles of seaweed. They each carried a pitchfork. Now that a few rainstorms had rinsed some of the salt from the smelly mounds, Mr. Nilsson said that it was time to work it into the soil. Joshua sank in the mud as he hauled his first forkful back across the area.

"You don't have to cover every inch of dirt," Mr. Nilsson said as he passed the boy, "just make sure you spread it around evenly."

The shoes were heavy, and the wet pants chaffed his legs. This wasn't a bad job, but Joshua wished that there was an easier way to move this seaweed around. After an hour or so of work, there were small piles spread over a third of the garden. Mr. Nilsson went in to get some water for them to drink. Joshua leaned on the pitchfork and pondered the journey of this seaweed. From the bottom of the ocean, to the beach, to the cart, to the yard, and then into the soil to make it rich so their vegetables could grow. His father would have been amazed at the idea of it. He was always trying to figure out better ways of making his own garden grow. Joshua's mind began to turn now. The story that Mr. Nilsson had told him about his younger brother was slowly starting to process in his head. Gardening and baseball had been his father's passions.

"Thirsty?"

Joshua turned and saw Mr. Nilsson approaching with two glasses of water and some pieces of bread. He reached out for the drink and gulped down half of it before coming up for air.

"Mrs. Nilsson and your mother are making the chowder and some loaves of bread. I was thinking that maybe I'd try to rig up a basket for the bicycle, so we could send you on your first errand later this afternoon."

"Where?" Joshua asked, finishing off the last of the water.

"I figured that we could tie the lid to one of the chowder pots, and you could bring it over to East Beach. If you don't mind moving some of this seaweed for awhile, I can get that started."

"Sure."

"Then maybe you could swing up to the Post Road and get a few supplies and maybe the New York paper. Talking about it earlier got me to thinking that I don't really know what's going on in the world."

"Do you think the newspaper would have anything about the Boston Red Sox?"

"A Red Sox fan, eh? We'll have to cure you of that," Mr. Nilsson said chuckling. "They probably have the box scores. I don't think they get the Boston paper until the summer people start to arrive. Maybe the Westerly Sun would have something."

Joshua handed him the empty glass and trudged back across the muddy field. The hauling of seaweed became a routine now. Trying to cover as much of the garden by taking the fewest steps was Josh's goal. His pants were almost dry now, and the squishing sound from the oversized shoes had ceased. Baseball and gardening... gardening and baseball. These two thoughts kept circling through his mind as he plodded back and forth. He would try to learn as much as he could about growing food; and go beyond what his father knew. That would be the way that he filled up the empty spaces inside of him. This would be the field that his father always wanted to start in Warwick. Joshua planned to tend to this garden as if his father were watching him; helping him. Now the spreading of the seaweed became a much more serious affair. He realized that what he was doing was feeding the garden; making the dirt fertile, so the vegetables could feed them. The cycle of the whole process started to make connections in his brain. He remembered what his father's garden looked like by August. The fullness of the green leafy plants overtook the backyard. Joshua rested for a moment and gazed across at the muddy dirt. He had a long way to go if he was ever going to turn this patch of soil into a lush garden.

Looking back toward the barn, Joshua saw Mr. Nilsson wheel the bicycle outside. There was a slatted wooden crate attached to the front handlebar over the wheel. Joshua walked up from the garden to better look at it.

"It should hold," Mr. Nilsson said. "I put a metal bracket on the bottom, and this fruit crate is sturdy, but not too heavy."

"It looks great."

"Why don't we finish up with the seaweed. It looks like you took care of a good chunk of it. Then you can change your clothes and try her out."

Joshua smiled and nodded. Taking one last look at the bicycle, he headed back over to the seaweed. They had started at the bottom of the field, where the water tended to drain. Now they were at the top, and the dirt wasn't so wet. This made walking across much easier, and within three quarters of an hour, Joshua was scooping up the last of the seaweed. Mr. Nilsson had brought one of the clam rakes out with him, and he was spreading some of the mounds out to fill in the bare spots.

"Do you want me to get the other clam rake?" Joshua asked as he came up behind the old man.

"No, I'm just fiddling around. Why don't you go put your own clothes back on and try out the bike. You've done enough work for today."

Joshua nodded and headed back up to the house. The smell of freshly baked bread filled the kitchen. He tore a corner off the loaf that Mr. Nilsson had cut from before and popped it into his mouth.

"Joshua, take those shoes off outside instead of tracking the mud all the way upstairs," his mother said as she came into the kitchen with a handful of dishes from the dining room cabinet.

Chewing the bread, Joshua walked out to the back porch and sat on the steps. The sun was sitting over the pond now, and the breeze made the water glisten as the light reflected down onto it. The incoming tide covered all of the rocks that had been breaking through the surface earlier. Joshua couldn't figure out where the water came from and where it went each day as the tides ebbed and then flowed back in. Mr. Nilsson said that it had something to do with the moon, but that made no sense to him at all.

Joshua felt much more comfortable in his own clothes. The salty chaffing of the old pants made the bottom of his legs red. Now he was ready to try out that bicycle. This one was bigger than the Joyces' bike, but it seemed much sturdier. Josh walked it down the driveway a bit before attempting to climb on. He had to swing his leg high over the bar. The seat was a little too high, so it made it hard for him to reach the pedal when it was in the lowest position. With a wobbling start, Joshua rolled out onto West Beach Road and down toward the ocean. The fruit basket on the front handlebars made steering an awkward affair, but once Joshua got used to weight of it, he was able to compensate.

He cruised down along the road next to the shore.

The beautiful blue sky above made anything seem possible. Trying a few quick turns, Josh veered from left to right. His balance was good. As he passed each of the cottages, he thought about what it would be like when people started to migrate down here for the summer. Part of him was looking forward to the new faces, but another side wanted to keep the beach to himself. Joshua paused at the path down to the sand, glanced down at the rolling waves, and then spun the bicycle around, and headed back to the Pond View. The wind flying past his face cooled some of the sweat that he was creating as he pumped the pedals.

When Joshua returned, Mr. Nilsson was coming out of the barn.

"How'd she ride?"

"Great," Joshua replied with enthusiasm.

"Good, I think Mrs. Nilsson has some errands for you, if you feel comfortable carrying things in the basket."

"Sure."

Joshua leaned the bicycle up against the barn and followed Mr. Nilsson into the house. She and his mother were working in the kitchen as usual.

"We saw you coming up the road," Mother said with a wide grin. "You looked pretty smooth."

Joshua smiled and poured himself a glass of water.

"Do you think that you can carry a pot of chowder in that basket?" Mrs. Nilsson asked.

Joshua thought about the bumpy road and wasn't sure if it was possible.

"I think maybe we can tie the lid down," Mr. Nilsson said, "and maybe then tie the handles right to the basket."

Joshua nodded, thinking that this would probably work.

"Then I need you to stop at the store up on the Post Road," she continued. "We're getting short on a few supplies. Mr. Crandall was supposed to stop by and take our order for when he goes back into Westerly."

"We may need to take the cart over to Cross' Mill if he doesn't show up fairly soon," Mr. Nilsson replied.

Joshua was still trying to figure out if the chowder

would spill out of the basket. He didn't want to let anybody down on his first official duty as the errand boy. Mrs. Nilsson put the pot on the table in the breakfast room. It was fairly large, but it didn't seem to be completely full. Mr. Nilsson grabbed some thick string from the pantry and began to wrap it around the pot. He strung it through the handles on both sides, and then through the small handle on the lid.

"There, that should hold it," he said.

Mrs. Nilsson handed him some coins.

"We need a five pound bag of sugar and flour. If they have salt, then you can get that also. Mr. Nilsson wants the New York paper if they have it."

"It'll probably be last week's, but that's okay," Mr. Nilsson said as he came back into the room after putting the string away.

"Where is the store?"

All three of the adults laughed as Joshua asked this question.

"Oh my, we were sending you out ill prepared," Mrs. Nilsson chuckled. "It just seems like you've been here for so long, that I forget that you haven't even been through one season yet."

"After you drop the chowder at the Thorntons' farm, just follow East Beach Road up to the Post Road and take a left. You'll see it as soon as you get up there. Then you can just follow the Post Road down to West Beach Road, and you'll end up right back here."

"Okay."

"The Thorntons can keep the pot for now. You can pick it up the next time you're over there."

Joshua nodded to Mrs. Nilsson. In many ways she was just like his grandmother. Actually, she was more like the way his grandmother used to be, before all the troubles began. Thinking about this, Joshua started to realize that he wasn't the only one who was suffering over the loss of his father and sister. He just hadn't really noticed how it had affected his grandmother. This led him to ponder how his mother must be feeling about the whole thing. He always thought that she was being strong, but the conversation last night up in their room gave him a completely different view of things.

Mr. Nilsson carried the pot out to the bicycle. Joshua followed, putting the money in his pocket.

"Hold this in the basket," Mr. Nilsson said, "and I'll get some rope from the barn."

A moment later the old man appeared with a short length of rope. He looped it through the handles, and then down through the slats of the fruit crate. Repeating the process, he then tied it tightly together.

"Now, take it easy as you're riding. I don't know how much jostling this crate will put up with."

Joshua nodded, and then climbed onto the bicycle. He almost tipped the whole thing over trying to keep his balance. The weight of the chowder made the handlebars heavier. Mr. Nilsson gave him a small push, and Joshua was off. He took a left out of the driveway, and then followed the road over to East Beach. The lid loosened a bit as Joshua rattled over the rutted road. He could hear the chowder sloshing around inside the pot. Trying to keep half an eye on the basket, and half on the road ahead, Joshua slowly made his way over to the Thornton farm. He had been there five or six times to deliver seaweed, and then to get the chickens, but this was the first time that he had been there by himself.

As he pulled into the driveway between the stone walls, Joshua slowed and tried to come to a complete stop before putting his foot down. On the way over, he knew that this would be the most difficult part of the journey. As the bike came to a halt, Joshua leaned to his side and dropped his left foot to the ground. Just as he was doing this, the front of the bike tipped up and the pot started to lean down. Joshua used all of his strength to heft it back to a standing position. Once he was off the bike, he untied the pot from the fruit crate and walked it up to the front door.

Joshua knocked, and for a moment there was no response, so he knocked again. Slowly, the front door opened, and the girl who he had seen before on the front porch stared at him with big green eyes. Joshua looked at her for a moment, not knowing what to say. Her face showed no expression.

"I brought some chowder from Mrs. Nilsson."

In one swift motion the door slammed shut in his face. Joshua wasn't quite sure what was going on, but within a minute or two, the door opened again, and the old man who had given Mr. Nilsson the chickens appeared.

"I brought some chowder from Mrs. Nilsson," Joshua tried again.

The man opened the door and let Joshua step inside.

"Thank you," he said in a quiet manner, "why don't you bring it into the kitchen and give it to Mrs. Thornton?"

Joshua was led through the front parlor and then the dining room. Mrs. Thornton was in the kitchen stirring something on the stove. The girl was over at a table, sitting and writing on a piece of paper as if nothing happened.

"Oh, what do we have here?"

"Chowder."

"Our first chowder of the season."

"Mrs. Nilsson wanted me to bring it over. Mr. Nilsson and I went clamming this morning."

Over at the table, a small snort came from the girl. Joshua couldn't figure out if she was laughing at him or if she was just strange.

"Would you like some peach cobbler? It's the last jar of peaches we have from the fall."

"Yes, please," Josh answered.

"Why don't you have a seat? This is our granddaughter, Elizabeth," Mrs. Thornton said as she reached for the cobbler. "She's doing her lessons for school."

Mrs. Thornton placed the dessert down on the table along with a glass of milk.

"Joseph, is it?" she asked

"Excuse me?"

"Your name... did Mr. Nilsson say that it was Joseph?"

"No, it's Joshua."

Again, a sort of chuckle came from the other side of the table. Joshua looked around for a moment, but the woman had retreated back into the kitchen. Elizabeth ignored him, keeping her eyes on the book in front of her, so Joshua just started to eat. The sugary taste of the fruit was delicious, and although the milk was a bit warm, it was the first glass that he had had since he was in Watch Hill on his day of arrival.

"Why aren't you in the school?" Elizabeth asked, not looking up.

"What?" Josh mumbled with a mouthful of cobbler.

"School, you know, where you're supposed to go to learn. Is there something wrong with you?"

"No, I just moved here, and I do my school work at the inn with my mother," Joshua replied defensively.

"Oh," she said and packed up her books and left the room.

Joshua watched her go, not quite understanding what was actually going on here. He finished the last of his peach cobbler and milk, and then brought the dish and glass over to the sink. Mrs. Thornton had disappeared, so Joshua started to walk back toward the front door. She came around the corner with a wicker basket in her arms.

"Oh, how was the cobbler?"

"It was delicious, thank you very much."

"Leaving so soon?"

"I have to stop at the store up on the Post Road."

"Well, tell Mrs. Nilsson, thank you for the chowder."

"Okay."

Joshua was back outside and on the bicycle in a moment's time. As he left the property and turned up toward the main road, he looked back at the farmhouse. In the upstairs window, behind a half opened curtain, Joshua could see Elizabeth looking down at him.

When Joshua arrived at the general store, he could see Mr. Crandall's truck parked out front. There were two oversized, stuffed chairs in the back. Josh leaned the bike against the building and went inside. The store was dark and musty smelling, and it took a moment for him to adjust his eyes. The walls were lined with shelves, but most of them were empty. Behind a counter, stood a man with a handlebar mustache. He was wearing an apron and talking to Mr. Crandall. Both men turned as Joshua walked up to them.

"Well, if it isn't my friend from the Pond View."

"Hello."

"Tell the Swede that I'll be down there in a few days. My truck's been on the fritz, so I'm runnin' a few days behind schedule."

Joshua nodded, and then looked at the man behind the counter.

"Could I please have five pounds of sugar and five pounds of flour?"

"Sure thing, young man."

Joshua watched as he moved down the counter and reached up to one of the shelves. He pulled down a sack marked 'sugar', moved down farther and grabbed one marked 'flour'.

"Anything else?"

"Some salt."

"How much?"

"Not too much. Do you have a small container?"

"I got a one pound box."

"Okay," Josh replied. "Do you have the New York paper?"

"Last week's."

"That's okay."

The man gathered everything together, and Joshua handed over the coins that Mrs. Nilsson had given him.

"The Pond View, huh."

"Yes."

"What's your name?"

"Joshua.... Joshua Keegan."

"Well Joshua, I hope to see you again."

"Thank you," the boy replied as he took back the three pennies in change and picked up his supplies from the counter.

"Remember," Mr. Crandall shouted as Joshua was going toward the door. "tell the Swede I'll be down in a few days."

Joshua just nodded his head and pushed the door open. The brightness of the day shocked Joshua as he stepped onto the boardwalk outside of the store. He placed the items into the fruit crate and eased himself onto the bike. Off in the distance, he could see an automobile coming over the hill from the north. Josh took a right onto the Post Road, and then a left a little way down onto West Beach Road. He cruised along as the pond appeared on his right. The salty smell got stronger while he pedaled. As he was riding, Joshua's mind drifted to what Mr. Nilsson had said about his brother. He filled up the empty spaces inside of himself with different parts of his brother. Pedaling up the small rise in the road and approaching the inn, Joshua wondered again how he was going to be able to do that very thing.

6

The tilling was harder than Joshua thought it would be. First, Mr. Nilsson had to attach all the rigging to Nettie. For some reason she didn't want to cooperate on this beautiful spring morning. She kept backing up or moving before Mr. Nilsson had everything lined up. When they finally got going, it seemed as if Mr. Nilsson's patience was just about all used up.

"Joshua, why don't you follow along behind, and if any rocks turn up that are bigger than a walnut, toss them off into the bushes."

"Okay."

Mr. Nilsson held onto the handles of the plow as Nettie slowly led him across the garden. The soil turned over as they made their way in a fairly straight line. The light colored dirt and seaweed was replaced with deeply rich soil. Again, Joshua made a game of scooping up the rocks and flinging them across the field. A few of them were big, and he had a harder time disposing of them.

It took them most of the morning to till the whole garden once. Joshua couldn't imagine what it would be like to cut into earth that had never been tilled before. This area had been a garden for years, and Mr. Nilsson still struggled with the plow.

"Let's get some lunch, and we'll go through it one more time this afternoon."

Joshua just nodded.

"Are you ready to give it a try?"

"I guess," he answered in a low voice. Inside though, Joshua wasn't sure if he could handle guiding the plow or Nettie for that matter. Over the last few weeks, the horse had become friendlier to the boy, but controlling her as she walked across the field was another matter.

They ate a quick lunch that Mrs. Nilsson had

prepared for them. Mother was stuck down in the basement with the laundry. As he was chewing, Joshua started to think about the process that they used to spread the seaweed out in the field. There was an easier way, that cut out one part of the operation.

"I had an idea about the seaweed."

"Oh, what's that?"

"What if we rinsed it off when we first got back from the beach? Remember how you flushed out the well to get it pumping again?"

"Yes," Mr. Nilsson said with a smile.

"Well, if we used that water to rinse off the seaweed, instead of just letting it run off down the yard, then we could just put it out in the field instead of mounding it up on the side, and then loading it up again and moving it."

Mr. Nilsson looked out the window toward the pond for a moment before responding.

"We might be able to do that for some of the loads. The timing is difficult though. You never know when a storm is going to hit and send us all that seaweed. I'm willing to give it a try next spring if you are."

Joshua smiled, and for the first time in awhile, he had a plan for the future. He was already looking ahead to putting his idea into use. He remembered his mother getting angry at him when he was younger. She would always complain that he would spend too much time trying to figure out an easier way of doing something. If he had gotten to the job when he was supposed to, then he would have been finished before he came up with his time saving method. It wasn't so much that he disliked work, Joshua just wanted to use his time and efforts more wisely. Now, that way of thinking was starting to pay off.

"Why don't I lead Nettie, while you guide the plow," Mr. Nilsson said as they were walking back out to the field.

When they came around the back of the barn, Joshua could see just how much work they had done. The area looked completely different now. The dark soil looked ready to be planted.

"What we'll try to do is turn the soil back over

again. Do you see how I left space in between each row?"

Joshua looked and could make out the rows of mounded soil all the way down the field.

"I want you to go right through those little hills that we made before. Then we can make some rows and get most of it planted before the sun goes down."

It was harder to control the plow at first because the handles wanted to go their own way. As Joshua looked back over his first pass across the field, he could see the wobbly line of soil. He tried to keep it straighter with each path, and soon he settled into a routine. Once, a large rock popped the plow right out of the ground. Mr. Nilsson stopped Nettie and came around to look at it.

"These things grow up out of the earth every year. It's an amazing thing."

He hefted the large rock up and slowly walked it over to the side of the field. Joshua's right shoulder was throbbing because of the jolt it took when the plow struck the rock.

"Looks like the plow's okay," Mr. Nilsson said when he returned.

Joshua finished up the plowing, and then he brought Nettie back to the barn. Mr. Nilsson was digging out rows with a shovel when Joshua returned. Most of the hard work had been done, so he was just touching up the furrows.

"The almanac says to plant your summer garden after the full moon in May. We're about two days ahead of schedule, thanks to all of your help," Mr. Nilsson said with a smile.

"Why the full moon?"

"I have no idea."

Joshua was trying to figure out the influence of the moon on tides and gardening. He couldn't see the connection. When he lived in the city, he didn't give the moon a second thought. He liked seeing it full, but that was about it.

"Let's see, I've got the seeds in the barn," Mr. Nilsson said as he walked up from the garden. "We'll plant about half of it today, and the rest we'll do in about a week or so."

Joshua followed the old man into the barn. He watched as Mr. Nilsson pulled a wooden crate out from under the work bench.

"We need lettuce, radishes, carrots, beets, cabbage, onions, corn, and peas. We should have gotten the peas in a few weeks ago, but I like waiting until the whole garden's plowed."

Joshua grabbed the small packets of seeds as Mr. Nilsson handed them to him. He watched as the man grabbed a flat hoe and a pointed one. They headed back out to the field to begin the planting. Joshua had helped his father do this same process in their backyard in Providence, but it was nothing like this large scale operation. This was almost like what Josh had pictured their farm in Warwick becoming someday. Although that dream would never come true, Josh started to think about what Mr. Nilsson had said about filling the emptiness inside of him. The idea had been playing in his mind since the first day Mr. Nilsson mentioned the garden. Joshua would be taking what his father had taught him about the farming and applying it to this field. All of the weeding and watering would culminate with the harvesting of their crops. In this way, the teachings of his father would live on. This was the exact thing that Mr. Nilsson was talking about with his brother, Lucas. Joshua could already feel something growing inside of himself at the thought of this.

"I'll start dropping the seeds in, and you fill in the dirt over them. Try to leave a little bit of the mound intact. Just scrape the top part over."

Joshua followed Mr. Nilsson's instructions, and they made their way through the rows. It was always an amazing thing to see these seeds go into the ground in the spring, and then pick the vegetables in the summer. Soon, this brown acre of soil would be bursting with green.

As the sun was slowly continuing its descent over the pond, the boy and man finished up with half of the garden. The seeds sat silently under the soil, waiting for water to get them started, and then sunlight to make the plants grow. Joshua was exhausted, and he couldn't wait to get some more of that chowder. Last night's dinner was delicious, and when Mrs. Nilsson said that they would be having it again tonight, Joshua just smiled.

"Let's head over to the cold frame and check out the tomatoes."

Joshua wasn't sure what Mr. Nilsson was talking about, but he followed him anyway. Around the far side of the tennis court, back behind some low bushes, sat a white wooden rectangular box. Joshua had noticed it before, but wasn't sure what it was. When they came around to the south side of it, he could see that there were three windows looking up to the sky. Inside, tomato plants were reaching up and touching the glass. Mr. Nilsson lifted the windows up and propped pieces of wood under each. The pungent smell of tomato plants assaulted Joshua's nose. There were at least three dozen plants inside the cold frame. They seemed ready to go in the ground.

"I planted these when we first came down here. The windows keep the frost off of them for the first week or so. The sunlight really heats them up."

Joshua just nodded as the old man spoke.

"I leave this open about a foot for the next week, then I'll take the windows off completely. They'll be protected from the wind here until we put them in the ground the following week."

They walked back into the house just as Mrs. Nilsson was ladling the chowder into bowls. The smell of another loaf of fresh bread filled the kitchen and breakfast room. Joshua washed up, and then sat down to eat. This was the latest that they had ever eaten dinner. After his third bowl, all he wanted to do was go to bed. Clearing his glass and bowl, Joshua headed upstairs without saying a word.

From the bathroom window, he could see the sun disappearing behind the woods on the other side of the pond. The blend of light blue, pink, and white in the sky made Joshua think of heaven. He walked back to his room, stripped down, and pulled out the trundle bed. His shoulder still ached from when the plow jerked away from him as it struck that rock.

81

Laying on his back, Joshua's mind started to drift. Mary was somewhere up in those pink clouds, and maybe she was looking down at him now. Mr. Nilsson's story about his brother had been gnawing at him for two days. It wasn't hard to figure out how to fill up the emptiness from the loss of his father. Baseball and gardening were the man's obsessions. Joshua had been meaning to look at that newspaper that he had bought up at the store, but he just hadn't gotten around to it. The new baseball season had started, and he wanted to see how the Red Sox were doing. They were supposed to be moving into a new ballpark this year. Mary was another matter though. He couldn't quite put his finger on what they had together, and the harder he tried to capture it, the more elusive it became.

Josh's mind focused on the clouds and the setting sun that he had seen just moments before. He drifted up from his bed, out the window, and into the sky. As sleep began to overtake his consciousness, he flew through the clouds looking for Mary. As twilight became night, Joshua remembered his sister. She would curl up in the big chair in the parlor and read books. It seemed like a different one every time he saw her. Josh remembered his sister's legs tucked under herself, and her head leaning against the side of the chair. The light coming in from the window shone on her hair and shoulder. He also remembered her sitting at the table in her room writing letters. She would write letters to Mother, Dad, Grandma, Uncle Kevin, and Uncle Steven. When the postman came, she used to put her letters in with the day's mail. Joshua remembered getting a few letters himself. At the time he didn't think much of them, but now he wished he knew where they were. She would write about little things that happened; like her walk home from school or what was going on outside of her window. She also wrote letters to Father Donovan and to her friends. She even sent some letters to Dad's relatives in Boston and Ireland; giving them news about our family.

A noise suddenly woke Joshua from his musings. It was pitch black now, and he could hear his mother's breathing. For a moment Joshua listened to the crickets outside of the window. It was opened a crack now since the weather was starting to get warmer. Just as he was drifting back to sleep, a shout came from somewhere off in the distance. Getting up, Joshua went down the hall to the bathroom. Outside the window off to the southeast, he could see lanterns and torches. The light was coming from the back path to the breachway. A sudden horror crept up Joshua's spine as he thought of the spirits that wandered through there. Could these be the slave hunters coming to capture the men who got away?

An engine started out past the path on West Beach Road, and slowly the line of torches meandered out toward it. Joshua watched as they gathered around the headlights. A few of the lanterns were extinguished. A moment later the vehicle started to move down toward the breachway. Joshua watched as the headlights cut through the dark night. The view would darken and then reappear every few seconds. By the time it got down to the breachway, Joshua couldn't really tell where it was going. Once the vehicle was out of sight, Joshua looked up to see the stars. Out over the beach he could see the almost full moon rising. He shuffled back to his room and tried to recapture his dreams about Mary, but was unsuccessful.

The morning brought a stiff breeze from the west. When Joshua got outside, he could see the windmill spinning at a good clip. With the crust of last night's bread in his hand, Josh walked over behind the tennis court to check on the tomatoes. Their leaves were jutting out from all sides now, getting used to the freedom of the open window. As he came back into the yard, he noticed the trail that his footsteps had made in the dewy grass. The lawn was starting to get long now. Mr. Nilsson had said that they would be hooking up the mower to Nettie pretty soon. They had to keep the grass short, so the bugs would go live somewhere else.

Josh headed over to the barn to feed Nettie. Kip came off the porch and met him at the door. As he pulled it open, Josh felt the ache in his shoulder throb. He got the horse's feed and quickly poured it into her trough. The nervousness of his first attempts to feed her had long disappeared. A lot of things had changed since he had arrived here. His muscles were getting stronger, and most of all, he had something to occupy his mind each day. Between all of the chores that he was responsible for and the learning of new things, Joshua hadn't had time to wallow in the sadness that had filled his days in Providence.

Curiosity got the better of him after he got a glimpse of the bicycle leaning against the wall. He wanted to figure out what was going on down the path last night. With Kip trailing behind him, Joshua rolled down the driveway and then cut over to the back path. His eagerness started to ebb as he approached the site of last night's torches. Up ahead he could see where the bushes had been trampled down. The wind was fluttering Joshua's hair as he parked the bike and slowly stepped toward the beginning of this new path. Kip walked along next to him, oblivious to the apprehension that the boy felt.

As he came around a clump of bushes, Joshua saw it and knew exactly what it was. Covered in grape vines about fifteen feet in front of him was a low stone structure. This was the old root cellar that the slaves had escaped to that fateful night a century ago. But why were there men out here last night? Josh stepped a little bit closer. He could see where they had gone around to the other side of the hut. Inching forward, Joshua could hear a low hum coming from somewhere nearby. As the wind kicked up, the sound turned into a mournful howl. As it built in pitch, Joshua stood frozen, waiting for the spirits to come take him. Kip barked and broke the spell. Joshua turned and ran back to the bike as fast he could. Trying to hop on the seat while still attempting to escape, he ended up spilling into the bushes on the other side of the path. The sound continued as he got back up, took a breath, and tried to maneuver out of this place. Once he got back on West Beach Road, Joshua dared to slow down and attempt a glance back. There was nothing following him.

Back at the inn, Mother was serving some oatmeal to Mr. Nilsson. Joshua sat down at the table as his mother did the same for him.

"I was thinking that we'd take a ride up across the Post Road today and get some wood," Mr. Nilsson said as he drained his glass of water.

"Wood?"

"Yes, firewood. We can cut down a tree or two and haul it back here. I just have to sharpen the ax and the saws."

"Okay."

"Mrs. Nilsson will pack us a lunch."

The old man finished up his breakfast and headed outside. Joshua had another serving, as well as some bread with jam spread on it. Mother sat down and had a bowl of oatmeal for herself.

"Where did you go off to this morning?"

"Oh, just riding the bike around," Joshua replied. "I fed Nettie first."

They both sat in silence for a moment.

"Do you think Grandma can send us some things from home?"

"What are you interested in?" She answered with a growing smile.

"I was thinking about my baseball glove and a ball... and maybe some of Mary's books."

"Mary's books?" Mother said with a slight shock in her voice.

"I've been thinking about her," he answered, "but not in a bad way," he said quickly. "I was talking to Mr. Nilsson, and he told me a story about his brother."

"What was that?"

"His brother Lucas died when their family first came to America. His Aunt Catherine told him that he had to figure out a way to fill up the emptiness inside of him. It took him a while to think of how to do it. He kept remembering him, and that made him sadder than ever. Like what happens to me. Then he figured out how to make his brother a part of him, and that helped to make him feel better."

"What are you going to do?" Mother asked with a little apprehension in her voice.

"I don't know yet, but I figure that Mary was

reading all the time, so maybe I'd start there."

"I've been meaning to write Grandma and tell her how we've been doing. I've let two weeks pass. If Mr. Crandall is going to show up like you said he was, then maybe he can take the letter to the post office."

They both cleared the table. Joshua felt good about sharing his thoughts with his mother. Often, she would just tighten up whenever he brought up the subject of Mary or his father. That night of the thunderstorm changed something between them. Joshua couldn't figure out where it was going to lead, but for once he was starting to feel a little more comfortable around his mother.

Mr. Nilsson was hooking Nettie up to the cart when Joshua came around to the front of the barn. Mrs. Nilsson had given him a sack with their lunch inside and a jug of water. In the back of the cart, there was an ax, a long saw with handles on both ends, and two smaller saws. Snapping the reins, Mr. Nilsson started them off. As they made their way up West Beach Road toward the Post Road, Joshua remembered meeting Mr. Nilsson for the first time. They passed the spot where the old man was fixing the wheel from the cart.

"The Boston Red Sox," Mr. Nilsson said out of the blue. "I remember when they were the Boston Pilgrims."

"That's when they won the first World Series," Josh replied.

"1903."

"I was there on my dad's shoulders."

"I remember seeing Cy Young pitch once. He was almost as good as Christy Mathewson," the old man said with a grin.

"Almost?" Josh laughed. "The Giants were afraid to play Boston in the 1904 series. My father always called John McGraw a bum for doing that."

"Well, let's not go too far. It wasn't McGraw's fault, he would've played. It was Brush, the owner, who refused."

"He called Boston a minor league team. They beat the Pirates the year before."

"We were ready for Boston, actually it looked like it

was going to be the Yankees up until the last week of the season."

"My father was so mad. He was ready to take me up to Boston to stay with his cousins, so we could see the series. He had it all arranged at work to get the time off."

"You can't possibly remember all that."

"I don't remember when it was happening, but he talked about it for years."

They were both silent for a few moments as Nettie pulled the cart up onto the Post Road. They headed north for about half a mile, and then went up a dirt road into the woods.

"No one is going to beat the Giants this year," Mr. Nilsson said.

"The Sox are going to be strong."

"With who?"

"Joe Wood. No one's got a better fastball... and Tris Speaker out in center with Harry Hooper and Duff Lewis on either side of him. They all batted over 300 last year."

"Nobody is going to beat the Giants with Christy Mathewson and Rube Marquand on the mound. No one's better on the bases than we are. Merkle, Herzog, Murray, and Snodgrass each had near 50 stolen bases last year, Josh Devore had 60. Don't forget about Larry Doyle at second base. He batted over 300 with 25 triples and 13 homeruns. How many did your Tris Speaker have last year?"

"Eight," Joshua said glumly.

"Joe Wood's a great pitcher, I'll give you that. He had over twenty wins last year, but Christy had 26, and Rube had 24. It takes more than one guy."

"He had 23 wins with an ERA of 2.02."

"Mathewson had a 1.99."

The cart wheeled on up a small hill. There were no houses up here. Off to their right, Joshua could see a white steeple from a church. Behind them, the ocean spread out wide, and Block Island sat beyond the shore.

"The Red Sox have got a new ballpark this year."

Joshua's ears perked up.

"I know."

"I read about it in the paper. I'm surprised they even had room enough to print it with all the news about the Titanic."

"What's the Titanic?"

"It's that ship that hit the iceberg... the biggest boat ever made... supposed to be unsinkable, but on its first voyage, it sank to the bottom. A lot of people went down with it."

Mr. Nilsson pulled the cart up onto a small path. Nettie was a little hesitant about moving, but the old man led her on. Once they got through a narrow area, a small field opened up with woods all around. Joshua could see that a lot of trees had already been cut down. Stumps lined the north edge of the field, and smaller branches were piled off to the side.

"The owner lets us take as much wood as we want. He and his family stay at the inn for a week in August. This is the trade we make. I think he's going to start building some houses up here soon, so we're just helping to clear the area out for him."

Stopping the cart in the middle of the field, Mr. Nilsson hopped down and unhitched Nettie. She slowly sauntered away and started to feed on the grass. Mr. Nilsson handed Joshua the ax and one of the saws. He grabbed the double saw and a smaller one. They made their way across the field and stopped at a tree that seemed to be a little bit over a foot thick.

"First we drop the tree, then cut away the branches, and then saw it to four foot lengths. We'll cut them down to size this fall, split them, and then stack them by the barn for next year."

Mr. Nilsson looked up and down the tree a few times. He walked around it, and gazed out to the field.

"The trick is to drop it where you can cut the rest up easily. This one seems to be fullest on the field side, so we'll notch it right here. You ever chop a tree down?"

"No."

"Well, the first thing that you do is cut a small chunk on the side where you want it to fall. It's called a notch. This way the tree has room to break free."

Joshua watched as the man swung the ax into the

trunk about a foot from the ground. Then he came around to the other side.

"Now I chop into the tree above the notch on this side, and with a little luck, it'll fall right out there."

Mr. Nilsson began swinging the ax into the tree. Joshua stepped back off to his left, keeping an eye on the sway of the branches. The man chopped in a downward motion, then switched to an upward one. Soon there was a V-cut forming on the trunk. After about five minutes of swinging the ax, Joshua heard a slight cracking sound. As Mr. Nilsson continued swinging, he could see the tree begin its descent. It swayed for a moment, then began to fall. A crack sounded as it broke away from the stump at the bottom. When the tree hit the ground, it bounced back up a few feet, then settled onto the grass. One of the larger branches snapped and dug into the ground.

"Now we cut away the limbs, and saw up the rest."

He handed Joshua one of the smaller saws, and they both got started from the top of the tree. Each working their way down a side, they were soon tangled in the pile of branches that didn't seem to have a beginning or end.

"Joshua, why don't you start dragging these limbs off to the side over there? We'll save some of the bigger ones once we get near the bottom, but the ones we cut aren't really worth hauling back to the inn."

Sweat was pouring off Joshua's face as he pulled each of the branches free. He didn't realize that so much work went into creating a fire for the stoves in the house. He thought the splitting and stacking were more than enough. Soon though, the tree was stripped down to its core. The trunk lay silent on the ground, all of its branches stripped away.

"Let's take a break before we start cutting it up."

They both walked over to the cart and sat on the back. Mr. Nilsson popped the cork on the top of the jug and took a big gulp of the water. He passed it over to Joshua who did the same. They sat there for a few minutes in silence, letting the breeze cool the sweat from their bodies.

"What position do you like to play?"

"Center field and pitcher."

"Tris Speaker and Smoky Joe Wood all wrapped into one, huh?"

"You know the Red Sox have a player named Olaf Henriksen? They call him Swede."

"I didn't know that," Mr. Nilsson said, taking another chug of water.

They started from the top of the tree, cutting lengths with the double saw. It was awkward for Joshua at first, but once they got going, they both fell into an easy rhythm. The first half of the tree was easy, then the wood started to get thicker. Joshua had a hard time keeping up with Mr. Nilsson. When they got near the bottom, Mr. Nilsson said that they should only cut through about two-thirds of the trunk, then they would try to roll it over to get through the rest.

Once the tree was cut, Mr. Nilsson hitched Nettie back up to the cart and brought it over to the logs. They each took an end and lifted the lengths into the back. Joshua was exhausted by the time they finished.

"Let's have some lunch," Mr. Nilsson said as he wiped his forehead with a rag.

Silently, they ate, each trying to get some of the strength back that the morning's labor had sapped from them. The water wasn't as cool as it had been in the morning, but to Joshua, the liquid felt just as good. He was sweating it out faster than he was taking it in.

"Did your dad teach you to play ball?"

"Yeah, he loved the game. He came from Ireland when he was in his teens, and when he got to Boston, that's all he did in his free time."

"What about the Providence Grays?"

"We went to a lot of games, but he couldn't get behind them. I think his heart was still with Boston."

"I remember taking my boys to the Polo Grounds to see the Giants. I'm not sure who got a kick out it of more, me or them."

They finished up their lunches and drank some more of the water.

"Are you ready for one more tree?"

"Not really, but I guess I'll have to try," Josh

responded.

They went through the same routine with the next tree, and when they finally loaded it up onto the cart, Joshua could barely lift it. The back sagged down the rear axles, and Josh wondered if the cart would hold up for their trip back. The thought of having to fix a broken wheel with this heavy load on top of it made Joshua very nervous. They would have to unload it, repair the damage, and then load it back up again. He wasn't looking forward to taking the logs off the cart when they got back to the inn. The way they had loaded it though; they would just have to roll the wood off the back.

The trip down West Beach Road was slow, and they traveled it in silence. Joshua was worn out, and he couldn't even imagine how the old man felt. His shoulders sagged as they approached the inn. When they started up the driveway, Joshua noticed that the door to the hay loft was open. As they got closer, a man appeared.

"Luther!" the man shouted.

Mr. Nilsson's eyes lifted up to the second floor of the barn, and he smiled.

"The Drabble brothers are here."

Thankfully, the two men came out to the other side of the barn and helped unload the wood. Joshua's muscles ached as he stepped down from the cart. As they were rolling the logs over the edge, he got a better look at the two men. The first one was missing his left hand, and he also had a scar that started under the ear and traced a white line along his neck almost to his chin. The other man was missing two fingers on his right hand and was stooped over to one side. Although they seemed beat up, both of the men had smiling faces as they dropped the lengths of wood onto the ground.

"Who's this fella?" the man with one hand asked.

"Oh, I'm sorry. This is Joshua. He's going to be working here this summer. The boy's a great worker."

"Hello there, Joshua. I'm Walter, and this is my brother Henry," he said, reaching out his one good hand to shake with the boy.

Joshua nodded, smiled, and shook the man's hand. He did the same with Henry, but the man's missing

91

fingers felt weird as Joshua gripped his hand.

"We're all set up in the barn," Walter said. "I think we'll get started on some of the scraping today, so we start painting bright and early tomorrow morning. We got two other places to get to in Quonny before we head back over to Weekapaug."

"You boys are keeping busy," Mr. Nilsson said with a smile.

"Winters are slow, so we got to make up for it when the weather's on our side."

Joshua's eyes began to fade as he listened to the men talk. Sensing the boy's exhaustion, Mr. Nilsson sent him inside to wash up and get ready for dinner. The boy trudged up the steps into the house, arms hanging loosely by his sides. His mother was in the kitchen when he entered.

"How did it go?"

"Good," he answered.

"Long day?"

"Yes."

"Why don't you go upstairs and wash up? There's some clothes on the chair that you can put on. I'll try to wash those tomorrow."

Joshua just nodded and slowly made his way up the steep stairs in the back of the kitchen. From the bathroom window, he could see the three men still talking away in the backyard. He stripped and washed himself off, and then made his way back to the bedroom. Thinking that he would just rest for a moment, Joshua dropped off into a deep sleep.

7

The Drabble brothers started painting the inn. They rigged up ladders and scaffolding that to Joshua seemed ready to topple down at any moment. Walter's missing hand didn't slow him down one bit. He carried the paint bucket around draped over his wrist while he covered the shingles with long brush strokes with his other hand. They chattered away all day long; laughing and singing. This brought a whole new life to the inn. Mr. Nilsson did some of the prep work, but the Drabbles did most of the painting. Joshua ran back and forth to get more paint or different brushes, but his mother wouldn't allow him up on the rickety platforms.

Mr. Nilsson gave Joshua the job of trimming all of the brush around the yard that was creeping onto or over the lawn. He had a pair of cutting shears, and slowly had made his way around the perimeter. Every half an hour or so, the boy would gather all the brush from the ground and dump it out past the cold frames behind the tennis court.

"Hey Joshua," called Henry Drabble.

The boy dropped the cutters and came running up the yard to where the men were painting.

"Yeah."

"Can you grab me another can of the white paint?"

"Sure."

"And see if there's another rag nearby, this one's shot," he said as he tossed the paint smeared cloth down to the ground.

Josh sped into the barn to where the Drabbles had stacked the buckets of paint. There were dozens of two gallon cans. Most of them were white, but a few were green. Coming back outside, Joshua could see the difference in where they had painted. The white shingles shone in the late morning sunlight.

For a week they painted. Mr. Nilsson kept ahead of them with the scraping. By the third day, Joshua's mother had loosened up enough to let him do some work on the ladder. She was adamant, though, about the scaffolding.

"If I see you even stepping onto any of those flimsy planks, then you'll spend the rest of the summer with me in the kitchen," she said wagging her finger at her son.

It was sad to see the Drabbles leave. Joshua was starting to get used to their presence at the inn. They were just moving down the beach near the Ashaway cottages, but things got a lot quieter when they left. Josh visited them a few times on the bicycle, bringing them lunch or water to drink.

By now the grass in the yard was getting long. Mr. Nilsson said that it was time to start cutting. In the barn, there was a mowing machine that looked very complicated. Joshua had glanced at the thing wondering when they would finally get it going.

"We need to grease it, and then sharpen the blades."

The old man showed Joshua all the spots where friction needed to be eased with the lubricant. They gave each spot a dab of the grease. There were four sets of rotating blades; two in the front and a pair right behind them. The old man used some type of file to bring out the edge of each blade. In the front of the mower, there was a small bench to sit on and a hitch for Nettie. Mr. Nilsson showed Joshua where the blades could be adjusted for height.

"We'll set it high this time, so we can get through some of the thick grass."

Joshua nodded, watching the man's every move. They pulled the mower out of the barn and hooked the horse up to it. Sitting on the bench, Joshua noticed how hard it was to see around Nettie to know where they were going.

"I'll take it around once, then you can try it. Whatever you don't cut with this mower, you have to do by hand with the smaller one."

Mr. Nilsson made a wide loop around the yard. The mower got most of the grass, but there were still some stalks and clumps that he missed. When he came back up the incline, he pulled Nettie to a halt.

"Are you ready to try it?"

"I guess so," Joshua answered.

There were rocks scattered all around the lawn, and Joshua wasn't sure if he would be able to maneuver around them. With a jolt, Nettie pulled ahead, and the boy tried to rein her in as much as possible. The ride was much bumpier than the cart. Josh traced the path that Mr. Nilsson had taken, and after two passes by the house, he was starting to get the hang of the mower. Looking back behind him, he could see the grass flying up into the air as he cut through the thick lawn. The wheels in the front turned as Nettie moved around in a big circle. The horse seemed to know how to get around the rocks enough for Josh not to worry so much about it. As he passed around and around, he could see where he missed some sections. By the time he finished the back yard area, he knew that he would have to go over it again.

They took a break, and Joshua got some water for Nettie. The lawn had a different look to it now. The grass was a deep green, and for the most part, it was cut evenly. There were tufts surrounding the rocks and some of the bushes, and scattered around the yard were places that he missed. While Joshua took the mower around to the front of the inn, Mr. Nilsson unhooked the fencing on the side of the tennis court. The days were getting warm now that they were into the middle of May. Josh made his passes around the yard again, and then led Nettie down the path to the dock. He had tough time turning the mower around once he got down there; getting hung up in some of the low brush on the side of the path. Mr. Nilsson soon came down to investigate.

"That's a tough turn," the man said. "I usually come down, cut, then unhitch Nettie and turn it around manually."

Joshua thought that would be a good idea for next time. Both of them tried to pull the mower free from the grape vines that had tangled into the blades.

"Go up and grab those shears from the barn."

Joshua ran up and found them sitting on the bench. He raced back to where he had gotten stuck and tried to cut the stringy vines away. They were gnarled and knotted, so it took Joshua a few minutes to even break through. Once started though, Mr. Nilsson was able to peel away most of the rest of the vines. They pulled the mower out by hand, and then hooked Nettie back to the harness. The horse waited patiently for the whole affair to resume. Josh then led her back up into the yard.

"Try to pull her into the tennis court. I usually do it by hand, but the first time it's better to get the bulk of it cut down with the big mower."

It was tough for Josh to maneuver through the fence, and then around the rectangular area. The poles for the nets made it even more difficult. The back wheel clipped the edge of one of the shafts and almost bounced Joshua off the bench. After pulling out of the court, he headed across the yard and through the opening in the stone wall. Joshua did a couple of laps around the garden, and then headed through the grove of fruit trees. A few weeks earlier, he and Mr. Nilsson had trimmed all the branches that were shooting straight up in the air. The old man had said that these suckers sapped the energy of the tree, and by cutting them down each spring, the fruit was able to grow in a healthier fashion. He wasn't able to cut as close to the tree as he would have liked because of the low hanging branches. By the time he swung back up to the barn, Mr. Nilsson was pulling the smaller mower outside.

They both took turns pushing the contraption around. Mr. Nilsson also held a small hand tool that had a blade shaped like a crescent. He would slice through some of the tall grass before Joshua pushed the mower through. This was hard work, and by the time dinner rolled around, Joshua was exhausted. They had just put all the equipment away when Mr. Thornton pulled into the driveway with his cart. His granddaughter, Elizabeth, was sitting next to him.

"Afternoon Lewis," Mr. Nilsson said. "What brings you out here?"

"I was just at Cross' Mill getting some supplies, and when I stopped to check the mail, there were a few things for the Pond View, so I picked them up for you."

"Well, thank you."

"I brought a few more chickens over too."

Mr. Nilsson walked around to the back of the cart as Mr. Thornton eased his way off. Elizabeth just stayed where she was. Josh walked up and stroked the nose of the white speckled horse.

"She looks thirsty," Joshua said to the girl as the men disappeared around the corner with the chickens.

"She's fine. We stopped and gave her some water before we came over here."

Josh didn't know what else to say.

"Is your last name Keegan?"

"Yes."

"Well, there's a package here for your mother. It's from Providence, and it's heavy," she said in a matter of fact tone.

Joshua came around to the side of the cart and waited for the girl to hand him the box, but she just sat there with a satisfied grin on her face.

"Can I have it?"

"My grandfather told the postmaster that he would deliver it personally, so I can't touch it. You'll have to wait for him to come back."

Joshua couldn't figure this girl out. He wasn't sure if she was being mean or just trying to have fun at his expense.

"The back path to the breachway is haunted," he suddenly said, hoping to scare her.

"You're not talking about the old stone shack are you?"

"It's haunted."

"That's just an old story to scare people away."

"Oh yeah, why?"

"I'm not telling. You figure it out for yourself."

The two men came back around the barn. They were talking about the upcoming summer season.

"Lizzie, why don't you hop down? Mr. Nilsson has invited us in for a cold drink."

She deliberately reached right over Joshua's head and handed the package to her grandfather. He in turn gave it to Mr. Nilsson, and they all walked into the house. Mrs. Nilsson welcomed them inside and introduced Mr. Thornton and Elizabeth to Mollie. They sat at the breakfast table, and Mrs. Nilsson served some lemonade and cookies to the guests. Joshua ate in silence, just staring at the package that was sitting on the counter.

"They've been catching some flounder over in our pond for the past few days."

"We haven't had a chance to get out yet," Mr. Nilsson replied.

"How's Mrs. Thornton doing?" Mrs. Nilsson asked.

"Oh fine, just fine. She hasn't forgotten about your pot. She told me to tell you that she's going to be making some fish chowder to send back over later in the week."

"Tell her, there's no hurry. I've got plenty of pots here."

"When are the Van Houttens arriving?"

"Mrs. Van Houtten should be here next week, and we never know when the mister will show up," Mrs. Nilsson said. "We'll have guests the first week of June, unless Mrs. Van Houtten brings people with her when she arrives. We haven't heard yet."

"A lot to do before then," Mr. Nilsson said.

"Well, I thank you for the drink, and we'll be seeing you soon," Mr. Thornton said.

"Thank you for the chickens," Mr. Nilsson said, "and the special delivery too."

Mr. Thornton and Elizabeth stood, and everyone else at the table followed. Mr. Nilsson walked them out to their cart. Just before climbing up, Elizabeth looked back at Joshua who was standing on the back porch. He waved, but she ignored him and just sat herself down on the bench.

When he walked back inside, Mother was opening the package. She pulled out a stack of books, some pieces of paper, and his baseball glove. He reached for his mitt and slid his fingers into the leather. Punching the palm of it a few times, he got into a fielding stance and waited for the ball to be hit to him. Joshua looked over at the pile of books and scanned down the titles and authors. On the top were two books by Jane Austen; *Pride and Prejudice* and *Sense and Sensibility*. The next few were books of poems by Emily Dickinson, Walt Whitman, and Sarah Orne Jewett; people he had never heard of before. There were three O. Henry books. Joshua at least recognized his name. The last two on the bottom were by Mark Twain, and they instantly brought a smile to his face. They were *The Adventures of Tom Sawyer* and *The Adventures of Huckleberry Finn*. Of course, he had remembered these two books. Mary had spent some time reading parts of them to Joshua. He recalled laying on her bed as she sat in her chair reading aloud. The Mississippi River flowed through his mind as he listened.

Joshua looked up from the pile of books and saw his mother staring at a piece of paper. Her chin rested on the palm of her hand, and there were tears flowing down her cheeks. She looked up at her son, and then handed the paper to him. It took a second, but soon he realized that this was a letter that Mary had written to him in March of last year. He put the mitt down on the counter and ran up the stairs to their room to read it.

At first Joshua just sat on the bed with the letter on the quilt next to him. It was like a voice from the beyond. Mary hadn't written him a letter for a long time before last March. In fact, he wasn't sure if she had even written him one since their father passed away. He missed her so much. Joshua wished that he hadn't been so mean to her. Taking a deep breath, he picked the letter up from the bed.

Dear Joshua,

It has been almost a year now since Daddy left us. I know that you have had a difficult time with his passing. Mother and I miss him so much too, but we are at a loss as to how to help you move on. I have watched you change from a happy and curious boy, who was the smartest student in his class, to someone who is lost or trapped inside of himself. Where did my brother Joshua go? We had thought that you would become the man of the house,

and in time, Mother and I hope this will happen. In the
meantime though, we have tried everything that we can
think of to help you emerge from the fog that you seem to be
floating through.

I had a thought the other day that I have been
attempting to develop in my mind. I want to sit down with
you, maybe on the front steps, and try to remember
everything we can about Daddy. I want to try to figure out
what he stood for. We could write these things down and
try to continue what he started. This would be his legacy. I
read about it in a book once. As his children, it is our
responsibility to do this for him. Maybe this will help you to
get back to the Joshua that we all remember.

Joshua turned the page over, but there was
nothing on the back. Mary hadn't finished writing it. He
went back to the top and read through it three more
times. The tears that Mother shed didn't well up inside of
him. He thought about his sister's words and her idea
about helping the memory of their father live on. This was
similar to what Mr. Nilsson had told him about his own
brother, Lucas. Over the past few weeks, Joshua had
been so busy with work around the inn, that he hadn't
really thought about it too much. Now he sat on his
mother's bed and tried to formulate a plan.

The idea of creating a legacy, as well as filling up
the emptiness inside of him seemed to go hand in hand.
Now that he had Mary's books and her letter, he could
begin. He lay back on the pillow and stared at the ceiling.
Not only would he have to create a legacy for his father,
but he would also have to do the same for his sister. Her
words echoed in his mind, and it was as if he could hear
her voice. Holding the letter up in front of his eyes, he
followed the words as they led him across the page.
Mary's voice was loud and clear; he had to become the
man of the house now. It was time for him to put all of
the crybaby theatrics behind him. Although he couldn't
control it in the past, Joshua now felt that he could be
strong and not wallow in self pity. Instead of being lost in
a confused state of mind, this creation of a legacy for his
father and sister would give his life some meaning. His

eyes and thoughts would be viewing the world, not only for himself, but for them too.

When his mother came into the room a few minutes later, Joshua had a determined look on his face. He turned to look at her, and suddenly he smiled. This seemed to catch her off guard.

"I feel a lot better now," he said.

"Well, that's good news," Mother answered as she came over to the bed.

"She must have written this right before it happened last year."

Mother just nodded.

"She didn't even get to finish it," he continued. "I think I know what I want to do now."

"What's that?"

"I'm going to write back to her."

She looked at her son with a strange expression in her eyes.

"I want to tell her what's going on in my life. She always used to write me letters, but I never wrote back to her. Now's my chance."

"Are you sure that's a good idea?"

"I'm positive," Joshua answered in a determined voice.

They were quiet for a moment; each feeling the weight of their discussion. The smells from the kitchen drifted up into the room, and this reminded Joshua how hungry he was. The day spent cutting the grass gave him quite an appetite.

"Well, I better get downstairs and help Mrs. Nilsson," Mother said. "Why don't you wash up and come on down?"

"Okay."

She left her son still lying on the bed. Joshua read the letter over again; the wheels in his head spinning with thoughts of his family. They had been fairly happy for a lot of years. Losing the babies cast a shadow over them, especially Mother, but they carried on nevertheless. That was what Joshua would do now. He would carry on, in spite of the loss of his father and sister. Their lives would become part of his, so inside of him, they wouldn't be totally gone. This thought breathed new hope into him, and as he made his way to the sink in the bathroom, Joshua made a commitment to himself, that he would not cave into the dark thoughts that had kept him down for so long.

The view outside the window was grand. The freshly cut grass on the back lawn was a beautiful contrast to the crystal water on the pond and the deep blue sky above. The lowering sun brightened the surrounding woods that encircled the pond, and the ocean in the distance gave Joshua a kind of hope that maybe things would turn out okay for him and his mother.

After finishing three helpings of dinner, Joshua helped clean up the kitchen with Mrs. Nilsson. He then went outside to get some firewood for the stove in the kitchen. They weren't using nearly as much as they had when Joshua first arrived. Poking through the cupboards under the bookcase in the hall later on, Joshua found a writing tablet that hadn't been used before. He thought that he had seen it there when he was rummaging through the piles of magazines and old newspapers.

"Would it be okay if I used this?" Joshua asked Mrs. Nilsson.

"Oh, I think so. I don't believe anyone will miss it," she answered with a smile.

Joshua went into the sunporch in the far end of the house. He lit a kerosene lamp as the last traces of sunlight disappeared from the sky. There was a small table tucked in the corner of the large room. Joshua had the nub of a pencil. He opened to the first page, and suddenly had no idea what he was going to write. He sat there alone, staring at the blank page, and thought of his sister. The only image that came to his mind was of the horse coming around the corner on Westminster Street. A crowd was gathered around the newsstand, and he and Mary were stepping out into the street. Taking the pencil into his hand, Joshua began to write.

Dear Mary,

I wish I never stormed out of the house that day. I have tried to take it back over and over again, but I just

*can't. When I woke up in the hospital, I didn't know what
had happened. I just remembered the horse and cart
coming around the corner. I was blind because I got hit in
the head. They held me down on the bed and shoved a
cloth with ether into my face. I didn't know what was
happening to me. I just kept telling Mother that I couldn't
see anything. Once things settled down, I just rested. One
night my vision came back. The room was very bright, and
you were standing there. I was so happy that you didn't get
hurt. When I woke up the next morning, I was blind again,
and I heard Mother and Grandma talking out in the
hallway. They were making plans for your funeral. I
sucked air into my lungs, and my heart stopped. I don't
think that it has been working right since then.*

     Joshua read over the words he had written. Now
the tears came. They rolled down his face and dropped
onto the page. He ran his fingers through his hair and
wanted to tear it out. Inside of him came a low moaning,
and then Joshua cracked his head down on the wooden
table. He rose and did it again. The lantern shook each
time his forehead came down onto the surface. Finally, he
got hold of himself and wrapped his arms around his
chest and tried to shake the tears away. He stomped his
feet on the floor, trying to rid himself of the pain that
Mary's memory created inside of him. Reaching out in
front of him, Joshua ripped the page out of the notebook
and crushed it into a ball in his hand.

     This definitely wasn't working. Joshua attempted
to get his breathing back to normal and be a man.
Stopping to think for a minute, he realized that he made a
mistake by going back into the past. He shouldn't have
written about that day. What did he expect to happen?
This was even worse than thinking about it. Now he had
it on a page before him. The crinkled paper in his hand
began to take on a weight that was beyond his
comprehension. Joshua tossed it onto the floor and
closed the writing tablet. He stood and walked over to the
large window that looked into the backyard. Twilight was
fading into darkness, and Josh could just see the stillness
of the pond.

He had to come up with another way of filling the emptiness. The faint images of baseball, gardening, books, and letters kept circling through his mind. Joshua decided to start again tomorrow. At dinner, Mr. Nilsson had mentioned that they might try a little fishing in the morning. Maybe he would tell Mary about that. It was going to be his first attempt at trying to catch fish.

As the darkness engulfed the outside world, the flickering of the lamp turned the window into a strange mirror. Joshua stared at his reflection. Half of his face was in the shadows, and the other side brightened and dimmed with the waves of light from the lantern. He saw himself for the first time as boy who was trying to climb out of the depths of sadness. There was a bit of hope as the flame beamed, but soon it faded into a murky shadow. Turning, Joshua picked up the crumpled piece of paper from the floor and grabbed the notebook and pencil.

Before going up to his room for the night, he dropped his first letter to Mary inside of the stove. He watched as the embers slowly caught the fringes of the paper. Within a few seconds, the letter was disappearing into an orange flame. Joshua Keegan walked right past his baseball glove and then up the stairs with a heavy heart and a smoldering spirit.

8

Joshua slept fitfully that night, tossing and turning with every thought of his sister. When the birds finally drove him out of the trundle bed at dawn, his sheets were strewn all about. His whole body felt clammy. Getting up and going to the bathroom, he looked out the window and saw Mr. Nilsson carrying a lobster pot down to the dock. Josh had asked the man what those boxes with the wooden slats were used for, and the old man said they were going to help them catch a seafood dinner. Quickly, the boy got dressed and headed downstairs.

Mr. Nilsson was walking up the path into the backyard when Joshua hopped off the steps with a crust of bread in his hand.

"Good morning, Joshua. Are we ready to go catch some fish?"

"Sure," he answered, still a little groggy from not enough sleep.

Joshua hauled a lobster pot down to the water. It wasn't too heavy, but the bulk of the crate made it difficult to carry. The old man followed with another one.

"Why don't you go pull that minnow trap? I set it last night," Mr. Nilsson said, pointing to a string at the end of the dock.

Joshua walked out to the end of the platform while Mr. Nilsson stacked the traps in the front of the dinghy. The boy pulled the string, and up from the bottom came a metal cylinder. Inside, Josh could see dozens of small, silver fish flopping around. They were each about two inches long. Tiny pieces of flat and soggy bread were scattered around them. Mr. Nilsson took a bucket and reached down into the water, pulling up a handful of seaweed. He brought it out to where Joshua was squatting down watching the minnows flip back and forth.

105

The old man unhooked the clasp in the middle of the trap and dumped the fish into the bucket.

"It takes a fish to catch a fish," he said as he turned the seaweed over, burying the minnows beneath.

Mr. Nilsson put the bucket and a small wooden box into the boat and pointed to where he wanted Joshua to sit in the back. Grabbing a fruit crate from the end of the dock, he untied the dinghy and pushed off, putting the box in the front of the boat. Quickly, the old man sat in the middle seat and began to row. The tide was high this morning, so the channel's shallowness wasn't an issue. They moved out past the island that lay about a hundred or so yards out, and then came around to a rocky shore.

"If we catch anything, we'll drop the pots right along here," he said with a nod.

Joshua watched the birds swooping all around. Out toward the middle of the pond, small white ones were diving out of the sky right into the water. As they approached the area, Josh could see that sometimes they came up with small fish in their mouths. All of a sudden a wave of minnows jumped out of the water and fanned out in different directions.

"This is where the fish are," Mr. Nilsson said, "probably stripers or small blues."

"Are we going to try and catch some?"

"We can try, but I don't think we'll get anything. I was planning on dragging the bottom for some flounder today."

They moved into where the fish had been jumping only moments before. There were only small ripples now, caused by the incoming wind. Joshua looked all around for signs of the fish, but didn't see anything. The birds seemed to have strangely disappeared also. Looking back over his shoulder, Joshua could see the sun coming up over the trees near the inn. This view of the place was different than anything he had seen before. It seemed to be some type of guardian for the pond. He could see a house farther down the shore, and to the north a few places were scattered along the road. At first he heard, and then saw a truck making its way up the Post Road.

Mr. Nilsson pulled up the oars and tucked them

into the sides of the boat. He reached for the wooden box and opened it up. Inside, Josh saw two sets of light brown string wrapped around a wooden square. The old man handed the spools to Joshua, and then reached back into the box. He pulled out some fishing hooks and some metal weights. Putting each of them on the seat next to him, Mr. Nilsson then pulled out some pieces of wire.

"We'll set a double jig on each of the lines,"

Joshua watched as the man fed the string through the middle of the wire. The metal weights slid through easily. On each end were small metal clips. He took the hooks and attached them.

"Pass that bucket over here, will you Joshua?"

The boy handed the pail over to Mr. Nilsson. He dug into the bucket and pulled out one of the minnows. Taking the hook, he speared it through the underside of the small fish, letting the sharp edge come out through its mouth. He repeated this process with the other hook, and then handed the whole spool over to Joshua.

"Alright, slowly let the line drop. Unwrap it as you go. Let it fall all the way to the bottom."

Joshua did as the old man instructed. The line floated on the water for a moment, but then the weight of the metal dragged it beneath. The end disappeared lower and lower into the pond. After unwrapping what seemed like a lot of line, it hit bottom. The drifting of the boat caused it to drag along. Each it time the line got slightly caught on something at the bottom, Joshua thought he had a fish. Mr. Nilsson rigged up his own line and dropped it over the other side of the boat. They floated along with the wind for a short time. Joshua began to wonder what he should do if a fish happened to get hooked on his line. His first instinct would be just to pull, but he wasn't sure what to do with all of the line that would come up with it.

"Got one," Mr. Nilsson said quietly.

Joshua watched as the man slowly rewrapped the line around the wooden spool. The fish kept pulling his hand closer to the water. The old man would compensate for it by giving the line a good tug. After about a minute, Joshua could see the whiteness of the fish flashing beneath the boat. It looked to be about as big as frying pan. With a quick yank of the line, Mr. Nilsson pulled the fish up and over the side of the boat. It was an odd looking fish; completely flat. The color was brown, speckled with dark spots. The strangest thing about it though, was the fact that its two eyes were next to each other on the top of the fish. When it flopped over in the bottom of the boat, Joshua could see that it was completely white. Mr. Nilsson picked it up by the gills, pulled the hook out, lifted the lid of the fruit crate, and dropped it in. He rinsed off his hands and grabbed a clump of seaweed that was floating by. He tossed that into the crate also.

Joshua was so busy watching what Mr. Nilsson was doing, that he didn't realize that there was a pull on his line. Within seconds though, the jerking became stronger, and Josh had to work just to hang onto the wooden spool. The fish pulled and pulled, without letting up.

"Just take the line in front of you with your free hand," Mr. Nilsson said in a calm voice, "and wrap it around. Keep doing that, and before you know it, the fish will be in the boat."

Joshua couldn't believe the strength of the fish. His line kept swinging back and forth, cutting through the water then swerving beneath the boat. Soon he could see the white belly moving under the surface. Joshua pulled the flounder out of the water, and for a moment it just hung in mid-air.

"Pull it in the boat before it lets go."

Josh had to half stand up to be able to swing the fish over the side of the boat. This one was bigger than Mr. Nilsson's, and Joshua watched as the man stepped on the fish and worked the hook out of its mouth.

"Not bad, good size," the man said.

The boy rebaited his hook and dropped the line down again. Within an hour or so, they had eight fish in the fruit crate. Each one came up easier than the next, as Joshua got used to the technique needed. When they sat without catching anything for awhile, Mr. Nilsson decided to call it a day. They switched seats, and the man let

Joshua row the boat. As they headed over to the small island, Joshua looked over toward the breachway. The houses and inns made up a small village. He looked forward to exploring the area again. This time he would do it more thoroughly; hoping that maybe there would be more people down there.

As they approached the island, Mr. Nilsson dropped the small anchor. He took a long, skinny knife out of the tackle box, and then reached for the fruit crate. Joshua watched as he pulled one of the flounder out and slapped it onto the top of the box.

"The trick is to cut along both sides, so you get a nice filet."

Mr. Nilsson dug into the fish with the sharp point of the knife and slowly cut away a section.

"All of the innards are on this side, so you get a smaller piece."

As he sliced the guts out, he dropped them overboard into the water.

"That will get the lobsters moving over here."

"What are you going to do with the rest?"

"We used a small fish to catch a big fish, now we'll use the parts of the big fish we don't want to catch a lobster."

Mr. Nilsson lifted the lid and put the two filets inside and took out another fish. He left the head, skin, and bones of the first fish on the bottom of the boat. He repeated the process a few more times before handing the knife over to Joshua. He was a little squeamish about slicing into the flounder, but once he cut through, it seemed to go a little easier. His filets weren't as well-shaped as Mr. Nilsson's, but by the time he got to the last one, he was getting the hang of it.

"Now we bait the traps."

Mr. Nilsson had Joshua reach around and lift one of the lobster pots up and put it between them. The man unclasped the top, and Joshua got a closer look at how the trap worked. One side of it looked like a spider web. There was netting with a big opening on the end. The hole got smaller and smaller up to the middle of the trap, then opened up wide again. Joshua watched as Mr. Nilsson put some of the remains of the flounder into the larger section of the pot. He closed it back up, unfurled the rope, and dropped it into the water. A small white buoy floated on the surface, and Joshua could follow the rope down a few feet before it disappeared into the darkness. They did the same with the other three pots, and then Josh started to pull on the oars to bring them back to the dock.

"We'll go out and check them in a few days."

The boy rowed them all the way into the dock. The tide had gone out since they left, but there was still plenty of water in the channel for them to get through easily. Josh brought the fruit crate up to the house and put it on the back porch. Mrs. Nilsson came out with a platter, and the boy dug the filets out from the seaweed.

"Oh, you did well out there today," she said with a smile. "I'll clean these up a bit more, and we'll have a nice fish dinner tonight."

Joshua just nodded, proud of his accomplishments this morning.

"Could you maybe grab a few eggs on your way back in? I'll need them to cook the fish."

"Sure," Joshua answered, not quite knowing how fish and eggs went together.

Josh went back down to the dock and helped Mr. Nilsson clean out the dinghy. The old man had already emptied the bucket of the extra seaweed and minnows. Now he was flushing the fish guts out. With the boat pulled up onto the shore, he was able to pull the drain plug and wash everything out. Joshua rewound the fishing line, taking the excess seaweed off as he went. He then cleaned off the hooks and metal leaders, and put them in the tackle box. They eased the boat back into the water, washed their hands, and headed up to the inn.

"We have got to do something about the varmints in the garden today," Mr. Nilsson said, looking over at the field. "As soon as those sprouts come up, they'll be all over the place."

"What kind of varmints?"

"Deer, rabbits, woodchucks..."

Joshua had seen a lot of rabbits in the area, and

once he thought he saw a deer at dusk one night, but he had never seen a woodchuck. He didn't think that he would even recognize one if he did. They walked over to the barn, and Mr. Nilsson put the fishing tackle away. Josh went over to the chicken coop and grabbed four eggs. When they got back into the kitchen, Mrs. Nilsson was putting out some sandwiches and lemonade for lunch.

After they ate, Mr. Nilsson grabbed some thick string and old pie plates from under the bench in the barn. They walked out to the field, and Joshua grabbed one end of the string.

"Take this and feed it through the thick branches of the fruit trees over there."

Mr. Nilsson had driven some stakes into the ground the day before. Joshua wondered what they were for. He now passed the line through little eyeholes that he had screwed onto each. Once they made a complete circle of the field, Josh saw that the string hung between two and three feet high off the ground. Mr. Nilsson then took his pocketknife out and cut some short lengths of string. Around the perimeter, he started to hang the pie plates in pairs.

"If a deer comes along, he'll touch the string and the pie plates will clang together. That'll scare most of them away. Sometimes the wind does the work for us, and they don't even come near the garden."

"What about rabbits?"

"Well, I've got something else in mind for them. They're just a bother. It's the woodchucks who can do a lot of damage. I hate woodchucks."

Back in the barn, Mr. Nilsson went to the far wall where some chain and other pieces of metal were hanging. As Joshua looked closer, he could see that they were small traps. He had read about these things in a story about trappers in Canada.

"The only problem with these is we have to put bait out on them, and that attracts more rabbits from all over. Once we catch one though, I'll let it rot out in the field. The smell usually keeps the others away for awhile."

Joshua watched as Mr. Nilsson put a little grease into the spring mechanisms of the traps. The squeaking

111

noise got less and less as he worked the jaws back and forth.

"We'll set these up tomorrow. I'll let the grease smell fade a bit. Maybe Mrs. Nilsson can save some greens from dinner, so we can set them in the morning. You have got to be careful around these. They'll take a toe if you're barefoot, and they'll mess up the mower if you're not paying attention. A few summers ago, one of the dogs from down near the beach wandered over and got his snout caught in one."

"What happened?"

"They had to put her down. It was a sad sight to see, but she shouldn't have been wandering around our garden in the first place."

Mr. Nilsson took one of the traps and put it on the floor, setting the spring so the jaws were set open. He grabbed a stick and handed it to Joshua.

"Here, tap this on that center piece right there."

Josh reached over with the stick and slightly touched the metal. Instantly, the trap snapped shut and cut the bottom part of the stick in two. The boy jumped as the metal bounced, and then fell back to the dirt floor.

"See what I mean? These things aren't toys to be played with."

Joshua just stared at the trap for a moment, not knowing what to say or do.

"If we see a woodchuck, then we can try to figure out where his hole is. He'll usually have two; one that he uses and one for escape. We'll block one hole and set one of the traps at the mouth of the other. They're not too smart, so we should catch him easily."

"Why are they so bad?"

"Two summers ago I had a row of beans that went from one side of the garden to the other. I had them all strung up on poles, and just when they were getting ready to be picked, they disappeared. In one night, that woodchuck devoured all my beans."

"Did you catch him?"

"I'm not sure. I saw him a few days later, and I might have clipped him with the shotgun, but I don't know. I didn't see him at all last summer, so maybe he's gone."

Mr. Nilsson started to gather some rags, paintbrushes, and a can of paint from around the workbench. He put it in a crate and walked out of the barn. Joshua took Nettie's brush down from the peg on the wall and ran it down the horse's back. Strings of hair gathered on the brush with each stroke. Nettie stood still as Joshua brushed her on each side. She tolerated the boy's presence now that he showed a little more confidence in the stall. Mr. Nilsson walked back into the barn just as Joshua was finishing up.

"Why don't you grab a couple of those sawhorses, and we'll get to those canoes today."

Joshua knew that both of the long boats needed to be painted. They were just waiting for a dry day to get it done. He hefted the wooden horses onto his shoulders and made his way down to the pond. The canoes were tucked into the underbrush about ten feet up from the dock. Mr. Nilsson followed the boy with two more sawhorses. They set them up on the flat ground on the grass near the water. Grabbing one end of the first canoe, both of them pulled it out of the brush. Mr. Nilsson tossed Joshua a rag, and they each made their way from the ends wiping it down. Joshua could see the scratches and nicks on the bottom of the boat. He knew that the bottom of the channel was littered with all sorts of jagged rocks, so he could easily imagine how the canoe could get banged up. They pulled the other one out and repeated the process. After hefting the boats up on top of the sawhorses, they got busy painting the bottoms.

"These canoes have gotten fairly popular over the last few seasons. People take them out and have a picnic on the island or somewhere along the shore. Sometimes they pull up to one of the docks at the breachway, and spend the day over there."

"What's it like over at the breachway?" Joshua asked.

"Oh, it gets pretty lively. We're a little isolated here, but over there, people are roaming about at all hours. A few of the places serve spirits, so they can get rambunctious. Mrs. Van Houtten doesn't allow any liquor

113

here, so sometimes the younger crowd will drift over to the Eldredge or the Worcester. Some of the braver ones make their way out to the back of the casino, behind the bowling alley."

"What's back there?"

"They used to call it the Blind Pig, but it's just a place some of the working men gather to share a drink and tell stories."

Joshua's mind started to drift back to the afternoon when he ran into Travis and Homer. He pictured them as the type of men who would spend an evening in a place called the Blind Pig. He wondered what other secrets the breachway held. Those late night torches on the back path were still a mystery that Joshua had yet to figure out. As his mind wandered, he continued his long brush strokes on the bottom of the canoe. Off in the distance he could see the buildings over at the breachway. The Eldredge Hotel stood tall with its five stories. The others looked like small replicas of the bigger place.

Later on, Joshua went for a bicycle ride down the back path to the breachway. Kip started out the journey with him, but soon got sidetracked in the brush. As the boy passed the area near the stone shack, he just couldn't get up the nerve to stop and investigate once again. He continued onto West Beach Road and followed it down to the breachway. There was much more life down there now. A big truck was backed up to the door of the place where he had peered into a few weeks ago. Joshua pictured the empty shelves slowly filling up. He wasn't sure if he would be going up to the Post Road for supplies, or if this would be the place where he ran his errands.

As he pulled closer to the breachway, he could hear some shouting. It was like some kind of rhythmic chanting. He wheeled the bike through a pathway and saw a large white rowboat drifting out toward the ocean. Seven men in white uniforms were inside the boat. One of them was sitting in the back near the rudder and steering them along. The others each held a length of rope. As Joshua watched, he could see that there were actually two lengths of rope that three men grasped on each side. On

114

the end of each line, there was a circular rescue float. Josh inched closer to the edge of the stone wall and watched what the men were doing. Floating out ahead of them, there was something in the water. Two objects bobbed along with the ebbing tide. They weren't humans, but they were shaped in a similar fashion. The man at the bow of the boat tossed the line out toward the object. The ring landed directly on top of it.

"Good throw, Nathan," a member of his group shouted.

The other man in the front of the boat threw his line. It landed just short of the other floating object. They came around the corner of the breachway, and the man at the back of the boat had to pull the rudder hard. Joshua stepped down from the stone wall and hopped up onto the wooden boardwalk. He followed the progress of the boat as it rode the outgoing tide. The men who threw the first ring were pulling in their rescued target. The other three men were hauling their rope back to the boat. Joshua watched as they tossed the line again. This time their aim was true, but they were flowing into the choppy ocean water as they began to draw their intended mark back to the boat. They bounced on the frothy water that was part ocean and part pond. The other three men sat down at their benches and began to row away from the outlet. Within a few moments, Joshua could see the men hauling the other dummy onto the skiff. A loud cheer went up as they safely completed their mission.

The men started back in toward where Joshua stood. A couple of them gave him a big wave as they passed. The boy watched as they pulled their boat up to the Life Saving Station across the breachway. There was a small cart that ran along a track. Once they got the boat on top of it, four of them pushed it up and in through the large doorway to the station. The other three men busied themselves with the ropes. They each methodically wrapped the lines in circles, and then twisted them into tight rolls. Within a few minutes, they all disappeared inside of the building.

As he pedaled back to the inn along West Beach Road, Joshua thought about becoming a Coast Guard member. He could work at the Life Saving Station and rescue people who ran aground. Mr. Nilsson had said that there were a number of times when the crew saved people on boats right off shore. Josh thought about all of the rocks that dotted the beach, and he was surprised that it didn't happen more often. He remembered the fog that came in during those first few days down here. What was it like to be out in a boat in fog that was so thick, you couldn't see twenty feet in front of you? The old man told Joshua about the cannon that they used to shoot a rescue line out to the boat. They had heard it a few times over the last few weeks, and now Joshua realized that they had just been practicing for the real thing. Mr. Nilsson said that once the line was attached to the boat, the crew members would string a rescue car onto it. They would haul people back from the boat until they were all safely back on shore. Joshua hoped that he would see this maneuver sometime over the summer.

The best part about coming back to the inn were the smells that seeped into Joshua's nose as he walked into the kitchen. Mrs. Nilsson was an excellent cook, and each night they had a meal that gave him energy throughout the next day. She was laying the filets of the flounder in some flour, and then eggs, and then finally into some crushed up crusts of bread. A few were already cooking in the big black frying pan on the stove. The fish sizzled as it cooked.

"Joshua, could you please go out and tell Mr. Nilsson that it's just about time for dinner?"

"Sure," he answered, as he turned and bounded off the back porch.

Mr. Nilsson was inside the barn straightening up the workbench. Both of the paintbrushes were cleaned and set out to dry. The paint was tucked away, and the traps were back on the wall, waiting for the oily smell to dwindle.

"It's almost time to eat."

"Alrighty," the man answered as he reached under the bench to put a rag down there. "How's that fish smell?"

"Great."

"Well, let's go in and eat what we caught."

They both entered the house as Mrs. Nilsson was setting out the meal. Mother had appeared in the kitchen and was now pouring drinks for everybody. The fish tasted even better than it smelled. It was amazing to Joshua that they could trap minnows at the shore, then row out using the small fish as bait to catch the flounder. He couldn't wait to see what the lobster pots held.

After dinner, Joshua walked out to the end of the dock with his notebook and decided to try to write another letter to Mary. He was worried about having one of his spells, but figured that he had to try and move on with things somehow. If he could just figure out the magic combination to make the darkness go away, then he would devote everyday to trying to see it happen.

The sun was hanging just above the tree line as Joshua sat himself down. His feet dangled over the incoming tide. Opening the notebook up, he could see the remnants of the torn page. Joshua tried to ignore the emotions welling up inside of him as last night's memories rose to the surface. Shaking his head to send those thoughts away, he started to write.

Dear Mary,

> *Mother and I are at the Pond View Inn. It is a nice place in the southern part of Rhode Island. The beach is called Quonochontaug, and it has taken me awhile to figure out how to spell it. We have been here for about two months. I like it, and Mother seems to feel the same way. We had to get out of Providence.*

Joshua paused here for moment, as remembrances of the city crept into his mind. He now knew that if he dwelt on the past, then it would haunt him. He decided not to even mention his old way of life again.

> *I've been learning a lot of new things here. Mr. and Mrs. Nilsson run the place. They don't own it, but they are the caretakers. Mr. Nilsson is teaching me how to work in the garden. We went fishing this morning, and I caught three flounder. We ate them for dinner. I helped to paint the*

inn, and I have been riding a bicycle all over the place. Mr. Nilsson has made me the official errand boy of the Pond View.

Mother has been very busy getting the inn ready for the summer guests. She has been doing a lot of laundry, but someone is supposed to come in June to take over that job. She works from early in the morning until after dinner. I think she likes it here.

There's a place nearby that they say has ghosts, but I don't believe it. I tried to explore the area once, but I didn't get too far. There's something strange going on there though. Elizabeth said that it is just a story they tell people to scare them. She is a girl who lives over in East Beach. So far, she is the only one around here that is my age. This isn't too good because she is sort of mean to me.

Grandma sent me some of your books, so I can read them. I think I will start with the Tom Sawyer one. I also read the letter that you wrote to me. I think that I will try to do what you said in the letter.

Joshua stopped here. He could feel the emotion welling up inside of him again. If he was writing about what was going on around the beach, he was fine, but once he started thinking about Mary or back home, then things started to change. The sun was now below the horizon, and darkness was beginning to fall. Joshua closed the notebook and stood up. He looked out at the still pond and wondered where things would lead. As he hopped off the end of the dock, he spotted a flat rock on the shore. Picking it up, he heaved it in a side arm fashion out to the water. He watched as it skipped five times before slipping beneath the surface. Scouting around, he found a few more thin stones. Before giving up to the night, he had set a record of eleven skips.

As Joshua slept that night, everything was perfect. Dreams made his world right again. His family was staying at the Pond View Inn in Quonochontaug. It was the month of July, and he and his father were playing catch in the backyard. Mary was lounging on a lawn chair under the shade of a tree. She was reading one of her books. Off in the distance, the garden was brimming with vegetation. All of the work that he and his father had done there was paying off. It all seemed just right. Suddenly though, as his father threw him a fly ball, Joshua could see his mother up on the scaffolding painting the trim at the top of the house. He tried to warn her, but she couldn't hear him. The planks collapsed beneath her, and she tumbled down through the rest of the boards. Strangely, she landed in the breachway. Joshua, Mary, and their father were in the boat from the Life Saving Station. Each of them was trying to throw a rope as Mother drifted out to sea. They watched helplessly as the current took her into deeper water. For some strange reason, the skiff that they were in couldn't go past the end of the breachway. Joshua stood at the bow of the boat and watched his mother disappear.

He woke with a start and sat up in his bed. The pitch blackness was a stark contrast to the bright sunlight at the breachway. For a moment, he thought that he was blind again. This took his mind back to the hospital when Mother and Grandma were making the funeral arrangements. As he slowly crept out of his dreams, Joshua could hear his mother's breathing nearby. His heart thudded with the memory of his dream. When would his mind finally let him be at peace? He lay there for awhile trying to keep his thoughts from where they wanted to go. The dream had been such a nice one before his brain took him into a nightmare. After a time, Joshua slowly faded back into a more peaceful slumber.

9

Mrs. Van Houtten arrived with much fanfare a few days later, and everything changed at the inn. She brought two other ladies with her and a small child. Mr. and Mrs. Nilsson acted differently, and suddenly, Joshua didn't feel as comfortable any more at the Pond View. He tried to stay out of their way as much as possible, but sometimes it was very difficult to do. Mr. Nilsson and Joshua hauled all of their bags and boxes into the house. The driver of the large motor car seemed to be happy enough just watching them unload everything.

"Mrs. Nilsson, I don't know why you haven't made up these rooms yet," Mrs. Van Houtten barked in her high-pitched voice. "We need clean linens up here."

"Yes, Mrs. Van Houtten, right away," the older woman said with a bow.

Mother became a frantic ball of nervous energy as she tried to figure out how to please the owner of the inn. She rushed to and fro with handfuls of dishes and silverware as Mrs. Van Houtten made her shift everything around.

"We need something new. I am getting weary of the same old arrangement season after season."

Mrs. Hosmer and Mrs. Vickery kept giving Mrs. Van Houtten new ideas, and it was up to Joshua, Mother, and the Nilssons to follow through with them. They had them rearrange furniture, move pictures on the walls, and change curtains. By the end of the first day, though, almost everything had been shifted back to its previous location. Joshua was exhausted, and looking around, he saw that he had gotten absolutely nothing accomplished. Frederic, the little three year old, kept getting in their way as they tried to maneuver things around the different rooms. Mrs. Vickery, the boy's grandmother, seemed to be oblivious to the problems that the little one was causing.

A formal dinner was served in the dining room, and Mother acted more and more like a servant as she waited for the women to finish each of their courses. Mrs. Nilsson slaved away in the kitchen, and Joshua wondered how she would be able to do it during the summer when there were thirty or forty people staying at the inn. He could tell that Mrs. Van Houtten made everyone nervous. Each time his mother came back into the kitchen, it seemed as if her jaw was set a little tighter. Joshua tried to help as much as he could, but every time he attempted to assist in the kitchen, it just seemed like he was getting in the way.

After dinner, Mr. Nilsson had Joshua help him carry a large box into the sun porch. As the old man opened it, Joshua saw that it was a phonograph player, but it seemed different than any that he had seen before.

"Oh, she's a beaut," Mr. Nilsson said. "I heard these were coming out."

"It looks different."

"They don't have those cylinders anymore to play the music. You have to get those new recorded disks. You see this needle here, you put the record on this spinner, and the needle sits on top of it, then it spins around and the music comes out like it always did."

Joshua couldn't quite figure how the whole thing worked. How could a needle play music? After Mr. Nilsson set the phonograph up on the back table, he left the room, only to return a few minutes later with a smaller box. He pulled out the circular disk and set it on the phonograph. Joshua looked down and saw that it was a Scott Joplin record performing some ragtime hits.

"You can either crank it manually or give it some electricity."

Mr. Nilsson turned the crank, and then set the needle down. The scratchy noise that came out was soon replaced by Joplin's upbeat piano playing. Joshua was amazed at the quality of the sound. This was the first music that he had heard since coming to the inn. A few minutes later, Mrs. Van Houtten and the other women came into the sun porch. This broke the mood that

Joshua was starting to get lost in.

"Oh, this is marvelous," Mrs. Van Houtten said to her friends. "Alfred didn't want me to purchase this, but I said that it would get some good use this summer. I want to have a masquerade dance, and this phonograph will just be the height of fashion."

Joshua eased his way out of the room and went back into the kitchen. The sounds of the piano could still be heard at the other side of the house. Mother and Mrs. Nilsson were cleaning up from dinner as Joshua entered.

"What can I do?" The boy asked, knowing that his mother was under some strain.

"You can dry these dishes and put them back in the cupboard," she answered, blowing a strand of hair out of her face.

It seemed like real work now. Mrs. Van Houtten's entrance into the house set a whole different tone. It was a strange feeling. Except for ordering them around and criticizing their work, the women acted as if the Nilssons, his mother, and himself weren't even there at all. All of Joshua's thoughts about this place being his new home were fizzling as the day and evening progressed.

After he finished putting all of the dishes away, Joshua went out to the back porch and sat on the steps. It was dark now, and thousands of stars lit up the night sky. If there was a heaven, then it must be up there somewhere. This reminded Joshua that he had to write to Mary. He didn't really want to say anything about Mrs. Van Houtten, but he figured that maybe Mary would understand. Mother probably spoke to her a lot about her job at the Hearn's home on the East Side, so maybe she would be able to grasp what was happening. Standing up and looking at the stars one last time, Joshua glanced over toward the end of the house. The bright lights were flickering out into the yard, and he figured that he would have to refill all of the kerosene lamps fairly soon.

Joshua poked his head into the dining room and saw that his mother was setting out a new tablecloth. She looked tired, but when she saw her son in the doorway, her face brightened.

"Thank you for all of your help today."

"Sure," he answered. "I'm going to head upstairs."

"Alright. I should be up before too long."

Joshua didn't know where the Nilssons were. They probably had to hover somewhere near Mrs. Van Houtten until she decided to call it a night. Maybe they were getting the guests' rooms ready. He headed up the back stairs and lit the lamp in their room. He pulled the notebook out from the closet and sat on his mother's bed. Looking down at the next blank page, Joshua thought for a moment, and then took the small pencil and began to write.

Dear Mary,

Everything changed today. Mrs. Van Houtten showed up with some friends. She is the owner of the inn, and I don't like her too much. Mother seems to be having a hard time of it, but I hope that she will get used to things here soon. At least I get to be outside for part of the day. She is stuck in the house with that woman. Maybe Mrs. Van Houtten will ease up as time goes on. She treated us like puppets today. We moved everything around and then put it all back where it was. I guess that's what we're getting paid for though. I'm just sad that things are beginning to change. I was just getting used to the routine of the place. I have to keep reminding myself that the reason we are here is to work during the summer season, so I suppose I knew things couldn't go on the same way forever.

Your Brother,

Joshua

He closed the notebook, and then put it away. Josh didn't want to continue complaining to his sister, so he decided to wait until things started to change for the better. He reached under the chair and took out Mary's copy of *The Adventures of Tom Sawyer* and opened it up to the first page. Although some of the language was difficult to understand, and the way they spoke was almost impossible, Joshua liked the story. He laughed as Tom outwitted his Aunt Polly. It reminded him of the way he treated his own grandmother sometimes. When his mother was working, she was the one who always took care of him, and Joshua tried to get away with as much as possible without her figuring out what he was up to. In the second chapter, when Tom tricked all those boys into helping him paint the fence, Joshua thought of himself the way he used to be. Boys would usually be hanging around at his house, swapping different treasures for other things. Joshua always thought that he got the best of all the trades. He read until his eyes could no longer stay open. He thought of this book as one of the *Pluck and Luck* stories; only a much longer version.

As the week went on, Joshua couldn't figure out if Mrs. Van Houtten was easing up on her demands, or if they were just getting more used to her. Maybe it was a little of both. Once the initial shock of her presence wore off, it was easy just to maneuver around her and deal with the woman only when it was necessary. Mrs. Nilsson took the brunt of Mrs. Van Houtten's wrath. The older woman filtered the owner's words, and then directed them to Mother, Mr. Nilsson, or Joshua. It was much nicer getting a list of things to do from Mrs. Nilsson.

"Joshua, the ladies would like to play some lawn tennis this afternoon. Do you think that you and Mr. Nilsson can get things set up for them?"

Joshua just nodded and headed out into the barn to give the old man the news.

"Okay, I think we'll have to go over the court with the hand mower, then rake it out. The lines will have to be set, and then we can put up the netting. The equipment probably needs to be shined up too."

Joshua went into the back of the barn, moved some other things, and then dragged out the small mower. He inverted it, and then wheeled the machine over to the tennis court. The grass hadn't sprouted too much since the last time they cut, so Josh was able to go over it rather quickly. Mr. Nilsson started the raking, but when Joshua returned from putting the mower away, he handed the rake over to the boy. Joshua made four piles near each of

124

the corners. Scooping up one at a time, he dumped it in the brush out past the cold frames. Mr. Nilsson came back with the lines and the net. He had everything in the wheelbarrow. Starting at the small pole on the pond side, the old man measured out the end of one side. He placed the white cloth line down on the ground and tacked it into the grass with hooked spikes. Joshua helped as they made their way around the court. The net was a little more difficult. It was tangled and ripped in a few places. Once it was strung across the middle of the court, Mr. Nilsson worked on a few of the knots to close up the gaps. They tightened the net, so it was taut.

Both of them dug the equipment out of the closet behind the kitchen and dusted it off. Joshua carried the rackets and balls out to the court while Mr. Nilsson dragged a bench over. Once they set the bench in place, they put the equipment on top of it. To Joshua, this looked like a country club. Only a week ago, this was just an overgrown fenced in area.

"Why don't you pull that mower out again and cut a large square on the flat area over by those maple trees? Make it go all the way over to those rocks in the middle of the yard."

Josh wondered what the man had in mind.

"The ladies like to play croquet too. They'll want to play tomorrow anyway, so we might as well get it done this morning."

Joshua just nodded and went back into the barn. If he was outside, he didn't mind doing all of this work. It was the confining walls and Mrs. Van Houtten's voice that caused him problems. She had yet to acknowledge his presence, and the woman had been at the inn for five days. When she spoke, it was as if he wasn't even in the room. If Mr. Nilsson worked with him outside, then things would be just fine. Josh decided that when they came outside to play tennis, he would use that time to ride up to the store on the Post Road to get the New York newspapers that Mrs. Van Houtten wanted. He wondered if the store down at the breachway was selling any papers yet. Maybe he would swing down there after he returned to check things out again. He hoped that the crew at the

Life Saving Station would be out practicing again.

Mr. Nilsson helped him set up the wickets for croquet. Josh had seen people playing in Roger Williams Park, but he had never played the game himself. He shined up the mallets and the balls. As he leaned everything up against the tree, Joshua looked out to the pond and could see fog beginning to roll in. The ladies came out a few minutes later in their white athletic wear, and Josh watched from across the yard as they attempted to play tennis. They hit the ball over the net, but really couldn't get a volley of more than three hits going. It seemed like they were always reaching down the pick up the ball. Frederic pulled up the line on the side of the court. His grandmother scooped him up and sent him outside of the court with one of the tennis balls. Mrs. Van Houtten tacked the line down back in place. This was the first time that Joshua had seen her lift a finger to do anything.

He went into the house to get some money from Mrs. Nilsson. She gave him a small list of things to get at the store. Hopping on the bicycle and not looking back, Joshua sped down the driveway and onto West Beach Road. By the time he got close to the Post Road, Josh could see the fog rolling in even denser over the pond. This reminded him of his first day at the Pond View Inn. As usual, the main road was empty. He looked up and down as far as he could see, but there were no signs of carts or automobiles. Most of the traffic passed during the morning hours.

Inside the store, Joshua pulled out his list. Mrs. Nilsson wasn't sure if they would have everything on it, but she said that he should try to get as much as possible. He got a pound of butter for 23 cents, two cans of sardines at 5 cents a piece, and a can of coffee for 31 cents. They didn't have any of the dried prunes or apricots that she wanted. Joshua grabbed three days worth of the New York paper and some penny candy. Mrs. Nilsson told him that since he had been such a big help, he could have a treat. After the man wrapped everything, Josh popped one of the hard candies in his mouth as he hopped back on the bicycle.

The fog was washing across West Beach Road when he returned, and the pond was almost out of sight. As he pulled back into the Pond View, the fog was rolling up the lawn. The ladies had given up on tennis, and Joshua figured that it took him about three times as long to set the court up, than they spent playing on it.

"They had everything but the dried fruits," Josh said as he came into the kitchen. "He figured that they should be coming in with the next delivery."

"Thank you, Joshua. Mr. Nilsson would like you to put all the equipment away before the dampness gets to it."

Joshua hopped off the back porch and gathered the tennis rackets and balls. He also rolled the croquet set up with him to the house. After storing everything back in the closet, he decided to take a quick spin down to the breachway before the fog got too thick. In the back of his mind though, Joshua really wanted to check out the stone shack off the back path. He followed the dirt trail along the side of the pond. As he got near the spot where he saw those lanterns that night, he slowed. Joshua peered over to where the hut was hidden behind the bushes. Just as he was about to stop, a large white spirit leapt out at him causing him to lose his balance and fall into the vines on the other side of the path. He struggled to get up and run, but brambles held him back. The more he tried to extract himself, the more tangled he became.

When Joshua finally got himself loose, he saw that it was just the fog coming up from the hut. He held his breath and squinted his eyes as he crept closer to it. He vowed to be able to explain what was in the shack to Elizabeth the next time he saw her. The look on her face when she told him that the stories were told just to scare people away gave him the determination to carry on. Puffs of fog were coming out of the window area of the shack as Joshua approached it. He couldn't understand how this was happening. He began to stomp his feet louder as he approached the stone hut. If there were any spirits in here, then he was going to scare them away. As he came around the front on the pond side, he could see where a door hung limply. The beaten down bushes led right up to the entrance.

The low wind made the door creak as it swung back and forth. Joshua couldn't take his eyes off the entry way. He stepped closer, wondering if it would be better to swing it open quickly or just ease it slowly back. Carefully he approached, not wanting to stir anything. As he reached for the dangling door, a low moaning sound came from within. Joshua jumped back from the structure and waited for the sound to disappear. The pond was only thirty feet away, and Josh remembered the peacefulness that he had felt when he was out on the boat. Now he just stared at the ominous doorway.

Without letting himself think too much about it, Joshua Keegan stormed the shack. He broke through the entrance, and before he could lose his nerve, he looked all around. The shelves were lined with bottles. Some were wrapped in cloth, but most of them were just set there by themselves. Counting, he saw that there were over forty bottles in here. As he stepped closer, he could see the words written on them. There were bottles of whiskey, gin, rye, rum, and vodka. This was a shack that was filled with spirits! He heard the moaning sound again from behind him, and quickly, Joshua turned to see a pipe coming up from the wall, down near the floor. Fog flushed out of it and into the shack. It wafted by Joshua and then out the window. The pipe was about a foot wide, and it must go down to the water's edge. Joshua couldn't figure out what it was used for.

The men must have either been delivering the alcohol to the shack that night, or maybe they were just getting some bottles to take down to the breachway. Either way, there was a lot of hooting and hollering going on when they were here. A few empty bottles littered the floor, and it looked like there were some broken ones in the corner too. Questions filled his mind as he looked back at the shelves. Why did they store the spirits here? Who was in charge of this place? What would happen to him if he got caught inside of here? This last thought sent Joshua on his way. He picked his bicycle up from the bushes and followed the path out to West Beach Road.

Joshua circled up to the Ashaway cottages and left

his bike in one of the yards. The Drabble brothers had moved on, and the house they painted looked the best. Joshua missed them, and wondered if they were still in Quonny, or if they had moved on to Weekapaug. When he came over the rise between the cottages, he could see that the fog was just as thick over the ocean. He could pick out some of the rocks, but beyond that, there was nothing but gray. As he hopped onto the beach, Joshua scooped up some stones that were lying about on the sand. He picked out a rock about twenty-five feet out in the water and began his target practice. The first few splashed to the sides of the rock, but after five or six throws, he was able to hit the rock almost every time.

The contents of the shack made Joshua think about life back in Providence. Some of the men in his neighborhood got too involved with drinking alcohol. His own father had overdone it on a few occasions; getting loud and merry, and then seeming to get angry over every little thing. He could hear his mother getting upset with his father up in their room. He would yell, and then things would be quiet for awhile. The next day getting ready for church would be like walking on eggs in the house. Mother would try to be quiet, but she would drop a pan or something, and Dad would start yelling again. For the whole day, he would be a grump, and everyone would just stay out of his way. When his cousins came from Boston, it was worse. They would stay for three or four days, and the party would never stop. Mother and the other wives would try to keep things steady, but the men would carry on late into the night. The worst thing about it, Joshua thought, was that he wouldn't be able to play ball with his father during that time.

Joshua made a collection of flat stones, and when he had about a dozen of them, he tried to find an open area where he could skip them. With his index finger wrapped around the outside of the stone, he flung it in a sidearm motion. Watching it bounce on the water, Joshua counted the skips. He promised himself that if he could get to ten, then he would eat the last piece of candy in his pocket. Each of the stones fell after seven or eight hops, but then he flung one that had a perfect curve to it. He watched as it bounced eleven times before flopping underneath the surface.

Joshua hopped back on the bike and continued his journey down to the breachway. Although it had broken apart, the lemony candy still tasted sweet in his mouth. Homer gave Joshua a wave as the boy pedaled past him. The man was changing the tire on an automobile outside of the garage. Travis was nowhere to be seen, which was fine with Joshua. Again, the lifesaving crew was practicing out in the breachway. A few of the men were in front of their station, while others had rowed across to the other side. Joshua put the bike down and stepped up onto the rocks a little way down from them.

"Hey kid, why don't you move down farther. Johnny's ready to fire the cannon."

Joshua looked down at the man who was yelling over to him. He wasn't sure what the guy was talking about. After he stepped back from the waterline, Josh looked over and saw the small cannon for the first time through the fog. It was sitting down near the water at the end of their launching area. There was a big metal box sitting on the ground next to it. Two of the men were looping rope together. Joshua watched as they attached it to something on the cannon. After a minute or two, the boy saw one of the men light the fuse on the top of the cannon. With a loud bang, it went off. As it did, Joshua watched as something shot out of it with rope trailing behind. The whole thing landed beyond where the other men were standing on the opposite shore.

Scrambling along the rocky edge, Joshua moved closer to see what was going on. The two men on his side were tying down the rope, and across the breachway, the other men were rigging the metal box to the line. As they tightened it, Joshua saw that they were going to send it across. One of the men hopped inside through the top and started pulling himself across. Another line dragged behind him in the water as one of the men fed it out. Josh crept closer. A few other people came out of various buildings after the cannon was shot, and now they stood around watching the maneuvers.

"Hey kid," the same man called over to him.

130

Josh just looked over, thinking that maybe he would be getting in trouble for being so close to them.

"What's your name?"

"Joshua."

"Joshua, you want to go for a ride across the breachway?"

The boy's eyes lit up, and he moved closer. The metal box was just getting to the shore, and the men were pulling it closer.

"What is that?" Joshua asked in a quiet voice.

"It's a rescue car. If a boat hits the rocks in a storm, we have to get the men off the ship before it goes down. You want to try it out?"

"What do I have to do?"

"Just climb inside, and we'll send it across."

Joshua made his way closer to the box. Rivets lined the sides of it. He wasn't too sure about getting in, but he didn't want to seem like he was afraid. There were two steps built into the side, and Josh hopped up after the other man climbed out. Once inside, the sea smell was strong in his nostrils. The man who had spoken to him before peered down in at Joshua.

"Are you all set? I'm going to close the hatch, and you'll be over to the other side in about two minutes. This will be smooth sailing. Try to imagine riding in this thing during a storm."

Joshua gave a slight smile and a nod as the man closed the hatch and slid the bolt into place. The darkness was instant and total. He could hear their voices outside, but Joshua seemed to be in another world. He started to get a little frantic, but soon he felt the box begin to move. The water surged along the sides as he was pulled across the breachway. The darkness crept inside of Joshua and made him think of his days in the hospital bed when he was blind. The shock of the accident was so powerful, that he didn't really have time to focus on a life without sight. But now, here in this damp and dark box moving across the breachway, Joshua imagined an unlit world. He would never have had the opportunity to see the view from the upstairs room at the inn or watch the powerful waves roll into the beach. He couldn't even conceive of the other sights that he would see in his lifetime. Just as he touched the rocks on the other side of the breachway, he began to be truly thankful that he was spared a life of darkness. He heard the latch being loosened, and then, like a new day, the foggy light came into the box.

"Ahoy there," the man said, "who are you?"

"I'm Joshua."

"I'm Willy, and this is Max. Two of the other bums are sleeping."

Joshua looked back over to the other side of the breachway. The men were undoing the line and putting the extra rope into the skiff. Joshua hoped that they would be giving him a ride back in the boat instead of in the box.

"Over there's Cliff, Ben, and Mason. Mason's the one who talked you into this ride. How'd you like it by the way?"

"Not too good," Josh answered, "but I guess if I was trapped on the rocks in a storm, I wouldn't mind it too much."

"That's the thinking."

Max wheeled the cannon back up to the station, while Willy pulled the box onto the launch area. The other men were coming across now. Fog was getting deeper and denser. It was hard to see very far into the ocean or back into the pond. Cliff and Ben were rowing, and Mason was at the rudder. It didn't seem like he had to do much work.

"You want a ride back, or do you want to swim?" Mason asked as the boat approached the landing.

Willy reached out and caught the bow just before it touched the launch area. Joshua waited; he wasn't sure what to do.

"Hop right up there," Mason said from the back.

Joshua scrambled up and over the side of the boat. One of his shoes stepped in the water, and he could feel the wetness soaking through his sock. He sat in the small seat in the front of the boat, and grabbed the line that Willy tossed when he cast them off. The tide wasn't too strong now; slowly ending its outward flow for the day. Joshua was starting to realize the cycle of the tides. It seemed like when it was high tide in the morning one week, then it would slowly catch up about a half an hour each day. By the next week, it would be low tide in the morning.

"Where do you live, Joshua?" Mason asked from the back of the boat. "I haven't seen you down here before, and this is my third year stationed in Quonny."

"I stay at the Pond View Inn. My mother works there."

"The Pond View, eh? We went to a dance there last summer. Nice place."

"Yeah, I like it."

"Luther... he was the old guy who takes care of the place."

"That's Mr. Nilsson," Joshua said with a nod.

"He's a good man."

They brought the boat around, so Joshua could hop out onto the dock. Ben held onto the piling while Joshua scooted up and off the boat. He stood and gave them a wave as they pushed away from the dock.

"Come on down anytime," Mason said, "we'll teach you about boating and the sea."

Joshua waved again and watched them row back over to the other side. Once they pulled the skiff up the launch and into the station, he headed back to his bicycle and hopped back on. He was bursting. Joshua couldn't believe that the men from the Life Saving Station actually talked to him, and then used him during their rescue practice. He started to feel like Tom Sawyer. He was having adventures of his own now. Joshua weaved back and forth on the road as he pedaled back to the inn. The fear that he felt going up to the stone hut, and then inside the metal box was gone now.

"How did you get your shoe wet?" Mother asked the moment he stepped back into the inn.

He told her the whole story; at least the part that happened down at the breachway. She was worried at first, but soon got caught up in his enthusiasm. Mrs. Nilsson's entrance into the kitchen broke the spell of Joshua's story, and soon his mother was back to fixing the dinner. Josh grabbed a heel of bread and went upstairs. He wanted to tell Mary all about his day.

10

With only a few days to go before the first guests arrived in early June, it was decided that Mr. Nilsson should go into Westerly for supplies. Ray Crandall was hired for most of the day, and when he arrived in his pickup before nine in the morning, Joshua couldn't wait to hop inside. A day without Mrs. Van Houtten seemed like a vacation to the boy. He was still upset with her for eating those lobsters that he and Mr. Nilsson caught. His mother had told him that he had better shape up and start to understand why they were there in the first place.

"Joshua Keegan, I think you've grown two inches since I saw you last," Mr. Crandall said as the boy walked up to the truck.

He just smiled. The faster they got on the road, the better. Joshua was worried that his mother or Mrs. Nilsson would find something for him to do and spoil this outing for him. He had forty-five cents burning a hole in his pocket, and he couldn't wait to hit the road. Mr. Nilsson finished up with what he was doing, and in a few minutes they were off. Maybe it was the weather, but the truck just seemed to ride a lot smoother than it did on that first day Joshua arrived back in March. So much had changed since then. For one, the view was much different. Once they got up on the Post Road and started to head toward Westerly, the stark land that he remembered was now filled with bright green. Instead of turning in toward Watch Hill though, they stayed on the main road. There weren't a lot of houses, but as they got closer to town, there seemed to be a little more life. They passed carts and automobiles. Ray gave each one a big wave as they went by. Mr. Nilsson was silent for most of the trip.

"How have you been keeping yourself busy these

days, Joshua?"

He thought for a moment. There was so much to tell, but the noise of the engine made a conversation difficult.

"I've been gardening... cutting the grass... fishing... just helping out around the inn."

"I knew they'd keep you busy once you got there. How's Mrs. Van Houtten treating you?"

"Good, I guess."

The man laughed, seeming to know something about the woman. Joshua didn't really want to speak ill of her. Although he didn't much like being around her, he knew that the Pond View Inn was a nice place. He figured that in order to keep it running in such a successful manner, there had to be someone who was demanding at times. He also felt like he wanted to protect the reputation of the inn. It was now part of him, and the running of it this year depended in some way on his efforts.

When they got into Westerly, there were so many things to look at, that Joshua had a hard time keeping up with what he was seeing. There was the Westerly Opera House and the Star Theater. Their first stop was the Westerly Furniture Company. Mrs. Van Houtten wanted two new beds for one of the upstairs bedrooms. Joshua figured that Mrs. Vickery was complaining about them, so they had to be replaced. He followed Mr. Nilsson inside. There were rows and rows of chairs and tables and sofas and beds. Josh wandered around while Mr. Nilsson spoke to the salesman. He wanted to get something for his mother, but there didn't seem to be anything here for her. He walked through the kitchen supply area looking for something she needed. As he thought about it more, he didn't think that a dust pan or dish drainer would be something that he would want to give her anyway.

Mr. Nilsson had a slip of paper in his hand, and he waved over to Joshua. Once they were outside, they found Ray Crandall across the street having a cup of coffee. He wheeled the truck around to the loading bay, and Joshua watched as the men from the store placed the iron beds, springs, and mattresses into the back. After tying it down, they moved on to their next destination.

Joshua looked up at the sign as Mr. Crandall wheeled in; the P. H. Opie Company. This place was more interesting, and Joshua followed Mr. Nilsson as he picked out what they needed. They got an American flag, two rolled up hammocks, and a dozen adjustable screens that could fit into the windows.

"We're looking for a large canvas canopy," Mr. Nilsson said to one of the clerks.

"What kind?"

"One we can set up for shade. I need poles, rope, and stakes to go with it too."

"I believe our largest one is sixteen by twelve feet."

Next, it was the Mechanics' Clothing Company. Joshua wondered what they would be getting here.

"Your mother wants me to get a few things for you."

Joshua looked at the man with a little bit of surprise.

"What things?"

"She said that you need a good pair of shoes, some pants, and bathing trunks."

"I only brought forty-five cents with me," Josh said as he sadly thought about how his money would now be spent.

"She already gave me the money."

They went in, and a salesman came up to them right away. Mr. Nilsson told him what he and Joshua needed. He had no idea what size he was, so the man had to measure. All Joshua could see were fancy shoes, and he wanted no part of them. Mr. Nilsson led him over to a different part of the store, and he immediately found what he wanted. They were a two dollar pair of work shoes that were on sale for $1.48. He tried them on, but they were very stiff.

"You'll break them in soon enough," Mr. Nilsson said as he saw the discomfort on Joshua's face.

He got two pairs of pants and some bathing trunks. Mr. Nilsson also bought him a straw hat.

"You'll need this out in the garden in the coming weeks."

They went over to the Mohican Company to buy

their food supplies. The prices here were cheaper than the store at the top of West Beach Road, and Joshua noticed that they could buy a lot of things in bulk too. Mr. Nilsson ordered large sacks of flour, sugar, corn meal, potatoes, onions, and some other kinds of grain. They found all of the other things that they needed around the store.

"We have to make this trip twice a month in the summer. This should keep us until the end of June though. We can get odds and ends at the breachway or up on the Post Road."

Joshua had never seen so much food. He couldn't picture them eating it all, but once he figured that the guests would be devouring most of it, then he started to comprehend the volume that they would be going through each day. Ray pulled the pickup around back, and the men loaded the big sacks into the rear of the truck. With all of the other food, Joshua couldn't imagine what else they could fit.

"Are you hungry?"

"Very."

"Why don't I buy you lunch?"

They walked over to a variety store that had a lunch counter. Joshua ordered a roast beef sandwich and a large glass of milk. It had been awhile since he had either. When the sandwich arrived, it was on two thick pieces of bread with juice dripping all over it. The sandwich was delicious, and the glass of milk washed it right down. When he was finished with his meal, Joshua wandered around the store. This would be the place where he would spend his money.

On one of the racks, he found a Boston newspaper. Opening it up to the sports page he saw that the Red Sox were in first place. They were 24 and 10 on the season so far, and they had just beaten the Washington Senators 21 to 8. Joshua decided to buy the newspaper, because he wanted to get a closer look at the box scores, and because the man at the counter was giving him the evil eye for just reading the paper. He looked over on the magazine racks and saw a Red Sox program booklet with Tris Speaker and Joe Wood on the cover. He also grabbed the newest copy of Baseball Magazine. Sliding down the row a little bit, he picked up a woman's magazine for his mother. This left him with three cents to buy candy. He brought everything to the counter, and the man rang up his purchases.

Mr. Nilsson had to stop at the hardware store for a few things around the inn.

"Do you need any help in there?" Joshua asked.

"No, you can sit out here and read about your Red Sox," Mr. Nilsson said with a smile.

Joshua watched as both men walked into the store. He grabbed the newspaper out of the bag and hopped onto the open tailgate around the back of the truck. The game against the Senators was a slugfest. Speaker had hit two doubles and gotten on base every time at bat. Of course, the great Walter Johnson wasn't pitching for Washington, so they had it a lot easier. Smoky Joe Wood kept them hitless for three innings until they started to get the hang of his fastball. Everybody contributed to the win. Harry Hooper and Duff Lewis, the two outfielders with Tris Speaker, each scored multiple runs while driving in others. Their new player/manager Jake Stahl scored three runs. Josh read and reread the articles in the paper. Before he knew it, Mr. Nilsson was coming out of the store with a box of supplies. Mr. Crandall was still talking to a man in the doorway as Josh folded up his paper and hopped back into the truck.

All the way back to the inn, he dreamt of baseball. A part of him wanted to be in centerfield like Tris Speaker, but sometimes he wanted to be on the mound like Smoky Joe Wood. Third base also had an attraction. Joshua liked the idea of scooping the ball out of the dirt as it bounced over the bag, and then turning to fire it over to first.

From the Post Road, Joshua could clearly see the pond before they made their turn down West Beach Road. The water's blue sparkle made him glad to be alive. He saw the spot where Mr. Crandall had dropped them off a few months before. He could see marshy grasses on both sides of the road. When they pulled back into the inn, Mother was outside hanging laundry on the lines. The sheets snapped in the breeze. Joshua helped Mr. Nilsson and Mr. Crandall unload everything from the truck. While they carried the beds upstairs, Josh brought the food into the kitchen. Mrs. Nilsson busied herself putting everything away. Josh put the hammocks and the flag on the back porch, and then carried his new clothes and magazines up to his room. Although he wanted to sit and read about baseball, he knew that he was needed elsewhere.

"Joshua can you hold the end of this frame while I slide in the runners?" Mr. Nilsson asked after Mr. Crandall had fired up his truck and ambled down toward the breachway.

They put both of them together, took the old ones from that room, and moved them to the bunk area on the third floor. With a little bit of a struggle, they then hauled the ones they replaced out to the barn. Mr. Nilsson set them up, and Joshua wondered if maybe he could spend the summer out here. The breeze blew through both ends of the loft area. He could probably find some screen to keep the bugs out. Maybe he would ask his mother about it that night.

They rigged up the pole and slid the new flag up. The wind caught it immediately, and just like the sheets, it flapped in the breeze. Although no one would probably be lying there any time soon, Mr. Nilsson set some rings in the trees in the back and side yards. They rolled out the hammocks and hooked them up. Josh climbed right in, immediately flipped out onto the ground, and then tried it again. This was the first time that he had ever been in a hammock, and once he got used to the tilting nature of it, he swayed peacefully back and forth. If he hadn't been so concerned about what Mrs. Van Houtten would think about it, he would have stayed there all afternoon.

Mr. Nilsson then had Joshua help him with the canvas canopy. They unfurled it and set the stakes in the ground outside the perimeter. Starting from the middle, Joshua pushed up the tallest pole and held it steady. Mr. Nilsson did the same with the other one. Josh held both as the old man pulled up the end pieces, and set them in place. He did the same with the other end. Although the wind was blowing at a good clip, the canvas shelter held strong.

"Mrs. Van Houtten wanted to get a new one this year. The other one we had was a little smaller, and it was starting to show its wear."

"Do we set it up in the yard?"

"No, no... this is for the beach. The Pond View Inn has a little section where we set things up, usually on weekends, but mostly everyday for the first two weeks of July. You and I will go down in the morning and put it up, and maybe bring some chairs along. Around lunchtime, I'll bring a basket with some snacks and drinks, and then in the evening, we'll take it down. Some people don't like the sun, and others like a break once in a while, especially on those hot days."

"What do I do during the day?"

"Like I said, you'll probably be the errand boy. You'll stay on the beach for part of the afternoon. People are always forgetting something or wanting more of something else. You just speed back on the bicycle and get it."

Joshua just nodded, thinking that it was going to be fun staying on the beach all summer. They let the hammocks and the canopy air out for awhile. Mr. Nilsson brought his box from the hardware store into the barn and began to sort out everything that he purchased. Joshua went and got his baseball glove and ball and headed out to the far side of the barn. He tossed the ball onto the roof and caught it again and again. He did this for awhile until Mr. Nilsson came out with two hoes in his hand.

"It's time to start keeping back those weeds."

They walked out into the garden. The traps were empty, and it didn't look like any animals had eaten any of the plants that were popping up all over the garden. It was amazing to see the lines of leafy greens growing up and down the rows. The weeds were scattered on both sides.

"If we keep up with it, the weeds don't take hold, but if we let it go, then we have a problem. They choke the plants, and weeding becomes a whole day affair."

They went at it strongly. Mr. Nilsson was able to move up and down the rows at a fairly good pace. Josh

141

was slow in the beginning, but once he got the hang of working the hoe, then he was able to progress at a good clip. For the first time, he noticed bugs starting to bother him. If the wind died down a bit or if he stopped for any length of time, they swarmed around his head. The more he swatted at them, the worse they seemed to get.

"Those are May flies. They came late this year because the winter was so cold. They'll be gone in a week or so. It's the mosquitoes that are a real bother. They come in July and August depending on the rain, and on those humid days without any wind, you are going to wish you were back in the city."

Joshua didn't think that he would want to be back in the city. His only dilemma was being outside with the bugs or inside with Mrs. Van Houtten. They finished the garden as the sun was hanging low over the trees on the far side of the pond. Mrs. Nilsson had dinner on the table when they finally came in. Joshua washed up at the sink, and then dove into his food. The roast beef sandwich in Westerly had been a long time ago, and his appetite seemed to be getting stronger as the days went on.

That night he tried on his new clothes for his mother. She seemed to be pleased with the choices. He walked around in the shoes for a short time, but they didn't seem to be loosening up any. When he handed her the woman's magazine, she smiled, and Joshua almost thought that he saw a tear forming in the corner of her eye. They both thumbed through their magazines for awhile. Joshua read all about the Red Sox new field; Fenway Park. There were a few pictures and some sketches of it. Joshua wondered if he would ever sit in one of the seats of that ballpark. He hoped so, but couldn't picture any situation in which he would find himself there. Since his father had died, his mother didn't keep in touch with their relatives up in Boston.

"Do you think it would be possible for me to sleep out in the barn once in awhile?"

"In the barn?"

"Yeah, Mr. Nilsson and I just set up some nice beds in there, up in the loft," Josh said as he tried to plead his case.

"Doesn't it smell out there?"

"No, I keep it pretty clean. I shovel out Nettie's stall every day. And now she spends most of the time outside chewing the grass, so she's not in there too much."

"I don't know, I'll have to think about it. I'll speak with Mrs. Nilsson."

Joshua went back to his magazine, thinking that maybe he would have a shot at living out there. Glancing through the pages, he saw that there was a profile on each of the players on the team. He didn't want to read too much of it, he wanted to savor the articles and make them last. He did read about Tris Speaker though, and as he drifted off to sleep, he had visions of sitting in a box seat in Fenway Park and watching the Red Sox win the World Series.

Just after sunrise, Joshua was up and outside. He walked down to the pond to skip some stones. The tide was high, so it was hard to find anything along the shore to throw. He saw a boat crossing the pond and wondered if it was Johnny Crandall. Mr. Nilsson had said that he was the local fisherman. Maybe he was Ray Crandall's brother or relative. Walking back up toward the inn, he could see his path in the grass where he had traipsed through the dew.

Joshua quickly went back upstairs, grabbed his notebook, and retraced his steps. With some bread in his other hand, Joshua sat on the back steps of the porch and opened up to a new page.

Dear Mary,

I went into Westerly yesterday to get some supplies for the inn. I also bought some baseball magazines. The Red Sox have a new ballpark, and I wish Dad was around so we could go see a game. I've been thinking about him a lot lately, but not in a bad way like I used to. You too. I have decided to look at things as if you or Dad were with me. I know that sounds weird, but I think that it is starting to work. If I start to remember all of the things that we used to do, then I get sad. But if I see new things and try to think of how you or Dad would feel about them, then it makes me feel better.

I'm going to try to follow the Sox as closely as I can this summer. I only did it once in a while for the last two years. The idea of baseball and the Red Sox always made me think of Dad, and then I would usually have one of my spells. Now if I think of it as sharing his love of the game with what is going on, then it makes me feel better. I don't know if that makes any sense. Now when I read my Red Sox program, I feel like Dad's with me. Just like when I'm reading about Tom Sawyer. I remember you reading it a few years ago, so now we have something in common again. I'm really starting to like Tom, but I'm not sure what is going to happen with that girl at Judge Thatcher's house. There is a girl down here who is just like her. Her name is Elizabeth, and I can't figure out why I want to impress her because she ignores everything I say. Either that or she says something to make me feel bad. I went and looked at this haunted shack that we have down here just so I could tell her what was inside. It turns out that it's not haunted, but filled with bottles of liquor. I can't wait to see her reaction.

Your brother,

Joshua

He read over his latest letter to Mary and was satisfied with what he had done. It was getting easier to write to her each time, and as he looked over the words, they seemed to have a calming effect on him. He now truly felt that Mary was with him. Sometimes when he was alone, he wondered if writing to his dead sister meant that he was losing his mind. He trusted Mr. Nilsson, and if the man was able to get over his brother's death by doing something similar, then Josh was all for it. Mary's unfinished letter to him put the whole thing in perspective, and his momentary lapse of confidence in his plan began to slowly fade away.

Joshua could see the long shadow of the inn shortening in the back yard as the sun rose higher.

144

Guests would be arriving today after lunch. There were some things that he had to do with Mr. Nilsson to prepare for their visit. Mrs. Nilsson said that there would be a few families coming. Some would stay for a week, while others would remain longer. More guests were to follow as June progressed.

Just before putting the notebook in his back pocket, Joshua saw some movement out near the garden. There was a brown animal that was bigger than a cat slowly ambling toward the leafy sprouts. The critter wobbled back and forth as it walked, and Josh figured that this must be the woodchuck. The boy slowly stepped to the side of the barn, and then came around near the windmill. The breeze was blowing up from the pond, so Josh didn't think the animal would pick up his scent. He watched as the woodchuck sniffed along the ground near the beans. There was no way that he was going to let some varmint eat up the garden that he was growing.

Joshua reached down and picked up some stones that were lying near the pump area next to the windmill. He stepped lightly to the stone wall, and then went along the edge of it to about the place where the woodchuck was starting to eat. Slowly, Joshua raised his body up and saw the animal about twenty five feet away. With the all of his strength and accuracy, Josh hummed the rock at his target. It bounced off the rear end of the animal. The chase was on. The woodchuck raced back toward the fruit trees, just as Joshua leapt over the stone wall and followed. Just before it went into the brush, Joshua threw another rock, but it bounced wildly a few feet away. He walked to the edge of the grass and tried to see where the woodchuck went. Mr. Nilsson said that if they could find the animal's hole, then they could set a trap at the mouth. They'd have to block up the escape hole first. Since he was barefoot, Joshua didn't want to go tramping through the woods, so he just marked the place where the woodchuck went in and ran back to the inn.

"I hit him," Joshua said to Mr. Nilsson at breakfast, "but he just took off into the woods."

"Where'd you get him?"

"Right in the back, near its tail."

"A head shot might have stunned him for a minute."

"That's what I was trying for."

"I'll have to get him with the shotgun, unless we can find his hole."

The guests arrived in the early afternoon. They were in the same kind of jitneys that Mrs. Van Houtten had arrived in. They had come up from New York and New Haven by train, but instead of stopping in Westerly, they went on to Bradford, which was closer to Quonochontaug. Again, it was women and small children. Joshua was hoping for someone his own age, but was out of luck this time. He and Mr. Nilsson took all of their bags up to their rooms. Mother and Mrs. Nilsson had prepared everything for them upstairs. When they were all settled, Mrs. Van Houtten became the hostess, and tea was served in the sun porch. Joshua climbed the tree next to the house, and he could hear their conversations from the branch that hung just above the low roof at that end of the house.

"What a glorious day..."

"The place looks beautiful..."

"...children to play with..."

"The height of arrogance..."

"...glad to be out of the city for a spell."

"Wasn't that terrible news about the Titanic."

"Those poor people in that frozen water."

"Just as bad as that fire in the shirt factory last spring."

"...those girls jumping to their deaths."

"That's why women should have the right to vote, to avoid sweatshops like that."

"Oh Ida, please, enough with the Suffrage... we're on vacation."

Joshua could only hear bits and pieces of their conversation. It wasn't like he was trying to eavesdrop; that branch was the most comfortable place he could read without falling asleep. He could sit on the thick branch just before it forked out, and lean back on another limb that ran just above the one he was sitting on. With his bare feet dangling, he almost felt like Tom Sawyer.

Joshua didn't really understand what they were talking about. The only thing that he knew about was the ship that had hit the iceberg. What did women's right to vote have to do with a fire in a shirt factory? He tried to go back to his reading, but their chattering voices hindered his concentration.

Mr. Nilsson suggested that they try some fishing later that afternoon. He said that the tide would be just right, and they could row over to where the breachway fed into the pond.

"Maybe we'll get lucky and snag a big one that's coming in to feed."

They got the tackle box out of the barn, and carried their gear down to the dock. Josh pulled the minnow trap, then Mr. Nilsson shoved off, and the boy started to row. Since the tide was coming back in, they didn't have to follow the channel.

"Cut behind the island, and we can make a beeline over through the edge of the flats."

"Okay."

Joshua rowed over the sandy, clayed bottom between the island and the marshy grassland, as Mr. Nilsson rigged the lines. The water was only about two and a half feet deep, but he was able to maneuver the bottom just as well. The only problem that Joshua had was when they were coming around the last bend before the breachway. The current was surging in, and Josh felt that he was losing more ground than he was gaining.

"Head out a little bit away from the land. The pull isn't so strong."

When they were out in front of the rushing water, Mr. Nilsson dropped the anchor. They drifted for a moment, before catching on something at the bottom. Water bubbled up at the front of the boat, as the rushing water bounced off the bow. Mr. Nilsson had four lines set up with minnows hooked on each. They dropped two off each side and waited.

"Don't let it drop to the bottom. We won't catch any flounder here. Let it dangle a few feet down, and maybe something will come along."

They sat for a short while, and then there was a

tug on Joshua's line. As he pulled it in, he could feel the strength of the fish. It was much stronger than the flounder. His line tightened around his hand. When he finally pulled it up to the surface, Mr. Nilsson was there with a net. He scooped the fish out of the water and plopped it on the bottom of the boat. It was whitish with black lines running from its gills to tail.

"You caught yourself a striped bass, young man," Mr. Nilsson said as he pulled the hook out, and then dropped the fish into the fruit crate."

It was about sixteen or seventeen inches long. Joshua watched as it moved around inside the crate; lifting its tail and head in a curling fashion. He dropped the line in again, and almost immediately, there was a strike. This one wasn't as big, and when he pulled it in, the fish looked different than the first one. It was long and skinny with a shiny skin. The top of the fish had a greenish blue color to it.

"That's a mackerel. Boy, you never know what the tide's going to send in."

Mr. Nilsson caught three fish before Joshua even had another bite. Two of them were stripers, and the third was a small blue fish. The blue was only about a foot long, and its teeth kept snapping as the man dropped it into the crate.

"Don't get your fingers near his mouth."

They caught one more striper each before heading back to the inn. Joshua rowed as Mr. Nilsson gutted them. He dropped the insides where they usually put their traps, so the lobsters would get used to feeding there. The old man said that they would set some traps in a day or so. When they got back to the inn, Mother and Mrs. Nilsson couldn't believe their catch.

"We were just starting to worry that we would have to come up with something else for dinner," Mrs. Nilsson said with a smile as she sliced the fish into filets.

Mother got the skillet going, and Joshua and Mr. Nilsson went to wash up. The thing that discouraged Joshua the most about catching the fish was that the guests got to eat most of it. He was trying to understand the concept of being the hired help, but it still hurt to see them shoving his food into their mouths. Even worse, they didn't even bother to thank Joshua and Mr. Nilsson for catching it. They just expected the food to be there for them. Joshua figured that he better start getting used to this, because when summer arrived, there would be more people here. Even if Mrs. Van Houtten didn't know he was part of the inn, Mother and the Nilssons appreciated what he was doing. He went to sleep that night trying to think of a way to deal with the guests without getting upset over their behavior. Maybe he would talk to Mr. Nilsson about it if the time was right.

11

After finishing breakfast and their morning chores, Joshua and Mr. Nilsson went looking for the woodchuck hole. They saw that the garden was still intact as they passed by and went around the fruit trees. Joshua showed the man where he had marked the spot at the edge of the bushes. He picked up the few stones that were there. Spreading about ten feet apart, they made their way through the brush.

"Look for a mound of light colored dirt. They just dig and push the soil out. You'll know it when you see it."

They worked slowly, scanning back and forth. Sometimes there was an opening in the brush, but mostly it was thorny and full of vines. Joshua had his new work shoes on, and they were suffocating his feet. Lately, he had been going around in bare feet, and now the shoes felt too confining. Although he knew that he could never make it through this brush without something on his feet, he longed for the freedom that he had without them. Off to the left, Joshua spotted a mound of dirt. It was right next to a rock that stuck up out of the ground about two feet high.

"I see it."

Mr. Nilsson made his way through the brambles and looked down at the ground.

"Yup, that's it. There should be another one around here someplace."

Josh found the other one in no time. It was only about five or six feet away. Mr. Nilsson walked straight out toward the field, and Joshua followed. They marked the entrance with a stick, but it was obvious where they pushed the brush over.

"Go find a big flat rock that will cover the hole, but one that you can carry. I'll get the trap."

Joshua found a rock out by the bottom of the garden. He put it right at the entrance to the woods, and then went up to the barn to help the old man. He was coming out of the house with some food. Mr. Nilsson grabbed the last trap off the wall and a hammer from the bench, and then they headed back to the woods. Joshua placed the rock firmly over the back hole. It had been difficult maneuvering it through the brush, but it fit over the exit nicely. Mr. Nilsson banged a stake into the ground and set the trap just inside the hole.

"If this doesn't get him, then maybe he deserves to have some of our vegetables."

Once out of the woods, they walked slowly through the fruit trees. Mr. Nilsson examined them for insects and disease. He had a pump sprayer that he filled with a foul smelling substance that he showered the leaves with every ten days or so.

"Do you like Mrs. Van Houtten?" Joshua asked out of the blue as they walked.

"Do I like her? That's a difficult question. She and Mr. Van Houtten are my employers. They pay very well compared to other places, but they expect a lot in return. So when you ask if I like her, my answer would be yes. Do I wish that her disposition was more pleasant? My answer would be yes to that also."

"Don't you get mad when she orders you around?"

"Joshua, you have to realize that jobs like this one are hard to come by. Mrs. Nilsson and I are very pleased with what we do. When we go up to Mrs. Vickery's winter lodge in Vermont, it's the same thing, but we know that we can easily be replaced. Your mother is lucky to have this position, and if things work out, then she may be able to take over both places when Mrs. Nilsson and I are ready to retire."

"Really?"

"Yes, Mrs. Nilsson is very happy with your mother, and you've been a great help to me."

Joshua beamed with the compliment. He hadn't really thought much beyond this summer. He thought that they might be going back to Providence in the fall, and he wasn't looking forward to that prospect. Following the Nilssons to Vermont seemed like another adventure worthy of Tom Sawyer.

"Mrs. Vickery owns the lodge in Vermont?"

"Yes, she's Mrs. Van Houtten's sister. Their father had both places built for them."

Joshua saw things in a new light now. He didn't even know that the two women were related. The boy and man strolled out of the small orchard, and then into the garden. They had put the tomato plants in and built small frames to hold up the heavy tomatoes when they arrived. Joshua never liked the smell of those plants, but he loved what grew out of them.

"I was mad when Mrs. Van Houtten ate the lobsters that we caught."

"That was bad timing on my part. We should have set the traps before that, so we could have had a taste before she arrived. Don't worry though, you'll get your fill of lobsters this summer."

They strolled up and down the rows of the garden. Mr. Nilsson gently lifting the leaves to see how they looked. Joshua did the same, but he wasn't sure what he was looking for.

"My mother says that I have to do some science and mathematics work to go along with my reading and writing."

"There's plenty of that right around here."

"What do you mean?"

They walked down to the pond. Mr. Nilsson snapped some vines that were growing out onto the path. When they got near the shore, they both grabbed an end of the canoe and set it into the water. They did the same with the other one. Mr. Nilsson tied the ends to the pilings.

"The whole place is full of science. Look at all of the animals and birds that are around here, not to mention all of the fish and clams and what not. There's some books inside that have information about all the wildlife and sea life in New England. Growing a garden and taking care of a horse is science. The weather changes fit the bill too."

"How about the tides?"

"They sure are. You've got yourself a real laboratory down here."

"What about math?"

"How long are our vegetable rows?"

"I don't know... maybe forty or fifty feet."

"And how many seeds can go in a row?"

"A lot."

"How much does a packet of seeds cost, and how much do you need of each kind to fill the garden?"

"I never thought of that."

"How many bushels of apples can you get from a tree?... or peaches?... or plums?"

Joshua's mind began to reel at the implications of all these mathematical problems. He couldn't even begin to comprehend the figuring that he would have to do to calculate all of those numbers. Thinking about it for a moment though, he knew that a smart farmer would have to make all of those estimates before the season started. Maybe that's what they did all winter while the fields were frozen. He wondered if his father had done any of this figuring when he had planned to buy some land in Warwick.

"The best part of this kind of math is that it's useful. By the end of the summer, you'll be telling me how many packs of seeds I'll need for next spring, and then figuring out how much I have to charge Mr. Van Houtten."

"I don't even know where to start."

"Why don't you go measure the field? I've got a fold-out tape in the barn. Once you get the dimensions, then the rest just breaks down easily. Who knows, maybe you can save us some money next year."

When they got back to the barn, Joshua found the measurer. It was made up of foot long pieces of wood, that were folded over and over again. The entire length was sixteen feet. Joshua went over to the garden and undid the tape measure. He marked each spot for every sixteen foot length. Once he got the proportions, he figured out the number of rows they had, and listed each different kind of vegetable. Over the summer, he planned to see what people ate more of, and then plan accordingly for next year. Mr. Nilsson gave him the prices on all the packets of seeds, and estimated how far each one would go in the garden. Joshua thought about making a chart to see how much food they got from each plant, and then comparing it to the price of vegetables at the store on the Post Road and in Westerly. This logical way of thinking was just what Joshua needed. He now had a distinct plan for the summer.

After talking with Mrs. Nilsson, Mother said that Joshua could try sleeping out in the barn. Although she wasn't too excited about the prospect, she said that she could understand the boy's need to be out of his mother's room. As soon as Joshua got the word, he started setting things up in the loft. He cleaned it out again; sweeping all of the dust and cobwebs out. Mr. Nilsson gave him some screening and helped him build a frame to put at each of the upper doorways.

"This will probably stop some of them, but you're going to have to live with bugs buzzing around your head at night."

He moved the bed that they had brought from the upstairs bunk room over to one side. Mr. Nilsson got him a kerosene lantern, and for the hundredth time explained how careful he had to be with it. Joshua had a small shelf nearby where he put his baseball glove and ball, Red Sox magazine, notebook, and Mary's books. From the house, he also grabbed the books on nature. One was devoted just to birds, and another for wildlife in the Northeast. There was also a book on marine life that Joshua instantly took a liking to. Inside were colored drawings of all kinds of fish and shells. Joshua thought about starting a collection of each of the different kinds of shells on the beach, and then figuring out what they were. There was plenty of room here in the loft, and Joshua's only worry was that he wasn't sure who would be living up here in the summer. He figured that his mother wouldn't be too keen about him sharing this place with the working men who came to the inn. He would have to move back inside when that happened. In the meantime though, he enjoyed his new sense of freedom.

On a large scrap of white paper, he drew out the

dimensions of the garden. Row by row, Joshua filled in the vegetables that were growing there. Beneath the large square, he listed out the different types of crops again. He planned to keep track of what they picked from the garden. He tacked it up on the wall near his bed. It was good to see that he was finally getting out of his stagnation.

Joshua heard the good news a day or so later. Mrs. Van Houtten and the other ladies would be returning home to New York City. Unfortunately though, they would be coming back at the end of the month to prepare for the many guests who would be arriving in July. Joshua and Mr. Nilsson helped pack up all of their stuff and haul it down to the driveway. Their fancy jitney arrived later in the morning, and as they drove away, Joshua breathed a sigh of relief. Hopefully things would get back to normal before too long.

"Do you want to go for a walk to the beach?" Joshua asked his mother later that afternoon.

"Oh, I don't know," she lamented, "I've got a lot of work to do."

"You haven't been to the beach yet, and we've been here almost three months."

"Well..."

"When Mrs. Van Houtten comes back, and when all of those guests start coming, then you'll never get a chance."

"Let me just finish up in here first," she answered as a smile broke on her face.

As Josh waited for his mother, he figured that she hadn't been farther than the clothesline. Since either Joshua went for supplies, or they were delivered, there was no reason for her to go anywhere. Looking over at the tennis court, he could see that it needed to be trimmed, and as he glanced about the yard, he thought that maybe it was time to get the big mower out again. He wondered how many times he would have to mow it over the summer.

"I told Mrs. Nilsson that I was going for a short walk with you," Mother said as she stepped outside, "but she told me that I deserved a long one."

Joshua smiled and then led his mother around to the front of the house. It was a beautiful afternoon with bright blue sky and a nice dry breeze coming from the west. They walked down West Beach Road, and then followed Surfside Avenue by the cottages that lined the shore. Josh took his mother onto the beach and was happy to see the smile break out on her face when she saw the ocean. Since the tide was out, they strolled along the hard packed sand near the water's edge. When Joshua passed the spot where he had his first mental breakdown after arriving at the Pond View, he didn't give it a second thought.

"You know, your father used to spend part of his summers at the shore when he was back in Ireland."

"He did?"

"Yes, the whole family would get the crop into the ground, and then pack up for a journey to the ocean."

"Did they have a house there?" Joshua asked in disbelief. All of the stories that he heard about life back in the old country were of a struggling family just trying to get by.

"No, they'd set up little shanties up on the beach. It would be his family, his cousins, and some other neighbors; like some big clan. They'd dig for shellfish or go out fishing during the day, and then at night, there'd be music and dancing around the fire."

They continued walking as Joshua tried to picture it in his mind. It seemed like there were a lot of things starting to connect now. Here he was, down at the shore, planting a large garden and going out and getting food from the water. He tried to imagine what life was like for his father when he was Joshua's age.

Large gulls circled overhead, as smaller sea birds chattered and chased each other by the watery edge. Joshua tried to notice as many details as possible as he looked at the birds. He wanted to be able to find them in the nature book when he returned to the inn. They came around a last turn, and Joshua's mother gasped as she saw the boardwalk and line of cottages.

"Oh, this place is grand."

It was at that moment that Joshua decided that he

would save as much money as he could, and someday buy a house down here for his mother and himself to live in. Joshua was already starting to learn about how he could make money down here. People needed vegetables and seafood, and they also had to have some type of transportation. All he would need was a pickup truck, a boat, and a house. Everything else would just fall into place. Actually, he would just need a plot of land. He could learn how to build a house easily enough.

They climbed up on the boardwalk and came around to where the breachway met the ocean. His mother just stared as the water was starting to flow back into the pond.

"That's the Life Saving Station over there," Joshua said, pointing over to the other side.

He could see the crew down at the far end of the breachway, all rowing in unison against the incoming tide. They moved closer as Joshua and his mother continued along where the houses and inns lined the waterway. Joshua gave them a wave as they passed by.

"Want to go for a ride, Joshua?" a voice came from the back of the boat.

"Not today," he shouted back, even though he really wanted to hop on.

Back up on the road, they walked through the small village area. All of the windows and doors were open at the casino. It didn't look like there were many people in there, but it had a lot more life than when he peered inside the last time. Although Joshua wanted to dawdle, he could tell that his mother was getting a little uneasy about being away from the Pond View for so long. They followed West Beach Road back toward the inn. He was tempted to take her down the back path, but he didn't really want to have to explain the shack with all of the alcohol to his mother. He hadn't told anyone about his find. Joshua was actually saving that bit of news for Elizabeth. For some reason, it was very important for her to know that he wasn't afraid to explore the haunted shack.

"How was your outing?" Mrs. Nilsson asked when they came back into the kitchen.

"Oh, this is a glorious place. I didn't realize how beautiful the shore really is."

Joshua poured himself a glass of water and nibbled on one of the biscuits that Mrs. Nilsson had just made. He looked out the back window and saw the four children playing in the yard. Their mothers were sitting on the bench under the tree, chatting away. Joshua didn't feel connected to the guests at all. It was like they weren't really part of the inn. He wondered what it would be like when the hordes of people started arriving. That day was quickly approaching.

After bringing in some firewood for the stove, Joshua made a tour of the grounds. Much of the brush that he had trimmed when the Drabble brothers were there was growing back. He would have to get the clippers out soon. The grass was growing at an incredible rate now. He could see the spots along the edge of the lawn where he didn't do a thorough job. Tufts of stringy green were folding over onto themselves. The weeding that he and Mr. Nilsson had done in the garden made it look very professional, but Joshua worried that there hadn't been enough rain. He couldn't remember the last good storm that they had. Looking up, he could see towers of white, billowy clouds pluming in the north. The trees were starting to bear fruit. Joshua ran his fingers over the small apples, pears, and plums that had formed on the branches. It was truly an amazing thing to see.

What Joshua really wanted to know was if they had trapped the woodchuck. He slowly made his way through the leafy brush until he came to the place where they set the trap. As he got closer, he could hear thrashing sounds, but Joshua wasn't sure what it was. Nearing the hole, he saw that the woodchuck was pulling at the chain. His front paw was caught in the trap, but he wasn't dead. It looked as though the stake was pulling out of the ground, and Joshua wasn't sure if he would have enough time to go find Mr. Nilsson and ask his advice. The animal was oblivious to the boy's presence as it attempted to twist and tear away at the trap. Joshua stepped over to the escape hole and picked up the large rock that he had placed there before. As he did so, the woodchuck spun quickly to face him. With the rock over his head, Joshua looked at the trapped creature. For a moment he felt bad for its predicament. He didn't think that he was giving the creature an even chance. At that moment though, the woodchuck pulled quickly to the side, and Joshua saw the wobble of the stake. If he didn't do this right away, then there wouldn't be another chance. With squinting eyes, he let the sharp edge of the rock fall onto the woodchuck. It cut into the back of its neck, and suddenly, the animal was still. Joshua couldn't look at what he had done, so he turned and slapped his way through the brush once again.

Out in the sunlight, things seemed different, and the hesitation that he felt back at the woodchuck hole didn't seem so significant. He saw the garden, with its neat rows, and Joshua knew that he had done the right thing. His father would have wanted him to do it. The woodchuck was just a varmint whose only mission in life was to eat up the vegetables that he worked so hard to grow. The animal didn't deserve to have any of it. As he walked though, Joshua kept focusing on the image in his mind of the helpless animal caught in the trap. There was something disturbing about the whole scene. He wondered if other animals would seek retribution for what he had done. As he walked down toward the pond, his mind pictured hundreds of woodchucks emptying out of the woods to come and get him. They all filed into the barn and up the ladder into the loft. Joshua tried to shake this notion out of his mind.

When he got to the dock, he sat down on the end and rested his feet on the end the canoe. His shoes were starting to break in now. After a few walks and days around the yard, he didn't even notice the tightness anymore. He bounced the boat up and down in the water; watching the ripples flow out into the pond. The crushed skull of the woodchuck reminded him of his sister. Although he had never seen what had happened to her, he knew there must have been some kind of serious head injury. He pressed harder on the canoe, and the back of it started to pop up out of the water. The boat banged against the dock without the boy even realizing it. When

159

the front of the canoe finally sunk beneath the surface on one of his thrusts, Joshua lost his balance, and fell off the dock. He tumbled into the front of the canoe and struck his head on the front seat. Quickly snapping out of his lost thoughts, Joshua tried to steady himself. The bottom of the canoe had some water in it, and Joshua's shirt and pants were soaked through to his skin. He tried to stand and hold onto the dock, but he couldn't steady himself. It was too awkward. The back of the canoe was out of the water, and the front was almost dipping into the pond. Grabbing both sides, Joshua slowly lifted himself up and onto the dock. He sighed a long breath and just lay back down.

After a few moments, Joshua picked himself up and sat at the end of the dock. In the distance, he could hear rumbles of thunder. Looking northward, there were mountains of clouds, darker now, building over the horizon. The sun sat above the trees on the far shore, but slowly, Joshua watched the clouds start to engulf it. Around the sun, the sky turned a deep pink, and it almost looked like a long finger was pointing out at him. With the storm approaching, Joshua felt the guilt again. His sister was dead because of him. There would never be a time when he would think about it in any other way. He could write to her all he wanted or read her books, but if it wasn't for him, then she would still be alive. She might as well have been the woodchuck, trapped in the mouth of its hole. The cart that came around the corner on Westminster Street was just like the rock he slammed down on the animal's head. As the clouds filled in around the sun, Joshua watched as the world darkened.

He could hear the rain before he could actually see it. It came across the pond and through the trees. When the drops finally hit him, they were big and falling at a rapid pace. He didn't want to move. Silently, Joshua wished that a bolt of lightning would come down and end it all for him. A flash burst somewhere in the hills on the other side of the Post Road, and a roll of thunder followed after a few seconds. The boy sat as the torrents of rain soaked him. The drops seemed to bounce off the pond, but the closer Joshua looked, he saw that the rain caused

160

the water in the pond to splash up. Thousands of the watery beads washed across the pond in front of him. Another bolt of lightning struck just beyond the small island. The thunderbolt was instantaneous. In the flash of light, Joshua thought he could see his sister standing on the island's shore. She was calling his name; beckoning him to come over. Just as the boy was about to drop into the channel and begin the walk through the water over to the island, something grabbed him.

"Joshua!" his mother screamed, "Get into the house."

She pulled him up from where he was sitting and led him away from the dock. He looked back across the pond to the shore of the island, but Mary was gone. The rain had washed her away. The tugging on his arm got stronger, but when he turned toward the inn, he didn't feel the pull as much. When they came through the door, Mr. and Mrs. Nilsson had looks of concern on their faces. Joshua ignored them and continued to be led by his mother. She pulled him up the stairs and into the bedroom. Looking deeply into his eyes, she attempted to get a read on where her son was. Joshua just felt the water streaming through his hair and down his face. She grabbed him by the shoulder and shook, but there was no response. The boy was lost in some far away world. She peeled the wet clothes from him, and tried as best she could to dry him off. Putting a nightshirt that he rarely wore over his head, she pulled it down and sat him on the bed.

"I saw her."

"Who?"

He was silent again; bewildered. His eyes were vacant, and his jaw hung loosely. Pulling the sheets back, his mother put him under the covers. She stroked the towel over his hair, trying to soothe as well as wipe away the dampness that still lingered. In Joshua's mind, there was only fog. He couldn't capture a thought, nor did he know how to try. His eyes were searching for Mary on the shore, but everything had disappeared. He tried to push through the gray to find her, but it was useless. He was blind again, in the hospital, alone with no hope. Joshua

161

kept trying to go back a little further in time, so he could grab Mary and pull her onto the sidewalk, but the ashen color that covered his world wouldn't allow him any escape.

Suddenly, it all cleared. The sun was shining, and Mary was standing on the shore of the island again. Joshua stood in the canoe as it floated across the pond to her. The stillness made the water seem like glass. She smiled and waved to him. Everything was going to be alright now. The boat started to move faster, and when he was just about to reach the shore, the pond opened up into a deep chasm. The water fell back into the misty fog and disappeared. Before Joshua could do anything about it, he plummeted over the edge. Reaching to grab a hold of something, he felt Mary holding him. He opened his eyes, and his mother was there with him. The room was mostly dark, but the low flicker of the kerosene lamp gave him a glimpse of his surroundings. She looked at him with concern, and as he blinked the remnants of the images of Mary away, he came back to himself.

"Are you okay?" Mother asked.

The boy stared at her with a sadness in his eyes.

"She was there, and then she was gone."

"Who?"

"Mary. I saw her on the island, but then I couldn't find her anymore."

She held her son, wrapping her arms around his shoulders. He cried, not knowing any other way to react to the loss. As the tears slowly turned into sniffles, Joshua realized that everything that he had worked for was slipping away. He thought that maybe his new method of dealing with his grief was going to work, but now he just figured that he would spend the rest of his life lost in that gray world of misery. The rain fell softly now on the roof.

"I don't think you should write those letters anymore," his mother said in a quiet voice.

"That was the first time that I saw her. Every other time it was just some memory."

"But it's affecting you ..."

"I don't know ... maybe it was a good thing."

"Why?"

"I'm not sure. I killed the woodchuck, and then I started thinking about Mary."

"I think we have to talk about what happened that day. We've never done that."

Joshua was silent for a few moments; putting his thoughts together. Maybe it would be a good thing to explain it all to his mother. His fear, though, was that reliving the incident would throw him into some kind of dark hole from which he could never climb out.

"It was all my fault ... she died because of me."

"Joshua, that's nonsense."

"I ran out of the house because I was mad at her for bossing me around. I was coming to tell you about it at the Hearn's, but then I figured you would just take her side."

His mother looked at him in silence. He had never confessed this to anyone. Grandma didn't even know that they had been arguing.

"Mary found me downtown when I was walking back. I wasn't too angry anymore, so we were just walking home. We had to walk out in the street because people were crowded around a newsstand. We were laughing."

Suddenly it came to him. He remembered.

"There was an old Italian lady yelling at the people. She had a crazy hat on her head, and we were staring at her. That's what we were laughing at. I could never remember that."

Suddenly, there was a strange easing to the pull in his heart. Just knowing that one fact seemed to comfort his burden. The image in his mind became clearer now.

"We were looking back toward the old lady, and suddenly the sounds of the hooves got louder. Just as we turned, the horse sped past us. The wheels of the cart just kept sliding closer. That's all I remember. The next thing I knew, I was waking up in the hospital, and I couldn't see anything."

Mother looked out the window into the darkness. She was quiet. The rain slowly dropped onto the roof.

"She just seemed so small when I saw her on that stretcher," Mother said. "She wasn't my Mary anymore.

All of the life had gone out of her. I can't get that picture out of my head."

They both cried; holding each other and rocking back and forth. This was the first time that they had ever talked about that day. It seemed to Joshua that his mother just wanted to go on with things, and not dwell on what had happened. He felt better that he could remember what made them laugh. Suddenly, she grabbed him by his shoulders and held him out in front of her.

"It wasn't your fault."

"But I ..."

"It wasn't your fault."

"She wouldn't have ..."

"It wasn't your fault. The crowd shouldn't have been all over the sidewalk. The cart shouldn't have come around the corner so fast. It wasn't your fault."

"I ..."

"Joshua, if you're ever going to get over this, then you have to know that it wasn't your fault. Things happen. Pat Joyce has never been the same since your father passed. He was supposed to have checked the load on the rail car, but there was a problem with another one."

"I don't know what to do though."

"Maybe you should keep writing letters to Mary. I thought that things were starting to improve before today."

Joshua sniffled and dragged his arm across the bottom of his nose. The image of Mary on the island's shore had faded, but still lingered in his mind. He was going to continue writing to her anyway. Now that his mother had agreed that it might be a good thing, Joshua was even more driven.

12

Joshua could feel the heat as soon as he woke up. The humidity had finally arrived. Mr. Nilsson had warned him that once the heat got here, things wouldn't be as pleasant. Joshua walked down the stairs and into the kitchen. His mother and the Nilssons were all busy doing their morning chores.

"Not enough rain," Mr. Nilsson said, "we're going to need a lot more soon."

It was strange. They all acted as if nothing happened yesterday. Joshua wondered if his mother had spoken to the Nilssons about their discussion. He ate a quick breakfast in silence, and then headed out to the barn. He wondered what it would have been like to sleep out there during the thunderstorm. Kip poked his head up when Joshua came inside, and Nettie started to weave back and forth in her stall. Josh fed both animals, and then climbed the ladder up into the loft. He opened the nature book and tried to find the section on seabirds. The small ones that scurried along the water's edge were called sandpipers. He added the name to his growing list. Joshua had already identified most of the birds that hovered around the property. There were robins, blue jays, cardinals, swallows, finches, and doves. Joshua had seen two or three different kinds of seagulls. When he turned the page, he found a bird that he thought he had seen somewhere before. It was called an egret. The bright white bird stood on long, skinny legs. He tried to think back to when he had seen one before. With a sudden jolt, Joshua pictured Mary on the opposite shore. As he thought about it, he realized that what he imagined was his sister, was really an egret.

Joshua tried to sketch the bird on a piece of paper. Although his drawing skills weren't that good, he was able to create a likeness. It was strange how his mind worked. How could he mistake a bird for his sister? Mary's presence was getting stronger. Now that he focused on telling her what was happening with his life, it seemed like she was with him. Yesterday's spell was a minor setback. In his heart, Joshua knew that he was doing the right thing. He had just let his mind wander too much when he killed the woodchuck.

Downstairs, Mr. Nilsson was fiddling with something at the workbench, so Joshua lowered himself back down the ladder. Since Nettie was done with her breakfast, the boy led her out of the stall and let her wander around the grounds. He wondered why she never went over to the garden.

"We need to start collecting some shellfish for our clambake," Mr. Nilsson said without turning around. "We've got less than two weeks before the Fourth of July, and by this weekend, the inn will be half full."

Joshua was silent. He wanted to talk to Mr. Nilsson about what happened on the dock, but he didn't know where to start. The old man grabbed the rakes from the wall, and Josh picked up the bushel basket. They put their tools in the yard and went inside to change. Since it was so warm now, Joshua just put on his new swim trunks and his old shoes. Just before heading outside, he grabbed the straw hat that Mr. Nilsson had bought for him.

The tide was low as they made their way down to the shore of the pond. Joshua kept an eye on the island as they approached the dock. The strange swirlings in his mind were no longer there, and the boy was at a loss as to how his brain worked. Why did it seem like he was insane one minute and completely normal the next? Josh hopped into the dinghy and placed the rakes and basket in the front. Mr. Nilsson pushed them away from the dock, and they floated across the channel. Far out at the point of the island, near where they dropped their lobster pots, Joshua saw the egret. Part of him was relieved at the sight of it, but another piece of him wished that his sister was really waiting for him over there. The bird stood on long legs, with its neck craned, surveying the water all around.

"This seems like a good spot," Mr. Nilsson said, breaking Joshua's wandering thoughts.

He dropped the anchor, and they both eased up and over the side of the boat. The old man put a rock in the bottom of their basket, just like last time, and they started their raking. For some reason, they must have hit a spot that hadn't been touched in awhile because they both started pulling up clam after clam. Without even having to move very much, they filled a quarter of the basket within a few minutes.

"Must have missed this spot last year."

Joshua still wanted to unburden himself, but he didn't know where to start. He silently scraped the rocky mud beneath the surface of the water, occasionally looking up at the egret on the distant shore.

"I got the woodchuck yesterday."

"I know, I went to check the trap this morning, and I saw what you had done. Good work."

Again, they were quiet. The sounds of the tines on the bottom and the drips of mud above the surface were all that could be heard.

"I had another problem last night."

"Yes, that's what your mother said."

"I thought I saw my sister out on the island."

"Why do you suppose that happened?"

"I guess I was thinking about her after I killed the woodchuck. She got hit by a cart, and the dead woodchuck just reminded me of what happened."

"There used to be a boy who lived near us. We were packed in like sardines in our first apartment. There was a small courtyard in the middle, so you could hear what was going all around. This boy, he had a cough just like Lucas did. Whenever I heard it, especially at night, I would think my brother was in the next room. If I was half asleep, then I'd picture myself going over and talking to him. I guess it was just part of a dream."

"How come your brain does that to you?"

"I guess you want the person back so badly, your mind tries to give you what you need."

They continued clamming for awhile. Joshua tried

to reconcile what Mr. Nilsson said with what had happened last night.

"It's like I go to a different world or something."

"Yes, a perfect world where everything is right again."

Joshua smiled. If he could just get himself to the point where he knew what was happening inside of his head, then possibly he could try to develop a way to avoid losing himself again. Just knowing that Mr. Nilsson had gone through a similar situation gave him some relief. He would continue writing to Mary, and if he fell back into that confusion again, then he would just have to know that it was part of the process. It was hard to imagine, though, if he could be strong enough to overcome the power of his torn up mind.

When they came back across the channel with their full basket of cherrystones, Joshua couldn't believe it when Mr. Nilsson dumped almost all of them into the water, creating a mound under the dock.

"Joshua, run up to the barn and grab that other basket, the one with the broken rim."

Joshua raced up to the barn, grabbed it, and sped back. Mr. Nilsson took it and started to pick the clams up off the bottom. He took handfuls of the shellfish and dropped them into the basket. There were about twenty-five clams left in the first basket, and Joshua was able to carry it up to the inn without any problem.

"Oh good," Mrs. Nilsson said, "we'll have some more chowder tonight. And don't worry, Joshua, I'll save some for you."

Josh smiled as he walked back down to the water's edge.

"We'll save our clams under here," Mr. Nilsson said. "I think we're going to have to go out almost every day to get enough for the clambake. We'll set some traps too for lobster. Whatever we can't get ourselves, I'll have to buy from Johnny Crandall."

"How much do we need?"

"I'd say about four or five bushels of clams and maybe two dozen lobsters."

Joshua was amazed at the amount of food they

would have to get. He couldn't imagine where they would cook all of it.

"How's Mrs. Nilsson going to do all of that?

"She isn't ... we are. Right up at the edge of the path, we'll dig a pit about eight feet long and three feet wide. It shouldn't be too hard, I do it every year, so the ground is all ready for it."

"Do we just put the pots on top of it?" Joshua asked a little bit confused about the whole thing.

"No, we cook it in seaweed. We need rocks and firewood at the bottom, then we toss in layers of seaweed. At each layer, we put in the clams, lobsters, and maybe some fish. We won't have corn on the cob for July, but in August we can get some up the road."

"It just cooks in the seaweed?"

"No, we'll drag a canvas tarp over it, and let it heat up for awhile. The top will start to puff up. When that happens, we know that it's dinner time," Mr. Nilsson said with a smile.

As they walked back up to the barn, Joshua could see the outline of where the clambake had been in the past. He had noticed the difference in the ground before, but never knew what it was from. He hung the rakes up on the wall, and they went in for some lunch.

"I think that some of the guests want to go down to the beach this afternoon," Mr. Nilsson said. "We'll hook Nettie up to the cart, and then I'll give them a ride. You can follow on the bicycle if you want to, and then stay on the beach with them."

"Are we going to set up the canopy?"

"No, maybe next week when some more guests start to arrive. I'll throw in a few umbrellas. They have some small children, and you never know what their nap times are like."

Joshua led the expedition. He wheeled ahead on the bike, as Mr. Nilsson followed in the cart. There were three mothers and seven children. None of them were over the age of five. Every time Joshua looked back, it seemed like one of the kids was about to go over the side. He escorted them down Surfside Avenue until they reached the bathing area. His trunks were still a little damp from clamming earlier.

Once Mr. Nilsson pulled Nettie to a halt, they both helped the women and children from the cart. Joshua lugged two heavy umbrellas down to the sand, and then came back for some small chairs. The women were fully dressed, and Joshua wondered how comfortable they were in this heat. The three sets of children had matching outfits on. They were much fancier than Joshua's bathing trunks, but he was happy with what he was wearing. It was so much better than those long pants. Now that the heat was here, he figured that he would be living in these clothes for the rest of the summer.

Small waves rolled in from about twenty feet out in the water. Joshua thought that maybe the thunderstorm from the night before might have stirred the surf up a bit. Once they got everyone settled, Joshua and Mr. Nilsson stood on the dunes watching the children play by the shore.

"When do we get the seaweed for the clambake?"

"Oh, probably a few days before. I'm hoping that we can get it on the beach while it's still wet. I usually set up a little area down next to the dock, so it stays wet until we need it. If nothing washes up on the beach, then we'll have to drag the pond. That's no fun."

"How do we do that?"

Well, I'll rig up a long net, and we'll scrape the bottom over at the end of the channel. We just have to keep walking back to the dock with each load. It takes most of a morning to do it. There's a cove down near the Ashaway Cottages where seaweed collects sometimes. Maybe you can go check it out on one of your journeys."

"Sure."

"I'm going back to the inn. I'll bring the cart in a few hours. Use the bike if anyone needs anything. Try to keep yourself busy. You can play with the children if you want to. The mothers will probably appreciate that."

Joshua watched as Mr. Nilsson turned the cart around and followed Nettie down the road again. The dunes were warm on his bare feet, so Joshua walked down to the shore. The wet sand glistened in the sunlight after each wave washed over the edge. He could see other groups of people on the beach now. Most of the cottages had been opened up for the season, and people were out on their porches. A few others were in the water. No one was much past their knees. Josh waded in a little way, and quickly noticed that the water here was much colder than the pond. A wave caught him unprepared and splashed up on his shirt. Backing away a little bit, he looked down the coastline. Joshua had come so far since that first day he was on the beach. Doing chores around the inn and exploring the area had given him a new life. He was no longer moping around the house on Foster Street waiting for something to happen. Joshua was now moving on. He didn't feel guilty about leaving them behind or not focusing on the past. His setback yesterday didn't seem like such a big thing now.

Turning back to the shore, Joshua saw the children playing in the sand. Although he didn't know any of their names, he went up and joined them. He remembered making sand castles with Mary and his dad when they went to Rocky Point, so Joshua knelt down near them and started to dig. Slowly, a few of the older children, the four year olds, drifted over to where Joshua was piling up sand.

"What are you doing?"

"Building a sand castle. Want to help?"

"Okay," they both answered.

Joshua quickly realized that this wasn't going to be much of a castle. At first he got a little upset when the children would stomp on one corner or swipe away a pile that he had just molded. Slowly though, he started to enjoy this time with these little kids. The parents were up on the beach talking, and they seemed to like having Joshua around to occupy the children.

"Put some more sand over on that one," he told one of them.

Joshua found that if he could give each of them a job, then things went more smoothly. He sent two of the older ones to find some sticks and strands of seaweed, but he couldn't do much with the younger kids. They were going to do whatever they wanted, and all of Joshua's efforts to control their actions, just made things harder.

In the end, they had mounds of sand with pieces of beach debris sticking out everywhere. The children seemed to think that it really was a castle, so Joshua just went along with it.

"Nice job," a sarcastic voice came from behind him.

Turning, Joshua saw that it was Elizabeth. She wasn't wearing a full dress, but she didn't have on bathing trunks either. It was something in between. The girl had her hands on her hips as she apprised the structure before her. Joshua had sand all over him, and the younger children were now starting to walk all over the piles that they all had created.

"Why are you down here?"

"I have a right to walk on this beach if I want to ... more than you do."

"I'm just asking, what brings you down here?"

"Oh, school's out for the summer. I did all of my chores, so I decided to take a walk on the beach."

"Do you want some company?"

"I guess I can't stop you."

Joshua hopped up, brushed the sand from his legs, and walked up to where the women were talking.

"Does anyone need anything from back at the inn?"

They all looked at each other for a moment. Joshua hoped that they wouldn't want him to go back.

"No, I don't think so," one woman answered.

Joshua nodded and trotted back down to where Elizabeth was walking. They were quiet as they walked around the rocks that appeared along the edge of the shore. Joshua didn't know how to start the conversation, or even understand why he wanted to walk with this girl who had yet to say a kind word to him.

"How come your mother doesn't make you go to school?"

"I don't know. When we moved here, it was just about springtime. I do my studies at the inn."

"What studies?"

"I read books, I study the animals in the area, I figure the mathematical problems around the inn, and I write letters to my sister."

Joshua gasped as he spoke these last words. He

didn't mean for it to come out, and saying it to Elizabeth made it seem like a strange thing to do. He hoped that she didn't pick up on it.

"Where does she live?"

"Um, it's kind of complicated."

She looked at him funny. He thought that maybe his voice sounded a little strange when he tried to explain, but Joshua tried to keep his composure.

"If you didn't want to talk about it, then why did you bring it up?"

Maybe it was the tone of her voice, or maybe Joshua just wanted to tell someone else. If she thought that it was a crazy thing to do, then he would just turn himself around and not look back.

"My sister, Mary, died last year, and I write to her and tell her what's going on in my life."

She stopped and stared at him for a moment.

"Why did you say that? Are you making fun of me?"

Joshua just stared at the girl. She had real anger in her voice, and it looked like she was going to hit him.

"Did my grandmother tell you? I told her not to tell anyone. Why are you making fun of me?"

"What?"

"Does it make you feel better to make fun of me?"

"I don't know what you're talking about."

Joshua stepped back in the sand as Elizabeth wagged her finger in his face. His heel jammed into a rock, and he fell over backwards onto the sand.

"Did you read my diary when you were at my house? That's it, isn't it ... you read my diary."

"No."

"Get away from me. Why are you following me? What's wrong with you?"

Joshua watched as the girl stormed off, back down the beach. He wanted to follow her and try to figure out what was going on, but her anger was so strong, that Joshua thought she might pick up a rock and hit him over the head. Her footsteps were in a determined line, straight in the opposite direction. Joshua stayed where he was for awhile. He skipped some stones into the water.

There was a seagull-stained rock out about fifty feet, and Joshua tried to hit it, pretending that the rock was the catcher at home plate.

Slowly, he made his way back to the wading area. Two of the children were crying, and the other ones were down at the water's edge. It looked like the mothers were ready to go, but there was no sign of Mr. Nilsson.

"Do you want me to go back and get the cart?"

"Yes, please. I think the little ones have had enough."

Joshua sped back on his bicycle. The cart was in front of the inn, and Nettie was a few feet away grazing on the lawn. The boy wheeled into the driveway and found Mr. Nilsson clipping the grass around the maple tree.

"We'll have to mow this lawn tomorrow or the next day," he said as Joshua approached.

"The guests are ready to come back. Do you want me to go get them?"

"Sure. Keep an eye on that back wheel. I thought I felt it starting to give a little bit when I was coming back."

Joshua nodded and headed back around to the front of the inn. He hooked Nettie up easily, and then slowly pulled out of the yard. The wind had picked up, and the heat was not as oppressive as it had been. The mothers were waiting when Joshua pulled up to the dunes. He helped them load their things, and then went down on the beach to retrieve the umbrellas and chairs. It took him two trips, and by the time he hopped back onto the seat, it seemed like the children were finally settled in their places. When he came around the first corner, Joshua looked back at the rear wheel. There was a little bit of a wobble to it, but he thought that it wasn't too bad yet. Mr. Nilsson would have to look at it later on this afternoon.

When everyone was safely home, and the younger children were put down for naps, Joshua helped Mrs. Nilsson in the kitchen. He peeled potatoes as she kneaded some dough.

"Is Elizabeth Thornton kind of strange?"

"Why do you ask that?"

"I don't know. She doesn't seem to like me very

much."

"That girl has had a difficult life. Her name's not Thornton, it's Elizabeth Whitten. She lives with her mother's parents."

"Where are her parents?"

"The poor girl. Her mother passed away during childbirth, and her father died a year or so later. He worked at the mill in Bradford."

Suddenly, Joshua understood things a little more clearly. He went on peeling the potatoes. Mother came in and started cutting them into cubes. The clams had already been boiled, and now they were sitting in the sink. Joshua peeled the meat out of each of the shells; putting the salty core into the big pot. Once Joshua was done with all of the clams, he took the shells outside and dumped them into the pond. Rinsing off his hands as he squatted by the shore, Joshua made up his mind what he was going to do.

"I'll be back before dinner, unless you have something else for me to do," Joshua said to Mr. Nilsson.

"No, tomorrow's your big day," the man answered as he carried in a bowl of fresh lettuce.

Joshua hopped onto the bicycle and made his way over to East Beach. He wasn't sure what he was going to say to Elizabeth Whitten, but he knew that he wanted to say something. Her rage toward him was out of the ordinary, but now he knew where it was coming from. Turning onto East Beach Road, he had the sudden fear that she wouldn't even talk to him. As he pulled into yard of the farmhouse, he could see Mr. Thornton walking around the front.

"Hello."

"Afternoon Joshua, what can I do for you?"

"Is Elizabeth here?"

"She's not feeling very well."

"I know. I was wondering if I could speak to her."

"Let me ask Mrs. Thornton."

The man disappeared into the house, and Joshua waited.

"What do you want?" An angry voice came from an upstairs window.

Joshua wasn't prepared to say anything yet, so her sudden words caught him off guard.

"I didn't read your diary, and your grandmother didn't tell me anything. I really do write to my sister. It makes me feel better."

The figure disappeared from the window, and for a minute there was no sign of any other life. Joshua watched the front door, wondering if the girl would come out. She appeared from around the side of the house, and as she got closer, it looked as if she had been crying.

"I'm sorry that I yelled at you," she said in a very formal voice.

"I shouldn't have told you about my sister. It just slipped out."

Joshua watched as she walked out to the road and sat on the stone wall. He followed her and did the same.

"What happened to her?"

"She got hit by a cart last year in Providence."

"How old was she?"

"Fourteen."

They were quiet, both staring into the meadow across the road.

"Why do you write letters to her?"

"I don't really know. I just started doing it. Mr. Nilsson told me a story about his brother, and I guess the idea came from that. She used to always write letters, so I decided to write to her."

"I write to my parents, but I never told anyone, except my grandmother. I didn't even know my own mother, and I don't remember my father. I sort of write letters to them, but not really. I guess I just write down what I'm thinking about, and in my mind, I'm telling my parents."

"Me too."

"Is your father back in Providence?"

"No, he had an accident at work two years ago, and the funeral was a few days later."

Again, they were quiet. To Joshua, this seemed like an unburdening. He had never shared these thoughts with anyone his own age. The boys that he hung around with in the neighborhood really didn't understand. They just stopped coming over to his house. He figured that their mothers made them come over at first, but after awhile, he was so miserable that no one wanted to be near him.

"Lizzie," her grandfather's voice came from the front door.

"I have to go and help with dinner."

"Me too."

"Come over and see me again soon," she said with a smile.

Joshua smiled back. Getting on to his bicycle, he pedaled off to the inn. Even the thought of the delicious clam chowder waiting for him couldn't get his mind off the encounter with the girl. He thought maybe he would marry Elizabeth Whitten someday.

13

Just as Mr. Nilsson predicted, the inn started to get out of hand. By the last weekend of June, people started arriving all day long. Joshua couldn't keep track of any of them. Mrs. Nilsson seemed to have everything under control, but Mother looked frazzled by the whole experience. The older woman knew where everyone was going. She sent Joshua up to their rooms with all of their belongings. Mrs. Van Houtten was back, but because of all the running around, Joshua didn't seem to notice her too much.

By the time Joshua hit the pillow that night, he fell fast asleep. It was nice being out in the barn now. He felt like he was in a separate place from all the goings on in the house. Now that the inn was almost full, his studies took a backseat to what had to be done. There was a thin film of dust on the cover of the Tom Sawyer book. He realized that if he hadn't cut the grass the other day, then he would never have had the chance to do it. People meandered all over the lawn now. They spent the sunny afternoons in the shade, but when it was a little cooler, the guests occupied themselves with all forms of recreation.

There were men now at the inn. Some were older, but others seemed to be in their early twenties. A few were university men; taking a quick break before going off to some summer office work in the city. They were active all day long. The tennis court had non-stop use, as well as the croquet area. They had baseball gloves and bats, along with golf clubs and tiny balls. Although there was no course, the men made a game of it. They hit the ball toward any grassy area and shot for some type of target. Sometimes it was a small tree, and other times it was a rock. After a few days of this, they set up markers in all directions up and down the road. Joshua never knew when a ball might be flying through the area. Unbelievably, no one was ever struck, nor were any windows ever broken.

"Can I play?" Joshua asked one early evening when the men were tossing around a baseball.

"Sure, sure ... go over by the bushes."

They tossed the ball lightly at first, but soon realized that Joshua was fairly good at the game. In time, Joshua was making diving catches onto the grass. He would hop up each time and fling the ball back as strongly as possible. He thought that he saw Mrs. Van Houtten up on the porch giving him a dirty look, so Joshua decided to call it quits. He jogged back into the barn, put his glove away, and grabbed the hoe on his way back out. Mr. Nilsson had always told him that if he got a free minute, he should head out to the garden and try to stay ahead of the game.

The vegetables were growing now, but the weeds seemed to come on stronger too. Joshua had to work a little harder to get the invasive plants out of the picture. He noticed that the more effort he put into the scraping, the more dust flew up into the air. He wondered when it would rain again.

"We might have to do something about the water," Mr. Nilsson said as he came up from behind.

"Like what?"

"A few years ago I rigged up a line from the pump. I ran a pipe out through the field over to the edge of the garden. I just let the water fill up each of the rows."

"What about the run off?"

"Well, that's the hard part. You have to mound up the rows so the water doesn't flow out. It's a lot of work, but it sure beats losing the crop."

"Do we have enough pipe?"

"No, we'll have to take a run over to the Thornton's place. Then we'll probably have to haul ours over there, so he can do the same."

Joshua had tried to get over to see Elizabeth, but since there were so many people at the inn, he hadn't had a moment to himself. Tossing the ball with a few of the

179

men had been his only time off. He finished the row he was on, and then took a walk around the garden. He thought maybe they could use planks to stop up the rows, and then channel it through to the next. If he could direct the flow in such a way, then they wouldn't have to rework the pipes so much. When he went back upstairs in the barn, he took a look at the diagram that he had made. Once the water flowed into the row, he would have to give it a chance to sink into the soil. He figured that he could use the planks for four rows before moving the pipes. That would cut down on a lot of attaching and reattaching of the line. Joshua wondered how Mr. Nilsson was going to send water to the garden without cutting the supply to the inn.

After dinner, Joshua filled all the kerosene lamps. Since it was staying light for so long at night, people didn't seem to be using them as much. Mr. Nilsson had the cart all set when Joshua brought the can back to the barn. The wind was just dying, and Joshua knew what that meant. The mosquitoes would be invading soon. They had arrived a week ago, but each day they seemed to multiply. Whenever the air was still, the tiny bugs covered the boy. As Mr. Nilsson pulled away from the inn, the cart's movement kept the mosquitoes at bay.

When they got to the Thornton's farm, Elizabeth was nowhere to be found. Joshua helped the two men load the pipes into the cart, while he kept an eye out for the girl.

"We'll bring them back when we're done. If you need it, you can use our extra pipe."

"Let's see if we get any rain first," Mr. Thornton answered.

Just as Joshua was climbing back onto the cart, Elizabeth came out with a small basket. She held it up to the boy, and he took it.

"It's cornbread that I made. You can share it with Mrs. Nilsson and your mother."

"Thank you," Joshua answered with a big smile.

Mr. Nilsson seemed to be oblivious to what was going on between the two of them. It was strange how things had changed between Joshua and the girl. Their shared loss seemed to connect them in a way that the boy couldn't have imagined. No one back home had any type of loss like his. Grandparents and infants had died, but no one's older sister or father had passed away. Here was a girl who had lost both of her parents. Joshua waved as Mr. Nilsson pulled away. Although he wanted to stay, he knew that there was much work to be done.

They drove right past the inn on their way back. Joshua wondered where they were going.

"We have to cheat a little."

"How?"

"I don't think we'll have time to go fishing, so I'm hoping that one of the fellas at the breachway got lucky today."

They rolled down West Beach Road, and Mr. Nilsson pulled up next to Wilson's carriage house. After tying Nettie to the post, the old man wandered across the dirt road. Joshua followed. When they got to the boardwalk, Mr. Nilsson looked up and down.

"Aha ... I thought so."

There was a long boarding house set down along the breachway past the Eldredge Hotel on the pond side. There were a bunch of kids at the water's edge around an old man who was squatting in ankle deep water.

"Good afternoon, Captain. I see you've been fishing today."

The man looked up with a big smile on his face.

"Not me, the grandkids took the boat down to the end of the breach," the man said as he pointed toward the pond. "The way they tell it, they couldn't pull them up fast enough."

"Must have been when the tide was coming in," Mr. Nilsson replied.

"No better time."

"I was wondering if I might be able take a bucket full of the remnants to bait my lobster pots."

"Sure help yourself. You've got that clambake coming up. Am I right?"

"Fourth of July. You're welcome to join us."

"We'll see. There's usually a lot of action down here that afternoon."

One of the children fetched a bucket, and the captain filled it with fish guts, skin, and bones. Mr. Nilsson thanked them, and he and Joshua were quickly on their way.

"Maybe we'll rig up the pipe, and then run it tomorrow afternoon when most of the guests are at the beach. I'd like to get these pots in the water before nightfall."

Joshua nodded as they pulled out of the breachway area. Dozens of people milled about now. This little village was so much different than it was a few months ago when everything was boarded up. Although he pictured it in his mind, Joshua really had no idea what things would be like. There was a woman hanging clothes on a line, a man lugging boxes up the stairs at the casino, children running back and forth across the road, and Homer and Travis pushing an automobile out of the garage. Dust drifted behind them as Nettie pulled the cart back to the Pond View.

"The pipes will leak, but we'll try to get them as tight as possible."

Joshua and Mr. Nilsson strung the line from the bottom of the windmill. The old man connected the pipes as Joshua fed them to him. After an hour or so, the line ran all the way up to the first row of vegetables. They dropped other pieces all along the edge of the garden, so they could attach it as they went along. Joshua brought some planks from the barn and formed a blockade at the end of four of the rows. He figured that he would dig away the ends when the water finally filled up.

With the wheelbarrow, they hauled six lobster traps down to the dock. They baited each of the traps before setting out. The dingy was so full when Joshua pushed out into the channel, that setting them up in the boat would have been impossible. Mr. Nilsson rowed out to the island; Mary's island. The egret stood on the rocky shore, watching them as they passed by. He remembered looking through one of the books that Grandma had sent down. It had stories about New England, and one of them was entitled *The White Heron*. Joshua thought about maybe looking it up that evening. He felt guilty about not reading lately, but he had been so busy that by the time he went to bed at night, he was too tired to even pick up a book. Maybe once he got into a routine, he could somehow fit reading into his schedule. He had spent a few afternoons in the maple tree. If the mosquitoes died down a little bit, then maybe he would try to fit it in.

As they came around the north end of the island, Joshua eased the traps into the water. The buoys bobbed in the gentle wake of the boat. After dropping the sixth one under the surface, the boy looked at the great orange ball that hung just above the tree line. The haze in the air dulled its brightness, but not its intensity. Here it was almost sunset, and heat of the day was still pronounced. Beads of sweat rolled down Joshua's back as he gazed across the windless pond.

"Your Red Sox are doing pretty well," Mr. Nilsson said as he turned the boat around.

Joshua had not had a chance to look at the papers that one of the jitney drivers had brought to the inn. Every time he headed in that direction, someone was either reading them, or he was given some type of chore to do.

"How well?"

"46 wins and 20 losses. Philly's only won 34. It looks like they're making a run for the pennant."

"I told you."

Joshua smiled as the old man rowed back to the dock. The view of the inn still amazed him every time that he saw it. The long shadows on the rolling lawn up from the pond looked to be out of some work of art. He had never seen colors like that before. Guests were milling about on the back porch, and Nettie grazed just outside of the barn. A sense of peace filled Joshua and quieted the guilty anguish that had grown inside of him. He breathed deeply, filling his lungs with the warm, humid air of late June. Joshua decided right there and then that 1912 was going to be a healing year. He was going to will his mind out of its murky depths and take control of his thoughts. The next time he fell down into the darkness, Joshua Keegan was going to pull himself right back up.

"Mr. Nilsson, I need you to take a look at the

tennis court before you come in for the night," Mrs. Van Houtten said in that critical way of hers.

The old man just nodded, and Joshua followed him back across the yard. The net was tangled and ripped in a few places. As they inspected it, the mosquitoes started to buzz in Joshua's ears. They landed on his forehead and arms. He swatted them away, but quickly the incessant bugs returned. Anxiety crept up inside of the boy as they started to feed on him.

"Let's just take it down for the night, and we'll fix it in the barn tomorrow morning," Mr. Nilsson said, seemingly unbothered by the insect assault.

Joshua unhooked one end, and then they rolled it up. He could see the tears in some of the netting and figured that they could patch it up in no time; just as long as the bugs stayed away.

There was music coming from the sun porch as they passed by. Twilight was holding onto the last glimpses of the day. Joshua could see his mother serving lemonade to the guests. As each took a glass, the boy noticed that none of them said thank you. He was starting to form some ideas about what kind of adult he wanted to be. In his heart, Joshua knew that he didn't want to be someone's servant.

Buggies were pulling up the driveway now. Mr. Nilsson met each one and helped the people down. Joshua wasn't aware of a party this evening, but figured that this was an informal gathering of guests from nearby inns and cottages. He helped Mrs. Nilsson in the kitchen for awhile and then retired to his room in the loft. Through the screens, he could see the kerosene lamps glowing in the sunroom. A few people were dancing to the music on the phonograph. Others talked in small groups. The men were gathered in the corners, and the women sat about in half circles on the chairs and couches.

Joshua went over to his little table and lit his own lamp. He looked over the diagram of the garden one more time; sketching in the piping that they had put down earlier that day. The vegetables longed for water, and Joshua was excited about the prospect of drenching all of his plants. Picking up his bird book, the boy tried to figure out the names of some of the smaller birds that he had seen around the yard. He was pretty sure that there were some chickadees flying about, but he wasn't positive. Studying the picture, Josh planned to look for one the next day.

Although he had planned to start reading the heron story, he reached for Tom Sawyer. As he lay back in his bed, he opened up to where he had left off before. Soon, Joshua was inside of the book. Tom and Huck were in a graveyard at night. The boy looked around at the shadows in the loft; fears creeping up his spine. Nettie's sounds in her stall beneath calmed him somewhat. Although he thought that it might be a mistake, Joshua read on. In the cemetery, there was some movement, and as the two boys crept closer, they witnessed a fight and a murder. It reminded Joshua of the torches that he had seen out along the path. He didn't think that he would ever have the nerve to sneak down there if those lights appeared again. Maybe if he had someone like Huckleberry Finn with him, then things would be different.

As the words on the page began to join together and disappear, Josh tried to continue reading. His dreams started to take over, and he pictured himself in the bushes by the shack as Travis brought a shovel down on someone's head. Josh woke with a start. The book was over his face, and a moth hovered around the kerosene lamp; casting strange shadows about the room. For a moment, he thought that he was still inside of the shack, but soon he came back to himself. Reaching over, Joshua turned the lamp off and quickly drifted off to a deep sleep.

Sunlight beamed in through the screen, and a cool breeze blew over Joshua. As he began to stir, he could hear Mr. Nilsson downstairs fiddling around. He put his bathing trunks on and lowered himself down the ladder. The old man had strung the netting across the barn, and he was tying part of it together. He used a shoelace to link it in place.

"I think we'll need a new net for next season," he said without taking his eyes off what he was doing.

"How does it rip so much?"

"It's old, and when the children are out there, they don't pay attention to what they're doing. Once a rip starts, it just wants to keep going."

Joshua held part of the net tight, as Mr. Nilsson looped the string through the little squares. Together, they were able to get it looking respectable again.

"We need to set the canopy up on the beach today. Mrs. Van Houtten wants to have a picnic. The ladies are inside getting breakfast together and filling the baskets for the beach."

Joshua went up the steps to the porch and peered in the dining room window. Guests were sitting at the long table, while others milled about. Mother rushed in with a platter of johnny cakes and took out an empty one. Mrs. Nilsson said that there would be some girls coming today to help out with some of the duties around the inn. The laundry woman was coming too.

The kitchen was a mess when the boy entered. He grabbed one of the cakes from another platter, rolled it up, and popped it in his mouth.

"What can I do?"

Mrs. Nilsson turned from her station at the stove with a befuddled look on her face.

"Just try to organize some of the plates. I need to get some more of these pancakes out."

Joshua separated the dirty dishes and made a stack of the empty platters right next to Mrs. Nilsson. She quickly filled one up, and when his mother entered the kitchen, Joshua swapped the full plate for an empty one. Mother gave him a quick smile, spun on her heels, and disappeared through the swinging doors.

"Mrs. Van Houtten wants to have picnic on the beach today. She started putting things together, and threw me off," Mother whispered when she returned.

Joshua saw the pile of supplies for the beach. He gathered them together and brought them all out to the table in the breakfast room. This gave Mrs. Nilsson a little more latitude to get the breakfast out. Quickly, he took the dirty dishes from the counter and began to wash them in the sink. He stacked them in the dish drainer after each rinse. They had more of a system now, and when Mother came in with another empty platter, she seemed to ease a bit at the sight in the kitchen.

Joshua put the dry dishes on the back counter and then started with the silverware. He laid everything out, so his mother could come in quickly and get more settings on the table as guests came down for breakfast.

"I have to go help Mr. Nilsson put the canopy up on the beach."

"Go ahead. Thank you very much for your help, Joshua. You saved the day," Mrs. Nilsson said as she smiled over her shoulder.

She didn't get frazzled too often, but when she did, Joshua made it a point to try and help Mrs. Nilsson as much as possible. He gave his mother a wave through the dining room window just before he hopped back off the porch. He had a handful of johnny cakes, and he was popping them in his mouth as he walked back to the barn. When Joshua entered, Mr. Nilsson was tightening the wheel on the cart. The canopy was stowed on the back, and he had piled some chairs from the yard in there also.

"Ready to string up that net for the tennis court?"

"Sure."

The cool breeze kept the mosquitoes at bay, so they were able to work without any swatting. Joshua firmed up the boundary lines as Mr. Nilsson clipped some of the stray tufts of grass. The tennis court looked perfect. If only the guests would keep it that way, then Joshua would be happy.

The ride down the beach was a pleasant one. There was such a difference from the muggy air of the day before. When they got to the dunes, Joshua could see that the surf was high. Waves rolled in like they did in the spring. They angled in from the west. Josh was starting to understand how the ocean worked. The wind had such big effect on the way that the water moved.

On the beach, they got to work right away. Josh held up the poles while Mr. Nilsson drove in the stakes. The tent went up without any problems, and although the breeze flapped the sides, the structure seemed sturdy. They hauled the chairs from the cart and placed them underneath the shaded covering.

"They've probably packed the picnic lunch by now."

"I bet some of the guests are ready to come down," Joshua replied as they both walked up and over the dunes.

Grabbing a little more to eat at the inn, Joshua helped load up the cart with supplies. There were three families ready to take the journey to the shore, and Mr. Nilsson said five or six more wanted to go down a little bit later. After the old man started down to the beach, Joshua followed on his bicycle. He whizzed by Nettie and gave the children a wave. In his basket, Joshua had stowed his bird book, Tom Sawyer, and his sketch pad. He didn't know how much work he would actually be doing for the guests. The main reason that he was there was so he could assist them or make runs back to the inn.

"Oh what a glorious day," one of the mothers said as she came down onto the beach with her two children.

Joshua lugged their things and tried to put them in neat piles around the canopy. He figured that they could work out where they wanted everything.

"Looks like a strong undertow today," Mr. Nilsson said as he and Joshua stared out at the waves.

"What's that?"

"See how those waves are breaking. There's a drop right where the wave crashes. It churns everything up and then drags it back out to sea. You keep an eye on the little ones. Sometimes the parents don't watch them too closely."

Joshua nodded and looked over at the seven children who were milling about at the edge of the high tide line. As Mr. Nilsson headed back up to the canopy, the boy watched the waves tumble in. Each one seemed to slowly build, and then peak quickly. Just at the last moment, the wave curled in onto itself and pounded down. The green water became a mix of white froth and upturned sand. After the waves spilled onto the beach, they quickly receded back to form more waves. There were a few gaps where the current seemed to rip out into the ocean. Joshua could see the brown tails of forced water streaming out forty or fifty feet. They seemed to follow a pattern of the low points that meandered along the shore. He felt the sense of danger that the ocean was conveying. The children played casually along the shore, oblivious to the power of the sea.

"I'll be back down in a while with some more guests," Mr. Nilsson said as he returned to where Joshua was standing.

"Do you think Mrs. Van Houtten will be coming down?"

"Yes, I'm sure of it. Don't worry though. Everything will be ready for the picnic. Don't get in her way, but make sure that you're available if she needs you."

Joshua nodded. He was slowly learning how to deal with her. She was full of demands and reproaches, but if he just followed her directions and tried not to think of better ways of doing things, then he was okay. Joshua walked over to the canopy and helped one of the mothers spread out a blanket. There were some in the shade and others in the sunshine. The late morning was starting to warm up, but the breeze that came up the coast made the day comfortable.

Once everyone was settled, Joshua decided to take a short walk. He didn't want to be too far away when Mrs. Van Houtten arrived. She would most likely be bringing more articles down to the beach. To the east, there was a small cropping of rocks that broke up the sandy shoreline. A large rock, maybe ten feet tall, sat in the middle of the group. Houses lined the beach just beyond. The shore curved outward a bit as he approached the rocky area. Looking back, Joshua had a good view of the waves as they crashed. If he stood in one specific spot, the break of each wave made a hollow booming sound. He could see water spray out of the curl as it rolled down the beach toward him. Mesmerized, the boy watched as wave after wave came up to the shoreline. How many years or centuries had this been happening? Generations came and went, yet the waves continued to pound the beach. They were a constant, like the stars at night.

"Good morning, Joshua Keegan," a voice came from on top of the rock.

The boy looked up and saw Elizabeth peering over the crest at him.

"Hi."

"What are you doing?"

"Oh, I'm just going for a short walk. I set everything up on the beach for the guests, and I have to wait until Mr. Nilsson brings some more down."

"Did the pipes work?"

"We haven't tried it yet. Probably after the picnic on the beach. Mr. Nilsson wants to do it when the call for water isn't too high at the inn."

"Want to climb up?"

Joshua smiled and looked for the best place to get a good footing. He pulled himself up and sat down next to Elizabeth. They watched the waves roll in along the beach. He could see that the children were up above the water line, and it looked like they were trying to build a castle. Joshua smiled, thinking of the one they had built before.

"That shack isn't haunted," Joshua suddenly said. "Everyone knows that."

"It's just a place to hide liquor."

"Who told you that?"

"No one."

"Then how do you know?"

"I went there. The howling noise is a pipe that comes up from the pond, and the ghosts are just the cool air that travels through it."

"You actually went there? Who was with you?"

"No one, just Kip."

"The dog?"

"Yeah."

"I never knew anyone who actually went down there. Some of the boys from school talked about it, but they never tried it. They live on the other side of the Post Road."

"They're having a picnic on the beach today. Do you want to come?"

"It's not for you or me. They do it for the guests."

"That's okay. We can go and sit down by the other rocks," Joshua said, pointing down the beach.

190

"No, not today. I have to go back and help my grandmother."

"Maybe we could do it another time."

"Maybe," she answered with a smile.

They looked back out at the ocean. Twelve miles away, Block Island was clear as day. Joshua's heart was pounding. Did he actually ask Elizabeth to go on a picnic with him? He had never done anything like that before with any girl. Actually, Joshua had never felt this way about any girl.

"Do you want to go see the old shack sometime?"

Elizabeth laughed.

"What's there to see?"

"Just so you could tell the boys at your school that you've been there."

"I'll have to think about it. I don't have a fancy bicycle to ride around on."

For a second, Joshua noticed that old tone that Elizabeth used to have in her voice. He decided to be quiet for awhile, and not ruin anything.

"I have to go," she said as she picked herself up from the rock. Elizabeth stepped down and hopped off before Joshua even realized that she was leaving. He stood and watched her walk across the sand. After she had traveled a short distance, the girl turned and waved to him. Joshua waved back and continued to gaze at her as she made her way over the dunes and onto the road.

He jumped down from the top of the rock and sunk into the soft sand. Running and bounding along the water's edge, Joshua made his way back to the canopy. Although he didn't come out and ask anyone if they needed anything, he made himself available to them. The guests seemed content. They continued their conversations as if he wasn't even there. Joshua started to think that this was a good thing. Going back down to the water, Joshua waded in a little bit. The water splashed up onto his shirt as the waves crashed in front of him, and he could feel the pull as the water receded from behind.

Before Joshua could do much else, he saw Mr. Nilsson pulling up to the beach with another cartful of guests. The boy sped up the sand and helped the old man unload. Mrs. Van Houtten seemed unusually calm as she glided onto the beach in a long dress with a small umbrella over her shoulder. Joshua carried the baskets of food and drink under the canopy. Mr. Nilsson had a small table, and he set it up in the center of the shaded area. Once the bulk of the supplies were in place, Mrs. Van Houtten took over the whole operation. Joshua watched her as she got everything and everyone in order. She had a keen sense of how to do the whole operation. After making sure that Mrs. Van Houtten had all she needed, Mr. Nilsson headed back to the cart.

"Stick around for a few minutes until everyone's settled in with their lunches and then ride back to the inn. We'll get that field watered down."

Joshua nodded and headed back to the perimeter of the canopy. All of the ropes were tight, and it seemed like the guests were comfortable. Mothers passed out food to their children. One little girl dropped her lunch into the sand, but Mrs. Van Houtten quickly filled another plate. She wanted everyone to be happy, and to Joshua, it looked like they were.

As people were finishing their meals, Joshua helped to gather everything together. The dirty linens went in one basket, and the used dishes went into another. The boy decided to see how much he could fit on the bicycle. He filled the basket with the dirty napkins and small towels. The dishes wouldn't fit, but he was worried that maybe they might chip on the bike ride home anyway. Before leaving, Joshua remembered that he had to get his books. Even though he didn't look at any of them once, it was good to have them just in case he got the time. He pedaled his way through the dusty roads and wheeled into the inn as Mr. Nilsson was heading over to the barn. He dropped the basketful of napkins in the kitchen and then made his way to the windmill.

Mr. Nilsson had rigged a faucet at the end of the pipe they used to flush the well out in the spring. Joshua turned the lever, and they both walked over to the garden. Small streams of water sprayed out at odd angles where each of the pipes were connected, but once they got to the end, the clear liquid was flowing out. The stream ran down the first row. Much of it soaked into the ground as it went. Joshua set up the plank at the far end and waited for the water to reach him. He began to get impatient, but soon was rewarded with a thin course of water against the wood. The mark crept up higher on the board, as the boy watched it penetrate the dusty soil.

Once it got beyond the halfway mark about four inches up, Josh slowly dug a trench to the next row. He worked his fingers into the ground and watched as the water began to spill over to the other side. The plank blocked it from flowing anywhere, but directly down the channel behind the first. Quickly, Joshua thought about the best method of continuing his progress. If he took the second plank and brought it over to the other side of the garden, then he wouldn't have to cut off the flow. Water could just run through the first four rows by zig zagging back and forth. Mr. Nilsson came back from the barn with two more long planks.

"I see you changed your mind about the direction."

"Well, if it flows this way, then the far ends of the rows won't get so washed out."

"Good thinking."

They watched the water fill up the first four rows, waiting until it pooled up to the top. Joshua ran back and shut the faucet off, and they quickly broke down the first pipe, reattached another one, and let the water run again down the fifth row. He repeated the process that they had started before. Once in a while there was a break in the mounds, but the boy quickly went out with a shovel and patched it before too much water could flow through. When they got to the next set of rows, Mr. Nilsson left Joshua on his own.

"I think you're getting the hang of irrigation. I'll be back in a little while after I bring some of the guests back from the beach."

Joshua just nodded and looked up from where the water ran. He was totally wrapped up in what he was doing. As the water continued to flow, he went back up to see how far it had soaked in. The dust was gone, and now mud covered the rows. This would give the vegetables another week of energy to grow. Joshua just hoped that some rain would arrive soon. Although this was an interesting way to pass his time, rainfall made things a lot easier.

As the afternoon wore on, a few guests wandered out to the garden. Their interest was sparked by the boy running to and fro with the planks. When he finally got to the bottom of the garden, Joshua thought that it would be more economical to use the watering can. The tomato plants weren't really in rows, so if he directed the water around the base of the plants, then he wouldn't waste so much time and effort trying to fill the entire area.

They left the irrigation pipes where they were. Mr. Nilsson just turned the faucet off and let the water flow back into the inn. Mrs. Nilsson had come out to the garden twice to fill up pots, and it didn't seem like she enjoyed doing that chore too much. Joshua thought about what he had done today, and decided that he would write to his sister and tell her all about it.

14

Dear Mary,

You won't believe what I did today. Mr. Nilsson and I had to irrigate the entire garden. It took all afternoon, but I think that the vegetables will make it now. We haven't had any good rain for awhile. Dad would have liked to have been a part of it, I'm sure. He always kept enough water on his garden. This one is different though. It's about twenty times as big, so it would take a lot of runs back and forth with his bucket to get it done.

A lot has happened since I last wrote to you. Mother was getting the notion that maybe this wasn't such a good idea. I had one of my spells. This one was strange though. I started to think about you, and then I thought I saw you across the pond on the island. I think it was just an egret. That's a tall, white seabird with a long neck. I can't figure out how I could have made the mistake. I thought it was a good thing that I saw you, but Mother had the opposite reaction. I've named the island after you, and if I ever get a free minute, I'm going to paddle one of the canoes over there.

Remember the girl that I told you about? Her name is Elizabeth. I thought that she was really mean, but since I have found out a few things about her, we seem to be getting along very well. Her parents died when she was small, and her grandparents raised her. She has a diary, and I think she writes to her mother in kind of the same way that I write to you. Since she found out that I write you letters, she has been treating me much better. I asked her to go on a picnic with me, but I'm not sure if it will ever happen. I'm going to ride my bicycle over there the next chance I get.

Mrs. Van Houtten is back, but I'm looking at her with

different eyes now. She doesn't seem as bad to me anymore. Maybe I'm just getting used to her. She has a wonderful inn here. I wish you could see it. Mr. Van Houtten hasn't appeared yet. Mr. Nilsson said that he might be down for the Fourth of July. He's a businessman in New York City.

Speaking of the Fourth of July, Mr. Nilsson said that we are going to have a big clambake. We've already started to collect the clams, and we just set out some traps to catch lobsters. I'm not sure how the whole thing works, but we have to dig a pit, and then fill it with stones and wood. We put the clams and lobsters and other things in with some seaweed and let it cook for a few hours. I'll let you know how the whole thing turns out.

I think this is the longest letter I've ever written. I'm going to put it away for now. I want to get back to Tom Sawyer before I go to sleep. Muff Potter has been arrested for the murder of Doc Robinson, but Tom and Huck know that it's Injun Joe who did it. I've been trying to remember the parts that you read to me. I thought there was something about Tom playing pirates on some island, and then another part in a cave. Maybe I'll get to that soon.

Your Brother,

Joshua

He read over what was written on the page, and it looked good. He wanted her to get a picture of what was going on at the beach. Picking up the Mark Twain novel, Joshua read until he couldn't keep his eyes open anymore. Just as he was drifting off to sleep, he realized that he forgot to tell Mary that the Red Sox were in first place.

Joshua was awake before anyone else the next morning. He went out into the yard and raised the American flag up the pole. In the distance, he could hear the rumble of the surf. From the sound of it, the waves were even bigger than yesterday. Joshua couldn't figure out why they were rolling in so powerfully. The wind was blowing the flag somewhat, but it wasn't incredibly strong.

Maybe there was a storm out at sea that was causing this surge to happen on the shore. The pond was low, so it meant that the ocean probably was partly on its way to high tide. There was a lag time between the inlet and the sea. Joshua figured that it had something to do with getting all of the water into and out of the breachway.

After getting something to eat in the kitchen, the boy put his old shoes on, grabbed the bushel basket, and headed down to the dock to go clamming. The Fourth of July was getting closer, and he didn't think that they had nearly enough cherrystones to have a respectable clambake. He tried to gauge about how far over they had last foraged for the shellfish, and estimated that it was just about straight out from the dock. With a gentle push, he drifted across the channel. The dinghy carried him until Josh could feel the bottom beginning to scrape on the rocks. He hopped out and pulled the boat the rest of the way across the shallow area.

With the rake in hand, Joshua began digging his way through the coarse sand. Just like the other day, he pulled up clam after clam. Mr. Nilsson must have skipped over this part during the last few seasons. Looking up, he saw the man walking back to the inn with an armload of wood. Joshua gave him a wave. He had never really known his grandfather very well, but Mr. Nilsson seemed like the kind of man that he would have been like. Mother had said that the war between the states took a lot out of him. He worked for years afterward building roads for the city of Providence, but he was never the happy man that Grandma used to describe. She would often point out the cobblestones that he had laid out around the city. Joshua was starting to think of Mr. Nilsson as the grandfather he never knew.

It was strange how families worked. A child became part of what his parents were like. Joshua tried to piece together his own personality as it fit in with what he had grown up with. His love for baseball definitely came from his father, and his interest in gardening came from him too. His mother was a hard worker, and as he thought about it more, he realized that his father was too. He had never really seen him in action down at the shipyard, but from what he did around the yard, Joshua imagined what he must have been like working on those rails. Just the fact that he was an immigrant who became the leader of his crew, made Josh realize how hard the man must have worked. It probably had a lot to do with his way with people. He could make them laugh, but he could also get them behind him to finish a job. Joshua looked down at the growing muscles in his arms; although he was much stronger now than when he came to the Pond View, he had a long way to go to be as big as his father. Books. He knew that he had gotten that trait from his sister. She had always said that she wanted to be a teacher. Joshua smiled, thinking that she had taught him many things; especially the idea that if you didn't understand something, then you asked questions or looked it up in a book. Mother and Dad hadn't gotten much schooling when they were younger. Times were different. It was their mission, though, to have their children educated. That's what was so strange about his mother not pushing him to attend school down here. He must have really been out of his mind for her to allow that. As he scraped the bottom of the pond, Joshua vowed to continue with his studies. He realized now that his parents didn't want him to grow up and be someone else's servant.

Joshua looked up and saw Mr. Nilsson wading across the channel with a rake in his hand. The water was up to his waist, but he had a big smile on his face.

"Good morning," he called out as he approached.

"I decided to get a jump on the clamming today, and the tide seemed to be right."

"Good thinking."

"I think you missed this spot too last year."

"Boy did I. How long have you been out here?" Mr. Nilsson asked as he looked down in the half full basket.

"Not too long. I'm pulling up two or three every time I drag the rake through."

"If the lobster pots are half as plentiful, then we won't have to buy anything from Johnny Crandall."

"Are we going to check them today?"

"I was thinking that we should go fishing with the

incoming tide. The guests have been asking for some seafood. I just dropped the minnow trap."

"Where do we put the lobsters once we catch them?"

"I've got a big wooden crate in the brush over there somewhere. I might have to fix it up a little bit. We can sink it under the dock and store the lobsters in there until the Fourth."

They filled the basket in no time, and when they got back to shore, Joshua took about one third of them for Mrs. Nilsson to make some more chowder. He stashed the rest under the dock with the others they had gotten before. While he brought the clams up to the house, Mr. Nilsson went to the barn to get the fishing tackle. Some of the guests were stirring, but not many. Joshua figured that they were on vacation, and he wasn't. Mrs. Nilsson stood at the stove, and she gave the boy a big smile when he came in with the shellfish. The woman reached over and handed him some pancakes, and Joshua devoured them as he followed Mr. Nilsson back down to the dock.

The minnow trap had a dozen or so fish in it, and Joshua dropped them in the bucket with some seaweed as Mr. Nilsson rowed away from the dock. The man's pants were still dripping from his walk across the channel.

"Have you ever been on that island?"

"I gathered driftwood there one day on a whim. The boat was sitting fairly low in the water. I don't think I'll ever do that again."

"Is there anything on it?"

"They say the Indians used to have ceremonies out there when they came to the shore for the summer."

"What kind of ceremonies?"

"Beats me."

They came around the far side of the island, and Joshua saw the buoys floating in the water. He had a good feeling about the traps. There were two other boats at the inland mouth of the breachway as they approached. Mr. Nilsson had to really pull on the oars to make any progress. They found a spot that wasn't too close to the others, but was right in line with the incoming rush of the tide. The man gave the fellow fishermen a wave, and they returned the greeting.

Joshua had baited the hooks as they were moving across the pond, so once he dropped the anchor, they were ready to go. He watched one of the men in the nearby boat pull in a very large fish. He couldn't tell what it was from this distance; only that it had some weight to it. Joshua figured that the fishing line would cut off the circulation to his hands if he ever caught one that big. Mr. Nilsson got a hit the second he dropped his hook in the water. The fish jerked his arm left, then right. Joshua looked over as the man pulled a large striped bass into the boat. It had to be at least two feet long, if not bigger. The old man put the fish in the fruit crate.

"It barely fits," Mr. Nilsson said. "We catch a few more of those, then we'll be done for the day."

Joshua smiled as something hit his line. He could feel the tug as the fish tried to pull away. The line did cut into his hand as he had imagined it would. As the boy pulled on the piece of wood that the string was attached to, he attempted to wrap it around. Standing up, Josh tried to get the fish under control. He saw it swirl up near the surface, and then dive down again. This one was just as big as Mr. Nilsson's.

"Go steady with it," the man said. "Don't try to force it."

Josh's muscles held firm, but he could feel the strain on his hands. Every time the fish gave a little bit, he tried to pull it in a little bit more. The splash was only a few feet from them, but to Joshua, it could have been a hundred yards. He had no idea how he was going to get this fish into the boat.

"Easy now ... just guide her toward you."

Joshua tried to settle his breathing down and get control of the situation. He sat back down on the seat and slowly, but steadily pulled the fish toward him. It fought with all of its might, but the boy focused on what he had to do. As the fish got closer to the side of the boat, Mr. Nilsson was ready with the net. With one final tug, Joshua pulled the fish partly out of the water. Mr. Nilsson got the net underneath it, and scooped it into the boat.

"This one's even bigger," the man said. "Where are

these fish coming from?"

"The surf's pretty high ... I figured there was a storm out to sea ... maybe that's what's sending them into the pond."

"Maybe you're right. I don't care what's doing it, if we keep this up, then everybody is going to get fish tonight."

For the next hour, they kept pulling in bass. None of them were as big as the first two, but by the time they started to head back in, the crate and part of the bottom of the boat were filled with fish. Occasionally they flopped, but mostly Joshua just watched as their gills breathed in and out.

"Why don't we head back in? This boat's too full to carry those lobster pots. We'll cut them up at the dock, and then go back out."

Joshua pulled on the oars as Mr. Nilsson wound up all of the line. He dropped the three remaining minnows into the water, and Joshua thought that he saw a fish come up out of the darkness to snatch one of them. With the tide still coming in, Joshua had an easy time getting the boat back to the shore. The wind from the west made the whole trip seem effortless.

They lined the fish up along the dock. There were fifteen of them. Joshua arranged them from biggest to smallest. When Mr. Nilsson came back from the barn, he had a large platter, two sharp knives, and a measuring tape. The biggest fish was twenty-nine inches long, and the smallest was seventeen. They had a pretty good morning for themselves.

"Don't get too used to this, Joshua. We won't see anything like this again until September."

"Why not?"

"It just doesn't happen. In the fall, we'll see them again."

They started to gut and skin the fish right away. The platter was full before they had even gotten to the tenth one.

"Oh my word," Mrs. Nilsson said. "I guess you did fairly well this morning."

"I need another platter, we've got some more,"

Joshua answered with a big smile.

Mother walked into the kitchen and saw the pile of filets.

"Where did you get all of that?"

"We caught them. I got the biggest one ... twenty-nine inches."

"I guess we're having fish for dinner tonight."

"Fish and chowder," Mrs. Nilsson said with a grin.

Joshua went back down to the dock with the empty platter, and saw that Mr. Nilsson was finishing up the last bass. He piled the fish on the oval plate and went back up to the house.

For some reason, Joshua felt an incredible strength as he rowed the boat back out toward the island. Mr. Nilsson had three buckets of fish guts and carcasses. He wanted the lobsters to eat well. As the boy came around the far side of the island, the old man began to drop bits and pieces into the pond. His goal was for all of the lobsters in the whole area to come and live in this one spot. The first bucket was empty as Joshua eased the boat up next to the buoy.

Both of them pulled the rope, and as the trap broke the surface, they could see movement, but it wasn't a lobster. There were three enormous crabs in the pot.

"Blue crabs, these are beauties," the man said.

Reaching in, Mr. Nilsson gently grabbed the first one in the rear of its shell. He placed it gently in the fruit crate, and then did the same with the other two. Joshua rebaited the trap and let it slide to the bottom. The next trap had two lobsters, and the third one had three. The last three traps had one lobster apiece.

"Not too bad," Mr. Nilsson said as he closed the lid on the fruit crate. "At this rate, we should have at least two dozen by the Fourth."

Dear Mary,

You wouldn't believe how well we did out in the pond today. We went three for three. The clams just kept coming up, and then we set a record for striped bass. We pulled eight lobsters out of the traps. The cherrystones and lobsters are under the dock now. Mr. Nilsson and I pulled a big crate out of the bushes and fixed it up. I floated it out to the beginning of the channel, and Mr. Nilsson put some rocks in the bottom. All of the lobsters and blue crabs went inside. They'll be there until the clambake on the Fourth of July.

We also cleared away the area for where the pit is going to go. I had to get the trimmers and cut through the vines. There were piles of rocks in the brush too. Those are going to be used to keep the pit cooking once the shellfish are inside. We'll bring some wood down as we get closer to the day.

Mrs. Nilsson surprised me with a lobster dinner tonight. Mr. Nilsson must have snuck it up to her when I wasn't looking. I don't know how they got it by Mrs. Van Houtten, but somehow they did. The whole house smelled like fish at dinner time tonight. All of the guests got to have some of the striped bass that Mr. Nilsson and I caught. I had a piece of it too, along with some chowder. I think I'm still full from eating it all.

After dinner I took the canoe out to your island. It was the first time that I had ever been in a boat like that. I thought it was going to ride smoothly, but I kept weaving back and forth every time I tried to paddle. I did much better on the trip back. Mr. Nilsson said that the Indians used to have ceremonies on the island, so I wanted to see for myself. After crashing through the brush on the edge, I came to the middle of the island. There was a large clearing with grass growing. A long, flat rock sat off to the side. I stood on top of it and could see the inn over the bushes. I was thinking about maybe cutting a path through to the middle and asking Elizabeth if she wanted to have our picnic out there.

When I came back to the house, I found four ticks in my hair, and Mother found two on my back. I've only had one on me so far this summer. Mother took them off and decided that this would be a good time for a haircut, since my hair has been getting fairly long. She trimmed it twice before, but this time she took a lot off. It feels funny, but I think it will be cooler when it's hot out.

I read about Tom playing pirates out on the island in

*the river. I knew that I remembered you reading that to me.
It seems different, now that I know Tom better. I'm not sure
what he and Huck are going to do about Injun Joe, but I
can't wait to find out what happens.*

*I added four more birds to my list of sightings.
Around the yard, I've seen catbirds and a wrens. I think
that I might have seen a bluebird too, but I'm not sure.
Down by the pond over near the marsh, I spotted a bunch of
terns and a plover. In my notebook, I've sketched them out,
but they don't look nearly as good as they do in the book
that I have.*

*I still haven't gotten to the White Heron story. I'm too
caught up in Tom's adventures.*

Your Brother,

Joshua

The inn was now completely full. Guests had been
streaming in all week for the holiday on Thursday. Mr.
Van Houtten arrived with two of his grown sons, their
wives, and children. His appearance seemed to settle Mrs.
Van Houtten down quite a bit. The man had a strong
quality, much like what Joshua imagined Abraham
Lincoln to be like. The owner was similar to the late
president in appearance; tall and thin, but without the
trademark beard.

Joshua's life fell into a routine of clamming,
fishing, and pulling lobster pots. He accomplished all this
before following the cart to the beach for the afternoon.
He usually took a short rest after he saw that everyone
was settled. After about an hour though, he would have
to speed back on his bike to retrieve various articles for
the guests. The children always needed more food or
drink. Sometimes he would come back to the beach with
a full basket and a dangling umbrella leaning on the
handlebars in front of him.

He took a long walk down toward the breachway
late one afternoon when most of the guests had gone back
to the inn. Mr. Nilsson would be returning soon, so he
had to go fast. When Joshua came around the bend after

the Ashaway cottages, he was rewarded with a wonderful sight. The high surf had sent mounds of seaweed up onto the shore. Since the tides hadn't reached up that far in a day or so, the dark piles just stayed there.

"There's a bunch of seaweed down by the breachway," Joshua said to the man when he finally pulled back up to the dunes.

"I was hoping that would be the case. We'll drop the canopy, go back to the inn with the last few people, and then head over there."

Mrs. Nilsson packed them some dinner, and they hurried off after unloading the beach gear. From the top of the dunes, the piles looked enormous. Mr. Nilsson wheeled the cart down a little way from the cove, and then pulled it up next to the heap of seaweed. They were able to get much more in the cart than they did in the spring. The seaweed was still soaking wet once they got down a few inches. It hadn't started to smell too badly either. Joshua was able to keep up with the old man much easier now. His muscles were strong, and he felt at home with the pitchfork. Once they got to the top of the sides of the cart, Mr. Nilsson said that they should take a break. The boy could have gone on, but he saw that the man was winded.

There was a jug of water and a greasy paper bag. Joshua looked inside, but couldn't figure out what was in there. The bag was half full of light brown balls. The delicious smell made it seem like some kind of fried food, but he didn't recognize the odor. Josh looked over at Mr. Nilsson.

"Clamcakes. Mrs. Nilsson fries them in some kind of batter. Try one."

Although they had been in the bag for awhile, they were still warm. Joshua bit into one and was immediately rewarded with a delicious taste. The flavor of the clam was obvious once he began to chew. Mr. Nilsson grabbed a couple as Joshua swallowed the rest of his. They couldn't eat them fast enough. Before long, the bag was empty, and thirst became Joshua's number one need. He chugged the water from the jug, and then handed it over to Mr. Nilsson.

When they got back to work, Joshua felt sluggish. His belly was full, and the seaweed felt heavier. They continued to mound it up until it began to roll off the sides. Climbing back up onto the wagon, the man gave Joshua the reins to bring it all home.

"This should be enough for the clambake. If not, then we can drag a net along the edge of the pond, but I think we're all set."

"How do we get this down to the pond?"

"Well, that's a little tricky. We have to unhook Nettie at the top of the path, turn the cart around, hook up again, and then slowly back it down. She doesn't like it too much, so I try not to do it often."

Joshua found it difficult just maneuvering through the backyard. There were trees and stones all over, and the guests spent this time of the late afternoon and early evening strolling around the grounds. The boy didn't want to disturb them, and to add to the problem, there was a croquet game going on. Some of the children followed the cart down through the yard, and Josh had to keep half an eye on them to make sure they didn't fall under the back wheels.

"Try to make a wide arc, so we can get some leverage when we have to push. Keep it on the high side too, so we can roll it some."

Joshua did as he was told and left the cart on a slight incline as Mr. Nilsson hopped down and unhitched the horse. Josh took the lead that had been attached to Nettie and pulled it into the brush. The wheels turned at an angle, and he and Mr. Nilsson were able to push the cart into the mouth of the path. He was amazed at how heavy the whole thing was, not quite believing how easy it was for Nettie to pull the vehicle. Mr. Nilsson reattached the horse and slowly led her backwards down toward the water. She bucked a little, but the man was able to keep her under control. As the incline got a little steeper, it seemed like Nettie was having a difficult time with the heavy load. She reared up and brought her hoof down hard on a small rock that was nearly buried in the ground. This made her swing to the side and into Mr. Nilsson. Her bulk knocked the man into the bushes, but

Joshua quickly grabbed the reins without really thinking about it. He held her still and stroked her nose.

"I've got her," Mr. Nilsson said as he appeared behind the boy. "Let's just unhitch her and let the cart roll back into the water."

Joshua hopped up and pulled the brake as the man led Nettie back up to the barn. She seemed to be walking a little peculiar as she went, shuffling to one side. Mr. Nilsson came back down a few minutes later with a big fishing net, some long stakes, and a large hammer. The guests, who had been watching the excitement, started to fall back into what they were doing.

"Okay, I'll hold the lead while you ease up on the brake. Don't let too much out at a time. The ground flattens out before we get to the water, so that should slow us down."

Josh let the brake out, and the cart began to roll. It seemed like it was picking up too much momentum, so he pulled back on it again.

"We're okay, let it out," Mr. Nilsson said as he held onto the wooden poles.

Again, he eased the brake off the front wheel, and the cart started to roll. Joshua was worried about the speed, but he let it go. The cart rolled and rolled closer to the shoreline. The boy pulled on the brake and slowed it down as the back wheels dropped into the water. As he heard the splashing sound, Joshua tugged hard on the wooden stick. The cart came to a halt, and the boy almost flipped over backwards into the pile of seaweed.

Mr. Nilsson waded out a few feet into the channel and drove two stakes into the mud beneath the surface. He then wound the net around the far side of each and brought the ends back to the shore. The old man put two more stakes into the edge of the water on both sides of the cart.

"Why don't you start unloading the seaweed. Something's wrong with Nettie's foot. I'm going to take the bicycle over to Old Cal's and see if he can come over and take a look."

"Who's he?"

"Old Cal? He quite a character. He used to take

care of the horses in New York City when Teddy Roosevelt was the police commissioner. He followed him down to Cuba for the Spanish-American War. They say he was never right after that. He keeps to himself over in East Beach tending to the animals there. He watches Nettie during the winter."

"Oh yeah, that's where I've heard his name before."

"He doesn't get out much, but I know he'll come over and see her; especially if he knows she's hurt."

Joshua took the pitchfork and started to unload the cart. He watched Mr. Nilsson walk back up the path and then into the yard. Never seeing such concern on the man's face, Joshua worried about the horse. Since the cart was at an angle, the seaweed came off a lot easier than it went on. He watched as the netted area filled higher and higher. The tide was getting low again, so he had a good idea how much would fit inside the net. Once Joshua saw that it wasn't going to be enough, he hopped down into the water and pulled one of the stakes. He stretched out the netting some more and drove the stake back in again. The mud on the bottom of the channel gushed through his toes. Before he knew it, the seaweed was emptied from the cart. Josh grabbed the bucket from the dock, rinsed it out, and then started to pour it over the back of the cart. The guests probably wouldn't be too excited about riding down to the beach with the smell of seaweed permeating from the boards.

As he walked back up into the yard, it was starting to get dark. His arms swung low by his side. What were they going to do with the cart? The tide would be coming in soon, and he didn't think the salt water from the pond would do it much good. Coming around the front, he saw a chestnut colored horse tied to the rail. Inside, Mr. Nilsson had a lantern in Nettie's stall. Next to him was an old, gray haired man in faded overalls. He was painting a thick tar-like substance onto Nettie's hoof. Josh watched silently as Old Cal brushed the foul smelling gel onto the horse. He worked it in with his fingers as he went along. Mr. Nilsson turned and saw Joshua standing there.

"Just a small split. Cal thinks she'll be okay in a day or two."

Old Cal gently put Nettie's hoof back down onto the hay. The horse was still for a moment, then she lifted her leg back up and tapped it down a few times. Josh went out and filled a bucket of water for her, and then brought it back in.

"Cal's going to stay with her tonight to make sure she doesn't do any damage to herself. He said that we can use Lucky for a couple of days until Nettie's back on her feet."

"What about the cart? The tide will be coming in soon."

"Let's bring Lucky down and pull it back up here."

That night as Joshua lay in his bed, he could hear Old Cal talking softly to the horse. The man hadn't said a word while he was in the barn, but he spoke to Nettie; trying to soothe her. Joshua drifted off to sleep as the man was singing her a quiet melody as if she were a baby.

15

It was Wednesday, the third of July, so that meant it was time to dig. Because the clambake pit had been dug before, Joshua had no problem working through the dirt. The shovel sliced through the soil with ease. Mr. Nilsson had told him he should put it in the wheelbarrow and haul the dirt around to the other side of the bushes. They would need lots of room to maneuver once the clambake got cooking.

"What are you doing?" One of the Van Houtten grandchildren asked. She looked to be about five or six years old.

"I'm digging a hole for the clambake."

"My grandpa says that our clambake is the best one at the beach."

"I bet he's right."

"What's your name?"

"Joshua. What's yours?"

"Mary Rose. I'm five."

Josh looked at the girl's curly blond hair. She didn't seem at all shy around him. Nodding and smiling, the boy went back to his digging. He was almost down to his knees now, and it was getting harder to toss the dirt up and over the rim of the wheelbarrow. Mary Rose sat down a few feet away and crossed her legs. She picked a small purple flower from the edge of the lawn, sniffed at it, and then stuck it in her hair. Josh smiled as he tried to square off the back corner of the pit. The whole thing was eight feet long and two feet wide. Mr. Nilsson had told him to go down about three and a half feet; much lower than that and he'd hit water. The hole had to be deep enough to make layers of wood and stone, as well as fit seaweed, lobsters and clams.

They now had twenty-seven of the big-clawed

creatures under the dock along with four bushels of clams. Mr. Nilsson had gone out beyond where they usually got the cherrystones, and dug up almost a bushel of what he called steamers. They were shellfish with a more oval and delicate shell. The strange part was the little neck that stuck out on the side. When Joshua had returned from the beach, he saw them on the dock, squirting water out. When he went to pick one up, the shell clamped shut. Mixed in with the steamers were some razor clams. They were long and thin with a brownish color to them. The day before, Mr. Nilsson had sent the boy down to the rocks at the beach to tear off clumps of mussels that hung at the bottom of the rocks. Josh had easily filled up a fruit crate and put it on the cart to head back to the inn. It was strange having Lucky pull them back, but Old Cal said rest was the best thing for Nettie. She would be ready on the Fourth of July.

Mary Rose followed Joshua when he lifted the wheelbarrow and took it around to the other side of the bushes. His pile was getting larger, and he didn't look forward to hauling the whole thing back.

"Why are you putting the dirt over here?"

"So it's out of the way."

"Why do you have to get it out of the way?"

Joshua figured that this questioning could go on all day.

"Because we have the best clambake around, that's why."

This seemed to satisfy the girl, and she picked a yellow flower as she followed Joshua back to the hole. This one went over her other ear.

"Hello, Mr. Nilsson," the girl said as the old man approached. "This is Joshua. He's digging a hole for the clambake."

"Well, it looks like he's doing a fine job."

The man watched as Joshua shoveled another load into the wheelbarrow.

"Joshua, why don't you take Mary Rose up to the house and have some lemonade. Your mother just made some. I'll dig for awhile."

"I don't mind."

"Get a drink and come back down. There'll be plenty of dirt left for you."

The girl followed Joshua up to the house and into the kitchen. He rinsed his hands off in the sink and was drying them on the towel when Mother and Mrs. Nilsson came back in. There were two other girls with them. They looked to be about eighteen or nineteen years old. For a moment, Joshua forgot all about Elizabeth as he stared at the dark haired girl in the doorway.

"You'll be serving breakfast and dinner each day," Mrs. Nilsson said, "and helping to take care of the linens upstairs. Mrs. Keegan and I will be doing most of the work, and you'll be assisting us."

Joshua just kept staring as the four of them made their way into the kitchen.

"I think your hands are dry now," Mary Rose said as she watched Joshua.

"Oh Joshua, I didn't see you," Mrs. Nilsson said. "This is Charlotte and Louise. They live up by the Post Road, and they'll be helping us for a few weeks."

Joshua just smiled at Louise. She was beautiful. Her long black hair fell over her shoulders, and her white teeth gave him a big smile.

"Joshua, there's some lemonade on the counter for you," his mother said.

The boy stumbled over to the pitcher and poured himself a drink. He got a smaller glass and gave it to the five-year-old, who gulped it down. Mrs. Nilsson gave them a quick tour of the kitchen area, and then the party of four went back out through the swinging door. Just as she was leaving, Louise turned and gave Joshua another smile. He thought his heart was going to burst through his chest. As the door swung back and forth, Joshua just stared at where the girl had been.

Mr. Nilsson had made some progress when Joshua got back down to the pit. He figured that it would take two or three more wheelbarrows full to finish the project. The man climbed out and handed the shovel back to the boy.

"Where's your friend?"

"Oh, her mother wanted her to get ready to go

212

down to the beach."

As the man walked away, Joshua turned back to the hole. He had a sudden vision of his father's grave. He remembered them lowering the casket down into it. Although this hole wasn't as deep, the dimensions had a certain quality that reminded him of that drizzly March morning. Joshua had been in such shock over the whole thing, that he was numb to any feelings that day. His mother and sister cried and cried, as did the other women, but Joshua just stared. His knees began to get weak as he looked down into the clam pit. Trying to shake it off, he dropped the shovel and walked over toward the garden.

Joshua had to learn to control his thoughts when they started to fall in that spiral motion. He saw the pipes still laid out next to the rows, and wondered if maybe they would have to irrigate the garden again. The blue sky above gave no hints of any rain to come in the near future. Ducking under the string that lined the whole area, Joshua made his way over to the tomato plants. There were small, green tomatoes growing out of each one. He counted thirteen on one plant alone, and the small yellow flowers meant that there were more to come. Although he couldn't figure out when they would be ripe, he knew that within a few weeks, he would be biting into a juicy tomato. The beans and cucumbers were climbing the wooden slats that Mr. Nilsson had driven into the ground. The growth was starting to come on strong now. Joshua was sure that the water he had directed through the rows was making a big difference. His father would be proud of him for what he had done in this garden.

Taking a few deep breaths, Joshua headed back over to the pit, hoping that he had successfully overcome the darkness in his mind. The hole was still there, but when he hopped down inside, his thoughts focused on the clambake that would be cooking in there the next day. As he sunk his shovel in deeper, he noticed the black soil and figured that it was the ashes from last year's clambake. Sometimes it was hard for Joshua to imagine that there was such activity down here before he arrived. Everything seemed so new to him, that he thought this was the first season that anyone had ever come down here.

A husband, wife, and two young children walked by Joshua as he was bringing the wheelbarrow back from the bushes. They had a picnic basket and a blanket.

"Good morning," he said as they passed by him.

They just smiled and nodded. Joshua watched as they went out onto the dock and loaded the children and food into the canoe. The husband helped his wife down into the boat, then he stepped in and untied the line, gently pushing them away. Both of the adults had a paddle, and they moved through the water in a very straight way. Joshua figured that in order to keep the canoe in line, there had to be two people paddling. At first he thought they were going to stop at the island, but at the last moment, they cut inside and headed over toward the breachway. Maybe he would do the same with Elizabeth someday. Maybe he would take Louise for a canoe ride. His daydreaming kept his attention focused on the pond, and his chin resting on the top of the shovel.

"How's our pit coming for the clambake?" A voice said, snapping Joshua out of his reverie.

"Oh, good. It's almost done," Joshua answered as he looked up and saw Mr. Van Houtten. He was carrying Mary Rose in his arms.

"That's Joshua, he gave me some lemonade."

The man smiled down at him, and then looked out over the pond.

"It's a beautiful day," the man said in his quiet, but powerful voice.

Joshua found it hard to imagine that this man could be married to Mrs. Van Houtten. He seemed so at ease with things, and she was almost always frantic. Maybe that was how they got along. They were complete opposites.

"How are we looking for lobsters and clams?"

"Mr. Nilsson says that we're all set. Do you want to see?" Joshua asked as he hopped out of the hole and walked down to the dock.

He laid down on the wooden planks and reached under the surface for the clasp on the slatted crate. Pulling it up slowly, Joshua looked down at all of the lobsters that littered the bottom.

214

"Twenty-seven. Mr. Nilsson said that you had two dozen last year."

"That looks great."

Joshua quickly scooted over to the other side of the dock and showed Mr. Van Houtten and Mary Rose the bushel baskets that were full of clams and other shellfish.

"The seaweed's right over there in that netting. We'll drag it up in the morning. The rocks are piled next to the bushes, and we just have to bring down the wood."

"Very impressive. Have you done a clambake before?"

"No, this is my first."

"Well, make sure you get yourself one of those lobsters; you're doing a great job. Mr. Nilsson speaks very highly of you."

"Thank you."

Joshua watched as Mr. Van Houtten and Mary Rose walked back up into the yard. Mrs. Van Houtten hadn't ever talked to him directly, and now here was her husband complimenting him on a job well done. It made the boy feel good to be appreciated, and as he dug down into the last layer of dirt, his visions of the hole as a grave had disappeared.

After getting everyone settled at the beach, Joshua and Mr. Nilsson came back to get things ready for the clambake. The boy hauled firewood down from the barn. He brought four wheelbarrows full and dropped them by the side of the pit. Mr. Nilsson was inside the hole, lining the bottom with the logs. He intertwined old newspaper with the wood. Once they had one layer of logs, Joshua started to hand stones down to Mr. Nilsson. Most of them were easy enough to hold in one hand, but others were bigger. The old man placed each rock in perfect rows on top of the wood. He climbed out of the hole, and both of them continued the process on the next layer. When their handiwork reached the edge of the pit, Joshua looked down at what they had done.

"Where are the lobsters and clams going to fit?"

"The wood will burn down to ash, and the stones will collapse down as the fire heats them. Once that happens, we'll start loading the seaweed across, then it's just layers again."

Joshua saw that Mr. Nilsson had left openings in all four corners. He figured that this was so he could reach down with a match or lit stick to start the fire burning at the bottom.

"How long does it take to burn?"

"We'll get it started at about 8:30 or 9:00. That'll burn until noon, then we'll load the shellfish and cover it for at least an hour. The canvas should start to pop up around then."

"Pop up?"

"Yes, it's an amazing thing to see. The covering will blow up like one of those hot air balloons. That's when you know it's ready."

Joshua just stared down at the now filled pit. He couldn't wait until the next morning. As he was walking back up through the yard with the wheelbarrow, he saw that some of the young men were playing ball. They were just tossing the baseball around, but it got Joshua's blood going. Although he had been working all day long, he suddenly felt energy come back into his bones. After dropping the wheelbarrow off in the barn, he came back with his glove and sat on a rock to watch them play.

One of the men had a bat now and was playing pepper with the three other men. He tapped the ball to one of them, and Josh watched as they tossed it back and forth; through their legs and around their backs. Joshua got a little jealous when he saw Louise stop and stare as she came around the side of the house with a basket full of clean sheets and pillow cases. He longed to go out there and play, but he wouldn't do it unless he was invited. They played with ease and laughter. It reminded Joshua of those Sundays he watched his father play ball down at the field in the South End.

"George, I need you," came a voice from the upstairs window.

"Georrrrge, I neeeeeed you," mimicked one of the men.

The man named George hustled up to the porch and disappeared inside of the inn. Joshua watched for a moment, waiting. He even put on his glove and started punching it.

"Okay kid, c'mon out," a voice said.

Joshua bounced off the rock and took the spot that George had vacated. The boy stood on the line of the arc and waited for the ball. The batter bunted it to the man in the middle, who bobbed it off the back of his mitt over to Joshua. The boy grabbed it in his glove and tossed it easily over to the last man.

"Let's go, Harry. Keep that ball moving."

Harry popped it off his bat again, and Josh caught it and quickly flipped it around his back.

"Fancy move. Here you go, Kenyon."

"Give it here, Edward."

Joshua got lost in the game of pepper. He totally focused on the ball as it moved from glove to hand to bat and back again. Some of the other guests gathered around and began to cheer as the ball moved faster and faster. It didn't matter if it dropped because someone would just scoop it up and let the ball fly again. Joshua looked up briefly and saw Mr. Nilsson looking on. The big smile on his face made the boy realize what he was doing was okay. The spell was broken, though, when Mrs. Nilsson came out to ring the dinner bell. The men kept the ball going for another minute or two, but it was obvious that everyone was hungry.

"Hey kid, what's your name?" Kenyon asked as he was walking back up to the house.

"Joshua."

"Well Joshua, we play ball down at the field down by the pump for the beach well. You should come down and watch."

The boy just nodded.

"There'll be plenty of people to play tomorrow, but as the weeks go on, we're always looking for a good player. Maybe you could fill a spot."

"Sure," Joshua answered as they stepped up onto the porch.

His whole body was bursting at the thought of maybe playing ball with the men. With sad realization, though, Joshua remembered that he would be working the clambake in the morning. Maybe Mr. Nilsson would let him ride the bicycle down there for part of the game. Another sudden insight hit him as he entered the back hallway and saw Mrs. Van Houtten. He wasn't a guest at the inn; he was the hired help.

It seemed like the days of late June and early July went on forever. It was light until well after dinner, and people strolled about the grounds. The breeze coming off the pond kept the mosquitoes at bay for the most part. Joshua spent some time walking Nettie around the yard. Old Cal's treatment seemed to be working. The horse wasn't limping or favoring her other legs at all. Mr. Nilsson said that Old Cal would be stopping by sometime this evening to check on her and probably take Lucky back to his place. The stall was getting a little cramped at night, but the two horses seemed to be getting along fine.

The boy fell asleep that night dreaming of Injun Joe on the loose. Tom had testified in court, and the murderer escaped out of the window before anyone could stop him. Joshua felt like he was being chased by Injun Joe around the island out in the pond. No matter how fast he ran, the killer stayed right on his heels. Suddenly though, he appeared on top of the big flat rock with a knife to Mary's throat. Joshua stood helplessly by, while he watched his sister scream for mercy. Joshua woke with a start and realized that he hadn't put the kerosene lamp out yet. Knowing that Mr. Nilsson would be upset with him, Josh let the loft fall into darkness. Remnants of the dream still haunted his mind, but voices outside in the driveway caught his attention.

Joshua got up out of his bed and silently stepped over to the screen on the other side of the loft. He could hear sounds of men talking and singing, but couldn't see anyone. There was some movement out on the road, and the boy tried to focus on the exact spot where it was coming from. He thought he recognized Kenyon's voice. He was singing a song, but Josh had no idea what it was. Harry and George's voices accompanied them, and soon the trio broke into uncontrolled laughter. Josh figured that Edward was probably out there too. The sounds of their voices drifted away as if they were moving down toward the beach.

Joshua pulled on his long pants, laced up his shoes, and quietly lowered himself down the ladder. The barn door squeaked when he opened it, but not enough to cause anyone to stir inside of the inn. The place was in darkness. Joshua had no idea what time it was either, but he could see the three quarter moon high in the sky, so he knew that it must be getting late. Up ahead on West Beach Road, Josh saw the four of them arm in arm, swaying down the road. He crept up behind them, but didn't get too close. They stopped every few feet, and from the bushes at the edge of the road, Joshua could see them taking long pulls from a bottle. He wondered if they got it from the old shack, or if maybe they had been down to the breachway.

As he got closer, Joshua realized that they were all singing different songs. There was no accompanying, it was just random lines from some of the latest tunes. He inched closer, not really knowing why he was doing it.

"... Hoo-oo ain't you coming out tonight ..."

"... By the light, by the light, by the light of the silvery moon ...," one of the voices sang as his body veered off and tripped into the bushes. The other three laughed uproariously, but continued with the singing.

"... Come, Josephine, in my flying machine ... my flying machine."

"... Put your arms around me, honey... "

"That'll be the day when some girl puts her arms around you, Edward," Kenyon's voice said.

"At least I'm not chasing after some hired girl at the inn."

"Who said I was?"

"...Any little girl, that's a nice little girl, is the right little girl for me ..."

"... Let me call you sweetheart ..."

The quartet burst into laughter again at the lyrics they were singing. They stopped and each took a chug from the bottle. One of them finished it off, and tossed it into the woods. They continued their progress down the road, and veered off toward the beach when they came to the fork.

"... All aboard for Blanket Bay ..."

219

"... I've got the time; I've got the place, but it's hard to find the girl for me ..."

"... She's under the yum-yum tree... the yum-yum tree..."

"... If you talk in your sleep, don't mention my name..."

Joshua scooted from bush to bush along the edge of the road. Up ahead he could see the men following the path down to the shore. Actually, it looked like they were just tramping over the grass and not paying much attention to the sandy pathway. Joshua waited until they were on the beach before he crept any farther. The moon shone down on the open area, and although he didn't think the men would notice him, he still wanted to be careful. This was the first time that he had ever snuck out at night, and he didn't want to get caught. Joshua was having too good a time, and he looked forward to going on other adventures after dark.

Once he got to the edge of the dunes, he could see that the men were gathering driftwood up along the high tide line. With a quick burst, Josh dashed over to where one of the larger rocks sat down near the water. He tried to map out a path that would get him closer, but give him enough cover to remain hidden. One of the men was trying to light the pile of grass and sticks as the others looked on. Joshua moved ahead a little bit as they focused on what they were doing. Within a minute or two, the flame was slowly building, and then roaring. Joshua could hear the crackling and popping of the driftwood as it burned. The men cheered at their accomplishment, and then sat around the fire and continued their singing. They went round and round, each adding to the song. What started out as a simple melody, soon became a mish mash of confused lines from many different tunes. Joshua listened to their enthusiasm as the fire burned in front of them.

"... Til the sands of the desert grow cold ..."

"... Til the sands of the beach grow hot ..."

"... When I was twenty one and you were sweet sixteen ..."

"... When the midnight choo-choo leaves for

Alabam'… "

"… It's a long way to Tipperary …"

"… It's a long, long way to Tipperary," everyone joined in, and they kept singing over and over again. "It's a long way to Tipperary… Tipperary… It's a long, long way to Tipperary."

"Hey, what's that?"

"What?"

"I just saw someone over there."

"Where?"

"Over by those rocks."

"You're seeing things."

"Maybe it's your new girlfriend, Kenyon."

Joshua sat frozen behind a small rock; crouched, but breathing heavily. He had just bolted across an open space that was bigger than he thought. One of the men saw him, and he wondered if they would come over and investigate. They were quiet now, and maybe they were walking toward him right this moment. He didn't know what he would do if they found him there. Out from the bottom of the rock, he dared to take a glimpse of what was happening by the fire. The men were all staring his way, but it seemed like they were focused a few feet behind him. There were some other rocks nearby that he could use to stay hidden, but he didn't dare move.

"I know what I saw," Harry said, and Joshua watched as he tried to get to his feet. The man couldn't keep his balance and quickly fell back down. The other men laughed at their friend, but Joshua used this moment to escape. He bolted up from where he was hiding and took off back down the beach.

"There!" A voice yelled from behind him.

Joshua ran with all of his might. The sand made it seem like he was running underwater. He couldn't get the speed that he wanted. All the boy kept thinking was that he had to get to the path. If he could reach the road, then it would be easy for him to duck into the bushes somewhere. The only thing that would give him away then was his heavy breathing.

"That way!" Another voice shouted.

They were definitely in pursuit. Joshua wasn't

sure what they would do if they caught him, but he sure didn't want to find out. Up the path he went, and as he made his turn, he could see all four of them running up the beach. Now that the ground beneath was getting a little more solid, Joshua was able to pick up some more speed. He tore up the dirt roadway and made it out to West Beach Road ahead of the pack. Instead of running back to the inn, Joshua took a left and headed into the direction of the breachway. He figured that the long stretch of road back to the Pond View would give the men ample opportunity to catch up to him. His plan was to get around the bend of the road and duck into the back path.

Joshua's feet had a mind of their own, and he sped along the road with wild abandon. He could hear the men now; they were at the fork in the road.

"There he is!" Joshua heard a voice yell just as he was getting around the turn.

He would have to pour it on if he wanted to get into the pathway before they made their way around. The road kept curving after the opening in the trail, so the men would think he was heading down to the breachway. Joshua would be well on his way back to the inn before they knew any better. Without looking back or even slowing down too much for that matter, Josh turned and hurried down the path. The roots that spread throughout the path made him stumble, and the branches that hung out slapped across his face. The moon's reflection didn't cut through the underbrush too well, so Joshua quickly found himself in almost total darkness. This forced him to slow down, and in doing so, he had a moment to think about his predicament. The men were chasing him from one side, and the dark haunted path lay ahead. Although he knew that those stories were just a myth, his mind started to play games with him.

Off in the distance, he could hear the men running down West Beach Road, so Joshua knew that he was safe for the moment. His slow trot became a walk, but with the quiet, came noises from deep in the brush. Mosquitoes swarmed around his head, and all attempts to swat them away were futile. He could hear rustling sounds nearby, but couldn't see a thing. As he got closer to where he thought the shack might be, he began to think about the possibilities of spirits floating about. Although he knew that the stories were made up to protect the liquor that was stored there, his brain wouldn't totally accept the idea. Again, Joshua started to run. Quickly though, he fell flat on his face and banged his chin. Just as he was getting up, Joshua heard loud thrashing behind him. Voices echoed through the path. The men must have realized that he didn't go down to the breachway. Once they got to the long straightaway, the moonlight would have showed an empty road.

He started to run again, picking his feet up high, so the roots wouldn't pull him down again. Before he realized it, Josh was out of the path and near the lower part of the yard to the inn. He sped up to the barn as quickly as his tired feet would take him, and went around to the front. He poked his head around to look into the backyard. Because he was breathing so heavily, he couldn't hear where the men were. There was no sign of them, but once his panting subsided a bit, he thought he could hear bushes being trampled off in the distance. He didn't think that they had made it too far into the path.

Quietly, Joshua opened the barn door and slipped inside. The creaking sounded ten times louder now, but he didn't think there were any ears near enough to hear him. Upstairs in the loft, Joshua looked out through the screen. He couldn't hear the men any more, and he didn't see them coming up into the yard. The boy figured that they must have gone back out to West Beach Road to continue their search, or better yet, maybe they had given up.

Joshua took his shoes and pants off and settled down in his bed. Although he was scared when he was running away, Josh was glad that he went out exploring. Maybe he would venture out again sometime; only he would be much more careful. He felt the bottom of his chin and winced. The fall on the back path had rattled him, and as he felt along where he banged it, he thought that he felt some wetness. The blood seemed to be just at the surface, and he reminded himself to wash it off when he got up in the morning.

Tom Sawyer would have been proud of him tonight. Joshua drifted off with thoughts of further adventures in the near future.

16

Kip's barking stirred Joshua from his slumber. When he opened his eyes, he immediately saw that the sun was higher in the sky than usual. He had no idea what time it was, but knew that it was late. Getting out of bed, he saw a child chasing the dog around the yard. There were a few other guests out there also. Down by the pond, Josh saw Mr. Nilsson pulling the seaweed out of the water. He looked to be having a difficult time of it.

Racing down the ladder, Josh went quickly to the big wooden sink and turned on the water. He gazed into the small mirror and saw the scrape on his chin, as well as a few welts on his nose and forehead. He figured that the branches were slapping him harder than he thought. With a hasty rinse and another glance in the mirror, Josh could see that some of the blood was washed away, so he headed out into the yard.

"Good morning, young man," Mr. Nilsson said in a stern voice.

"I'm sorry that I slept so late."

"Grab the other end of the net, and we'll pull this seaweed closer to the shore."

The rope felt tight on Joshua's fingers, but slowly the large mass of seaweed began to drift in toward them and mound up in the shallow water. There was an odor coming off the pile, but it wasn't nearly as bad as the heaps of seaweed out by the garden in the early spring. This still had a fresh, salty scent to it.

"I set the canvas next to the pit, so now we have to haul this over there."

Joshua didn't ask any questions. He knew that Mr. Nilsson was angry with him, and understood why. The Fourth of July was the biggest day of the summer, and the boy should have been up two hours ago, so he

225

could help out. There was no reason for him to go sneaking around the beach the night before. Kenyon and the others could sleep as late as they wanted to; they didn't have the responsibility down here like Joshua did. With a quick grab of the pitchfork, Joshua immediately began to haul as much seaweed as he could up to the canvas. Water dripped in thin line as he made his way up the path, and a puddle steadily built in the low points of the tarp.

Sweat poured off Joshua's body. The humidity was back, and the boy felt the sun's heat, even though it wasn't much higher than the trees in the front yard. It was going to be a hot one today. Josh tried to imagine what it would be like with the fiery pit below him and the burning sun above. Shaking off those thoughts, he continued to carry forks of seaweed from the pond. Mr. Nilsson was huddled over the far corner of the pit with a long match in his hand. Reaching down beneath the layers, he attempted to light the paper on the bottom. He was crouched on the grass with his arm buried up to his shoulder. Although Josh wanted to stop and help, he continued back and forth from the pond. Swirls of smoke came out of the corner as the old man moved over to the next one.

Joshua couldn't believe how much wood was stacked inside of that pit. It reminded him of the day he and Mr. Nilsson had chopped down those trees up on the other side of the Post Road. The pit seemed to hold at least one whole tree within its domain. Josh could hear the crackling of the logs when he approached the pit now. It echoed the sound of the fire on the beach the night before. He wondered if the men had seen who they were chasing last night. Joshua couldn't figure out why he was running from them or why they were chasing him. Maybe it had something to do with the empty bottle that they threw into the bushes. Joshua knew that alcohol made people behave differently. When he saw them playing ball in the yard the day before, Joshua looked up to them, but seeing them stagger down the road gave him a whole different image.

"How much do you have left down in the pond?"

"I think that I got most of it... maybe a few more trips," the boy answered as he went back toward the water.

Joshua pulled on the netting and dragged the rest of the seaweed up onto the shore. Untangling the line, he set it off to the side and continued with the pitchfork. The mound ran the length of the pit and was piled higher than Joshua's knees. Mr. Nilsson headed back up to the inn as the boy hauled the last of the seaweed up to where the fire was starting to burst through the top of the stack of wood. Waves of heat came out of the hole, and Josh could feel it on his face. He watched it burn; mesmerized by the whole thing. The fire snapped and sent small embers flying in all directions. Joshua knew this wood was dry, and that it would burn nicely.

"Here you go," Mr. Nilsson said as he handed Joshua a large glass of lemonade and a plateful of johnny cakes.

"Thanks," Josh said as he took the peace offering from the man.

"I'm sorry that I was cross at you. I keep forgetting that you're not a twenty year old, even though you work like one."

"It's my fault I woke up late. I heard some noises last night, and I got up to investigate. Then I couldn't get back to sleep."

"Oh, that hooting and hollering. Sometimes the young men around here get a little out of hand."

Joshua ate his pancakes in silence. He didn't want to go into too many details about what happened the night before. He wasn't as innocent as he made himself out to be, and he didn't want Mr. Nilsson to know that he was roaming around the beach after midnight.

"We'll let this burn for awhile. After the fire goes down, we'll start to pull the clams and lobsters from under the dock."

Joshua nodded as he shoved the remains of his breakfast into his mouth. As the man went up toward the house, Joshua drifted down to the dock for a moment. It was the Fourth of July. So much had happened in his life over the last three and a half months. He had found a new home and a new way of life. Quonochontaug breathed a new spirit inside of him. This was so different than the existence he had in Providence. Joshua couldn't even imagine what life would have been like this summer if he was still there. He would probably be huddled in some corner of the house waiting for something to happen, but knowing that nothing would. His mother and grandmother would try to get him going, but their pity would overshadow any assistance that they could possibly provide. Now his mother treated him like she used to, before everything happened. Thinking about it for a moment, he realized that there was more to it than that. She acted as if he was all grown up now; like he was providing for the family; like he was the man of the house. Mary's hopes for him were finally coming true. Joshua vowed not to let Mr. Nilsson down again. His plans for further adventures during the nighttime hours faded as he realized the obligations that he had to his mother, the Nilssons, and the Pond View Inn.

Walking back up to the porch, Joshua saw that Mr. Nilsson was unfurling some red, white, and blue cloth. He went up to help and found that they were big half circles of material resembling an American flag. They draped each section over parts of the porch railing and then tied the ends off.

"Go out in the yard and see if it's even," Mr. Nilsson said.

Joshua bounded off the top step and went out by the flagpole.

"The left hand side is drooping a little bit."

Mr. Nilsson reached over and pulled up the banner.

"How's that?"

"Better," Joshua answered as the man tied it off again.

Mr. Nilsson also had a pile of smaller flags that were attached to three foot long dowels. He handed them to Josh and told him to set each one in the ground around the yard. The boy took the armful of flags and walked down the steps. He looked around and tried to figure out where the best places to put them would be. He counted fifteen, but soon saw that one of them was ripped down the middle. He placed two at the front corners of the tennis court and did the same at the four corners of the croquet area. Six of them lined the front section of the porch, and he put the remaining two at the sides of the step onto the dock. The fire was now burning down nicely. From the edge of the pond, Joshua looked up and the inn became a wavy blur. The heat that was coming out of the pit was unbelievable.

Guests wandered down by the fire after they finished up their breakfast. Mothers and fathers warned their children to stay clear. As Joshua looked into the pit, he could see the rocks shifting their positions as the wood burned away. Mr. Nilsson came down with a couple of clam rakes, and handed one to Joshua.

"Try to even everything out. We'll start putting the seaweed on in a little while."

Joshua looked up from his scraping and saw the four young men slowly walking out into the backyard. They all had baseball gloves with them, and Harry was carrying a bat. He watched as they walked around to the front of the house and disappeared. With a sudden longing, Joshua wanted to follow them and watch their game. He continued to rake the pit though, as sparks flew into the air. Heat drenched his body in sweat, and he hoped that the actual cooking of the seafood wouldn't be so brutal.

"Do you think it would be okay if I went down to the ballgame after we load everything?"

"I don't see why not. We'll just be waiting around. Why don't we go set up some of the tables and chairs now, so the ladies can start setting things up in the yard."

Joshua finished up in the far corner of the pit, and then dropped the rake onto the edge of the mound of seaweed. The smell was getting stronger, so he hoped that they would be feeding it into the fire pretty soon. They hauled some tables from the barn and the inn out to shady parts of the backyard. The wind had risen slightly, but the morning was still heating up. Mr. Nilsson had mentioned that there was going to be an ice delivery today, and Joshua couldn't wait to run his hands over the large blocks. Most of the chairs came out of the dining room and sun porch, and lined up nicely along both sides of the tables.

Mother came out with some tablecloths, and she and Louise clipped them down to the tables. Mrs. Nilsson and the other girl started to bring out dishes and glasses as well as, large empty platters. Josh and the old man set an old beat-up table a few feet from the pit. Mrs. Nilsson placed the platters on top of it, and then peeked in the fire.

"Oh my, it's coming along isn't it?"

"I think we're almost ready to start," Joshua answered.

The boy and man went down to the water's edge to start retrieving the clams. They each grabbed one side of the first bushel basket and hauled it out. Water spilled out through the slats as they carried it up to the pit. Mr. Nilsson led them over to the opposite side from where the seaweed was sitting. He had placed six metal trays out on the ground. They were just under two feet square and came up about three inches. The bottom and sides were lined with metal slats in a criss-cross fashion.

"Place the clams in these bins carefully. Try not to crack any of the shells."

"Can I pile them on top of each other?"

"Sure, fill each one up to the top."

Joshua took handfuls of the clams and gently placed them on the metal trays. As he filled each one, Mr. Nilsson brought another bushel basket up and gave him the next tray to fill. After a short while, all of the cherrystones, steamers, razor clams, and mussels had been distributed in all of the bins.

"Go up and fetch that fruit crate, so we can put the lobsters in. And grab those gloves under the workbench."

Joshua raced up to the barn. The excitement of the clambake was starting to build inside of him. Mr. Nilsson had explained the process to him a number of times, but he still wasn't sure how the whole thing was going to happen. Banging into the doorway on the way out, the boy stumbled for a few steps, and then continued his dash back to the pit.

Mr. Nilsson had pulled the large crate out from under the dock, and when Joshua got down there, he could see the clawed creatures moving about beneath the surface. With the right hand glove on his hand and the left one on Mr. Nilsson's hand, they started to pluck the lobsters from the crate. The movement of the box had stirred the bottom up, so it was difficult for Joshua to tell where one ended and the other one began. He leaned his other hand on the side of the crate and reached in with the glove. Grabbing at what he thought was the back of a lobster, Joshua felt the claw clamp down on the glove. It got him between the index finger and the thumb. Although there wasn't any pain, Joshua panicked a little bit. The lobster had his glove firmly in its grasp, and Josh tried to shake it off.

"Don't let it get away. Step out of the water and work it off."

Joshua did as he was told, and once he was away from the other lobsters, he began to settle down a bit. Grabbing it by its back, he twisted and turned it until the lobster let go. Actually, it was more like tearing the material on the glove than anything else. Joshua popped the lobster into the fruit crate and tried for another. The water had cleared enough for him to be able to pick out the different body parts of the creatures, so he was able to clamp down on them much more easily. The blue crabs gave them a little difficulty, because by the time they got to them, all of the lobsters were already out of the crate. This gave the blue crabs ample room to move around. They seemed to able to fly through the water. After a minute or two of trying snatch at them, Mr. Nilsson decided to just pull the crate out of the water. This worked much better, and they were able to resume their duties quickly.

With everything lined up on both sides, they were ready to begin. A small crowd gathered nearby to watch the start of the clambake. Joshua and Mr. Nilsson evened out the rocks again inside of the pit. They were glowing now. Most of the wood had burned away, so an open pit of hot stones sat before him. He prayed that he wouldn't fall inside as he was heaving the seaweed in, because he knew that it would either mean instant death or a life of pain and misery. They each grabbed the pitchforks and got ready to start. Mr. Van Houtten came down through the yard with Mary Rose in his arms. Mr. Nilsson waited until the man came to the front of the group of people before tossing anything in.

"Are we ready to begin our Independence Day clambake?"

"All set, Mr. Van Houtten," Mr. Nilsson answered.

He turned to the crowd of guests who were looking on with anticipation.

"Are we ready to start our celebration?" He shouted to the crowd.

A loud cheer arose, as people applauded the clambake and their country.

"Okay, Mr. Nilsson, let's get our clambake going."

With these words of encouragement, the man and boy began to toss clumps of seaweed onto the hot stones. The sizzle was immediate, and then the steam blinded Joshua for a moment. He wobbled a bit, but felt Mr. Nilsson grab him by the back of his trousers and pull him back.

"Watch out for that steam; don't look right at the seaweed when you throw it in."

Joshua nodded and wiped at his eyes. Blinking, he turned and filled the fork again. This time he just tossed it into the pit and turned back for another. He gave it some more, and then Mr. Nilsson put his pitchfork down and picked up the clam rake. Joshua did the same, and they both smoothed out the mounds of seaweed. Once everything was even, Mr. Nilsson handed Joshua the glove, and they began dropping the lobsters into the pit.

"Spread them out along both sides," the old man said.

Steam was getting into Joshua's eyes as he placed the creatures on top of the seaweed. When the fruit crate was empty, Mr. Nilsson picked up his pitchfork again and started to cover the lobsters. They fed a thinner layer into the pit. Again, they smoothed everything out with the rakes. Grabbing the sides of the trays that were filled with the clams, Mr. Nilsson and Joshua placed them on top of the next layer of seaweed. They were able to each stand on opposite sides of the pit as they performed this maneuver. Soon the entire hole was covered with shellfish filled containers. They tossed in the rest of the seaweed and brought the mound up and over the edge of the pit. As soon as the canvas tarp was empty, the old man and the boy pulled it over the pit. Mr. Nilsson pressed down on the middle with the back side of the clam rake. He tried to get everything even. Gathering the few remaining stones from the area, Joshua lined all four sides of the canvas to hold it down.

They stared at the tarp for a moment. The guests started to drift away, now that the excitement was over. Joshua figured that they would go down to the beach for awhile before everything was ready. As Joshua stared at the canvas, he could see tiny puffs of steam escaping from different spots. He went down to the pond and pulled a few more stones from the edge, and then plopped them down on the steam holes.

"It should take about an hour and a half or two before it starts to pop up. Then we really go to work."

"Do you think I should stay here?"

"No, I'll be around. People know that I'm not giving rides down to the beach today. They'll be strolling around. A lot of them will be down at the ballgame. Some of the women were talking about some kind of parade today too."

Joshua just nodded. He felt a little guilty about deserting Mr. Nilsson, but he really wanted to see the baseball game. He hadn't been to one all year. Last summer, he had walked by the field down in the South End, but he didn't have the heart to sit and watch. Josh casually kept track of the Red Sox last year, not really getting into the season like he had in the past. This year was going to be different. He knew that the Sox were going all the way. No one could catch them in the American League, and he had a feeling that McGraw's Giants were getting too old.

The boy's heart was pounding in his chest as he made his way back up the yard and into the house. He had to wash up a bit before going down to the field.

During his journeys through the roads around the beach, he thought that he could make out a mound and a diamond near where some of the cottages got their water supply. When he went by there in the past, the only thing around the pump was a field of high grass. Joshua hopped on the bicycle and pedaled as fast as he could. Dozens of people were walking around; families, as well as small groups of men, women, and children. Quonochontaug was finally fully alive. He could feel it as people waved to him as he sped by.

The field had been mowed and informal baselines had been drawn. A crowd of thirty or so people lined the right side, while a group of kids around Joshua's age and younger hung over by the pump at the well. He could see the men warming up out in the field. Kenyon was at third base, Harry at short, Edward in left field, and George behind the plate. Joshua didn't recognize the pitcher, but he quickly noticed how fast the man could throw.

"Yeah, yeah...Charlie... fire it in, fire it in!" yelled George from behind the plate.

The other players were a mystery to Joshua. He didn't know where any of them came from. He looked for Homer and Travis, but they weren't here. The men from the Life Saving Station didn't make it down for the game either. He tried to get a full glimpse of the men who were sitting on the bench, waiting to bat, but none of them seemed familiar.

"Play ball!" the umpire barked from behind the plate.

The practice balls dribbled in from the field, and Josh immediately wished that he had brought his glove with him. The first batter came up, tapping the bat on the bottom of his shoes. Joshua focused on the pitcher's wind-up and then follow through, as the ball whizzed into the catcher's mitt. The batter just stared as it sailed past.

"Strike one!"

The fielders cheered for their pitcher, and a few members of the crowd clapped as Charlie wound up again. The bat connected with a crack, and the ball cut foul into the bushes beyond third base. Joshua watched as the kids, who were at the pump, raced into the brush to retrieve it. The game continued, and the batter tapped a slow roller to third. Kenyon stepped forward, expertly scooped it up, and then fired it over to first for the out. The ball went around the horn, and then back into Charlie's mitt as the next batter came up.

"Let's go, Charlie ... no batter, no batter," Harry chanted from shortstop.

As the second man went down with three pathetic swings, Joshua thought that maybe he would be able to handle playing in this game. If that guy was allowed to play, then maybe he would get a chance. Before the next batter could come up, one of the boys came bouncing out of the bushes with the ball held high. He went over to the umpire and handed it to the man. Joshua watched as the umpire took a coin out of his pocket, and with a pat on the head, gave it to the kid. Joshua figured that he must have gotten a penny for finding the ball. He wondered if anyone could do that. Watching as the boys gathered back at the well, he thought that possibly he would do the same the next time he was at the field. Maybe he would ask Kenyon, if the time was right. Josh still worried that the men might have recognized him the night before.

The sides were changing before Joshua realized who had made the third out. His daydreaming about earning pennies made him lose his focus. If he was going to be part of this game someday, then he would have to learn to keep his concentration. Edward stepped to the plate, but before he could take the first pitch, a noise started to build from down the road. Heads turned as the drumming and clanging got closer. Joshua stood up on the rock he had been sitting on, and saw a strange sight. Women were marching toward the field with drums and bells. Many were holding large signs that said, 'VOTE' or 'SUFFRAGE'. They were singing a song, but Joshua couldn't make out the words because of all the noise from the clanging bells and beating drums. As they came over the hill, a few women cheered, but most of the crowd laughed at the parade that was going by. Josh recognized a few faces from the inn, but didn't see Mrs. Van Houtten among them. The group of twenty women marched on by, and the game continued. Joshua could still hear the beating and clanging as they wove through the streets.

Edward poked a single up the middle, and when the first pitch came into the second batter, he stole second. After a pop foul to the catcher, Kenyon came to the plate. Josh noticed the respect that the fielders gave him as they stepped back deeper in to the field. The pitcher for the other team wasn't as powerful as Charlie, and when the ball came in, Kenyon slapped it deep down the third base line, foul. Again the boys raced out, but the left fielder retrieved the ball from the high grass. With a few groans and kicks to the ground, the boys returned to the pump.

From the way the pitcher came around on his next throw, it looked like a curve ball was coming at Kenyon. He shifted his left foot into the plate and sent the ball flying to the opposite field. It bounced by the right fielder, and Edward easily crossed home plate. Kenyon rounded second as the ball was coming in. The relay was right on the money to the third baseman, but somehow, Kenyon slid under the tag. The crowd cheered as the young man stood up and dusted himself off. Shouts of praise and encouragement came from the bench. Kenyon scored on a sacrifice fly to center before the side was retired.

Joshua watched the game for a few more innings. The day was heating up, and Joshua wasn't looking forward to putting his face down in that pit again. He tried to look for gaps in the field as each batter hit the ball. The infield seemed to play in too close, while the outfield played it safe. The shallow spots in all three areas seemed like opportunity knocking. Even when a few hits dropped in, the fielders really didn't make any adjustments. Tris Speaker would have been mortified to see those hitters get to base. His speed in the outfield was beginning to be legendary. Who else, but him, could make an unassisted double play from centerfield?

Although he wished that he could stay for the whole game, Joshua knew that he had responsibilities back at the inn. Slowly, he climbed back on the bicycle and tried to ride away. He sat and watched as another batter was thrown out at first base. Forcing himself, Joshua wheeled the handlebars around and left the field.

He knew that there would be other days for baseball, but he just wished that he didn't have to leave. As he pedaled away from the field, Joshua made a plan to play ball around the inn as much as he could get away with, so the men could see that he had some talent. Maybe one day, when they were short a player or two, he would get the nod to join them.

Guests were all around when Joshua pulled back into the inn. They were playing tennis and croquet, as well as just strolling or sitting around the yard. He could see that both canoes were gone from the dock, but couldn't find them anywhere on the pond. Josh figured that they must have been over at the breachway. Mr. Nilsson was down by the clam pit, but there was no noticeable bulge in the canvas tarp. He walked down to where the old man was raking away some of the extra seaweed.

"How long?"

"I'm not sure. It could be any minute."

"I'll go see if they need any help up in the kitchen."

"Just make sure you keep half an eye down here. When it pops, we've got to get moving fast."

Joshua walked by the table with the empty platters and figured that they would need twice as many to fit all of the food that was going to come out of the hole. In the kitchen, Mother and the two girls were feverishly filling bowls with an assortment of food. Mrs. Nilsson was by the stove over a large boiling pot.

"Can I do anything?"

"I thought that you were going to help Mr. Nilsson." Mother answered.

"It's not ready yet."

"Oh ... You can bring some of these bowls out and put them on the tables. Grab some of those salt and pepper shakers too. When you come back, you'll need to bring more bowls and platters down to Mr. Nilsson."

Joshua nodded and walked back down through the backyard. A slight breeze was coming off the pond. The flag waved over his head as the boy passed under it. Spreading the bowls on the tables, Joshua looked down toward the pit. He could see the tarp beginning to swell slightly. Mr. Nilsson looked up at the boy and gave him a nod. Josh sped back to the house, grabbed the rest of the empty serving plates, and brought them down to Mr. Nilsson's table.

They both stared as the canvas began to rise higher and higher. People started to gather around them. It was an amazing thing to see. The hot stones were cooking the seafood and making the covering bloat. The rocks on the sides started to move a bit, and gaps started to leak out steam.

"Now?" Joshua asked.

"Not yet, we'll give it another minute or two."

Joshua watched as the bursts of steam seemed to be panting along the ground. The swollen tarp looked ready to burst, and the smell of the pressure cooked seaweed was starting to escape. For a moment, Joshua thought that the whole thing was going to explode. He watched as Mr. Nilsson kicked away a few stones and let the hot air out. Joshua could just imagine what this experience was going to be like.

17

Dear Mary,

You won't believe what happened yesterday. We had this great big clambake at the inn. Mr. Nilsson and I have been getting clams, lobster, and other shellfish for awhile now. We loaded everything in the pit and waited for it to be ready. When we finally pulled the tarp, it was amazing. The steam was rising through the seaweed like crazy. When I raked the top layer of seaweed away, the clams and mussels and steamers were all open and cooked. We had gloves on as we pulled the metal trays from the steamy pit. I couldn't believe how hot it was. Mother, Mrs. Nilsson, and the hired girls helped carry the platters of food as Mr. Nilsson and I unloaded the racks.

People were so excited by the whole process. They cheered us on as we lifted each thing from the pit. Mr. and Mrs. Van Houtten were directing the festivities, and for awhile, it seemed like we were all part of the same team. Mr. Van Houtten even grabbed one of the rakes when we finished with the clams. He peeled back the next layer, and a whole line of red lobsters appeared. Mr. Nilsson and I grabbed them and filled the platters as Mother handed them to us.

I felt like a grown up while I was working the clambake. People treated me differently for the rest of the afternoon. I was grimy from all the labor, but it was worth it. Kenyon came and patted me on the back, and I told him that he had great game down at the ballfield. I saw him get a triple and make two double plays. He also made a diving catch of a sharp line drive right down the third base line.

I got to eat one of the lobsters. Mrs. Nilsson sent me into the kitchen for some more dishes and told me that there was a surprise for me behind the bread box. She had made a plate of lobster, clams, steamers, and mussels. There was even a small cup of melted butter to go with it. I loved the lobster, clams, and steamers; but the mussels had a funny taste to them. When I came back outside with the napkins, I thought the whole day was going to be ruined. Dark thunderheads lined the horizon to the north. We could even hear some rumbles, but the sea breeze that kicked up later in the afternoon kept the rain away.

After I helped clean up and changed my clothes, I joined a game of catch that the guests were having. Mr. Van Houtten even put on a baseball glove. He threw me a few pop fly balls. Mr. Nilsson gave me a toss when a stray ball rolled down to where he was talking to one of the older guests. Since I had worked so hard all day, Mrs. Van Houtten didn't even give me one of her dirty looks when she came out back with a pitcher of lemonade.

The night was the best part of the holiday though. Mr. Nilsson and I hooked up Nettie to the cart and a bunch of the guests hopped on board. The horse's hoof seemed to be healing up fine, and I noticed that she wasn't favoring her other legs when she pulled away from the inn. We dropped off everyone at the beach and went back for more. After three trips back and forth, I settled down on the sand and watched the fireworks. Some men from the Bennett house set up a whole display for the crowd on the beach to watch. Others had rifles that they fired off in between.

I could see another display exploding in the sky over the breachway, and back the other way, there were fireworks bursting over East Beach. The whole sky was lit up. I wish you could have seen it. Mr. Nilsson brought some of the children and mothers back to the inn and told everyone else that they would have to walk back. Nettie seemed to be getting a little jittery with all of the excitement.

I walked down toward East Beach and found Elizabeth standing with some of her friends near a fire. She smiled when she saw me, and came over to stand next to me. We watched the fireworks together, and as I was looking up, she held onto my hand. No girl had ever done that before. It felt strange to feel her fingers moving in mine. After a few minutes, my palm started to get sweaty, and I was a little embarrassed. One of her friends came running over and grabbed her other arm and pulled her away. She said that she had to leave, and she gave me a smile and a wave as she disappeared into the darkness. I thought about following her, but decided that since I was out so late the night before, it was time for me to head home too.

I wandered along the beach through different groups of people. The fireworks display was starting to dwindle, and I was getting very tired. I wanted to get to bed, so I could wake up early and write to you before I had to go finish cleaning up around the yard. We left the stones in the pit, but I have to pull them out and then fill the hole back in. Mr. Nilsson and I also have to take all the shells and dump them back in the pond. He said that we would fill some buckets, row out a ways, and then empty them. I thought that we could bury them in the pit, but Mr. Nilsson said that it would cause too much of a mess for our clambake in August.

When I told mother about the Suffrage parade that I saw, she said that she's got her mind on too many other things to worry about voting.

Well, I have to get to work. It's nice and cool today, but we didn't get any rain. We could have used some for the garden, but I'm glad that last night wasn't spoiled. Mr. Nilsson is starting to get nervous now. He thinks that we might have to wet down the garden again, but he's not sure if the well can take it. I'm just hoping for some rain.

Your Brother,

Joshua

The next few days passed in a frenzied madness. Guests were all over the place by the weekend. Every single bed was filled, and some of the families even had to have their children sleep on the floor of their rooms. Mrs. Van Houtten was totally in her element. The more frantic things got at the inn, the calmer she seemed to be. Maybe it was the influence of Mr. Van Houtten that kept her at ease.

Joshua went nonstop from when he woke up in the morning until he dropped back down on his bed at night.

During the afternoons, it seemed like every other person on the beach forgot something back at the inn. Joshua sped back on the bicycle to retrieve a child's toy or blanket, and by the time he returned, he would have to ride back and get some snacks. He didn't mind it so much, he just wished that he could bring everything back at once.

After the beach, there were rides up to the store on the Post Road or down to the breachway. Mrs. Nilsson always needed a little something for the dinner. Joshua was sure that Mrs. Van Houtten had put her up to something unexpected, so the boy didn't blame the older woman for all the running around he had to do. This was his chance to get the newspapers. Every time he bought the Boston or Providence paper, Josh would stop along West Beach Road where the breeze from the pond cut across from west to east, sit on a big flat rock, and read the sports section. The Red Sox were having an amazing year. Their hitting was incredible, and their fielding and pitching were just as good. Tris Speaker was the team leader by example; doing amazing things in centerfield, as well as behind the plate. As Joshua read, he could just imagine what was happening at Fenway Park.

"I think we need to irrigate the field again," Mr. Nilsson said. "I'm worried about the well, but I don't think the vegetables will make it if we don't give them some water."

"It's getting pretty dry again."

"We'll need to get those pipes back over to Mr. Thornton, too."

"When do you want to do it?"

"Let's say Monday afternoon. Mrs. Van Houtten is having that dance tonight, and by late tomorrow afternoon some of the families and most of the men will be heading out to Niantic Station in Bradford, so they can be back to work."

At dusk, the guests started to congregate in the large sun porch, as other people began to arrive in carts and on foot. They were wearing masks over their faces. Mrs. Nilsson had said that Mrs. Van Houtten liked to have a masquerade dance each summer. Mother was dressed in her best attire as she served lemonade and plates of light snacks. Louise and the other girl were there also. From the lawn in the backyard, Joshua couldn't keep his eyes off her. She was wearing a dress that Joshua had never seen before, and she seemed to glide across the floor. Although there were other young ladies talking to Kenyon, his eyes seemed to follow Louise across the room. He was wearing a red mask with feathers coming out of both sides.

Mrs. Van Houtten was at her phonograph player, cranking the handle and playing her new records. People chatted for awhile, but as the darkness fell, they started to dance. Now he was behind the maple tree in the front yard. Mosquitoes buzzed in his ears, but the attraction of what was going on inside kept the boy glued to that one spot. Off by the barn, Joshua heard some giggling. Barefoot, he stepped lightly over to where he thought the sound was coming from. Around on the back side, near the windmill, there were two people. The moon was rising over the ocean, but its light was caught in the shadow of the barn. Josh was afraid that they might see him, but as his eyes adjusted to the darkness, he thought he recognized Kenyon and Louise. She was leaning against the wall of the barn, and he had one arm leaning against it.

"I have to get back inside," she giggled.

Joshua watched as Kenyon leaned in and kissed her. She pushed him away slightly, but then kissed him back. Joshua stood frozen, not knowing how to react. Before he knew it, though, Louise was walking directly toward him. Joshua turned and tiptoed around to the other side of the barn. It was his plan to hide on the pond side until they were both inside. He leaned against the barn and watched Louise walk onto the porch and into the kitchen. A sudden light broke Joshua out of his trance.

"Anything interesting going on?" Kenyon asked as he lit a cigarette.

Joshua's heart stopped. The man was smiling as he inhaled. Josh could see the embers of the cigarette brightening.

"Huh?"

"See anything interesting?"

"I was just going to bed, and I heard some noises."

"I'll bet you did. Was that you the other night on the beach?"

"When?"

"You know when. I don't mind that you're sneaking around, but if you run into someone who doesn't like it, then you might get yourself into some trouble."

Joshua just stood there as Kenyon took another drag on his cigarette. He began to stroll down toward the dock, but stopped and turned back to Joshua.

"Well, you better get to bed now," he said with a smile.

Joshua saw this as his dismissal, so he turned and headed back toward the front of the barn. There was some kind of a game going on inside the house, but Josh couldn't tell what it was. The guests were laughing and raising their arms above their heads. The boy stopped briefly, looked for a moment, and then disappeared inside the barn. Sitting on his bed, Joshua's heart was beating. He wasn't sure what was going on in Kenyon's mind. Was he angry with him or just trying to give him some advice?

Laying down, Joshua picked up Tom Sawyer and began to read. It took him awhile to be able to focus on the words, but slowly his mind drifted back to the reading. Tom was taking Becky on a picnic. Josh saw this as being a sign. As soon as things settled down, he planned to cut a path to the middle of the island, so he could bring Elizabeth out there. They could eat lunch on the big flat rock. Because he couldn't get back into the book without thinking about Elizabeth, Josh turned out the light and tried to go to sleep. The sounds from next door kept his mind going for awhile, but slowly he drifted off.

It was a good thing they irrigated the garden, because by the middle of the next week the heat became intense. Someone said that they heard that the temperature hit one-hundred degrees in New York City. It wasn't much cooler at the beach. The breeze was coming off the land, so the only escape was in the water. Joshua had only waded in up to his waist during the other times he was at the beach, but with this heat, he decided to dive right in. Other people had the same idea. Joshua had never seen so many bodies in the water at one time. Mothers and children were in up to their knees or thighs, but the men were out as far as Joshua. The waves weren't very big, so it was like they were swimming in a lake. The water was so refreshing that Joshua didn't want to get out. He practiced the swimming strokes that his father had taught him when he was younger. The muscles in his shoulders and arms pulled tight as he made his way back and forth in the chest high water. Although he didn't want to get out, he knew that the guests would be needing something or other.

Dripping, he walked up to where the ladies were sitting. Since they knew he was the errand boy for the inn, he didn't have to ask them if they needed anything. Joshua just made himself available. He checked the ropes on the canopy and rearranged some of the cups and snacks that were on the table. After a minute or two, the boy drifted back behind the canopy and let the sun dry the salty water from his body. There were some new faces at the inn, and Josh tried to remember their names. Two families from Springfield came in on the Monday train. Joshua thought their names were Peabody and Spellacy, but he wasn't sure. He didn't have enough actual interaction with the guests to get to know them very well.

As Joshua looked down the beach, he saw that people were getting up and walking down to the shore. Out in the ocean to the west, three or four miles, a fleet of white ships was coming around the point from Watch Hill. Four large boats cut through the water with a powerful force. As they got closer, Joshua saw that they were Navy ships. Some of the men had spoken about these boats at the clambake. They were making a tour of the east coast and doing training exercises out at sea as they went. People waved from the shore as the ships passed by. Joshua knew that the sailors wouldn't be able to see anyone, but he joined in anyway.

One of the ships fell back behind the others, and it looked like it dropped anchor. A launch came out from behind it and started to head in toward the beach. When it was about two-hundred yards offshore, the smaller boat came to a sudden halt.

"It hit a rock," someone said.

Joshua thought that he had heard a crunching sound just before, but he wasn't sure what the noise was. The sailors scrambled around the launch, trying to rock it back off. All attempts were unsuccessful. Joshua suddenly had an idea, and he ran up and over the dunes. Hopping on his bicycle, he raced down toward the breachway. Mason would be happy to know that he had the opportunity to rescue the United States Navy. Joshua couldn't pedal fast enough down West Beach Road. His legs seemed sluggish, and the bike just wouldn't move along. When he finally pulled into the little village, he dropped the bike and ran to the boardwalk.

The crew was out in their launch area with all of the equipment spread out onto the lawn. Joshua waved his arms, but no one seemed to notice.

"Mason!"

A few heads turned, and the man smiled over to Joshua. He waved.

"There's a boat stuck on a rock."

The man jumped to his feet and came over to the side of the breachway.

"Where?"

"Out in front of the beach. It's a Navy boat."

Mason nodded and turned to the other men. They had heard Joshua's words and were scrambling to get everything in order. Joshua watched as they rolled the rescue skiff down the cement launch area and into the water. Two of the men threw ropes and other equipment into the boat as the rest of the crew jumped in and began to row out from the breachway and into the ocean. A man came running onto the boardwalk, waving to the crew.

"There's a boat stuck out in front of the beach," he called.

Mason waved to the man as he hung onto the long handle of the rudder. The other six men were sitting with their backs to the direction they were traveling. Only Mason could see where they were going. He shouted directions to them as they rowed. Joshua trotted along the end of the boardwalk, watching the boat move through the water.

"Do they know about the boat?" The man asked.

"I just told them."

"Good work."

Joshua just smiled, knowing that he had thought quickly and acted on it without hesitating. Once he got to the end of the boardwalk, the skiff was pulling away from the shore. Joshua knew that there were rocks sitting just below the surface. The west wind helped to speed the skiff along. As they moved around the point, Josh ran back to the bicycle and hopped on. Homer was wiping his hands on a rag at the end of his driveway when Joshua sped past.

"Where's the fire?" He called out.

"There's a boat stranded out in front of the beach. The Coast Guard crew is going out to rescue it," Joshua yelled over his shoulder as he sped around the corner.

He could hear an engine fire up, and then before he could get back to the beach, Homer came speeding by in the automobile. Dust clouded Joshua's vision for a moment, but as Homer pulled ahead, he quickly gained his sight back. A large crowd had gathered on the beach by now. There must have been about a hundred people on the shore. The ship had sent another launch out, and it was trying to give the first boat some assistance. No one really knew what was going on, they just watched, waiting for something to happen.

A loud cheer went up when the boat from the Life Saving Station came around the corner. Joshua smiled to himself as he realized it was his doing that had brought the rescue boat out in front of the beach. When the skiff reached the other two boats, there looked to be much discussion, and then ropes were tied together. A few men climbed out of the stranded craft. The second launch and the rescue boat rowed a short distance away. As the ropes became taut, each of the crews began to pull on their oars. Within a minute, the launch eased off the rock and into the water. Again, the beach erupted in applause.

Both boats began to row in toward the shore, dragging the damaged one behind. As they got closer, a few members of the Coast Guard boat hopped out into the water. They pulled all three vessels onto the shore and assessed the damage.

"What's going on?" A voice said from behind Joshua.

"A boat was stuck on the rocks," he answered as he turned around and saw Elizabeth. She was in a full body bathing suit. The blue ruffles made her look different than Joshua was used to. "The crew from the Life Saving Station just pulled them off."

They watched as one of the Navy sailors pulled a box from the second launch. There was a gash in the bottom of the boat where it had rested on the rock. While the other members of the crew lifted it up from the sand, the sailor with the box scrambled under and began to patch it up. Joshua looked out at the ship that was still sitting out in the ocean. He could see other sailors lining the rails.

"That should hold it," he said as he crawled out from underneath. The man's accent was different; like he was from the South.

The Navy men dragged their boats back into the water and shoved off. Joshua didn't know why they were coming ashore in the first place, but he figured that they were so embarrassed about getting stuck on the rock, that they didn't want to stick around. They just got beyond the surf line and continued rowing back out to their ship. There wasn't a wave or any acknowledgement that they were thankful for the help that they had received.

People gathered around the crew that was still on the shore. Mason was telling them something, but he couldn't hear what it was. Joshua inched forward through the crowd with Elizabeth following him. Once he got to the front, he could see two other crew members looping the rope back together again. They had satisfied looks on their faces; knowing that they had come to the rescue.

"Here's our hero," Mason said as he pointed to Joshua.

Everyone looked over at the boy.

"He's the one who was smart enough to come down and alert us. We'd already done our sweep of the beach before the boat got stuck. Joshua here, came down and signaled us."

Joshua just smiled as he felt pats on the back from the people around.

"And young man," Mason continued, "that entitles you to dinner at the Life Saving Station. We can give you a ride over there right now."

Joshua felt his face starting to turn red. He didn't like all of this attention, and worst of all, he didn't know what to say. A ride back in their boat over the ocean would be an unbelievable adventure, but he knew that he had responsibilities, so he couldn't just leave the beach.

"I have some work to do down here, but I can ride my bike down to the breachway later on."

"That sounds great, we'll save a seat for you."

With that, the men pushed their boat back into the water, hopped in, and began to row back toward the breachway. The crowd gave them a big cheer as they popped up and over the waves that were rolling in. When Joshua turned back around, Elizabeth was just staring at him with a big smile on her face.

"What?"

"Oh, nothing."

Encouraged by Mason's words, Joshua worked up enough nerve to ask her on a picnic.

"We can do it next week when some of the guests start to leave. Mrs. Nilsson said that the inn won't be as crowded. We can go to the island right in the pond, and we can take the canoe out. In the middle, there's a big flat rock where we can eat."

"Maybe ... I'll have to ask my grandmother."

Joshua just nodded. She seemed like she wanted to go. Although he would have liked to spend some more time with Elizabeth right now, Joshua knew there was much work to be done to get the guests back to the inn. Mr. Nilsson would be arriving fairly soon.

"Do you want to go for a swim?" Elizabeth asked him just as he was about to turn and head back up to the canopy.

"Ummm ... let me go check and see how everyone's doing first, and then I'll meet you at the water."

249

Josh stared at the girl as she walked down to where the waves were washing up onto the beach. Breaking himself out the reverie, he shook his head and walked up to the canopy. Joshua started to pack up some of the supplies that were scattered around and under the table. He hauled one of the chairs up and over the dunes. Mr. Nilsson was nowhere in sight, and none of the guests had asked him for anything, so he decided to go for a quick swim.

Elizabeth was up to her knees when Joshua came running by, diving beneath the surface. He swam around back to her.

"Don't you splash me, Joshua Keegan."

He had a big smile on his face and pretended to slap his hand into the water. She ducked backwards a little bit, and when she did, a wave caught the front of her and sprayed her with salt water. Giggling, Elizabeth squatted down up to her shoulders and paddled over toward him.

"Okay, I'll go on a picnic with you, but it has to be an afternoon when I don't have to work around the house all day."

Joshua smiled and spun around in the water. Over at the dunes, Mr. Nilsson was carrying a chair up and over. With a sad realization, Joshua hopped up from where he was.

"I have to go, Mr. Nilsson's here, and I need to help."

"Okay, bye."

"See you later," the boy answered, wishing he could stay there until dark.

Dripping, Joshua grabbed another chair as the old man came back over the dunes.

"What was all the excitement that I'm hearing about?"

Joshua explained everything that had happened. Mr. Nilsson seemed especially interested in his quick thinking and his invitation to dinner.

"Why don't we get the guests back and unloaded. I think that Mrs. Nilsson is all set for dinner. The girls were getting things ready when I left."

Joshua raced ahead of Mr. Nilsson. He wanted to tell Mother what had happened before anyone else got there, and he would have liked to have Louise overhear it, but his mind was set on Elizabeth now. As he wheeled into the yard, he could see his mother taking clothes off the line. Joshua held the basket while he told her all of the details.

18

Mr. Nilsson had suggested taking the canoe over to the Life Saving Station, but Joshua wasn't good enough at paddling it, so he didn't want to embarrass himself. He rode his bike instead. As he pedaled his way down toward the breachway, Joshua was full of expectation. The crew seemed so proud of him, and Mason made it sound like the rescue was all his doing. Mother complimented her son on his quick thinking, and a few of the guests commented on what happened at the beach. Mrs. Van Houtten seemed pleased that her employee was smart enough to go alert the crew at the Life Saving Station. She talked as if Joshua had been part of the inn for years.

A group of nine and ten year olds were chasing each other through the street in front of the casino when Joshua wheeled in. They kicked up dust as they scurried by him. Leaning the bicycle up against a pole, Joshua walked over to the edge of the breachway. He didn't see any of the crew members outside, so he paced up and down the boardwalk while he waited. A few people were milling about. A man's hard shoes echoed as he hurried by the boy. At the dock just outside the porch for the Eldredge Hotel, a boy sat in a rowboat putting fishing line in a tackle box. He looked to be a little bit younger than Joshua.

"How about a ride across the breachway?" Joshua asked as he got closer.

"Where ya goin'?" The boy answered back as he looked up through squinted eyes.

"I'm going to have dinner at the Life Saving Station."

"How come?"

"I told them about the Navy launch that was stuck on the rock today."

"Oh, that was you?"

"Yeah."

"I woulda charged you a penny for the lift, but since you helped them out, I'll row you over for nothin'."

Joshua just nodded and climbed down into the boat. The boy undid the rope and pushed them away from the dock. It was less than fifty feet across, and since the tide wasn't coming in too strong, the boy only had to give it four or five strokes before they were across.

"What's your name?"

"Josh. What's yours?"

"Samuel."

"Hi Samuel, glad to meet you."

"I wish I was going to have dinner with the crew. They took me out in the pond one day. I sat in the front of their boat, and boy they got that thing moving across the water."

"I went across here in their rescue car. They shut me inside and pulled me back across."

"I saw them do that once. They fire off the cannon and a hook flies out."

"Yeah."

"Wow! Well, here we are, have fun."

Thanks," Joshua answered as he climbed out of the small boat and onto the cement launch area.

After pushing Samuel's boat back into the breachway, Joshua turned and slowly walked up toward the Life Saving Station. The large door was closed, so the boy walked around to the other side of the building. He could hear voices and laughter as he approached the screen door. With his hands cupped over his eyes, Joshua peered inside. Three of the men were in the kitchen area doing various tasks. It looked like Max was stirring something in a large pot, and Willy and Cliff were chopping things at different counters.

"Hello," Joshua quietly said.

"Hey, it's the kid," Max declared as he wiped his hand on the apron that he was wearing.

"C'mon in," Willy said as he walked over to the door. "Mason, the kid's here!"

Mason came in from another room with a short

length of rope in his hands.

"Hey Joshua, how're you doing?"

"Good."

"Great, come on in here; I was thinking that I'd show you how to tie some knots. You want to learn?"

"Sure."

Joshua followed Mason into what looked like a living room. There were pictures of boats and different crews lining the walls. A large window looked out to the ocean, and Joshua could see the small waves rolling into the shore. Mason actually had two lengths of rope in his hand, and he gave one to Joshua as they sat down on two wooden chairs by the front window.

"Okay, this is the working end, it's where all of the knots begin. You either have a loop or a bight."

Joshua watched as the man demonstrated the two styles.

"The rest is just called the standing part or standing end. Alright, the first one I'll show you is a standard bowline. You take an overhand loop, then pass the end through the loop, around the standing part, and then back through the loop."

Joshua watched as the man expertly flipped the line around and through. He had watched and listened, but Josh wasn't sure how the man did it.

"Just follow along with me."

The boy tried to mimic each movement and turn of the rope. The first knot just slipped away from him, but the second one held.

"Got it."

"Good, let's try it again, and then you're on your own."

Joshua watched Mason tie it, then followed along with him. Again the bowline held. When he tried it without Mason's help, though, he couldn't remember the last part. They went through it a few more times until Joshua was able to quickly tie the knot on his own. They worked through a buntline hitch and an end loop in much the same way. By the time dinner rolled around, Josh was able to tie a reef knot, a slippery sheet bend, and a sheepshank.

Dinner was a seafood feast. Joshua came to find out that the local fishermen treated the men of the Life Saving Station very well. Mason said that they had a meal allowance for the station, but that the local guys always gave them extra. Sometimes Max or Ben could get twice the amount that they paid for. A few fishermen had been hung up on the rocks during stormy times, and the crew had always come through for them. There was chowder and tuna steaks for everyone. The men seemed at ease with each other, and the ones who sat around while dinner was being prepared were the ones who cleaned up afterward. Since Joshua was Mason's guest, the man got off kitchen duty that night. They brought the boat down the ramp, and Joshua practiced his knots again. Mason let him keep the length of rope, and even showed him how to moor a boat to a pole with a tarbuck loop and then hitch a line to a cleat.

Five of the men gave Joshua a ride in the pond. Mason called out knots from the back of the boat, and Joshua tied them in the front. Of course, the boy couldn't use the terms front and back anymore; it had to be bow and stern. Left and right were port and starboard. Mason let him take the rudder, and he learned how to turn the boat from side to side. The man set a mark for him to shoot for; such as the buoy from a lobster pot, and Joshua had to take the boat around in as tight a circle as he could manage. Cliff gave up his seat, and let Joshua row for awhile. The oars were much longer than the ones on the dinghy at the inn, and he had to use both arms to pull it through the water. The men had a rhythm to their movements, and it took Joshua a few minutes to catch up to it.

"Do you want us to drop you at the inn?"

"My bike's at the breachway."

"How about if we go get the bicycle, put it in the boat, and row over there?" Mason asked.

"Sure."

"We have to do certain exercises each day in different locations."

"Oh."

"I log in all of our travels, and I noticed that we

haven't been to the east end of the pond for quite awhile."

They pulled back into the breachway and landed just beyond the King Cottage, where Joshua and Mr. Nilsson had gotten the fish guts for the lobster pots. The boy bounded out of the boat and raced to where he had left his bicycle. Riding it back, he tried to lift it up and over the rocks that lined the waterway. Cliff came to Joshua's assistance, and the young man easily hauled the bike over the bow and placed it on the bottom of the boat. Joshua scampered aboard, and just as quickly, they were back in the pond again.

Mason got the other crew members to really dig their oars into the water. Joshua could feel the breeze as the boat dashed across the still waters of Quonochontaug Pond. His neck jerked a bit as the crew pulled through the water. Mason coaxed them on, and before long, they were on the far shore on the Post Road side.

"Okay, Joshua, we're going to row along the bank here and look for any signs of debris. You need to keep your eyes open for rocks that might lurk beneath the surface."

"Alright."

"It's high tide, so we shouldn't have a problem."

The men took the boat along the shore. Joshua had never been to this side of the pond before. There were some rocky outcroppings along the edge that hung ten to fifteen feet over the water. He had seen them before, but being up close gave the boy a different perspective. Mason guided the boat into some small coves. The edges were marshy, and it seemed like water flowed into them from somewhere. Joshua tried to keep an eye on the water in front of them, but the scenery was too distracting. When he did look down, he could see long, stringy eel grass growing toward the surface or a shell-strewn, sandy bottom.

"What's that?" Joshua said as he pointed to a dark brown, shelled creature with a long pointy tail.

"That's a horseshoe crab. It's pretty strange looking," Mason answered from his standing position in the back of the boat.

Along the shore they went. Occasionally Joshua

looked up to see where they were. First he had to find the inn, and then he could gain some perspective on their location. They glided along almost silently for awhile. The only sounds were the dipping of the oars into the water. Mason kept his eyes on the shore.

"Rock!" Joshua yelled, probably too loudly, as he pointed ahead of them.

Mason easily steered around the boulder that lay hidden beneath the surface. Joshua could see the seaweed that clung to its sides as they passed by.

"Good job, Joshua. I forgot about that one."

They passed between the shore and an outcropping of rocks. The largest one was about forty feet long and looked like a giant loaf of bread. Joshua thought that this might be a good place for a picnic too. It was directly across the pond from the inn. All he would have to do was row over there, or maybe they could both take the canoe over. He wasn't sure if Elizabeth had any experience with paddling before.

As they approached the far east end of the pond, a smell started to creep into Joshua's nose. Beyond the shore, he could see a truck slowly working its way down West Beach Road. The odor got stronger as Mason wove between the rocks that were jutting out.

"What's that stink?" Max asked from where he was sitting.

"I'm not sure," answered Mason.

Joshua saw it first. The brown fur with black speckles was a distinct contrast to the bloody gash that ran along its side. Mason brought them into the grassy shore, and they all looked down at the small seal that lay still on the water's edge. Crabs scurried about as the boat skimmed the sandy bottom. The animal had been here for awhile. Some of its body had been eaten away by the crabs and other creatures. The smell was offensive, and Joshua's stomach began to feel nauseated as he looked down at the poor creature.

"What happened to it?" Joshua asked.

"I don't know. It could have been a boat or maybe a shark," Mason said.

"Probably happened out in the ocean, and she

drifted in here," Cliff added.

"Yeah, we've had that west wind for a few days," Willy said as he looked back to where the breachway was located.

Mason took out a long pole from the port side of the boat and reached over to the seal. Probing the deep cut on the side of the animal, he stared at its length. The man turned the seal over, but there weren't any other wounds.

"I don't think it was a shark ... probably a boat, or maybe a fisherman's gaff."

They left the seal where it was and continued their journey around the pond. The sun was starting to get low now. Joshua couldn't get his mind off the poor seal. The crew eased its way through the channel, and before Joshua even realized it, they were at the Pond View. Guests started to stream down toward the dock. The crew's appearance at their shore was a novel sight. Cliff handed the bicycle up to Joshua after he climbed up onto the dock.

"Thanks for dinner and the ride ... and for showing me how to tie knots," Joshua said almost mechanically.

"Thank you for coming down and alerting us today," Mason replied with a smile.

Joshua felt empty inside now. As he stood on the dock, balancing his bike, he just wanted to get away from everyone. The guests seemed to be surging down at him, and Joshua didn't know if he could get off the dock in time. He wheeled the bike to the end of the boards and let the wheels bounce down to the grass. A few mothers smiled at him as they led their children out toward the boat. Joshua pushed the bike a little way up the path, and then stopped to look back. The dock was crowded now, but when he waved goodbye, Mason gave him a wink and a nod.

Mother was up on the porch wiping her hands on a small towel when he came up into the yard. She smiled at him, but he didn't have the energy to respond.

"How was your dinner?"

"Good," the boy mumbled.

"What's the matter?"

Joshua continued over to the barn. Mother followed him and quickly caught up.

"What's the matter, Joshua?"

Tears were rolling down his cheeks now, and when he turned to her, a weak cry caught in his throat.

"We found a ... we found a dead seal in the pond."

"Oh Joshua," she said, as she put her hands on his face. "Leave the bike and come inside the house."

She led him into the kitchen and sat him down at the table in the breakfast room. She pulled another chair over next to him. His tears had stopped, but he had a vacant look in his eyes now. His mother smoothed his hair back and rubbed his shoulders. The look of concern in her eyes was slowly giving way to pity. Joshua looked over to her and blinked.

"I have to go bury it," he said in a determined voice.

"What?"

"The seal. I have to go bury it," he repeated with a little more enthusiasm.

"Not now, it's getting dark."

"In the morning then.

"I'll talk to Mr. Nilsson. Maybe he'll go over with you."

"No, I have to do it myself."

She held him by the shoulders and looked into her son's eyes. The empty look was gone, and there seemed to be some life coming back into the boy. He stood up and went over to the sink. Pouring himself a glass of water, Joshua didn't stop chugging until it was empty.

"I'll do it in the morning. There's a wide board in the barn that I can use, and I'll just bring a shovel," he said as he began to walk out the back door.

"Joshua, would you please help me put some things away around the kitchen?"

"Sure," he answered, suddenly with new life in him.

For the next half hour, Joshua related every single detail of his adventure with the Life Saving crew. He stopped at the point where he had alerted Mason to the rock beneath the surface. Mother seemed a little more at ease when Joshua left the inn to go to bed for the night. He fell fast asleep without another thought of the dead seal.

Dear Mary,

> *I had a very important thing to do today. I got up just as the sun was rising and went over to the end of the pond to bury a seal that we found yesterday. Mason thinks that it was hit by a boat or something. He's the head of the Life Saving Station. I had dinner over there yesterday.*
> *I brought a shovel and a board to lift the seal. I couldn't believe how wide awake I was as I started to head over there. It must have caught up with me when I got closer to where the seal was, because all of a sudden, I felt all the energy drain out of me. The tide wasn't fully in yet, so the seal was just laying on the muddy shore. I broke down, but it was a good thing. I cried and cried, but it felt different this time. I wanted to cry, and I just let it happen. It didn't feel like my brain was trying to control me anymore.*
> *When I was done, I just got out of the boat. At first I sank down in the gray mud, but once I got used to it, I just walked over to the dry land. My biggest problem was being able to dig down without hitting water. I had to keep moving back from the shore. I found a little mound that was sitting up higher than the rest of the ground. The digging was a lot harder than the pit for the clambake. I kept hitting rocks every time I put the shovel into the ground. After awhile though, I had a fairly decent hole. It was about two feet wide, two and a half feet long, and almost three feet deep. I felt the ground start to get muddy, so I decided to stop digging.*
> *Getting the seal over to the hole was hard. First I had to roll it onto the board. If the tide was up a few more feet, then things would have been easier. I tried not to think about the smell, but it was bad. Once I got the seal onto the board, I had to drag it about sixty feet over to the hole. It dropped off a few times because the ground was uneven. I had to work my way around some bushes too. When I finally got it to the hole, I didn't know what to do. I thought that I should say a few words, but nothing came into my*

mind. I tried to put the seal into the hole as gently as possible, but the whole thing just slid in when I tilted the board. When I was filling the hole back in, I tried not to look down.

Instead of going straight back to the inn when I was finished, I rowed over to your island. The egret wasn't there like I had hoped, but I sat on the shore for a few minutes and looked over at the inn. It was very quiet. I didn't even see Mr. Nilsson anywhere. A strange wave of energy came over me as I sat there, so I decided to do something. Taking the shovel, I started to clear out a path to the middle of the island. Vines and brush were all over the place, but I sliced through it with the shovel. Once I made my way to the middle, I went back and cleared it out some more. I kicked the brush to the sides, and before too long, I had a nice little path to the clearing in the middle. I'll have to go out there again with a clam rake and some clippers, but it looks pretty good now.

When I came back to the dock, I was sweating and smelly. The muddy clay from the other end of the pond really stinks. I went under the windmill and pulled the chain under the big wooden tub. Ice cold water sprayed all over me and washed the mud off. With dripping clothes, I went into the barn and changed. By that time I was starving, so I went inside and had my breakfast.

This seemed to be a good way to start my day. I finally feel like I'm getting some control of myself. If I had seen that seal two months ago, then I would have had a tough time of it. I'm just trying to stay positive about things now.

Your Brother,

Joshua

P.S.   I just finished reading Tom Sawyer. I'm glad everything worked out for him. Maybe I'll find a box of gold in my travels.

Once in a while, in the evening when there wasn't any dance going on, Mrs. Van Houtten had whist parties.

There were usually about sixteen ladies from the inn and other cottages. Joshua had to set up the four card tables and the chairs around each one. He dug the decks of cards out of the drawer at the end of the sun porch, as well as the pencils and pads of paper to keep score. He was starting to learn how to play the game, but the overall strategy still eluded him. Joshua couldn't figure out how each of the players knew what cards to play, especially since they teamed up with a partner. The basics of winning each trick and trying to stay with trump were easy, but the actual winning of the game was the hard part.

The ladies didn't seem that concerned about who won or lost. They just used the time as a social gathering. Joshua sat inside the sunporch with them, or just outside on the back porch, waiting to see if they needed him to get more refreshments. Although he tried to watch how they were playing the game, he couldn't help but overhear their conversations.

"... Harriet's doing just peachy after her operation. She should be down to the shore within a few weeks."

"... Myriam Eider sure was peeved when that classy automobile she was riding in broke down on the way in from Westerly."

"... Now when Kenyon gets married in the fall, he'll be able to start right away at her father's office."

Joshua's ears perked up at the mention of Kenyon's name. He had a sudden vision of the man and Louise on their wedding day.

"... Of course, they'll live in the city for awhile. It'll be a cinch for them to get an apartment."

"... Oh, what do you know about that? You haven't had to look for an apartment in New York for years."

Joshua was confused. He wasn't sure why Louise's father would have an office in New York City. He thought they were talking about Westerly.

"... Sure, sure... Helen will make a beautiful bride. Kenyon's such a fine young man."

Helen? Who was Helen? Joshua's mind reeled at the memory of Kenyon kissing Louise out by the barn. How could he do something like that if he was to be

262

married in the fall?

"... What's trump this hand?"

"... Hearts."

"... I hope they don't have any of those animal dances at the reception. I won't stand for them at my inn," Mrs. Van Houtten complained.

"... They've banned some of them at the dance halls, and some of the better families have refused to go to certain places until they do."

"... I don't see how these young people have the nerve to display themselves like that."

"... That kangaroo dip is obscene."

"... I've heard that the chicken scratch and the bunny hug can get you arrested in New London."

"... The whole thing is distasteful."

Joshua had never heard of these dances before, but the mention of them sparked his interest. He knew that he would never see such things at the Pond View, but maybe some of the other inns down at the breachway allowed it; especially the ones that served alcohol.

When the ladies broke up for the evening, it was Joshua's job to walk them back to their cottages. He carried a lantern in front of them while they walked. There were seven ladies who had to get to various places around the beach. They all walked together, and said their goodbyes as they walked down paths to where they were staying. None of them were guests at the breachway, so Joshua had to just make the rounds through the road to the beach, and then a short way down West Beach Road.

As he walked back to the Pond View by himself, Joshua couldn't get his mind off the fact that Kenyon was kissing Louise, while at the same time, planning to be married to someone named Helen. It just didn't make sense to the boy. He was sure there was some explanation, but he couldn't figure out what it was.

Back at the inn, Mother was cleaning up the glasses and small plates that were around the card tables. Joshua put the chairs back where they belonged and folded up the tables.

"What's on your mind, young man?" Mother asked

him as she was putting glasses on a platter.

"Nothing."

"I know when something's bothering you, now what is it?"

"Can you plan to marry one girl, but still be interested in another one?"

"What do you mean?"

"I heard that Kenyon is supposed to get married in the fall, but I think he likes Louise."

"He's getting married?" Mother asked in surprise.

"That's what the ladies were talking about."

"Rich people do things a lot differently than you and I."

"How's that?"

"Well, when your father and I were courting, there were certain responsibilities that each of us had to follow."

"Like what?"

"He had dinner at our house, and we went to certain functions together and had to behave properly. If he stayed out late with his friends, word always got back to me or my mother. It was a time when the two families were getting to know one another. By the time our wedding rolled around, we knew that we were right for one another."

"How is it different for the rich?"

"Well, for one thing, we never really left the neighborhood. Many of these people travel up to a hundred miles to spend time here. Also, we didn't have much free time. Your father and I worked sixty hours a week, sometimes more."

"Oh."

Joshua felt a lot better about things when he went out to the barn that night. He started to think about what he and Elizabeth might go through if anything developed between them. Before falling asleep that night, he vowed never to agree to marry anyone and then go behind the barn to kiss someone else.

19

When the rain finally came, it fell with a fierceness that Joshua hadn't seen or heard since the early spring. It started at night with a steady shower, but by morning, the wind was howling, and the rain was coming in torrents. Joshua had to close up the door on the pond side of the loft because water was streaming in. He ran over to the porch and then into the inn, and was dripping wet as he stood in the breakfast room. Mr. Nilsson was trying to shut the windows over the table.

"Joshua, why don't you run upstairs and close the windows in any of the rooms that don't have guests in them? I think there's two."

The upstairs hall was dark. The usual sunlight that streamed in wasn't to be found. Joshua entered the first room and pulled the windows shut. He went to the bathroom and got an old towel to dry off the windowsill. The rain had pooled up and was dripping down the wall. The other room was farther down the hall and on the street side, so Joshua didn't think that there would be too much water in there. He was wrong, but it was a different kind of water. As he came into the room, he could hear a noise. Off in the corner, there was someone sitting in the large, stuffed chair. In the dimness, he couldn't tell who it was. Although he didn't want to intrude, Joshua wanted to find out if there was a problem. As he moved closer, he could see that it was Louise, and she was sobbing into a handkerchief.

It didn't look as if she noticed Joshua yet, and he didn't really want to disturb her. He just went over to the window and pulled it down. The noise seemed to startle the young woman out of her crying, and her sobs slowly became sniffles.

"Are you sure that you heard them right?"

"What?" Joshua answered, not understanding the girl's tearful question.

"Is he getting married in the fall?"

"Kenyon?"

"Of course, Kenyon."

"That's what the ladies were saying."

"Your mother warned me. I don't think she wanted to, but she probably thought she had to."

"I'm sorry."

"What's her name?"

"Helen."

Joshua stood frozen in the middle of the room. Louise's face was red and puffy from her crying. She just sat there and stared at the rain outside. Joshua looked at her, and then out the window. The wind was whipping the green maple leaves back and forth on the tree outside in the front yard. The whole thing seemed to sway, like some great beast, but the limbs thrashed in a frenzied fashion that made Joshua wonder if they would snap off and fall into the house.

"Helen. That's a nice name. I went to school with a girl named Helen."

Louise didn't seem to be talking to Joshua. It was like she was trying to piece the whole thing together in her mind. He didn't know whether to stay in here with her or leave the girl alone. Someone walked by outside the room and broke the spell. Louise wiped her eyes and stood up from the chair. Joshua stood in the same spot as she fixed her hair and then began to walk out of the room.

"Thank you for telling your mother. I don't like being the fool."

Joshua watched her as she turned the corner and strode down the hall. He wasn't sure what she meant by those words, but it was good to see that she had gotten herself back together again. Joshua took one last look around the room and then went up the stairs to the bunkroom. Young men were still lying around in their beds. A few were still asleep, and others were looking at books and magazines. Without a word Joshua went over to the windows and shut them. Kenyon was propped up on a pillow, looking at a sports magazine. Joshua felt like he betrayed the man that he looked up to. On the other hand, though, he tried to imagine if someone treated his mother or sister in the same manner. Joshua knew that he had done the right thing, but it didn't make his insides feel any better when Kenyon gave him a smile and a nod as the boy was walking back toward the stairs.

Joshua grabbed some eggs from the platter that Mrs. Nilsson was filling and went out on the back porch. Even as he stood against the outside wall of the house, he could feel the water splashing him. The pond had whitecaps coming in toward the shore, and rain kept falling in sheets up the yard. He decided to go eat his breakfast on the front porch. The wind wouldn't be whipping right at him, and Joshua could still sit and watch the rain come down. He thought of all the water seeping into the ground around his plants. This rain was exactly what his vegetables needed. The irrigation that he and Mr. Nilsson had done kept the plants alive, but this downpour would fatten those tomatoes right up.

In the front of the house, Joshua could see the little rivers of water running down the driveway to the road. He ate his eggs and watched the silvery raindrops fall onto the lawn. Large puddles formed all about the yard, as the soil couldn't keep up with the amount of water that was falling. This storm looked different than the ones in the spring. Maybe it was all the green on the bushes and the trees that made it seem odd. The deep, dark colors of the outside of the leaves contrasted with the lighter shades on the back of them. The wind's fury made them flap in such a way that the woods across the street seemed to be alive.

The inn felt smaller as the morning went on. With all of the guests milling about, waiting for the rain to end, Joshua started to feel the walls start to close in. They finally settled into various activities once it became clear that the rain wasn't letting up any time soon. The clouds seemed to get darker over the pond as the morning wore on. A box of toys was pulled out for the children, and they took over the sun porch; marching and jumping all around. Some of the mothers stayed in there, but most of them just ventured in and out when things got too noisy or too quiet. Joshua helped to get some of the board games out of the cupboards in the front hall. Guests set them up around the dining room table. Others read or chatted in the two parlors, while some stayed upstairs in their rooms.

Joshua tried to be of help, but when he realized that he was just getting in the way, he decided to head back over to the barn. Waiting for a lull in the storm, he sped over the soggy grass and let himself inside. Nettie was a little spooked in her stall, but when Joshua gave her some food and then water, she seemed to settle down. Kip only put his head up when Joshua crossed the barn and when he finally climbed back up the ladder. It was a lazy day, and the boy plopped himself back down on his bed and listened to the rain hit and then roll down the roof. Its trickling sounds hypnotized him as he stared up to the rafters.

Joshua let his thoughts wander. The seal was safely buried in the ground. She wouldn't be pounding against the shore in this storm. Crabs and other scavengers wouldn't get to her now either. He thought of his mission out to the east end of the pond as sort of like penance; a tribute to Mary. He had done it for her. Joshua's sister would have appreciated his efforts. He remembered her doing the same thing for a robin that had died in their backyard. The bird had lain on the ground near the house for a day. Flies buzzed around the dead bird's body, and a cat had attempted to steal it away. Mary made Joshua dig a hole in the back corner of the yard, while she made a marker with two sticks. She was so solemn about the whole affair, that Joshua got caught up in the ceremony.

Back in Providence, Father Donovan was always talking about atonement for sins. Joshua decided that he would not only write to Mary, but try to find ways of making things right in the world; the way his sister would have done. She could never walk by a crying child in the neighborhood without stopping and trying to soothe the youngster. Mary always helped people in need. If Mrs. Callahan was struggling with her packages or trying to get her children in the house, Mary would be the first to offer assistance. The more he thought about it, the more Joshua realized what a good person his sister was.

As the guilt started to well up in his throat, the boy fought it off with plans to seek forgiveness. He thought about the things that he did around the inn. When someone needed help, he was usually there to lend a hand. The money he was making for working here didn't really play a role in his motivation. Mother held onto most of his wages anyway, so he usually didn't even think about it. As the rain continued to fall, Joshua realized that he was like his sister in many ways.

Thunder off in the distance broke the spell, and Joshua rolled off his bed and opened the door on the pond side just a crack. The screen was coated with droplets of water, and the wind sprayed some of it inside. Closing the door back up, Joshua went to the other side and swung the opposite door open. He went to his small table and looked through the sketches that he had drawn. Touching up one or two pictures of the birds, he then flipped through the pages of one of the nature books, not really able to focus on anything. Joshua mindlessly picked up and put down each of the books in the stack in front of him. He finally came to *The Adventures of Huckleberry Finn* and decided that this was going to be the book he read next.

Joshua went over and dropped himself back onto his bed and began to read. Immediately, he was taken back to the Mississippi River. It seemed to pick up right after Tom Sawyer ended. The boys were rich now, but Huck didn't like the respectability of it. Huck had been adopted, and the Widow Douglas tried to raise him properly. As lunch time drew near, Joshua's stomach started to growl, but he didn't want to put the book down. He was riveted to the words on the page. This one started to seem much darker than Tom Sawyer. Huck was afraid of his Pa, and he didn't want him to steal his money. His father held him captive until Huck was smart enough to escape by faking his own death. Closing the book, Joshua realized that the rain had tapered off to a slow drizzle, so he decided to head inside the house and get something to eat.

As he walked back across the yard, Josh could hear the thunderous roll of the waves down at the beach. He made a quick decision to grab some food and go down there to have a look. Mrs. Nilsson and Mother were in the kitchen cleaning up the lunch dishes when he came in.

"Where have you been all morning?" Mother asked.

"Reading in the barn. I started Huck Finn."

"Well that's good news."

"I think I'm going to take a walk down to the beach. It looks like the rain's about to stop."

"I want you to have something to eat first."

"That's why I'm here," he answered with a big smile.

Mrs. Nilsson gave him some bread and a few pieces of beef that were left over from dinner the night before. Joshua put the meat between the slices of bread and began eat while he was standing there in the kitchen.

"How about if you have a seat in the breakfast room and slow down a bit?" Mother said as he gulped down the water that she had just handed him.

Joshua put on his straw hat before heading outside again. He partly wanted to keep the rain out of his face, but he also had taken a liking to what Huck Finn wore. There was no one on West Beach Road when he walked out there. Joshua tried to stay on the edges because the mud was squirting up between his toes when he stepped onto the road. The sound of the waves built with each step toward the sea. When Josh finally came over the dunes, he was amazed to see the unbelievable force of the surf. The waves were crashing about fifty feet out, but then rolling up to the back steps of the cottages along the beach. He could see that the tide was very high because most of the rocks were covered out in the water. People stood on their porches staring at the angry water.

As each wave crashed, wind blew spray off the peak. Farther out, large swells broke in the open water. Joshua couldn't even imagine what it would be like to be out in the Life Saving Station's dory on a day like this. Walking along the edge, where the wave line met the beach, Joshua kept staring out to the water. The ground shook as each mass of water pummeled the shore. He could see where the sand had been washed away. In the valley that was formed, water rushed out, only to be churned back up with the next wave. Joshua grabbed a piece of driftwood and chucked it over to where the water drained back to the sea. The stick thrashed about in the tumult, and then was swept back into the ocean. Josh saw it wash up again fifteen feet down the beach, and then repeat the process again and again.

He walked down toward West Beach, but found himself trapped when the waves started to crash onto the seawall in front of the Ashaway cottages. Looping back around, he went through the backyards and continued to follow the shoreline from above. The drizzle was now a mist, and more and more people started to appear behind the houses and along the dunes. When he got to the boardwalk down by the breachway, the water was flowing beneath it. Joshua could hear the rocks rolling over one another as the waves pushed forward. They crashed over picnic rock and surged through the mouth of the breachway. Boats were banging against the docks that sat in front of the inns and cottages along the waterway. Guests were on the rocks and porches, but none ventured down to the docks below. Water was washing over the boards, and to Joshua it looked like the boats were sitting low in the water. He could see the men from the Coast Guard Station. A few were down at the edge of the water where the launch area came out, and the others were up on top of the hill next to the building. They were all looking out to sea in different directions. Joshua turned and looked too, but thankfully, there were no boats to be seen.

He waved to them from the opposite shore, and a few returned the greeting. It seemed as if they were too busy to really acknowledge him, so Joshua continued walking down the breachway toward the pond. At the Eldredge Hotel, two men had stepped out onto the dock. They were trying to untie the skiff, but Joshua had no idea why. Once the rope was off, one of the men pushed it out into the water, while the other one held onto the line. The dinghy swiftly swung around to the other side. With the water in the bottom of the boat giving it weight; combined with the strong incoming current, the men had a difficult time trying to keep it steady. The first man attempted to tie the boat down, but the flow was too strong. Joshua jumped down onto the dock and immediately felt the water racing by his ankles. Grabbing the loose end, he pulled along with the pair of men. The boat was drifting about ten feet out, and white water pushed up against the bow. Once they hauled it a few feet closer, the pull wasn't as strong, so they were able to tie it to the piling on the other side. The view from the dock was incredible when Joshua turned back around. The mouth of the breachway looked out to the high surf, and Joshua watched as it rose and sank with each swell.

"Thank you, son," one of the men said. "We best get off this dock, though, before it gets swept away."

Joshua led the other two men off the planks and back onto the porch in the back of the hotel. Most of the storm must have been out to sea, because even though the squall was ending on shore, the darkness lingered out as far as Joshua could see. One of the women handed him a glass of lemonade as thanks for his assistance, and Joshua gulped it down. All eyes were focused on the ocean. There was a strange attraction to the force of the sea. Joshua could feel it as he watched another wave crash over the rocks at the entrance to the breachway.

As he headed back, it almost seemed as if the water was getting higher. Joshua got caught off guard once, as a wave stretched onto the beach and splashed up on his leg. The sky was gray now, and the only water in the air was the spray coming from the ocean. Beads of mist clung to his clothes and dripped off the brim of the hat. The Mississippi River had nothing on the Atlantic Ocean today. This was a dangerous place to be. Up ahead, Joshua saw a wave crash on a tall rock. The explosion of the impact sent water splashing twenty feet in all directions. The rock stayed in its place, and the wave kept rolling in.

Joshua's mind started to drift again as he thought about the ocean. All of the smooth stones that lay in front of him on the sand had at one time been jagged rocks. The water's movement over the years shaped each of them into their present form. As the waves pulled back out into the ocean, Joshua could hear this taking place. Hundreds of stones were dragged back into the deeper water by the potent force of the waves. It sounded like an army of horses galloping into battle. With each break of the swell, this course repeated itself. How many times would a stone have to roll in the tide before it was deposited on the beach as a polished piece of granite? Joshua remembered trying to dig around those rocks in the backyard of the inn. The shovel wouldn't even chip away a piece. Yet, here was the ocean, seemingly without thought, grinding rock down to its most basic shape. He looked out to where the large boulders sat in the water. The waves pummeled them, slowly breaking pieces off, and then sending them into the trough to be worked on. Joshua stood and just stared out at the awesome power of the sea.

When he got back to the inn, Joshua noticed that a number of small branches had fallen onto the grass. He went around and picked them up, tossing handfuls into the brush on the side of the yard. The sky was brightening a bit, but there was still no sign of sunlight. Walking over to the garden, Joshua saw that the rain had beaten down some of his plants. The damage wasn't too great, but Joshua was a little worried nevertheless. As he stepped into the garden, his feet sank down into the mud. He laughed as he realized how wet the ground actually was. Deciding to wait for the soil to get a little more solid, Joshua walked around the perimeter. The injury to the plants seemed minimal. A few of the limbs on a couple of tomato plants were sheared off, but that seemed to be the extent of it. Leaves that had been blown off were scattered around the area too.

"Well, you got your rain," Mr. Nilsson said as he walked up behind the boy.

"My foot sank right in," Josh responded, showing the man his muddy toes.

"This should keep us for awhile. Once the sun starts to heat up again, this place is going to fill right out."

The two of them walked down to the dock to see if there was any damage. Everything seemed to be in order.

The only thing that Joshua had to do was bail out the two canoes and the rowboat. As he sat down in the skiff with a small can, Joshua looked out to the pond. There were no longer any whitecaps, as the wind had died down considerably. There looked to be over two inches of water in the bottom of the boat. The rainwater became muddy as the dirt from Joshua's feet started to wash off. He filled can after can, dumping each load over the side of the boat. It didn't seem like he was getting anywhere, but in time, he eventually started scraping the wooden bottom.

"The sun will dry out the rest," Mr. Nilsson said as he walked back to the dock area.

Joshua hopped out and started on the canoe. This went much quicker, but the faster he went, the more the skinny boat rocked back and forth. On one long reach, Joshua felt like the whole thing was going to flip over. He slowed his pace down a bit, so he wouldn't end up in the bottom of the channel. Guests began to spill out of the inn and spread out over the grounds. A few wandered down to where Joshua was working, but most stayed up in the yard. The children ran around the trees as if they had never been outside before. All of their pent up energy from the day released in quick sprints around the yard. Women strolled about, some with their husbands, stopping occasionally to chastise an errant youngster. The party seemed to converge out near the tennis courts, and after a few minutes of discussion, they wandered out toward the road, and then down to the beach. The lure of the waves had called to them.

Joshua finished at the dock, and then went into the house to see what he could do to help out. The place was a mess; especially the sunporch. It looked like the children had just thrown everything around. Papers and toys were strewn all about the floor, and the cushions from the chairs were mounded up in one corner. It looked as though they had built some kind of a fort with them. Glasses and empty bowls were on every table, and there were remnants of popcorn scattered throughout the house. Mother and Mrs. Nilsson looked exhausted. This rainy day had thrown them off of their routine. They stood in the parlor, looking around. It didn't look like they knew where to start.

"If you need to start making dinner, I'll clean up in here," Joshua said to both of the women.

"Oh Joshua, that's not necessary," Mrs. Nilsson said.

"I'm serious. I'll do it."

They both looked at each other for a moment, and then back at the boy.

"Okay, we'll get things started in the kitchen," his mother said gratefully.

Joshua quickly made a game of it. He gathered all of the glasses as quickly as he could; taking three in each hand. He ran them out to the dining room table and placed them there. After six or seven trips, he switched over to plates. He came back next with the large popcorn bowls. Half of the table was filled when he went back through the downstairs one more time, looking for stray plates or glasses. He was disappointed to find that he had neglected two glasses that were sitting on the floor behind one of the chairs in the back parlor. Next, Joshua put the toy box in the middle of the sun porch and scurried around, gathering each plaything that the children had left. He tossed most of the unbreakables from where he found them. About half of the toys went into the box, and the others fell nearby. Although he wished that everything went in, he knew that he could gather everything quickly as he moved closer to the box.

"What are you doing?" Mary Rose asked from the step of the sun porch.

"Cleaning up. Want to help?"

"Okay," the little girl replied.

"Take all of those toys next to the toy box and put them inside."

Joshua watched as she walked over in a very determined way and started to pick up the stray objects that had missed the mark when the boy tossed them. She was very precise with each placement of the objects. Josh watched for a moment, and then continued with his cleaning. He started with the cushions; racing back and forth by Mary Rose. She seemed oblivious to his movements as she squatted and picked up each toy in her small hands. After folding up two small tables, Joshua went over to help the girl finish up. They dragged the box over to the corner of the room.

"Thank you very much for your help, Mary Rose."

The girl just smiled up at him. Josh left the room and came back a moment later with a broom and a dust pan. Mary Rose watched as the boy swept up all of the stray popcorn and other crumbs into different piles. She held the dustpan, while Joshua whisked the piles into them. When he came back through the house to empty the debris, he saw that someone had taken all of the glasses and plates into the kitchen. Mrs. Nilsson was at the stove, and Mother was up to her elbows in soapy water by the sink.

"It looks much better out there," Mother said.

"I had help," Joshua answered as he emptied the dustpan into the garbage.

Mary Rose stood at the entrance to the kitchen. It looked like the swinging door was about to knock her over. Mrs. Nilsson handed her a cookie from the tray, and then gave Joshua one too. The two of them went back into the parlor and swept up. The rug on the floor made things a little difficult, but after he was done with the two rooms, they looked a lot better. Guests were starting to trickle back into the house. Joshua was putting the board games back into the cupboard in the front hall as they filed passed him.

Although he had a great sense of accomplishment, Joshua's heart began to sink as he realized that they were coming back to make a mess again. Sometimes he wished that he and his mother had a place of their own, so it wouldn't seem like all they did was pick up after, feed, and take care of other people. Deep down, he knew the day would come, but in the meantime, he would have to be someone else's servant.

20

Dear Mary,

  *Today was the best day of my life. The sun was
shining and the sky was blue. The guests wanted to get
down to the beach early since they had missed out on a day
in the sun yesterday because of the storm. I went down
with Mr. Nilsson in the morning and set up the canopy. I
had to clear away a lot of debris that washed up on the
shore. The high tide mark was in the grass by the edge of
the dunes. Even though it was about middle tide then, the
waves were still powerful. The ocean was smooth and
shiny, but the surf was high. I found a nice wooden bucket
that wasn't damaged at all, so I threw it into the back of the
cart when I went back for some chairs.*
  *Since I had my bicycle, I stayed on the beach while
Mr. Nilsson went back to get some of the guests. Others
had just walked down while we were setting up the tent. It
wasn't like them to be on the beach in the morning, but I
guess that's what happens after a rainy day. I just kept
rolling the piles of seaweed away from the area where
people sat. Mr. Nilsson said he would bring back a clam
rake, but I wanted to get moving before too many people
showed up. A dead seagull turned over in one of the piles
that I was moving, so I just buried it under a few inches of
sand. There were loads of sticks and pieces of driftwood. I
piled them up off to the side, because Mrs. Van Houtten has
been talking about having a marshmallow roast on the
beach one of these nights. I figured they could use the
wood.*
  *It was strange how differently the beachfront was
shaped today. As I walked along the shore, the beach rose
and fell where the water had rushed out at high tide. There
were shells and rocks and crabs and starfish all along the*

edge. I tried skipping some of the stones, but the water was churning up too much to get an even surface. Although I was a little scared about the undertow, I still wanted to go into the water. For some reason I wanted to feel the power of the waves coming in. Three older boys went crashing into the surf in front of me, so I watched them get tossed around for a few minutes. Since Mr. Nilsson hadn't returned from the inn, I decided to take my chances. I waded out up to my waist, the first wave crashed onto my chest and sent me under the water. I turned over and over underwater until I could get my balance and come up for air. I surfaced just in time for another wave to smack into me. Getting a mouthful of saltwater, I coughed and choked until another one washed over me. I knew that I had to get out right away. It was just too rough out there for me. I had hardly been in the water this summer, and when I did, the waves had been less than two feet high. This was just too much. I got caught by one more wave before I struggled back to the shore and sat down.

The older boys seemed to be having a great time. They were wading just beyond where the waves were crashing. I figured that if I had gotten out that far, then I would have done alright. I just didn't have it in me right then to try going out again. Sometimes they would get caught off guard and sent beneath the surface. They just laughed at the whole thing though.

Seeing the cart pull up, I went up over the dunes and helped the guests with their things. Most of them were happy just to sit on the sand or walk along the water's edge. I played with some of the little kids, but the tide kept coming up higher, so we had to keep moving back. I was playing ball with a boy named Stevey when I saw a wave crash in and knock Mary Rose down. The force of the wave tumbled her down into one of the small valleys formed by the storm. As the water crashed over from the other side of the mound, I saw her get sucked out into the water. I yelled to the parents up on the beach, and then ran down to where I saw her go under. She was gone. I looked and looked, but there was nothing but more waves coming in. It seemed like a lot of time was passing. As another one crashed, I saw her hand and a bit of her arm a little farther down the beach. I ran and jumped at where she was and grabbed onto her leg. A wave knocked me back, but I didn't let go of Mary Rose. As I came up, another wave hit me, but as soon as I got a firm footing, I pulled her to me. Mr. Van Houtten grabbed the two of us as another wave rolled in. He pulled us out, but I would not let go of Mary Rose until we were on the dry sand. I was coughing, but she wasn't moving at all. Mr. Van Houtten took her over his knee and slapped her on the back. He did this a few times before she came back to life and coughed up a lung full of water.

When I saw that she was breathing, I fell back onto the beach. People were gathering around the little girl and hugging her. I was trying to finally catch my breath. Mr. Van Houtten came over and told me that I had saved her life. He said that if I hadn't held onto her, then she would have been lost under the waves. If she had been down there for any longer, then she might have drowned. For some reason I started crying. I was sitting up, and I put my head between my legs and sobbed. Mr. Van Houtten's daughter, Mary Rose's mother, came over, hugged me, and wrapped a blanket around my shoulders. I just couldn't stop crying.

At dinnertime tonight, Mr. Van Houtten called me into the dining room and thanked me in front of all the other guests. Mary Rose was sitting next to him, and she gave me a picture of a rainbow and some flowers that she had drawn. The picture meant more to me than anything anybody else said or did. After awhile, I went back to the barn and hung the picture up on the wall. I really didn't want to answer any more of the same questions or tell the story again.

I'm going to put this letter away and get back to Huckleberry Finn. He and Jim are floating down the river now. It's getting very interesting.

Your Brother,

Joshua

For the next few days, Mrs. Van Houtten was very attentive to Joshua. She went out of her way to acknowledge his presence at the inn. A few times, she almost made it seem like Joshua was part of the family. Although the boy liked the attention, he wished that everyone would just get back to normal. In his heart, he knew that he had saved Mary Rose's life, but the more people talked about it, the worse he felt. Joshua couldn't explain why this was, but he knew that he didn't want to think about it anymore. The feelings he had for what he had done were powerful, but he wanted to keep them inside. Now there was a special connection between Mary Rose and him. Because of what he had done, Joshua began to feel the first glimpses of absolution for what had happened sixteen months before.

Mother seemed to sense what Joshua was going through, and she made it a point to praise him at first. As the days went on though, she attempted to get his mind off his renown and back to the matters at hand.

"Joshua, I need at least sixteen eggs from the coop this morning."

"I don't know if there's that many out there."

"Well, talk to your chickens and tell them what we need."

They both laughed as the boy went outside with the basket. When he went into the chicken coop, he grabbed all fourteen of the eggs that were there and whispered to them that he needed more. Joshua remembered the first few times that he had done this job. The chickens squawked and flew everywhere; their feathers flying about and sticking to him. Now he was able to ease his way inside, get the eggs, and retreat without so much as a cackle.

When he came back outside, Mr. Nilsson was setting some stones on the ground above where the clam pit had been. He laid them out in a rectangular fashion, leaving the front side open.

"Good morning, Joshua."

"What are you making?"

"Mrs. Nilsson wants to have a fish fry this week. I've got a metal grate that will fit on top of here, that is, if I can get these stones level."

"Are we going fishing?"

"No, I don't think so. All the fish are out to sea now. I'm afraid our big haul at the breachway was a fluke. Johnny Crandall is supposed to bring us a boatload when he comes in again."

Joshua hauled some stones from the nearby bushes and helped Mr. Nilsson set them in place. He had to get some smaller rocks from down by the pond to balance the larger ones. They worked for an hour or so, and as the old man was putting the final touches on the wall, Joshua went up and got some wheelbarrows full of wood for the fire.

"I collected some driftwood from the beach the other day and put it in a pile. I thought that Mrs. Van Houtten wanted to have a marshmallow roast."

"We'll put some in the back of the cart when I drop the guests off down there later on. I'm sure that she would like to have the children roast some marshmallows after the fish is cooked. We can just lift up the grate and let the little ones have some fun. They'll like the crackle of the salty wood from the beach."

Joshua collected the pile of driftwood once he got down to the beach. The sand was strewn with more wood than he could carry. After a few trips back to the cart, he walked along the high tide mark, looking for larger pieces. There was enough for quite a bonfire. After Mr. Nilsson left, Joshua came back over the dunes and found his spot on the sand. He was still a little reluctant about going out into the water, even though the waves had dropped back to normal size. The children at the shore kept most of his attention. Joshua now felt like their guardian; ready to spring forward at the first sign of trouble. Today, they peacefully played up above the water's edge.

Out over the water, Joshua watched a bird slowly circle back and forth in front of the beach. It wasn't a seagull; the wings beat in a different fashion. They seemed to bend in an unconventional manner as it flew over the water. Suddenly, Joshua saw the bird drop into the free fall; its wings tucked in partway, but guiding the plummet. It plunged into the water with great force. Joshua stared as the bird came back up and slowly flapped its wings a foot or two above the surface. With

281

much effort, it started to climb, and when it did, Joshua could see that the bird clutched a good sized fish in its claws. He watched this creature come in toward the shore and fly directly above his head. Joshua scrambled up the dunes to watch where the bird went. Up over the freshwater pond and into the marshy area beyond it went. Joshua could see the bent tail of the fish hang loosely under the bird. Finally, it began its descent and Joshua lost sight of it as the bird landed somewhere in the marshes.

The boy wished that he had brought his bird book down to the beach with him today because he wanted to figure out what he had just seen. It was a dark color with some lighter marks on it. The bird almost looked like an eagle, and Joshua was sure that he had never seen anything like it before. For the next hour or so, he was very antsy; waiting for someone to send him back to the inn for something. Finally, without being asked, Joshua decided that the children needed some lemonade. He hopped on his bicycle and rode back to the house to get some.

Mother made a container of lemonade and found a top for it. She handed Joshua some cups for the children. He had grabbed the bird book while she was preparing the drink, and he stuffed everything in the front basket of the bike for the ride back to the beach. As the children drank, Joshua thumbed through the pages of the bird book. He looked at all of the eagles, but none were similar to the bird he had seen diving into the sea. On the next page though, he found what he was looking for. The bird was called an osprey, and one of its main sources of food was fish. He decided that he was going to sketch it that night. The drawing in the book had the bird flying away with a fish in its talons, much like what Joshua witnessed from the beach.

Dear Mary,

We had our first fish fry of the season this weekend. Johnny Crandall brought us about forty fish. There were stripers, blues, and blackfish, but also some fluke. They

282

were just like the flatfish we caught in the pond, only much bigger. Mr. Nilsson and I set up the sawhorses down by the dock and put planks on top of them. We used this as our cutting board. It was messy work, but I didn't mind. Once I started going, it seemed like we whizzed right through all of them. I'm getting pretty good with the knife. Mr. Nilsson saved the guts and other remains, and once we brought the filets up to the kitchen, we headed out to set some lobster traps.

The iceman arrived just in time, and Mrs. Nilsson stored everything in the box by the back pantry after she wiped the sawdust from the blocks. I just can't figure out how he keeps all that ice through these hot summer days. He must live in some cave up on the other side of the Post Road where he comes from.

Saturday was beautiful, and after we lit the fire, Mr. Nilsson and I went down to the beach to pick up the remaining guests. Mr. Van Houtten is leaving on Monday morning, so I wanted this fish fry to be a success. He'll be traveling up to Massachusetts, and then back through Connecticut before heading to New York City for a couple of weeks. We'll do the August clambake when he returns. Mrs. Van Houtten will be staying, and I'm worried that she'll go back to her old self after her husband leaves.

Mother and I husked some corn on the back steps, and then set a huge pot to boil on the back corner of the grate. This was the first good corn of the season. The ears we got earlier in the summer were small and not very tasty. I also helped Mr. Nilsson stir the fire as we got ready to put the fish on to cook.

The strangest thing happened as I was walking back up to the barn. I heard a truck coming up from the breachway, and when I looked out at it, I saw what looked like a giant bottle of Moxie set in the rear of it. He continued to drive past, but slowed when the driver saw the large group of people gathered in the back. He reversed the truck and blew his crazy sounding horn...AAA-OOO-Gah. The guests moved up from the yard and came around the house to see. The man climbing out of the front seat was dressed like Uncle Sam. He even put on a top hat when he got out. A pretty girl in a fancy, but short dress hopped out from the *other side and gave everybody a big wave.*

I walked up behind the truck and looked at the giant container of Moxie. It was only a wooden form shaped like a bottle, but it looked grand, just the same. The man started shaking hands with everyone who stood around the truck, telling them what a great place America is. Mr. Van Houtten enjoyed the show, and when the salesman handed him an ice cold bottle of the drink, he shared it with Mary Rose, who sat on her grandfather's shoulders. I was waiting for him to pull more bottles out of the bottom door of the strangely shaped wooden storage bottle in the back, but he just kept on talking. He convinced Mr. Van Houtten to purchase four cases, and I helped to carry them into the backyard. Unfortunately, these bottles weren't cold, but we made do. Mr. Nilsson pulled a big tub out of the barn and filled it halfway with water. Mother washed the fishy smell from the rest of the ice, and I dropped the shrinking blocks into the water. Mr. Van Houtten, Mary Rose, and I placed each of the bottles into the water. He said that the Moxie would go along great with our fish fry, and I have to say that it sure did. I drank two bottles of the stuff.

There was more than enough fish to go around, and we even had some left over. I ate to my heart's content. Mrs. Nilsson said that she was going to make some fish chowder. She shaved corn off the four remaining cobs and saved that in a small container. I don't worry about what Mrs. Van Houtten thinks of me anymore, because she was the one who handed me the second bottle of Moxie, and smiled at me too.

Mr. Nilsson and I used a combination of fishing gaffs and boards with nails in them to pick the hot grate up off the wall foundation. We carefully walked it down to the pond and dropped it in the water. You should have seen it sizzle. We left it there for a short time while we cleaned up the area and brought the driftwood down from behind the barn. Just as the old man said, the wood snapped and popped the minute we piled it onto the embers of the fire. After only a short time, the fire was roaring again. The sun had set, and dusk was slowly turning to night when the children gathered around the fire. They had spent the last few minutes of daylight scavenging the brush for sticks long enough to reach the fire.

Everyone gathered around the glow of the flame to roast the marshmallows. Mothers and fathers helped their kids, and calmed them when the treats either fell into the fire or started to blacken and burn. I wish you had been there. I started to think about that for a moment or two, and then had to walk away because tears started to fall down my cheeks. I wish I had a family to sit around the fire with and roast marshmallows. Mother was so busy inside the house, that she didn't even have a chance to come down and see the fire. The guests had made quite a mess of the yard, and by the time we cleaned most of it up, she had to wash all the dishes and glasses in the kitchen. It was probably a good thing that she was up there, because if she started to think the way I did about our family, then she would have felt sad too.

I couldn't go back to the fire, so I went up to the inn to help Mother and Mrs. Nilsson in the kitchen. Louise and Charlotte were putting everything back in the cupboards, while Mother and Mrs. Nilsson were at the sink washing and drying. I collected some of the dirty things that were still on the breakfast room table and the counters, and brought them over to the sink. Outside on the porch, there were a few more glasses and plates, and in the yard I picked up whatever I could see. The flame from the bonfire gave off a nice orange glow, and I sat on the back steps and watched it from a distance. People cheered every time the fire popped.

When the guests started to wander back up to the inn, I went out to the barn to call it a night. My face still felt hot from standing over the fire while I flipped the fish over. The cold water that I splashed on my face helped for only a short time. When I came up the ladder, I decided to write to you because it's been a few days now. As I read over what I've told you, I can't believe how much I've written. I'm glad that I'm sharing my adventures in Quonochontaug with you. Speaking of adventures, I have to get back to Huck Finn before I fall asleep. The last thing I read had Huck and Jim exploring a steamboat that had crashed. They escape from the thieves who are on board by stealing their boat. I'll tell you more next time I write.

Your Brother,

Joshua

On Sunday morning, Joshua went down to the
ballfield to watch the men play. He joined the other boys
at the pump to wait for fly balls to carry out into the brush
or the woods. The game had already started, and it didn't
look like the boys wanted anyone else competing with
them for pennies. Joshua didn't recognize the man who
was pitching, but he had a Giants hat on his head, so he
took an immediate dislike to him.

"Who are you?" One of the boys asked.

"Joshua."

"Where do you live?" Asked another.

"At the Pond View," Josh answered, trying to keep
his eyes on the game.

The runner at first looked like he wanted to steal
second, but the pitcher kept him on the bag. When the
fastball came in, the man started to go, but hesitated. The
catcher popped from his crouching position and fired the
ball to first. The runner stepped right on top of the glove;
a perfect throw. The crowd cheered and even poked a
little fun at the runner as he slunk back to the bench.
The boys near Joshua seemed to be engrossed in the game
again, so they left him alone.

When the next batter fouled off a pitch into the
brush, all seven boys took off after it. Joshua trotted
behind them. He didn't know what the proper etiquette
for retrieving balls was, so he hung back and observed.
The boys scrambled into the tall grass, and then the
bushes without any care. One smaller boy tripped and
was left behind and forgotten. When they got to the spot
about where they thought the ball might be, they spread
into pairs; sweeping through the underbrush in a fierce
competition for the lost ball. Joshua followed them, and
kept his eyes open. Since they had slowed down their
pace, he caught up to them easily. Just as Joshua
spotted the ball underneath a small blueberry bush, one
of the boys kicked it by accident. Another one scooped it

up and started to run back to the field. The boy who kicked it chased after the boy with the ball and tackled him.

"That's my ball! I saw it first," he yelled as he dragged the other boy to the ground.

"Did not, you just kicked it, and I got it," the boy with the ball responded.

They wrestled for a moment until the ball rolled loose. It rolled over between Joshua's feet. Everybody froze for a moment and stared at Joshua as he reached down to pick it up. The little boy who had tripped was standing next to him.

"Go give this to the umpire," he said as he handed the ball to his new, little friend.

The other boys stared coldly, especially the ones on the ground. They reminded him of the younger boys from his old neighborhood, fighting over scraps in the street. Joshua really wasn't interested in chasing the balls into the woods, and he didn't want any part of these battles. He was making some money at the inn, so the pennies that he made here wouldn't amount to much. Joshua followed the little boy over to the umpire, serving as protection from the others. When Joshua saw that the kid had the attention of the older man behind the plate, he sauntered back around, past the players and sat on the bleachers with the other fans. Here he could concentrate on the game without being bothered by the fighting and questioning boys.

Joshua watched Kenyon at third base as the young man stared at the batter. Just as the pitch was coming in, he would get up on his toes and wait for the batter to connect. His knees were bent, and he leaned forward with his glove out in front of him. As soon as the ball was hit, he reacted. Although it flew out into centerfield, Kenyon was yelling to the other players; leading his team. The throw came into second base, and when Kenyon called for the cutoff man to let it go, Joshua watched as the shortstop grabbed the bouncing ball and put the tag on the runner. When a grounder did finally shoot from homeplate out to third, Kenyon expertly scooped it up and fired the ball over to first for the third out.

Joshua watched the rest of the game with rapt enthusiasm. Although nothing spectacular happened, he focused on each player at bat and in the field. When there were runners on base, Joshua went through the different scenarios for where the ball would go, depending on where it was hit. A couple of the players didn't seem to have enough sense to throw the ball to the right place, but Kenyon barked at them enough, so they would know what to do the next time. When the game ended, people gathered about for a short time and talked to the players. Joshua watched for a bit, but then realized that many of them would be coming back to the inn very soon. He wanted to have lunch before he had to bring them down to the beach for the afternoon.

When he arrived back at the Pond View, he saw Mr. Thornton's cart in front of the barn. Racing into the kitchen, he hoped that Elizabeth was there. He hadn't seen her for awhile and was anxious to be with the girl. Mr. Thornton was in there with Mr. and Mrs. Nilsson, but his granddaughter was nowhere in sight. He stood at the counter and waited for some information about her whereabouts. Mr. Thornton was talking about some lumber that he brought over, along with two more chickens. Joshua couldn't figure out why Elizabeth wasn't here. Mr. Thornton looked over at the boy and smiled.

"Hello Joshua, how are you these days?"

"Fine."

"Elizabeth sent over some sugar cookies that she made," Mr. Thornton said as Joshua nodded. "She's off to see Mrs. Thornton's cousins in Kingston. They should be back in a few days."

Joshua's heart sank at the thought of not seeing her. Since he had been so busy at the inn, he had neglected to go over to East Beach to visit with her. He would be sure to set up a time for the picnic when she returned. Now he was beginning to realize that chance meetings on the beach weren't enough any more.

21

As July became August, the guests at the inn started to change. The larger families who had spent a month were now replaced with different ones. Kenyon left for New York City, and Joshua had mixed feelings about his departure. He was a great ball player, but his dealings with Louise made the boy uneasy. It took a while to get used to the new people. There was a group of college professors and their families, and Joshua couldn't understand what they were talking about most of the time.

Joshua and Mr. Nilsson had to make another trip into Westerly for supplies. Once again they filled Ray Crandall's truck with stock needed for the inn. While he was in town, Joshua got another Red Sox magazine, as well as a small present for Elizabeth. The boy felt strange purchasing a necklace, especially since he didn't want Mr. Nilsson to see what he was doing. He felt awkward buying something for a girl. On the ride home, he suddenly realized that he hadn't gotten anything for his mother. She wouldn't be expecting a gift, but it would be nice to see the look on her face.

"Can we stop somewhere on the way? I forgot to get something for my mother."

Joshua felt guilty about the present in his pocket for Elizabeth. Both of the men smiled at Joshua as they pulled into the hardware store along the river's edge.

"There's a little shop across the road," Mr. Crandall said, as he pointed over his shoulder. "You might find something over there."

He counted fifty-three cents in his pocket as he scurried across the road. Once inside he realized that it was a women's shop, and he immediately felt awkward and foolish.

"May I help you?" An older woman inquired.

"I ... ah ... I need a gift for my mother."

"Oh, we have an assortment of lovely gifts."

Joshua followed the woman as she made her way through the small shop. There were fancy bottles of perfume and other toiletries placed in an ornate manner on tables and shelves. Joshua couldn't even begin to figure out what he wanted to get. She pointed out combs and brushes and hair pieces, but the boy was too confused. Another customer came into the store, so Joshua was able to spend a moment alone, thinking about what he wanted to purchase. He knew that his mother tied her hair up, but he had no idea how she did it. There didn't seem to be any anything on her bureau that resembled the items before him now. Joshua did see some hair pins, so he picked up four of them, and then as he walked back toward the front of the store, he noticed a fancy tin of powder. The grand total would be forty-seven cents, so he would be able to swing it.

The woman placed his purchases in a flowery, little bag, and Joshua felt even more silly as he walked back to the pick-up truck. The men were still in the hardware store, so he tried to fold the bag up a little bit, so he could hide what he had bought.

"Oh, you smell nice, Joshua," Mr. Crandall said with a teasing smile as he climbed back into the truck. Mr. Nilsson was silent, but had a slight grin on his face.

Back at the inn, all of the supplies had to be unloaded, and then stored around the kitchen and pantry. Mother and Mrs. Nilsson pulled out the almost empty containers of flour and sugar, as Joshua brought in the new sacks to replace them. Mrs. Nilsson was planning the big dinners that they would have, now that there was ample food in the house. Joshua was starting to think that the guests who were there at the beginning of the month ate much better than those who were there at the end.

Another clambake was coming up in a little more than a week, so Joshua and Mr. Nilsson had to head out into the pond to begin their process of collecting bushels of shellfish. Although the excitement of gathering clams was gone, Joshua still liked being out on the water. To be able to get food for the table at no cost was an amazing thing, and as the boy daydreamed of owning a small house down here someday, he was comforted in the fact that he and his mother would never starve. A garden and this pond would give him more than he would ever need. The problem would be saving enough money to purchase a piece of land. As he raked for the clams, Joshua looked around at the shoreline. There was plenty of open space around. Fields and low brush were interrupted by the occasional house, but Joshua knew that he wouldn't need much. His father's garden back in Providence wasn't very big, but it sure produced a lot of vegetables.

Joshua turned around all the way and looked over toward the island. He knew that he would have to go back over there and trim some of the path that he cut out with the shovel. Although he still wasn't sure if Elizabeth would go with him, he decided to work on the area before he even asked her to go on a picnic. He wanted to clear as much as possible, so they wouldn't have as much chance of getting ticks on them. Plus, he wanted to impress her with an island that he cleared just for her.

The first bushel basket went under the dock, with plans of adding to it the next day. Walking by the mound where he would have to dig the pit again, Joshua suddenly got excited. Mr. Van Houtten would be back soon, and he would surely toast their efforts like he did the last time. The stones were still in somewhat of a rectangle from where the fish fry was cooked, so they would have to be moved and set inside the hole along with the logs. The only part that Joshua wasn't looking forward to was the collection of seaweed. Luck was on their side last time, with those huge mounds down on the beach, but he feared that they would have to go out in the pond and scrape the bottom this time, the way Mr. Nilsson had described it.

Dear Mary,

So much has happened since I last wrote to you. Mr. Nilsson and I are getting ready for the next clambake. We

*went fishing and caught a dozen flounder out in the pond.
We cut them up into filets, and then took the remains out to
the lobster pots. Mr. Nilsson dropped me off on your island
on the way back in. I brought a clam rake and a pair of
clippers. Raking up what I chopped before, I cleared the
path all the way to the middle of the island. It must have
been almost a hundred feet long. I went back through it and
trimmed the sides, so the walkway seems like a tunnel into
the clearing. Some spots were difficult, but I got through it
okay. There were some vines hanging near the big flat rock
in the middle, so I worked there for awhile. I raked away all
the branches and leaves from around the clearing, until it
looked almost like a park. There were stones scattered all
about, so I collected some of them and made a circle for a
fire. With the rest, I lined them around the edge of the
clearing where the brush started. The place looked great as
I walked backwards down the path, admiring what I had
done.*

    *Mrs. Nilsson made chowder with about a quarter of
the clams we got. She put some in a pot, and I rode it over
to the Thornton's. Elizabeth was out in the garden when I
got there. She waved to me as I pulled through the opening
in the stone wall. After handing the pot to Mrs. Thornton, I
went over and helped Elizabeth in the garden. She had a
hoe and was cutting through the rows. I tried to pick out the
weeds and shake the soil off of them to help her. She told
me about her trip to see her cousins. They spent some time
in the gardens at the agricultural college near where they
live, and she came back with some new ideas.*

    *I asked her if she was interested in going on a picnic
to the island. It was strange. She seemed to try and
change the subject a few times, but finally she said yes. I
didn't want to stay there too long after she agreed to go
because I didn't want to give her a chance to change her
mind. I dumped a few handfuls of weeds into the brush
next to the garden and told her that I had to go.*

    *I picked her up in the cart today after I brought a
group of guests down to the beach. Mr. Nilsson said that it
would be alright, and Mrs. Nilsson helped me pack up a
basket of food. Mother would have helped, but she was so
busy upstairs. Louise's friend came down with a cold or*

something, and couldn't make it to the inn today. She gave me a big smile though when I came back to the inn with Elizabeth. We tried the canoe, because I thought that I could do better with two people paddling, instead of one. The rowboat had the scattered remains of fish guts in it anyway, and I didn't want to take Elizabeth out in that. The island was pretty much the way I left it when I cleared everything out. From the shore you couldn't tell that there was a wide open space in the middle, or even a path for that matter. The egret watched us get out of the canoe and carry our things to the shore. I pulled the boat up and then grabbed the picnic basket. Elizabeth brought a small one of her own, and she followed me as I walked into the pathway.

We didn't say much at first. It seemed too much like a special occasion, until I spilled some grape jam from a biscuit onto my shirt, and we laughed. She brought a small booklet for me. It was from the agricultural college, and I thumbed through the pages. There were all different methods and tips about gardening. When I gave her the necklace, she almost cried. We held hands as we walked back to the canoe. We never did get to make a campfire, but I took her for a short tour of the pond. We paddled by the buoys for the lobster pots, and I told her about the clambake that was coming up. I'm planning to ask Mr. Van Houtten if it's okay if she comes and joins us. The tide was at a lull, so we slowly made our way through the breachway. There were seven or eight other boats rowing along as we drifted down the waterway. We waved at everyone. I didn't want to get too close to the mouth of the breachway at the ocean end, so I slowly turned the canoe around. It almost felt like we were going to tip over, but I steadied us before we did. I didn't see any of the men from the Life Saving Station, so I wasn't sure how close help would be if we went over. Plus, I didn't want to spoil a perfect day by having to get rescued.

When I brought Elizabeth back to her grandparents' house, she made me stop on the road just before we came into view of their property. She gave me a kiss on the cheek. I could have stayed there for the rest of the afternoon, but it looked like she was ready to go home. I raced the cart back to the inn afterwards, and almost threw the back wheel coming around a corner. I slid a little bit in

*the dirt, and my mind jumped to that day last March. I took
it slow the rest of the way home. Because of what I did in
the cart, I've been a little sad, but since I've been writing
about my time with Elizabeth, things don't seem so bad
now. I'll write again soon.*

Your Brother,

Joshua

Mr. Van Houtten returned, and he brought gifts for
his family from his travels. He added to his wife's record
collection, which brought some new music to the house.
Mr. Nilsson and Joshua were out in the barn at the
workbench when Mr. Van Houtten came out to pay them a
visit. He gave the old man a double headed faucet to put
on the bottom of the windmill, so Mr. Nilsson wouldn't
have to break all the piping down when they had to
irrigate.

"When I was up in Boston, I was thinking about
my granddaughter, Mary Rose, and you came to mind,
Joshua. I picked these up for you along with a pair of
train tickets. I figured that you and Mr. Nilsson could use
a break in September," Mr. Van Houtten said as he
handed the boy two tickets to the Red Sox game against
the Washington Senators.

Joshua just stared at the tickets for a moment.
The game was to be played on Friday, September sixth in
Fenway Park. He couldn't tell where the seats were
located, but he didn't really care.

"Thank you, Mr. Van Houtten. How did you
know?"

"I like to find out a little about my employees," he
said, waving off Joshua's thanks. "How are we fixed for
the clambake?"

"Right on schedule," Mr. Nilsson answered. "Just
as long as those lobsters are crawling inside of those
traps, then we should be fine."

"Good to hear, good to hear. Well I'm afraid that I
have to go back inside and listen to some Irving Berlin on
the phonograph."

With a nod and a smile, the man walked through the doorway and out of the barn. Joshua reached over and showed Mr. Nilsson the tickets. They would get the train at the Niantic Station in Bradford and ride all the way up to Boston.

"Box seats," the old man said as he read the tickets, "that Mr. Van Houtten is quite a man."

Joshua walked around in a daze for the rest of the day. He couldn't believe that he was actually going to Boston to see the Red Sox. He quickly became fanatical about keeping track of the team. At the table up in the barn, he sketched out a ballfield and drew in the names of each of the players in their positions. One of the pictures in his baseball magazine gave him a fairly good vision of what Fenway Park looked like. Joshua listed out the batting order and went through the newspapers as much as he could to get batting averages and other statistics. Mrs. Nilsson never used the sports pages to start her fire in the stove each morning, she always saved them for Joshua. As he read through the articles, he looked for strengths and weaknesses on the team, and tried to figure out how to make the Sox play better. In his dreams, Joshua pictured himself at the game, and then part of the game; out in the field with Tris Speaker. Not only was the centerfielder a great player, but he was smart. Speaker was one of only a few professional ball players who had been to college.

When opportunity finally knocked for Joshua, his mind was totally focused on baseball. He had gotten into the habit of bringing his glove down to the ballfield on Saturdays after a foul tip smacked off of his palm during a previous game. He sat on the benches and watched as the men gathered on the field to warm up. Kenyon's words from earlier in the summer echoed in his mind. Today looked like one of those mornings when they might be short a few players. Joshua counted fourteen men on the field and two out on the road having a conversation with a couple of young ladies.

"Where's Walter and Lloyd?" A voice called from behind the plate.

"Too much sun yesterday," another voice

answered.

"Too much moon, I think," came a third voice from behind second base.

The men all laughed at this last comment, but Joshua wasn't sure what it meant. He looked up and down the dirt road to see if anyone else was coming, but there was just an old woman walking with a young child.

"Hey kid," Harry yelled from shortstop.

He was the only one left of Kenyon's friends. The others had all gone back to the city. Joshua just looked out to where the man was standing.

"Yeah, you, from the Pond View," he pointed. "We need another player."

Suddenly, Joshua froze. His body couldn't move and his thoughts couldn't react to what he was hearing. This was what he had been waiting for all summer, but for some strange reason, he blankly stared out into the field. Why was he just sitting there?

"C'mon kid, head out to right field."

A nudge from next to him brought Joshua out of his uncertainty.

"I think they want you to play," an older man's voice said from beside him.

This was enough to get Joshua up off the bleachers and out into the field. Before Joshua even realized it, the centerfielder was tossing him a fly ball. He got under it and made an easy catch. With a step forward, he threw it back to the man, but embarrassingly, the ball bounced and then trickled to a halt ten feet in front of him. Joshua dropped the next throw, but was able to reach the other fielder on one hop. After a few more tosses, Joshua almost felt like he was ready for a game.

"Play ball," the umpire yelled from behind the plate.

The practice balls dribbled in, and the pitcher stood on the mound, ready for his first batter. For the first inning, Joshua just watched the game take place. There were no hits out to him, and he sat on the bench, while five batters came up. Alone in rightfield, he was starting to feel like he wasn't really part of the game, when Chester Dunbrow came to the plate. He was the

296

handyman at a lot of the inns and cottages around the beach. If Chester couldn't fix something, then it was time to buy a new one. The man was big, with huge forearms. Joshua was thankful that the man was right handed, especially after the first pitch came in. Chester slapped the ball hard down the third base line. It was foul, but the speed with which he hit the ball made Joshua fear for the safety of the third baseman. From his view in right field, Joshua could see the boys running from the pump at the well out to retrieve the ball. Joshua almost felt like a grown up, being part of the game now.

"Charlie, Charlie... let's go Charlie... no batter, no batter," the third baseman chanted.

The next pitch shot from Charlie's arm in a weird sidearm motion. Chester looked surprised by the delivery and couldn't quite bring his bat around quickly enough. The ball hit wood and lined right at Joshua. It seemed to arc, then dip, and rise again. Josh's body was moving to where he thought the ball was going, but its odd flight was throwing his balance off. He got to the ball too soon; before he could get his glove up all the way, and it thudded painfully into his chest. Joshua was knocked back, but had enough presence of mind to surge back forward, pick the ball up, and throw it into second base as best he could.

"Way to get in front of the ball, kid," a laughing voice came from somewhere.

Joshua tried not to rub his chest, but the pain was throbbing with each heartbeat. He shook it off and tried to refocus on the game. He didn't recognize the next batter coming up to the plate, but with three quick swings, Charlie sat him down. After a pop up to Harry at short, and slow grounder back to the mound, the side was retired. Joshua was thankful that Chester didn't get to move to second base. His error hadn't cost the team anything.

When Joshua finally got to bat, he was a little nervous once he stepped to the plate. The men seemed so big to him now. All of the holes that he had seen in the field when he was a spectator, now seemed to be filled. The pitcher had a big smile on his face as he went into his windup. Although he didn't throw the ball as hard as he did with the older men, the ball still came in fast. Joshua could barely get his eyes focused on it before the thing was in the catcher's mitt.

"Strike one."

Joshua choked up on the bat a little bit and bent at the knees, just like his father had taught him. When the next pitch came in, he was a little more prepared. He swung away and felt the bat make a connection. Joshua watched as the ball slowly dribbled down the first base line. Just as he was about to drop the bat and run, it skittered into foul territory. Behind on the count, he didn't have much choice, but to swing away at the next pitch. He got a piece of this one too, but it popped up behind him, and the catcher easily let it fall into his glove. So much for glory on his first time at bat. Joshua slunk back to the bench and sat down, keeping his eyes on the ground.

As the next few innings passed, the game stayed fairly even. His team got two runs on four hits, and the other team had one run from a pair of doubles. Although Joshua got a good piece of the ball the next time he got up to bat, it bounced right to the shortstop, and he was easily put out at first. The only action Joshua got out in right field, were a few ground balls that slipped through the infield.

When Chester came back up again, he cracked a line drive between short and third for a single. With only one out, the tying run was on base. The next batter who came up was Henry Stimpson. He ran the bait shop down at the breachway, but they said that he was the barkeep out back at the Blind Pig each night. That was the place where the working men went in the evenings. Henry's fat torso gave him the look of a giant duck waddling up to the plate.

"Easy out... easy out, Charlie... no hitter!"

The first pitch came in fast, and Henry snapped the bat from the wrist. The ball was already by him by the time he came fully around. Seeming to almost feel bad for the man, Charlie lobbed the second one in. As it released from his hand, Chester took off from first base. Henry connected with his jerky swing, and the ball sailed slowly over the right side of the infield, sending the first baseman back, back until he tumbled to the ground. Joshua raced in as the arcing ball began to descend. He trailed its every movement, not letting his eyes fall onto anything else. With a confident lunge, he dove. Joshua's arm extended out as far as his tendons would allow, and the glove skimmed the top of the grass as the leather covered ball dropped in. Rolling as he clutched it in his mitt, Joshua popped and raced toward first base. Chester was doing the same thing as he realized what was happening. The first baseman was still on the ground, and from the corner of his eye, Josh could see Charlie racing over from the mound to cover the base. All three of them sped for the bag.

Everything slowed in Joshua's mind. A picture of his father floated inside somewhere, looking out at his son. He had to get to first base; nothing else mattered. With a strength that came out of all the days of pent-up grief, Joshua leapt and landed on first base just as Chester slammed into him. His cheek hit the powdery dirt with a brain ringing blast as the runner tumbled over him. Blinking away the pain, Joshua found himself lying in a cloud of dust. The wind slowly pushed it out toward centerfield. He felt for it, and there it was; the ball was safely hidden inside of the glove that Joshua clutched against his chest. From where he was lying on the ground, he held up his mitt to show the umpire that the ball was still there. A cheer went up from the crowd as he did this, and the other players on his team made their way over to help him up.

As he stood, Joshua smiled, knowing that he had made an unassisted double play from the outfield; just like Tris Speaker. More than any other time in the last two years, Joshua wished that his father was here to see this. He rolled the ball back out to the mound and started to walk over to the bench. A wave of dizziness washed over him, and when he felt the side of his head, Joshua could see blood on his fingers. There was a ringing in his ears, but he didn't feel any pain. With a cautious step, he tried to get his balance back, but the boy stumbled and almost fell to the ground. Suddenly, there was woman next to him holding him under his arm.

"Are you alright? Is your mother here?"

"No ... I mean, yes, I'm okay. My mother is back at the Pond View."

Joshua tried to walk away from her, but his world spun again. It reminded him of when he was in the hospital last year. With a sudden fear, he realized what a head injury could do to him. The woman handed him a handkerchief, and the boy held it to the side of his head.

"Nice play, kid," Harry said as he walked over to Joshua.

"Thanks," he replied, looking down at the blood in the handkerchief.

"Why don't you call it a day, Joshua? Lloyd just showed up, so he can take your spot out in right."

"But..."

"He's right," the woman said. "You need to have your mother look at that."

Joshua nodded, knowing that they were probably correct. He wouldn't be much good if his world kept spinning. The boy wasn't looking forward to showing Mother his injury. She got very nervous any time he got banged in the head now. Joshua tried to hand the cloth back to the woman.

"You keep it," she said, looking down at the blood.

Joshua walked back through the path. He didn't feel ready to hop on the bicycle, so he used it to lean on as he made his way back to the inn. As he walked, the speckled sunlight through the leaves put his mind into kind of a reminiscent daze. He had proved something out on the field today, and it reminded him of those games he watched down in the South End of Providence. When he was smaller, Joshua always pictured himself making a great play. As the men were out on the field, he would watch and imagine himself in each of the positions. He could picture the perfect play for each spot. Today's unassisted double play from right was probably the best thing he could do as a fielder.

Louise saw him first when he came into the kitchen, and her gasp made Mother turn around. She rushed over to her son with a wet cloth and wiped away the new blood that had trickled down as he walked home. She was quiet until she could see exactly what the damage was. He told her what had happened, but she didn't seem the least bit interested in his great play. The only thing she focused on was his collision and fall to the ground. Mother finally said that the cut wasn't too bad. It looked like the flap of his ear was torn a little bit, and it just kept bleeding. Since there was no crack in the skull, she seemed to relax a little. Mother sat him down at the table in the breakfast room and told him to keep the cloth held to his head. Louise brought over some lemonade and cookies for Joshua to eat while he waited for the bleeding to stop.

Harry sought Joshua out when he came back from the field a little while later. Joshua was sitting on the back steps of the porch staring out to the pond. The sun was high overhead now, and he was just waiting for everyone to finish up with their lunch, so he could go down to the beach.

"Here you go," Harry said as he tossed a baseball to him.

Joshua caught the ball in his bare hand and stared at the man. It didn't seem like he wanted to play or anything, so Joshua wondered what was going on.

"It's the game ball. The boys decided that you should have it after that great play."

The ball in his hand suddenly took on a greater meaning. He stared down at it, and let his fingers rub over the seams. Joshua smiled up at Harry.

"How's your head?"

"Not too bad," he answered. "Did we win?"

"We sure did ... three to one. Everett Taylor doubled to center, and then went to third on an error. I sacrificed him in with a fly to left. Your play saved the game. Chester would have made it to third, and they had two fairly good batters coming up next if you didn't retire the side."

Joshua tossed the ball up and down and back and forth from hand to hand. This was a treasure. Who would have thought that Joshua Keegan would get a game

301

ball after his first time playing with the men? With a pat on the boy's back, Harry walked up the steps and went into the house to get some lunch and change into his bathing trunks. Joshua sat on the back porch and thought about his life. It was as if the darkness was fading away now, and he was coming back into the world again. He wondered why it was happening. Was it coming to this place in Quonochontaug, writing the letters to Mary, keeping himself busy, or just the passing of time? As these thoughts flowed through his mind, Joshua realized that it was probably a combination of these things. All he knew was that now it seemed that life was worth living.

On the beach that afternoon, Joshua took out the small piece of wood from his bag that he had gotten from under the workbench in the barn. With Mr. Nilsson's old carving knife, he made a little indentation in the middle of it. He dug until the baseball fit into it without rolling off. He then flipped the piece of wood over and carefully started to carve in the letters. The work was slow, and Joshua wasn't happy about the craftsmanship, but he knew that the feeling was strong enough inside of him to let the small mistakes be forgiven. Just as it looked like some of the guests were getting ready to pack up their things to head back to the inn, Joshua blew off the last remnants of the shavings from the piece of wood. He looked down to read the words he had carved, and had to hold back the tears that wanted to fall.

FOR DAD
AN UNASSISTED DOUBLE PLAY
FROM RIGHT FIELD
AUGUST 13, 1912

22

Dear Mary,

    I put the game ball that Harry gave me on a little stand that I made. I've decided to dedicate it to Dad because he taught me everything I know about the game. Speaking of baseball, the Red Sox are on an unbelievable tear. They're pulling farther away from Washington and Philadelphia with each game. Smoky Joe Wood can't lose. He just won his twenty-fifth game, and should have no problem breaking thirty this year. The next stop is going to be the World Series against the Giants. Mr. Nilsson and I are going to a Red Sox game in a few weeks. It's against the Senators. Wouldn't it be something if Smoky Joe went up against the great Walter Johnson? They're neck and neck in the league for earned run average, strikeouts, shutouts, and wins. The hero of the team is Tris Speaker, though; he's leading the league in homeruns with six and batting .372. So far, he's got forty-five doubles and forty-two stolen bases. Since he's so good behind the plate and in the field, Speaker's got to win the Chalmers Award. 'The Gray Eagle' is the best all-around player in baseball. He had a hitting streak of over thirty games this year, and there's no one better in the outfield. I can't wait to get to Boston and see Fenway Park.

    The Nilssons have been very excited about the Olympics this summer. They were held in Stockholm, Sweden, which is not too far from where both of them were born. I don't think they were that excited about the actual games, but whenever there were articles about the city, they loved to read them. Jim Thorpe, the American, was the prized athlete of the games. I didn't read too much about it because I spent most of my time when I had the sports page reading about the Red Sox.

Mary, you can't believe the garden that Mr. Nilsson and I have. Just about everything is ripe now. We have vegetables for lunch and dinner everyday. Mrs. Nilsson spends part of each afternoon canning different things. She says that they'll take some of the jars with them to Vermont. Speaking of Vermont, Mother and I have been asked to go with the Nilssons to the lodge this winter. It's somewhere up near the mountains. Mrs. Van Houtten's sister runs the place, and the Nilssons take care of it. Mother sat down with me, and we talked about it. I'm all for it, but I expect that Mother wants to think about it some more. We would close up here in early October and then take the train up there. I don't really know what to expect, but I'm sure that there will be a lot of wood chopping.

The clambake we had was just as good as the one in July. At least I knew what I was doing this time. I invited Elizabeth, but she didn't think it was proper for her to attend. I got a burn on my hand because I wasn't paying attention, and now I have a big blister. We had a bunch of corn on the cob. This meant that Mr. Nilsson and I had to make another layer in the pit. First there were the lobsters, then the shellfish, and on top of that we put the corn. We didn't even have to take off any of the husk, it just cooked that way. The guests peeled it off when they were ready to eat it. Mr. Nilsson said that was the way the Indians did it. In fact, that's where the whole clambake idea came from a long time ago.

Well, I have to get back to Huck Finn. He left the Grangerfords after all the trouble, and now he's hooked up with the Duke and the King. I know there's going to be trouble with those two.

Your Brother,

Joshua

Now that the clambake was done, Joshua didn't have to spend his mornings out in the pond scraping for shellfish. The boy now focused on the harvest. The blueberries were plump, and he was able to pick all of the ones that the birds missed. Joshua tried to come up with

a way to keep them off the bushes, but he couldn't think
of anything. The apples, pears, and plums were getting
bigger everyday, and he was able to start picking the ripe
ones. The woods beyond the orchard were lined with
blackberries and grapes. He couldn't believe the size of
the juicy purple fruit that grew within the thorn bushes.
Both of his forearms were soon lined with red scratches.
The grapes hung in amazing, bright green clumps. They
wouldn't be ready for another month, but the sight of
them made Joshua's mouth water.

　　　The best part about picking the fruit was that
Joshua got to bring portions of his yield over to the
Thorntons in East Beach. This was part of the deal with
getting the chickens from them. Every other day or so, he
would load up the basket on the bicycle and head over
there. Sometimes Mrs. Thornton would make him lunch,
and the boy got to eat with Elizabeth. They spent a lot of
time together now. Joshua helped her in the garden when
he could, and when they had a chance, they would take
walks together.

　　　"What do you write about to your sister?"

　　　"I don't know, lots of things, I guess."

　　　"Like what?"

　　　"Just stuff that's going on around here."

　　　"Do you ever write about me?"

　　　"Aaah," Joshua stammered.

　　　Elizabeth laughed as she waited for the boy's
response.

　　　"Well, do you?"

　　　"A little bit. I wrote about our picnic, and what a
great time I had."

　　　"Does anyone else read it?"

　　　"No. It's just for me."

　　　"Oh."

　　　"You could look at it if you wanted to."

　　　The girl was silent for a moment. She looked over
at him and then stopped walking.

　　　"You don't mean that."

　　　"I don't mind. There's nothing really that special in
it."

　　　Again they started walking. The two of them were

at the far end of the Thornton property, right near Ninigret Pond. Quonochontaug sat between the two large salt ponds. Joshua and Elizabeth looked out into the water. This pond was much more wide open than the one by the inn.

"What are you going to do at the end of the summer?"

"We might be going up to Vermont. My mother hasn't decided yet, but I think we will. The Nilssons want us to go up there with them. I think it's their plan to have us be the caretakers of both places when they get too old to do it."

"What about next summer?"

"I hope to be back down here."

This was awkward for the two of them, and they fell into silence again. Joshua reached down and picked up a flat stone. Because the wind was from the west, this side of the pond was flat. The ripples didn't start for about thirty feet out in the water. The boy threw the rock in a low side arm motion and watched it skip eight times before dropping beneath the surface of the water.

"What about school?"

"I don't know. It seems like I'm doing more schoolwork now than I've done in the last couple of years. I finished reading Tom Sawyer, and now I'm over halfway through Huck Finn. Mr. Nilsson's got me doing all sorts of math problems with the garden and all the fruits and vegetables. He wants me to figure out the best way to plant the garden next year for the least amount of money. I'm learning all about the animals around here too. I have a lot of the birds sketched out."

"You do?"

"Yeah, there's a book at the inn that I use. I try to figure out the names of the birds that I see, and then I use the picture in the book to make my drawing. The best one I have so far is an osprey that I saw at the beach one day. It was diving into the water and getting a fish. I think it lives in the marsh on the way back to the inn from here."

"How many drawings do you have?"

"Oh, I'd say about forty-five."

"I never knew that you did that."

306

"The only thing I don't really have is American history. There's a few books back at the house, but they're too complicated."

"I have a book that we used in school. It's about the colonies and the Revolutionary War. You could borrow it if you wanted to."

"Okay."

They started walking back up toward the house. Elizabeth took Joshua's hand in hers as they made their way through the path. When the two of them reached the open yard, Elizabeth let go. Mr. Thornton was carrying a load of wood into the house. Joshua went over to the woodpile, grabbed a few pieces, and followed the man to the door.

"Oh, thank you Joshua."

He put them next to the stove in the kitchen. Mrs. Thornton was pouring some lemonade into a glass as Joshua stood back up. She handed it to him, and then one to Elizabeth as she came into the room.

"How was the clambake?" The woman asked.

"I burned my hand, but other than that, it was good. We didn't have as many lobsters this time, but there weren't as many guests as there were on the Fourth of July."

"I suppose not."

"The hardest part was getting the seaweed. We got some from the beach, but there wasn't enough. Everything from the storm was all dried out. We had to scrape the pond along the channel. I think if there's a storm next year, we'll go get it when it's still wet, so we just keep it in the pond until we're ready to use it."

The woman just smiled at Joshua. Elizabeth disappeared upstairs for a few minutes, and then returned with the history book. Joshua thanked her for it, told Mrs. Thornton how delicious the lemonade was, and then decided to hit the road. Mr. Nilsson would be needing him at the beach soon, so he wheeled the bicycle in that direction.

The families in August seemed a little more self reliant than the ones in July. There weren't as many young children, so Joshua didn't feel the need to keep a constant watch on the shoreline. The professors kept to themselves. They were very serious, but once in awhile, they all broke out in laughter. Joshua could overhear what they were saying, but he couldn't understand what was so funny.

When the wind was up, Joshua started to make a habit of reading Huck Finn in the tree next to the sunporch. The mosquitoes didn't bother him as long as there was a breeze cutting through the branches. The air was starting to get cooler and drier now, and on a few mornings, it almost felt like fall. One afternoon, he was hopping down, when one of the professors happened to be walking by.

"What have you got there?" The man asked as he pointed to the book.

"Huckleberry Finn."

"Ah Twain... his passing was a great loss to American literature."

Joshua just stared at the man. He had wild, white hair and sideburns that led into an even more unruly beard. His fingernails were a little bit longer than they should have been, and the man stood as if pulled to one side.

"The great Samuel Leghorne Clemens... he came in with Haley's Comet, and left when it returned."

"Who's Samuel Leghorne Clemens?"

"Why, that's Mark Twain's given name. He got his pen name from working on the riverboats. Every time they'd measure the depth of the Mississippi, they'd yell, 'mark twain'."

"I didn't know that."

"What else have you read?"

"I finished Tom Sawyer last month."

"Another masterpiece. Some of my colleagues wouldn't agree, but they've been too steeped in the Europeans to even give any American writer a chance. I've heard the man speak on a number of occasions."

"I liked it."

"As you should... as you should. Every American boy should read about Tom and Huck. Their spirits are what have made this country great. We should never forget about their adventures, especially in these modern times when life seems to move too fast."

As if on cue, a loud truck came rattling along West Beach Road. The professor bristled at the interruption. Although Joshua didn't totally understand what the man was talking about, he still enjoyed listening to him.

"What else have you read?"

"I got some books from my sister, but I haven't gotten to them yet."

"Who are the authors?"

"There's some poems by a guy named Whitman."

"Ahhh, Whitman."

The man stared out to the pond, lost in his own thoughts for a moment. Joshua waited, but it didn't seem like he was going to say anything else.

"There's some short stories. I'm not sure who wrote them, but there's one about a white heron."

"Sarah Orne Jewett. I've had the pleasure to meet that fine woman. She's a true American treasure."

"Um, and there's a couple of books by O. Henry."

The man wrinkled his nose when Joshua mentioned the name.

"Oh, he's very popular, I'll grant you that. We're all still waiting for something a bit more substantial from him. Now how far have you gotten with our friend Huckleberry?"

"The Duke and the King are run out of town, and now they're trying to cheat some money out of three sisters."

"Ah yes, the King and the Duke. You won't find another pair of foolish scoundrels quite like them in all of literature."

Joshua started to try to figure out a way to walk away from the professor in a polite way. He was starting to think that the man could go on for hours on the subject.

"I have to go help my mother."

"Very good, very good. You keep up your reading now. Your sister seems to have good taste in literature. Make sure she keeps sending you books."

Joshua just nodded, not wanting to explain things

to this odd man. With a quick wave, he scooted around the house and hopped up the steps onto the porch. In his mind, Joshua kept repeating the professor's strange pronunciation of the word, 'li-tra-chure'. Mrs. Nilsson was cutting some of the cucumbers Joshua had picked that morning. He went over to the counter, grabbed a slice, and looked for the other knife. Snatching one of the plump tomatoes from the basket, Joshua started to cut it up. He couldn't believe how juicy it was. Before they irrigated, the boy didn't think the plants would even have a chance for survival. But now, with his efforts and a few rainstorms, the tomatoes were just bursting.

"What's the lodge in Vermont like?" Joshua asked Mrs. Nilsson as he grabbed another tomato.

"It's quite a place. The house doesn't have as many rooms for guests, but it's bigger. There's a wide open great room in the middle of the lodge that goes up to the roof, and the fireplace is grand. You could stand up inside of it."

"What do people do up there?"

"Well, the men come up in the fall for the hunting and the fishing. There are animal heads mounted all over the lodge. They give me the willies at night. Some of the same families who were here this summer like to visit for a week or two. Mr. Nilsson gives sleigh rides through the country. Snowshoeing is becoming popular; there's ice skating on the pond. Oh, there's lots of things to do."

Joshua thought about this for a moment. He could almost picture the place, but not quite.

"What would I do, though, if we go up there?"

"I imagine you'd work with Mr. Nilsson cutting the wood and clearing the snow off the paths. There are two horses and a few milking cows. They need to be taken care of," she said as she paused to scrape the cucumbers onto a platter.

"What else?" Joshua asked. He was starting to get excited about the possibilities.

"Well, Mr. Nilsson sets traps and goes hunting for food. The general store is about five miles away, near the train station, so sometimes it's hard to get there on a regular basis."

Her mention of traps immediately made Joshua think of the woodchuck that they caught earlier in the summer. He drifted back to the episode he had right after killing the animal. As he thought about it some more, he realized that was the last time he really lost total control of himself. His mind had tried to send him into the darkness a few times after that, but he had kept himself in check. Maybe he was getting better. His mother's last ditch effort to save him by coming down to Quonochontaug had actually worked.

Later that day, when his mother went upstairs, Joshua followed her. She was going up for the short nap that she tried to take each afternoon between cleaning up from lunch and getting ready for dinner. She turned and saw her son walking in the room. Her confused look was only added to when he came up to his mother and hugged her. When they broke their embrace, she looked at him with a smile.

"I think I'm all better now," he said, choking back a swallow.

She looked into his eyes as they started to well up. They became puddles, and then tears fell down his face to his chin.

"I think you may be right. I've been hoping for the last few weeks, but trying not make anything of it."

"A few times I felt bad, but it seems like I can control it now."

"That's what I was thinking."

"The letters to Mary are helping. I know she's gone, but it doesn't seem like it so much anymore. I miss her, but I feel her with me too."

Mother just smiled down at her boy.

"Dad too. When I made that catch, I think he helped me get to the ball. And every time I pick something in the garden, I look up into the sky and show him. Does that sound strange to you?"

"No, it sounds perfectly fine. I think you've come up with a very good way of thinking about this. I'm glad Mr. Nilsson was able to help you find your way. He's spoken to me on a number of occasions, and told me how well you're doing."

Joshua wiped his face with the sleeve of his shirt. He now felt like the man of the house, and the amazing part of it was that he wasn't even trying.

"Do you think it would be okay if I showed Elizabeth my letters to Mary?"

"She seems like a nice girl. I think she might like that."

"I told her about my sketches of birds, and it sounded like she wants to see them."

His mother just smiled at him again. It didn't seem like they had these moments alone very much anymore. Since there was always so much to do at the inn, their quiet times together were few and far between. Part of him missed the nights they spent with each other in the beginning of the summer. He loved his bedroom in the loft, but once in awhile, it was nice to be in here again. When they had arrived in the spring there was talk of hired help staying in the barn during a few of the busy weeks, but since Joshua had worked out so well, Mr. Nilsson decided that men weren't needed. Joshua was proud of his accomplishments, and when he left his mother, so she could take her nap, she gave him a kiss on the top of his head.

When Mr. Thornton came over with three chickens the next day, Joshua saw that Elizabeth was sitting next to him on the cart. She told him that she could stay for awhile if he promised to walk her home. Quickly, Joshua agreed, and the two of them walked over to see Joshua's garden.

"This looks great. How do you get those tomatoes so big?"

"Water and sun. I think the seaweed helped it too."

They walked around the yard, stopping at the fruit trees and then looping around to the dock. Both he and Elizabeth looked out at the island. Although it had only been a picnic, Joshua knew that their time together was the beginning of something more. As they walked back up the path, Joshua had an idea.

"Let's go this way," he said, leading her toward the ironwood trees off to the left.

312

"Where are we going?"

"You'll see."

Joshua led her through the overgrown path that led to West Beach Road. The branches hung over them, and the light started to fade with each step. He hadn't been down here since late that night when he was running from Kenyon and those other men. As they got closer to the shack, Elizabeth seemed to sense that there was something sinister about the path they were taking.

"I don't think I want to go through here."

"It's only a little farther."

"Is that shack down here?" Elizabeth asked in a nervous voice.

"Follow me. It's right through here."

Joshua turned off the main footpath and followed the thin trail back toward the pond. He slowed because he knew she would be timid about venturing down here. All of her boasting in the beginning of the summer was gone as they approached the small hut. Joshua really wanted her to have something to tell the other kids at school when she went back in a few weeks. He held her hand now, but she pulled back with each step.

"What's that noise?"

"It's just the pipe that comes up from the floor. I'm not sure what it's for."

The shack came into view now. There was much more leafy growth around it, than there was earlier in the summer. The green made it seem not so haunted anymore. Even the path was overgrown; like no one had been down here for awhile. Joshua led Elizabeth around to the pond side where the door was. It still swung loosely on one hinge. Just as Joshua was about to push it aside, the girl pulled on his arm and tried to run away.

"It's okay," he said.

He knew that if he let go, then she would flee back up the path. Joshua wanted to show her all of the bottles that lined the shelves, so she could describe the place when she got back to school. The strange echoing sound was stronger now; like there was water lapping against the mouth of the pipe in the pond. Josh pulled the door back and peered inside. It took a second for his eyes to focus, and when he looked again, he saw that the shelves were empty. The bottles were all gone. Stepping further into the shack, he let go of Elizabeth's hand and stared dumbfounded at the barren planks along the walls. Down in the far corner, Joshua saw something, and when he reached for it, he found an empty whiskey bottle. For a moment he couldn't figure out what had happened, but soon he realized that it was getting close to the end of the summer, and the guests and residents down at the breachway must have worked their way through all of the bottles. He couldn't imagine that happening; there were so many of them here in the beginning of the summer. Elizabeth looked at the blank shelves too, and then glanced over to where Joshua held the empty bottle.

"They're all gone," Joshua said in disbelief.

"Well, they say that crowd down by the breachway is a rowdy bunch," she answered in a more comfortable voice.

Outside of the shack, Joshua followed where he thought the pipe went under the ground. He had to thrash through some thick underbrush, but he finally came out to clear skies at the edge of the pond. He could see the tube coming out of the bushes. The tide was high, and the ripples in the water were collapsing right into the mouth of the pipe. That was what was causing the strange sounds inside. Joshua tried to figure out what the pipe was for, but couldn't come up with anything. It was obviously old, and since he knew how hard it was to dig around here, he was sure that there was a good reason for it.

He made his way back to the clearing next to the shack where Elizabeth was waiting, and silently, they walked back out to the main path.

"Do you want to go down to the breachway?"

"No, I don't like it down there too much. I want to see your sketches," she answered in a firm tone.

Dear Mary,

Elizabeth came over today. I showed her the haunted shack in the woods, but it wasn't too exciting. The place was empty, but I think I figured out what the pipe was for. It might have been some kind of a slaughterhouse for pigs or sheep. The blood must have drained down and out to the pond. Elizabeth wanted to see my sketches, so I brought her back to the barn. She seemed interested in them and even told me that they were pretty good, but I think she really wanted to read my letters to you. I've gone back and forth on the idea of sharing them with her, but in the end, I let her see them. As she read, I could hear her laugh a little, and then I think she was crying a bit. It must remind her of what she writes in her diary. After she finished, she gave me another kiss on the cheek. I'm not really sure how I'm supposed to react to that.

We took Nettie outside and brushed her down. Elizabeth asked if I would write letters to her if I went to Vermont for the winter. I agreed, but the more I thought about it, the more worried I got that I would neglect my letters to you. I figured since the days are cold and the nights are long up there, then I would have plenty of time to do both.

Tonight, when I was washing the dishes with Mother, I asked her if we were going to head up North with the Nilssons. She was quiet for awhile, and then told me that she had written a letter to Grandma and told her of our plans to go to Vermont. She was still waiting for a response. I remembered their argument before we came down here in March, and I don't think Mother was asking permission. I think she was just telling Grandma what we were going to do. When Mother talks to me now, it seems like she's treating me more like a grown up.

I'm slowly getting to the end of Huckleberry Finn. The King and the Duke, who I hate now, have sold Jim back into slavery, and it just happens to be to a relative of Tom Sawyer. I think it's too much of a coincidence, but I'm still reading. It's funny when he pretends to be Tom, and then Tom Sawyer actually shows up. I might finish the book tonight. If not, then definitely tomorrow.

Your Brother,

Joshua

315

23

When most of the guests left at the end of August, Joshua had a week to prepare himself for the trip to Fenway. There was much to do before that happened, though, so he kept himself busy each day. He and Mr. Nilsson cleaned out the rest of the vegetables in the garden. They gathered up everything they could, so Mrs. Nilsson could do her canning. After removing all of the wooden stakes and other debris, they tilled the soil. Mr. Nilsson said that they would get some seaweed after the next storm and till the garden one more time.

Since all of the children had left, and the only guests remaining at the inn were older couples, Joshua didn't have to spend time on the beach in the afternoon. He and Mr. Nilsson repaired and sharpened all of the tools in the barn, and got them ready for next season. Two of the lobster pots needed fixing, so Joshua pulled some slats off a broken one. The netting also had to be mended, and Mr. Nilsson showed the boy how to do it. He had convinced Mrs. Van Houtten that a new net was needed for the tennis court next year, so they used the old one to work on the lobster pots. There was rarely any waste at the inn.

The canoes were pulled and washed down, before being stored in the barn for the winter. They kept the rowboat in the water because Mr. Nilsson said that the big fish would be returning soon as they headed south into the warmer waters. Mrs. Nilsson made batches of peach cobbler when the fruit ripened on the trees, and Joshua brought some over to the Thornton's in East Beach. Elizabeth was getting ready to return to school, and they both knew that it would be difficult to see each other much after that. Joshua promised her one more picnic, and they decided to have it on the beach on a Saturday afternoon in September.

After finishing Huckleberry Finn, Joshua started to read the history book that Elizabeth had given him. He wasn't sure if she needed it for school, so he wanted to get through at least some of it before she asked for it back. Mother and the Nilssons tested him on the facts whenever there was a spare moment. He could easily name the thirteen colonies, and even knew a little bit about each one of them. He focused on Rhode Island, but paid special attention to Boston. Each time he saw that word on the page, though, he thought of Fenway. Once that happened, it was difficult for him to focus on the Revolutionary War era.

Dear Mary,

I just got home from Boston, and it was the most amazing thing that has ever happened in my life. Ray Crandall picked us up bright and early Friday morning and took us to the train station in Bradford. Mr. Nilsson bought some newspapers, and we read until the train came. The Senators dared Jake Stahl to pitch Wood against Johnson, and even though he wasn't due to throw until Saturday, the Red Sox accepted the challenge. Walter had won sixteen in a row, but his streak had been broken. Smoky Joe was going for his fourteenth victory in a row. I couldn't believe all that they wrote about in the papers. It was like some kind of prize fight or something. They compared every statistic and physical feature of the two pitchers. The greats in baseball were going up against each other. During the train ride, I kept rereading the articles as my heart raced with each mile. It was strange when we pulled into Providence. I recognized everything that I could see out the window, but somehow it seemed like a place out of the past. It was like someone else's life. I was happy to finally pull out of the station there.

We got to Boston just before noon and took a trolley that let us off on Ipswich Street, right near the ballpark. I could see the crowds starting to build on the sidewalks. They all seemed to be heading for Fenway. We bought some lunch from a street vendor and ate as we walked.

When we came around the last corner, Fenway Park appeared in front of me. The brickwork was brand new. There were thousands of white brimmed hats in the sea of bodies, and as we got closer, all I could see were the backs of the men in front of me. Mr. Nilsson figured out which gate we had to go through, and we slowly made our way underneath the grandstands. When we came up the stairs and I saw the field for the first time, I thought that I had never seen anything so green. The Senators were out holding their final batting practice as we inched toward our seats. Mr. Nilsson had to keep nudging me to move because I couldn't take my eyes off the field.

The crowd roared when the Red Sox took the field for the first inning. In my dreams, I had pictured this day, but this was far beyond anything that I had imagined. The fuzzy photographs in the magazine that I had back at the inn didn't do justice to the beauty of Fenway Park. There were people everywhere. They had to tie ropes along the foul lines and in the outfield to hold all the extra spectators in. Cops had to push them back so the pitchers could warm up. The teams couldn't even sit in their dugouts, so they were on benches along the foul line. Our seats were high above the first base line. Cigar smoke was thick in the air, and the stomping of fans above us made the metal roof echo. We had a great view of everything that was happening.

Smoky Joe's warm up pitches were unbelievable. I didn't think a man could throw a ball that fast. My spine tingled as I looked out onto the field. Harry Hooper, Tris Speaker, and Duffy Lewis guarded the outfield, while Jake Stahl, Steve Yerkes, Heine Wagner, and Larry Gardner watched over the infield. Rough Carrigan was behind the plate catching Smoky Joe Wood's fastballs. It was all like a dream. A few times I thought Dad was next to me, but it was Mr. Nilsson. Even though he's a great man, I kept wishing that Dad would somehow appear.

The first few innings seemed to fly by. The crowd cheered for each put out by the Sox, and then moaned when they got thrown out at first. Smoky Joe kept striking the Senators out, and by the time the sixth inning rolled around, the fancy electric scoreboard had a string of zeroes lined on both sides. With two outs, Tris Speaker came to the plate. The crowd had all their faith in the Gray Eagle as he looked out to right field. Washington was playing him to pull it, but I thought I saw him take a quick look down the third base line. When Johnson's fastball came in, Speaker stepped into it and slapped it into left field. The ball disappeared into the crowd, and the umpire called it a ground rule double. Duffy Lewis came to the plate next, and the Senators shifted over to left. Just like Spoke, he hit to the opposite field. The whole crowd held their breath as the rightfielder raced for the ball. As it tipped off the edge of his glove, all eyes turned to Speaker as he came around third and headed for home. Fenway Park went wild as he crossed the plate.

I watched Speaker in centerfield for the rest of the game. I almost wished a runner got to second base, so I could see him sneak in for the attempted pick off. It was an amazing thing to see him play so shallow. Just as Wood was throwing the ball from the mound, Tris would begin to move, like he knew where it was going to go. He was in constant movement, and the balls just seemed to drop into his glove.

For the rest of the game, we sat silently as each batter came up for Washington, and then cheered when he sat back down. There were no real threats, and by the end of the game, they had a mere six hits, and Wood had himself nine strike outs. Speaker's one run was enough to win the game for the Red Sox, and when Mr. Nilsson and I started to file out of the stands, I knew that I had witnessed something special. We came out and then walked around the park along Landsdowne Street. Mr. Van Houtten had suggested a place for us to stay before catching the early train back this morning. We kept with the crowd for awhile, and when it started to thin out, we looked for a place to get some dinner. For a Giants' fan, the man seemed pretty impressed by what the Red Sox did. He kept the box score, just like Dad used to, and while we ate, Mr. Nilsson and I went through each play of the game. It was a true pitcher's duel, with great support in the field. Once again, Smoky Joe Wood and Tris Speaker were the heroes. I can't wait for the World Series.

We walked through the streets of Boston, as we made our way back toward the train station. The hotel that we were to stay at was only a block or two away from it. Mr. Nilsson kept asking about our relatives in the city, but I had no idea where they lived. I really didn't want to drop in on them either. I figured that they would bring back a lot of memories that might cause me some problems. Even though it seems like I'm getting better, I still have an uneasy feeling that I could slip back into my old ways without warning.

I was so tired that I fell asleep almost right away once we got to the hotel. I was reading the program that I got, and when I woke up this morning, it was still on my chest. I had this idea that I was going to get it signed by Tris Speaker and Joe Wood, but I couldn't even imagine trying to get through the crowd yesterday to get near them. Seeing them playing will always be in my mind, and I don't think that I will ever forget it as long as I live.

We bought newspapers for the ride home, and we kept reliving the game again with each sentence either one of us read. I tried to keep my head down when we stopped in Providence, but I got a quick glimpse of the skyline as we were pulling out. I feel strange about trying to block the place out of my mind, but I think that it's for the better. I had some money left, so I told Mr. Nilsson that I was going to pay for the jitney back to the inn. He must have seen the seriousness in my face because he didn't even argue about it. When the train pulled into Niantic Station, it felt like I had been on the adventure of a lifetime. Nothing could beat it. I was in a daydream for most of the ride down the dusty roads back to the inn. When we pulled in, Mother came out and gave me a great big hug. Two of the couples were leaving the inn, so we loaded up the jitney, and off they went.

I spent all afternoon and evening telling mother about the game, showing her the newspapers, and reading through the program with her. I know that she isn't too interested in baseball, but she listened as if I was telling her the great secrets of the world. I think she was just so pleased that I was so excited about life again, that she put up with it. Mrs. Nilsson even got caught up in the excitement. Both of the women asked silly questions, but I *answered them as if I was the most informed baseball expert around. Mr. Nilsson let me do most of the talking. He reminded me of different incidents, and then let me explain them.*

This letter has given me a chance to relive the game again, and I'll probably do the same thing with Elizabeth, even though I know she is about as interested in baseball as Mother is. Maybe the guys down at the Life Saving Station would appreciate a description of the game. I just want to tell the world that I was at one of the best games in the history of baseball.

I think I'll go back and reread the newspapers from yesterday and today. I know that I'll pick up something that I missed. I'll write to you again soon.

Your Brother,

Joshua

The next couple of weeks in September brought a freedom back to Joshua's life that hadn't been there since the spring. It was different now, though, his mind was in the right place, and he felt like he was more a part of Quonochontaug now. When the storm came up from the south and dumped an inch of rain on them, he knew that the surf would bring in seaweed. Joshua and Mr. Nilsson went down and filled the cart and brought it back to the garden. Things weren't new to him anymore. They seemed to be in a comfortable routine. The boy was able to plan his days around the chores that had to be done.

When he suggested that they widen the path to the pond a little bit and plant some more grass, Mr. Nilsson thought it was a fine idea. Joshua didn't even have to remind him of the problems they had with Nettie when they tried to get the seaweed down to the pond for the clambake. There was an understanding now between the two of them. It didn't seem so much like a teacher-student relationship any longer; they were more of a team now. Joshua could see the years that lay ahead, and he looked forward to them, like he had never done before.

Now that many of the cottages and inns were

empty, Joshua had the beach to himself again. He rode through the streets like the place was his; as if he was in charge of taking care of the whole beach. Instead of taking the boat out, he pedaled down to the breachway with his fishing tackle, and tried his luck from the rocks along the edge. Mr. Nilsson was right; the big fish came back in the fall. Joshua sent his line out only a few times and was able to pull in three, twenty inch stripers. Gutting and skinning them in the shallow water, he wrapped the filets in the newspaper that he had brought, put them in the basket on the front of the bicycle, and rode back to the inn. Mrs. Nilsson said that he should bring a couple of the filets over to the Thornton's place, so that's what he did. Elizabeth was still in school, but Joshua didn't mind going over there anyway.

Another day, the crew from the Life Saving Station was practicing along the breachway when Joshua pulled up on the bike. He watched them row down toward the pond against the outgoing tide with a power that only six men could muster. They flew back toward the ocean with the current, and Mason gave Josh a big wave as they passed.

"Want to go for a ride out in the Atlantic?"

"Sure," Joshua answered.

They pulled up to the edge of the breachway a few yards down from where the boy was standing. Mason picked out a nice spot where the rocks formed a small inlet. Joshua hopped up and over the bow, and then placed himself on the triangular seat beneath him. The ocean was fairly calm, but Joshua felt a little nervous as the dory bumped through the mouth of the breachway and out into the open water. They rowed along the beach, and Joshua was amazed at the view. The inns and cottages all lined the beach in an odd symmetry that seemed just right.

"What have you been doing?" Mason asked from the stern. "Besides pulling my dinner out of the breachway," he said with a smile. "I saw you hauling those stripers out."

Joshua knew that he was just kidding around, but he never thought of it that way before. The breachway was the crew's backyard. When Josh caught fish down there, it was like he was taking food off their table. He decided that the next time he went out in the boat, he would make an effort to share some of his catch with these men.

"I went and saw the Red Sox play in Boston."

"The Red Sox," Max said from where he was sitting with his back to Joshua. "That bunch of upstarts are going to get the tar beat out of them in a few weeks when they come up against some real ballplayers."

"Oh yeah, who?" Joshua answered with a little bit of irritation in his voice.

"Christy Mathewson, Rube Marquand, Fred Merkle, Josh Devore, Josh McGraw and the rest of the greatest baseball team in the history of the world."

Joshua was a little taken aback by the venom and challenge in Max's voice. He didn't really know how to respond to this man without getting out of control. He took a deep breath, and then smiled to himself.

"We'll see," the boy finally said in a calm voice. "I heard they're going to make the Polo Grounds a museum because the players are so old."

A few of the other members of the crew laughed, but Max turned around to look at Joshua. This threw their rhythm off a bit, and Mason had to compensate with the rudder.

"Easy Max," Mason said. "Joshua, you can't understand how this New Yorker's brain works, so you might as well not even try. You'll never get him to change his mind."

"We'll see what happens in October," Joshua said, suddenly feeling like he was the spokesman for Red Sox fans everywhere.

"I hear that Joe Wood is quite a hurler," Cliff said to continuing the baiting.

"Walter Johnson even said that no man alive can throw harder than Smoky Joe Wood," the boy answered quickly.

"You weren't at the game against the Senators, were you?" Mason asked in disbelief.

"I sure was," Joshua answered with pride.

"The papers said that was the greatest ballgame ever played."

"You better believe it, and I was sitting right up over the first base side. I watched Tris Speaker cross the plate for the only run, and I watched Walter Johnson walk off the mound in the eighth, knowing that he lost to the next World Series champions."

Max snorted at that comment, but didn't join in the discussion. They continued their journey along the coast, well beyond where Joshua had ever walked before. The houses disappeared, and there was just open beach. He could tell that the pond, where Elizabeth lived, was on the other side of the dunes. As he scanned the shoreline, his mind drifted to the plans he had made with her. They were going to go on a picnic soon. Joshua decided that he would ride over to her house very soon and set a date. He knew that his days were numbered down here, and he didn't want the time to slip away. Mother had made the decision to go to Vermont with the Nilssons, and although he didn't want to leave the beach, he was looking forward to the adventure of the north country. She was going to go back to Providence for a few days to visit with Grandma and bring some warm clothes and other things back to the Pond View. Joshua was very happy when she gave him the choice of going back or staying at the inn. The memories of pulling into Providence Station on the train with Mr. Nilsson made him sure that he didn't want to visit the city any time in the near future.

Mason turned the boat around after they came to what looked like an opening to the pond. It didn't look like the breachway in Quonny Pond, but it was some type of waterway nevertheless. Joshua enjoyed the view just as much on the way back, and as they got to the houses by East Beach, he tried to notice things that he missed on their first pass. Some of the cottages' windows were already boarded up, and it made Josh think of what it was like in the springtime. A few men stood on the beach with long fishing poles, but they weren't close enough for the boy to recognize any of them. A couple of times, a school of fish bubbled out of the water as they chased the baitfish to the surface. Joshua watched as blues and stripers snapped at the smaller fish. Seagulls hovered above the fray, diving down and snatching a meal for themselves. Joshua thought about the dismal lives of these tiny fish; bigger ones attacked from the bottom while birds assaulted from the sky.

When they came back into the breachway, the men looked tired. Even Mason had a weariness to his movements. They dropped him off where they had picked him up. Joshua gave the crew a wave as they rowed back across the channel.

"Thanks for the ride," he yelled as he went to where he had left his bicycle.

"Come down and see us again," Mason called over his back.

Fall was in the air. The dryness felt good as Joshua thought about those hazy summer afternoons when a breeze was hard to come by. He had to get back to the inn and start picking grapes for Mrs. Nilsson. They had started to turn a deep purple color only a few days before, and he promised her that she could start making the jam. He grabbed a basket from the barn and walked out to the other side of the garden. The seaweed odor was still very strong. It amazed Joshua that this foul smelling substance could be so good for the vegetables. Once he got under the vines and the big green leaves, he was able to easily pull the clumps down. Sometimes the bunch would crumble apart, and a few stray grapes would fall away, but there were so many, that Joshua didn't worry about it. He ate them as he went along; sucking the juices out of each one before spitting the skin and pit out. Once in awhile he would get a sour one, but for the most part, the taste of them made his mouth water even more.

"Joshua, I need you to take a ride up to the store on the Post Road and get me a few bags of sugar," Mrs. Nilsson said to the boy as he came back into the house with a basketful of grapes.

"How much?"

"Why don't you get me three, five pound sacks. That should keep us until we have to head north."

Joshua was on his bicycle and flying up West Beach Road within two minutes. Mrs. Nilsson had given him the money, and the boy was off. He had greased the wheels of the bike a few days before, so the squeakiness was gone, and it just seemed to move smoother. The shelves of the store were getting bare again, just like the ones in the shack. The summer people had come through and consumed their fill. When he got back to the inn, Mrs. Nilsson had the whole operation set up. There were pots on the stove and empty jars on the counter. She and Mother were getting ready to begin their jam making. Joshua stuck around for awhile, but realized he was just getting in the way. Two people could handle the project a lot better than three.

He took Nettie out of the barn and let her graze in the backyard. Joshua knew that he would have to cut the lawn one more time before they left, but he wanted to wait until they were getting closer. The boy sat on a rock next to the horse. She chomped on the grass while Joshua looked out over the pond. He remembered his first glimpse of this view back in March. So much had happened since then. The way he thought about life and dealt with it were the biggest changes. Now, he had a sense of being so much more in control of what was happening. Days and nights weren't spent waiting for the next episode or recovering from the last one. Joshua felt stronger; physically and mentally. As the cool north wind blew through his hair, Joshua felt confident in himself for the first time in his life.

"Now, I want you on your best behavior while I'm gone," his mother said as she prepared for her trip back to Providence. "I'll be gone for four days, and I want you to help the Nilssons in any way that you can."

"I already do," Joshua answered. He couldn't figure out why his mother was acting this way.

"I know you do. I'm sorry," she sighed, "I just don't like leaving you. Part of me wants you to come with me, and part of me knows that you should stay here and help out. I guess I'll just miss you, that's all."

With a smile and a hug, his mother walked out to the driveway where Mr. Crandall was waiting for her. Joshua put her small bag in the back, and all three of them waved as his mother left the inn for the first time in almost six months.

"Joshua, why don't you bring a few jars of jam over to the Thornton's place?" Mrs. Nilsson said.

She didn't have to ask the boy twice. He wheeled the bicycle out of the barn, and she went inside to wrap the jars up in some towels. Setting them gently in his bicycle basket, Joshua rode over to East Beach, hoping this time that Elizabeth would be home from school. When he passed through the opening in the stone wall, he could see that she was out on her front steps reading a book.

"Hello," he called out.

She closed what she was reading and smiled over to him. Joshua stopped the bike and pulled the jars out of the wrapping. He handed them to her.

"My mother and Mrs. Nilsson made this for you and your grandparents. I picked the grapes."

He followed her inside the house and watched as she placed them on the counter. Mrs. Thornton was making something on the stove when they came in.

"Oh, hello Joshua. What do we have today?"

"Grape jam."

"Mrs. Nilsson makes the best jam," she answered as she wiped her hands on a small towel. "Why don't you two sit down, and I'll fix you a snack?"

They sat for awhile at the table, but Joshua knew that he had to be getting back to the inn soon. He had noticed that Mr. Nilsson had been taking naps in the afternoon more often now, and the boy wanted to give the man a hand around the inn when he woke up. It seemed like he was exhausted from everything that they had done over the summer. Sometimes Joshua worried that all of the work was wearing the man out.

They made plans for a picnic on the beach. Elizabeth was going to make everything. All Joshua had to do was come over to the house and escort her down to the shore. Joshua left the Thorntons with a loaf of nut bread that Elizabeth and her grandmother had made. He cruised back to the inn filled with regrets about leaving Quonochontaug, but with plans for the future.

24

Dear Mary,

We've been closing up the inn for the season. Mrs. Nilsson and I have put sheets on all of the chairs in the upstairs rooms, as well as the furniture downstairs that we don't use. It's starting to get chilly out in the barn at night. I'm not sure if I'm going to stay there until the end or move back into the house. The walls are filled with my bird sketches and my Red Sox drawings and lists. I haven't decided if I'm going to take some of them down and bring them to Vermont, or if I'll just leave everything here until next spring. Mr. Nilsson and I put the garden to rest for the year. We tilled in one more load of seaweed. I've already made some changes in how the vegetables are going to be arranged next April and May. Mr. Nilsson says that it's up to me, so I guess I'll keep thinking about it. I'm going to spend the winter trying to figure out the best way to lay out the garden for the least amount of money. I have my chart of what people ate the most of, so I'm going to try and match that up with how I want to set the garden up.

I went on a picnic with Elizabeth. Mr. Nilsson was working on the cart, so I decided to walk over there. Even though she said that she was going make everything, I brought over some biscuits and another jar of the jam. She was still in the kitchen putting everything together when I got there, so I sat with Mr. Thornton on their back porch. We talked about the weather this summer, and how our gardens almost took a beating because of it. He told me a little about the pond behind their property, and I compared it to the pond behind the inn.

I carried the basket down to the beach as we walked. There didn't seem to be anyone around now. Everything was so quiet. Elizabeth talked about what was going on in school, and for a few brief moments, I wished that I was there with her. I had always liked being in a classroom before everything happened, but my memories of the last two years made me shiver. She said that I could keep the American history book because her group was working on the old civilizations now, and her teacher hadn't asked for it back yet. I told her that I would mail it back here if she needed it. This reminded both of us that I would be leaving soon, so I tried to change the subject.

As we came onto the beach, there were more people around. Men were along the shore with makeshift fishing poles. We could both see the fish working just beyond the breaking waves. One of the men pulled in a big striped bass. It was bigger than anything I had ever caught. Elizabeth and I continued down the beach, away from the other people, and set up our picnic just beyond where the people from the Pond View usually sat during the summer. The air was a little cool, but the sun shining on the ocean seemed brighter than ever. Elizabeth kept asking me what I thought it would be like in Vermont, but I didn't know. I repeated what Mrs. Nilsson had told me, but I didn't really have a good picture of the place myself. It's hard for me to even imagine so many feet of snow.

Elizabeth's lunch was delicious. She made some chicken sandwiches on thick slices of bread. We ate, and then went for a walk on the beach. As we climbed over the rocks, it seemed like we were still kids, but when I thought about it, I realized that we were getting serious about our relationship. The boardwalk down by the breachway was empty, and the crew for the Life Saving Station wasn't even around. The place was becoming a ghost town again. We ran up and down the walkway, and I skipped stones out into the water. As we walked back, it felt like summer was really over. I wasn't sure if we would see each other again before I headed north. Elizabeth was crying a little bit as we packed up the basket and started back to the road. I promised her that I would write her letters, and she gave me another kiss on the cheek before we got to her house. I waved to Mrs. Thornton, who was hanging out clothes, as I was leaving. The walk back to the inn seemed longer than usual, and even though I'm looking forward to Vermont, I

329

hope those five months pass quickly.

Mother returned from Providence this afternoon. She seemed a little sad about the trip, but she tried to hide it. There was a lot of news from back in the neighborhood, but I really wasn't interested in any of it. Mother noticed this, so she started talking about something else. She brought some warm clothes for me, but hardly any of them fit anymore. I'm not sure how much I've grown since last winter, but almost everything I tried on was either too tight or too short. Mother wasn't sure what to do. Mrs. Nilsson said that we could probably get some new clothes in Westerly before we leave. She said that Mr. Nilsson likes to go in at the end of the season to get some deals on the summer supplies that didn't sell. Ray Crandall is going to be coming around in a day or two, so maybe I'll be sitting in the back of the truck, while we cruise into town. I think I'll buy an American map when I'm there. I'm reading about the Revolutionary War right now, and I can't get a picture of the whole thing. The book just gives small diagrams of different battles, but not the entire war. I also want to get a good look at Vermont.

Well, I'm going to head out into the pond for the last time tomorrow. I want to go fishing once more before we pull the boat out of the water. I think I'll invest some of my money in a fishing pole for next year.

Your Brother,

Joshua

Rowing for the last time in 1912, Joshua made his way across the pond. He stared at the inn as he moved through the water. It was changing again. Some of the leaves were starting to turn yellow, and the whole area didn't look as green as it did after the rains in August. Joshua thought about the first time he rowed the boat, and he couldn't believe the ease with which he pulled on the oars now. The tide was coming in at a fairly good clip into the pond, but the boy was able to move the dinghy through the current without much of a struggle. He dropped anchor at the inside mouth of the breachway and expertly rigged his line.

The pond was quiet. The only other boat was off in the distance, down by the Weekapaug end. Joshua sat with the line in the water for awhile. For some reason, nothing was biting. He saw the water explode about thirty yards away with larger fish going after the little ones. He figured that by the time he made his way over there, they would be done. After looking for a minute or two, he saw the splashing move away from him, and then slowly fade to nothing. The water settled back down into an almost stillness again. He hoped that the fish would be heading back this way soon. The strong, incoming current, though, made that idea seem farfetched. Within a few moments though, Joshua heard a thrashing sound behind him in the breachway. It was another school of fish looking for food. As the large mass drifted toward him, he felt like the whole thing was going to consume his boat. The frenzy spread out twenty feet in each direction, and Joshua couldn't even imagine how many fish were involved. The bubbling water got closer to him, and he could see the huge fish jumping all around him. As the white water passed by both sides of the dinghy, Joshua was amazed that nothing grabbed onto his line.

Since the baitfish were near the surface, he pulled his hook up closer to where they were feeding, and suddenly there was an enormous pull. It ripped his arms at his shoulders and just kept tearing away. The small twine of fishing line in his hand thrashed with the whim of the escaping fish. It was almost too much to hold onto. Joshua's finger got wrapped up, and he felt like it was going to get severed from his hand. With an unexpected turn, the fish leapt out of the water right behind the boat. Joshua's eyes had trouble connecting the sight with his brain. The striper was so big, that the boy was a little afraid of it. The fish's huge mouth swung back at Joshua almost in a growl. The thing must have been over three feet long. It was as big as Mary Rose. In a daze, Joshua tried to hold on, but the striper's quick movements as it splashed back into the water ripped the line and wooden holder from his hands. It landed in the water, and for a split second, Joshua thought he could reach it, but the whole thing disappeared beneath the surface. It had

331

happened so fast, that Joshua didn't even know what had taken place until the water settled down again. He sat back down on the bench and just stared into the water. There was no sign of the fish or the line. Somewhere underneath him was a huge fish, but he wouldn't have a chance to catch it now.

Without anything else to fish with, Joshua just looked out at the pond. The school had disappeared somewhere, just like his line. He dumped the remaining baitfish into the pond and started to row back. A fishing pole would definitely solve his problems, and he promised himself to get one for next season. He wondered if there would be places to go fishing up in Vermont. He pictured lakes and rivers all around. He rowed back to the dock, searching the water for his fishing line. When he pulled up, Mr. Nilsson was there waiting for him.

"How'd you do?"

"Not too good."

When he explained what had happened, the man started to laugh. At first Joshua was offended by the man's reaction, but when Mr. Nilsson related similar incidents, the boy was able to laugh along with him. Joshua's plan for sharing his catch with the crew from the Life Saving Station was shot as he and Mr. Nilsson carried the boat up through the yard. He had his chance, but he had blown it. In his mind, Joshua pictured their reaction to the sight of his huge fish. That one striper could have fed the whole crew. Next year would be different, he wouldn't let the big one get away.

Dear Mary,

The last time that I saw Elizabeth before we left Quonochontaug was when I walked Nettie over to Old Cal's place. I had to go by the Thornton's house anyway, so I decided to stop. Elizabeth was sad, and so was I, but I was really looking forward to next spring. She said that winters down here aren't too exciting. The cold wind really bites into you in January. It was me who gave her a kiss good-bye this time, and I promised to write to her at least once a week. After I dropped Nettie off and walked past the house again, I just gave her a wave. I could see Elizabeth through the window. It reminded me of the first time that I was at the Thornton's place in the spring.

Everything has been a hustle and bustle for the last day or so. Mr. and Mrs. Nilsson kept remembering things that had to get done before we actually closed the place up for the year. I was trying to keep track of all the details too, so I could remember next time. Mr. Nilsson and I drained the big tank under the windmill. We used the water to wash off the boats and some of the equipment. He was very insistent about making sure all the metal was properly dried off. The worst part was cleaning out the chicken coop. Mrs. Nilsson cooked up the last one the other day, but the mess they left was disgusting. We used buckets and buckets of water to flush the coop out, but I still had to do a lot of scraping.

Mother and I packed. All of my new clothes for the winter made it seem like I was a different person. The trip we made into Westerly the other day was interesting. Mr. Nilsson spent a lot of money, but we got all new furniture for the back porch and a new net for the tennis court, among other things. The salespeople were willing to almost give the stuff away. Mother and Mrs. Nilsson did their own shopping, and they came out with bags and bags when we drove around to pick them up. I had to go through the pain of trying on outfit after outfit. Mother even bought me some clothes for next summer. They were about three sizes too big, but she said that I would grow into them. Mr. Nilsson and I rode in the back of the pick-up, while Mr. Crandall and the ladies were up front. It was a fun ride into Westerly, but on the way back, the truck was so full, that I thought we were going to fall out each time we hit a bump. Instead of spending my money on baseball magazines, Mother was happy to see that I bought three Mark Twain books and a map of the United States.

Baseball is still on my mind though. As I sit here in the Springfield train station, waiting to make our final connection up north, I keep thinking about the World Series. Last Tuesday in New York, the Red Sox stole a game from the Giants. Tris Speaker's triple in the sixth got Boston moving, and Harry Hooper's unbelievable catch and throw

to the plate in the bottom of the ninth saved it for them. I
didn't get back up to the store until Friday, so I had no idea
what was happening. Because game two in Boston went so
late, they had to call it a tie because of the darkness. It was
like the game never even happened. They played game
three in Boston too, but the Giants won 2-1 to tie the series
at one apiece. That fielder, Devore, robbed the Sox with a
great catch in the bottom of the ninth.

I told Mr. Nilsson on Monday that I wanted to go up
to the store and buy a newspaper before we put the bicycle
away in the barn. He's just as interested in the series as I
am. I'm starting to think that I'm turning him into a Red Sox
fan though. The Sox won game four and game five to give
them a three to one lead in the series. I knew that they were
going to win it all. There was no news until Mr. Crandall
arrived this morning after we closed everything up at the
inn. I took one last walk down to the beach and then
around the grounds of the Pond View. The leaves are really
turning colors and starting to fall now. Mr. Nilsson had me
rake some of them up yesterday and spread the leaves over
the top of the garden. He says that we'll till it in with the
seaweed next spring.

Mr. Crandall knows that I'm a big Red Sox fan, so he
didn't want to tell me the news, but he could see that I was
bursting. The Giants won game six by three runs, and they
tied the series in Boston. He said that the Red Sox played
the worst game in the history of baseball. The only good
play all game was an unassisted double play by Tris
Speaker. It was like Smoky Joe Wood forgot how to pitch.
When we got to the train station in Westerly, I bought a
newspaper, but I really didn't want to read it. The articles
talked about the Red Sox just falling apart.

We've been sitting in Springfield waiting for our train
to Vermont to arrive. The deciding game of the series is
being played right now in Boston, and every so often, an
update comes across the telegraph lines. In the third inning,
the Giants scored a run when Devore came across the plate
after Murray doubled. Harry Hooper saved more runs with
a great catch over the wall. I started to jump up and down
in the seventh when Olaf Henriksen came up to the plate to
pinch hit. I told Mr. Nilsson that The Swede was going to

save the day for the Red Sox. I think when Olaf got a hit to score Jake Stahl, Mr. Nilsson officially became a Red Sox fan. For the rest of the game, he cheered them on. The rest of the people in the station went into wild applause when Smoky Joe Wood came in to pitch in the eighth inning. At the end of regulation play, the score was tied one apiece. The man who was reading off the telegraph line started to call the game play by play. The whole place groaned when the ball got by Speaker, and the Giants scored a run. In the bottom half of the inning, Clyde Engle sent a fly to centerfield, and Fred Snodgrass just dropped it. With Tris Speaker up and men on first and third, I knew that he was going to win the World Series for them. After a foul ball dropped without anyone catching it, he sent the ball out to rightfield for a hit. The game was tied with runners on second and third. All was quiet in the train station while we waited for the next batter. Mathewson walked Duffy Lewis to load the bases, and when Larry Gardner sent a shot out to the field, Steve Yerkes tagged from third and beat the throw. I jumped off the bench and gave Mother a hug. The Sox had won the World Series.

For some strange reason I felt like it was Dad who was sending those messages across the telegraph line. I know it sounds weird, but he seems to be the connection between me and the Red Sox. It's the same way with the newspaper articles that I read. In my mind, Dad is writing all of them to me. When I was at the game in Fenway, I kept thinking that he was sitting next to me. The more I think about what Mr. Nilsson said about his brother, the more I think that Dad is inside of me now. It's my mind that carries him around. All of those late afternoons playing catch and talking about the Sox are coming back now. It's like he's still talking to me. Dad's voice is what I hear when I picture the game in my mind. The sound used to scare me, but now it makes me feel stronger, like I'm finally getting through this thing that's been haunting me for over two years.

Our train just pulled in, so I'll finish this up once we get going again. I have to help Mother with the bags.

Well, we're on our way now. The next time I get off this train I'll be in Vermont. I'm a different person than who I was six months ago. I'm embarrassed when I think of what I used to be like, but I'm starting to picture it in a different way now. I think it's like when I was blind, and it took a while for me to mend. My brain was wounded by what happened to Dad and to you, and I had to spend some time healing. The only problem was that I had to come up with a cure for what was wrong with me. If it wasn't for Mr. Nilsson, I don't know what I would have done. I'm also thankful for Mother. If she hadn't taken such a chance by moving down to Quonochontaug, then I don't think I would have survived. I really think that I would have hurt myself in some way if I didn't get out of Providence. They kept me so busy at the inn, that I didn't have time to feel sorry for myself.

I can't wait to get to the lodge in Vermont. The view outside the window is beautiful. The trees are bright orange and red and yellow. This is so much different than our ride to Quonochontaug in March. I didn't know what was going to happen back then. Now I feel ready to take on the world. I'll write to you again once we get there. Thank you for listening.

Your Brother,

Joshua